*1*

# CHAMPAGNE

# STEEPLEJACK

A Novel of Manipulation and Obsession

*SHEILA DIBNAH*

2QT Limited (Publishing)

First Edition published 2014 by
2QT Limited (Publishing)
Tatham Fell Lancaster LA2 8RE, United Kingdom

Copyright © Sheila Dibnah 2013
The right of Sheila Dibnah to be identified as the author
of this work has been asserted by him in accordance with the
Copyright, Designs and Patents Act 1988

The author has her own website: http://www.sheiladibnah.com/

Author/Publisher disclaimer:

While historical details are believed to be accurate all the characters
in this book have no existence outside the imagination of the author,
and have no relation whatsoever to anyone bearing the same name or
names. They are not even distantly inspired by any individual known or
unknown to the author and all the incidents are pure invention.

Cover Design by Hilary Pitt
Main Photo: Tony Smith , @HotpixUK
Other cover images: Shutterstock.com

Printed in Great Britain by
Lightning Source UK

A CIP catalogue record for this book is available
from the British Library
ISBN 978-1-910077-24-5

# IN MEMORY OF FRED, A KING AMONG MEN

*'People see me on telly messin' about with them big factory chimneys and think I'm the only steeplejack who ever lived! They never realise there were dozens of these wild blokes over a hundred years ago doing this caper and half of 'em were bloody mad! Some were quite famous, too. Men like Joseph Ball of Oldham, who owned a menagerie and built a castle in a row of terraced houses. And that other one as well, from Rochdale, Joseph Smith who had a Pullman carriage built and always dressed like a gentleman. "The Lancashire Steeplejack" they called him...'*

Dr. Fred Dibnah MBE.
A famous 21st century Victorian steeplejack.

# BEGINNERS PLEASE

*J*oseph Wragg's life was hanging by a thread.

The legendary Master Steeplejack and past manufacturer of lightning conductors trod the boards then dangled, spider-like, from a fragile staging encircling the top of the factory chimney. Once, part of the job he loved best —

King of his own world up here in the sky.

Before life got complicated.

And he fell from grace.

Never far from Joseph's thoughts were the three important women in his life: his devoted mother, Violet Wragg; his first love Tabitha Stark – and celebrated society beauty Lillie Langtry, once the mistress of HRH Albert Edward, Prince of Wales, and the sole reason Joseph lost his fortune.

Or perhaps four women, if he counted his wife Nellie, too.

Joseph kicked back from the masonry and contemplated his perilous predicament. Messrs Longhorn & Co Spinning Mill was the highest stack in Lancashire, governing the industrial skyline at a formidable 350 feet. He knew the exact measurement because he'd designed it himself.

Only a brave man would have nerve to tackle it and Joseph certainly was fearless – as well as being heartbroken, disillusioned and almost bankrupt.

He'd last scaled Longhorn's iconic chimney during the mid-nineteenth century shortly after it was built, erecting ten levels of wooden staging for a firework display to celebrate

Queen Victoria's visit to Oldham, festooning its elaborate corbelled top with hundreds of explosives. That night as they blazed, the glittering tiara of the textile trade, its polished carbon diamonds flashing with fire against the dark, smoggy industrialized sky, lit up the Queen's loyal subjects below who were celebrating the royal visit. Joseph clapped and cheered with his family, awed by the spectacle.

The sooty rain rattled down like iron rivets on his soaked cloth cap, dripping off the grimy neb and trickling down his nose, casting grey dust across his strong features like a veil. Then the warm sun came out for a while and turned it all to steam.

Rainfall never bothered him. But on days such as this, he knew the job was a young man's game. He was middle-aged now and felt it whenever the storms broke through.

He tapped at grimy masonry, ensuring the courses of brickwork were sound, his slender hammer moving with grace, catching scant rays of sunshine like treasured silver jewels.

Joseph pointed several cracks with red mastic made to his own recipe that he'd developed thirty years ago. Below, mill operatives toiling to the mechanised thrum of a steam engine, laboured at their spinning frames producing cotton thread for the Great British Empire. Above him, created by blasting fires of hell from a bank of eight boilers, the thirty-foot-diameter chimney spewed forth its thick, sulphurous smoke. It fell like inky teardrops in sadness for Joseph and for this weary northern mill-town trapped in the harsh factory system.

Since boyhood, Joseph had wanted to escape. He enjoyed taking risks and possessed a keen aptitude for successful entrepreneurial ventures as well as for steeplejacking. Against all the odds, he'd built a grand, modern palace of entertainment, the likes of which had never been seen outside of London. But ultimately it was all at a great cost to himself.

Working skilfully with his prized trowel, presented to him

by Oscar Wilde, he contemplated his failure: the spectacular demise of his theatre, The Red Rose Variety Palace on Union Street, Oldham. With its opulent style it was a palace fit for any Queen of Hearts – as he had intended.

Built from his obsession with an unattainable woman, his theatre complex was far closer to his heart than any unwise business investment but it had destroyed him emotionally and financially.

He'd learned the hard way that all things have their place.

Joseph tugged harshly at a rope fall line supporting his bosun's chair. The iron pulley wheel dropped him several more feet down the slippery chimney face. Tapping at the wet brickwork, testing the mortar again, he tried to ignore his disappointment. Broken hearted, his confidence in tatters, he realised his stupidity and once again turned to the steeplejacking trade for help – much to the curiosity of the periodicals and the general public, who wanted to be part of this historic day.

This was his first chimney-climb in years.

Joseph was the most legendary steeplejack of all time, and people across the land followed his antics with interest. He peered at the crowd gathering below. Small groups assembled, sheltering under the engine-house canopy. A magic lantern on a tripod would capture the moment his life began again. He counted at least twenty journalists with pads, scribbling away, taking notes, and several soberly-dressed men in black bowler hats – who could be bailiffs.

Within minutes, he would descend the red-painted ladders and talk about his return to the trade at his age. Then he'd slip back to the public house, avoiding bailiffs (if that's what they were), perhaps getting drunk with the regulars before staggering to his humble rooms above.

Joseph Wragg was once a wealthy man. '*The Gentleman Steeplejack of Chadderton Hall*' they'd called him. Then his home, a grand, stone mansion on the outskirts of Oldham, its tall rooms bulging with the finest furniture – and at one time a well-stocked menagerie within its extensive grounds

– was repossessed to pay off his debts. Everything except his disused chimney mending tackle had gone; that was now stored at the works yard, ready for action on this day.

His two sons Logan and Rudy, both apprentice steeplejacks, had suggested this climb at Longhorns. Their penniless father needed to drum up extra business and get back on his feet.

But it was many years since he'd laddered or mended a factory chimney.

Or climbed one.

And the effort almost killed him.

His stout, middle-aged body, now unused to demanding physical labour, ached with dull fatigue. But he was still tough. After tethering his bosun's chair to the wooden staging, he assumed a wide smile, a jaunty angle of the head and descended the ladders to meet his waiting public, waving on the way down to the cheering crowd.

People still loved 'their Joseph.'

Composed as always, forever more 'The Gentleman Steeplejack'.

And after the storm passed, the sun lit up the moving scene like limelight and his life began again.

*It was showtime...*

# PART ONE

# ACT 1

' *I*t's no use; tha's got to pull tha'sen together, our lass,' said Aspen Wragg, concerned at his wife's greying pallor which seemed worse each day. 'I know you're jiggered, but tha'll never get reet if tha don't eat a bit of summat and keep tha'sen warm.'

He had worried constantly about Violet since their son was born two months ago. Baby Joseph Wragg arrived when Britain's cotton industry was beginning to spread like a thick, snug blanket, covering the world with fine products from thousands of Lancashire spinning mills and weaving sheds. The industrial revolution gathered momentum in the grimy northern mill towns; the soft silence of peaceful human slumber and a tranquil day's rest were now as rare as steam power had been a few years previously.

Oldham, the Wraggs' home town, once a sleepy, peaceful hamlet at the edge of the Derbyshire Pennines, was now an important manufacturing centre leading the way in producing yarn for a proud nation. Imported from the slave-driven cotton fields of southern America to the capitalist-driven factories and spinning companies of northwest England, the raw material it depended on was lauded as 'King Cotton'. It was helping Britain to become 'great' and boast an empire that ruled the world.

The life-blood of the land that formed Joseph pumped through veins of black fossilized minerals that comprised the building blocks of its rigid, sprawling skeleton. Its soul was

held together by great clunking sinews of railway sustained by coal, and deep within its body the mines were its bowels.

Its womb was fed by polluted rivers and complex canal systems. Later, as a growing boy, Joseph would bathe in mill lodges used to slake the constant thirst of all this iron technology. He heard the beat of its cold steel heart as he swam amongst breeding rats. Machines, their muscles made of various leather straps and systems of super-heated pressurized steam, became merciless monsters snatching people from their rural homes, giving birth to human fodder for industry.

*'Here, you shall be my slaves or starve'* these engines rumbled tirelessly, in their tickerty-clank, tickerty-clank language that only a skilled engineer could decipher. Vast spinning mills and weaving sheds, iron works, foundries, engineering and machine shops, factories, bleach works, coal mines, gas works and giant smokestacks made up the northern aspect of Britain's unsightly, unnatural skyline.

Violet picked up baby Joseph, and attempted to feed him but her milk was slow. He screamed in frustration. She had hardly strength enough to hold him, and fretted he too would become weak.

'Here, Aspen, I can't. Give him some of that sugared water instead,' she said.

Aspen cradled his baby son, and wrapped him protectively in an old overcoat to keep out the freezing cold.

To survive in this life, a baby needed to be strong. And Joseph was born strong. He supped the sugared water, taking sustenance from the little nutrition that it offered. It was as though he already realised that he was a tiny part of the human powerhouse that forged ahead, making Britain the manufacturing force it was.

Lancashire's lads and lasses worked hard while the industrialists thrived.

Never the twain shall meet.

Not for ordinary folks, at any rate.

For them, neither ambition nor any number of viaducts,

bridges and aqueducts could span England's cast-iron social class system. And the lower classes, such as the Wraggs, struggled continually through their short lives, mostly in poverty. They survived in the shadows of tall industrial chimneys belching forth thick choking smoke like fiery demons, covering buildings and people, blackening everything with their poisonous fumes.

Only a few climbed out of the poverty and filth, if they were lucky.

Baby Joseph clutched at the tatty overcoat with a tiny fist and closed his eyes. His dreams would begin later.

The long row of red-brick, two-storey, terraced houses with a works at each end was called Potts Street after the cotton baron who built them. With an iron foundry yard at one end and Spinnercheck's Weaving Shed at the other, Potts Street was a row of modest dwellings where residents lived cheek-by-jowl with industry. Built solely to house factory operatives, the houses were cramped, confined and damp. In houses like these, usually owned by private landlords or factory owners, folk like the Wraggs risked becoming destitute if they fell ill or couldn't find their weekly rent.

The Wragg family fared worst of all on the workers' social scale. They lived in squalor, amid vermin and filth in a humble cellar almost on the iron foundry's doorstep. When the wind blew in one direction, the noise and fumes from the iron works filled the air with acrid smoke that seemed to eat the back of their throats raw.

Aspen Wragg, a dour but kind-hearted chimney sweep and his bonny wife Violet had married just over a year before, and this was the best they could afford. Aspen stood tall and proud, with a great handlebar moustache of ginger whiskers and a thin, red face. His merry expression belied the fact he'd known nothing but hardship all his life, with his mother dying of typhoid, and his wild, dullard father dragging him and his five brothers up as best he could. With his deep-set blue eyes, broad shoulders and a proud disposition, even when covered with soot as he mostly was,

Aspen cut a formidable figure.

Violet met him when she was working as a nursery maid for a local silversmith and his family who lived just outside Oldham in a smart new villa, set within an acre of land. Aspen came to sweep the front parlour chimney and, noticing her beautiful eyes as she walked past, he made polite conversation. Violet immediately fell head over heels in love with the handsome chimney sweep. When he left, she sneaked into the parlour and ran her hand across the marble mantelpiece, lovingly trailing fingers through a light covering of soot as if it were part of him.

The couple soon started courting, meeting for a walk down by the canal after church on her Sunday afternoon off. But the silversmith's wife did not approve of the union and banished Aspen from calling.

Soon afterwards, starry-eyed eighteen-year-old Violet, dreaming of having her own children and a husband to look after, left her employment. Within three weeks Aspen had proposed, saying he could afford to keep them both. The wedding on her nineteenth birthday at the local church had been a very humble affair. Her parents didn't approve of the match and didn't attend. Her father, a school teacher of good standing, had hoped that Violet might do better than a grimy chimney sweep who never seemed to have much about him.

Hopelessly in love, they moved into the gloomy cellar in Potts Street on the afternoon of the wedding and were happy, even though it broke her mother's heart. Her father said sorrowfully, 'You'll regret it one day, mark my words. You've ruined your life now, girl.'

'But we love each other, Father. How can that be wrong?'

'Love won't keep you warm in a hovel, lass.'

Married life came as a shock. With her comfortable upbringing, she had never known such hardship. One wall of the cellar dwelling was obliterated by black mildew and rising damp and the only water source was a temperamental cold tap in the outside yard, crudely lashed to a wooden post which stood upright like an evil totem and regularly froze

in winter.

Baby Joseph was born within the year to a worn-out and delicate Violet, whose chest had been badly affected by the damp living conditions and who also suffered chronic headaches and indigestion.

Her mother turned up with some clothes for when the baby came; seeing how the couple lived, she begged her daughter to return home. 'You can't have a child in these conditions, Violet,' she said.

Her daughter was willing to make the best of it. 'We'll be all right. I can't abandon Aspen. Besides, others cope.'

The place swarmed with lice and bedbugs.

In her condition Violet struggled, fetching pails of water and coal so she could have a hot meal prepared for her husband when he returned home. In worn clogs, she padded around the damp, stinking flagstones, which often flooded with sewage in wet weather. The sour, foul air of the cellar made her cringe and she thought of the beautifully ordered calm of the silversmith's nursery, where she once sat by a warm fire toasting crumpets or reading stories to her two young charges, Agnes and Jennie.

Then one day Aspen came home from work and found her unconscious. He carried her on his shoulders the mile and a half to her parents' house.

The birth was difficult; as the midwife pulled and tugged and tried her best, Aspen stood in the yard of his in-laws' home, pacing, listening to the screams of his wife indoors. He was alarmed to see all the blood when the midwife came to fetch him. The baby was weak, no-one had much hope and Violet remained in her parents' care for six weeks until she could stand being apart from Aspen no longer. She returned to the squalid conditions to be with the man she loved. Her parents pleaded with her not to go and baby Joseph shrieked and screamed all the way back to Potts Street.

Violet was suffering from what later would be described as post-natal depression as well as acute anaemia. The fetid air seemed much worse and she experienced several attacks

where she began weeping uncontrollably and couldn't stop. Aspen was anxious, and her parents urged her to return home again at once, but she wouldn't hear of it.

All her world was here with Aspen and Baby Joseph.

But as her father had predicted, love wouldn't keep them warm in a hovel.

Now Aspen came home once again to no hot supper. Violet glanced up as he moved towards the ancient table riddled with woodworm. He put Joseph down in the crib, then removed his grimy top coat and began unfastening a broad cummerbund around his waist. He glanced at the half loaf of bread and felt his stomach pinch. 'Get some of this down yer, lass. It'll make you feel a bit better,' he said, cutting a slice for his wife.

She smiled wanly. 'I'm all right, luv, just a bit tired is all,' she said, struggling up out of the chair near the cold, empty grate. 'Mrs Reeves gave me a lift down wi't coal, and I was just about to make the fire.' She went over to give him a big hug, wrapping both arms around his stout frame and pulling him close as she kissed him. He smelled of soot as always and some of it came off on her cheek.

'Don't be daft. Here, sit down our lass, I'll do it for thee,' he said affectionately, fiddling with the front fire bars and some sticks of kindling.

Violet sighed and flopped back wearily into her chair. 'I'm sorry, Aspen…' she said, gathering her woollen shawl around her thin shoulders.

The wood crackled and a weak flame took hold, casting a yellow glow over the dim room. Baby Joseph, still swathed in the threadbare coat, protected from the constant chilly draught, gurgled from his apple-crate crib. Aspen smiled at the child and the baby's face lit up. Because Violet had almost died in childbirth, the midwife had advised them not to have more children. Aspen was greatly saddened; he'd had visions of his own family business of chimney sweeps, run by tall, strong sons who would take over one day. In his dreams, he saw them having the biggest and best firm in the

entire North West.

But at least he had some good news today…

'Talkin' ter't landlord this morning,' he casually remarked as he piled little cobs of coal around the burning sticks. 'Reckons yon house at end is coming empty next week, the one with the big window,' he said, thumbing up towards the street with a big daft grin on his face. 'Where the Bickley family lived,' he added for good measure, bursting into a smile which wasn't at all like him.

Violet looked puzzled. 'Aye – well? Do they want you to do some repairs ter't chimney pot or summat?' she enquired, glad he seemed pleased about it.

'Better than that, mi' luv,' he said, pulling himself up to his full height as the fire in the grate caught hold and blazed. Straightening his scarf and jutting out his chin he said, 'We're 'avin the place. We're movin' in!'

Proud that at last he'd been able to afford new lodgings for his little family, he waited for his wife's reaction.

'Eee, by heck!' Violet exclaimed and jumped up from her chair. Her mouth dropped open, her eyes shone, and for once he saw the woman he'd married beneath the pallid, ailing features.

'All right, keep yer hair on!' he laughed, pleased to see her so happy for once. 'Aye, it's ours all reet. I've been and given word on it this mornin'.'

'It's champion news is that, Aspen,' Violet cried, flapping her shawl like a pair of faded wings. 'I can't believe it! I won't have to walk up and downstairs for coal every day and the baby can have some fresh air and daylight too.'

Despite her parents, who thought him shiftless, she'd never doubted her husband, knowing that he was a hard-working, careful man. The trouble with Aspen was he just lacked a bit of ambition, she thought. Violet didn't realize his dreams about having his own company of sweeps would be as far as he got. But he wasn't a dreamer in other ways and this latest news wouldn't be given lightly.

She looked around their tiny dwelling and few mouldy

17

possessions. 'But what are we to do for furniture in a house that size, Aspen?' she asked worriedly. 'We have nowt, have we?' The only thing they had of any quality was the brass bedstead given to her after Uncle Albert recently passed away, in which the three of them slept huddled together each night.

'Now don't go worrying tha'sen about all that palaver,' Aspen replied. 'The house has some stuff in it already an' what we 'aven't got, I'll get us,' he said, still puffed up like a butcher's turkey at Christmas. Work was good at present and he was gaining a reputation as a reliable, jobbing chimney sweep. He could afford this step up in their lifestyle.

Within the week, the Wraggs were the new tenants at 190 Potts Street. Aspen carefully stored his brushes and chimney-sweeping paraphernalia in the lean-to privy in the back yard while Violet wandered around inside the house examining dry walls and the foggy view across the street from the front parlour window, which was draped in discoloured lace. A horse and cart pulling a wagon stacked high with iron grid lids from the foundry passed by. No more fumes from that place, she thought. We'll be all right now.

The two-up, two-down, back-to-back house boasted a small scullery with great oblong slabs of rough-hewn stone for a roof. It had a small brass tap over a brown slop-stone in one corner; Violet turned it on and watched water gushing forth as if by magic, thinking how nice it would be in winter. In the downstairs rooms, they had gaslight like the rest of the street. No more of those dreadful tallow candles which gave off an unpleasant, greasy smoke and made her chest worse. There was even a colourful peg rug made from scraps of old cloth in front of the kitchen range in the back living room. Violet was pleased to discover two good-sized bedrooms with small cast-iron grates, and looked forward to seeing her beautiful brass bed installed later.

The house soon felt cosy and welcoming, and Violet's health greatly improved over the next few weeks as the family settled in.

\*\*\*

'Yoooo-hoooo!'

Violet was busy hanging out washing across the narrow back street which ran parallel to Bickershaw Street. She saw a pregnant woman with her sleeves rolled up on the opposite side, leaning against her own back gate. She was dressed similarly to Violet and was wearing an oversized mob-cap. 'Want a lift with them sheets there, lass?' the woman shouted.

Without waiting for an answer, she came striding across the cobbles and took several pegs from the basket. She was much taller than Violet and, despite being heavily pregnant, didn't struggle getting the sheet over the washing line. She looked at Violet. 'You're new 'ere. Ain't seen yer before,' she said, pegging them in place and smiling at her new friend.

'We've been living in a cellar further down the street. I'm Violet Wragg.'

'Uh-uh, and now you've joined the gentry, eh, Mrs Wragg?' the woman laughed. 'I'm Martha Crebbes, by the way, and them two little urchins theer are mi' girls Lizzy and Anne, and I don't know who this one is yet!' She pointed at her large tummy.

When Martha returned with the pram, Violet noticed that the girls were identical twins. Two children ran up to stare in the pram, abandoning their game of poking a spinning top with a stick.

'How old are they missus?' one of the small boys enquired, examining a tiny hand.

Martha smiled and replied, 'They're almost ten months and I'm expecting a sister or a brother for them in a few weeks.'

'We only have our Joe and he's a nipper as well,' said Violet.

'You'll be expecting again soon, I'll bet.'

Violet smiled gently and continued cooing at the two

girls, ignoring the comment.

Martha, she later discovered, was kind-hearted, a bit of a character and was popular with all the neighbours on account of how she selflessly looked after Mrs Sale next door. The elderly widow had been crippled by a runaway horse shortly after her husband died. Martha did all Mrs Sale's washing and cooking, despite having her own family to see to.

'So, what does yer ol' man do, then?' Martha asked, wiping her hands on her apron. 'Is he in't mill like my Cedric?' Her husband worked as an operative spinner at Barron & Cloughs Mill two streets away, she explained.

'Chimney sweep,' replied Violet, unable to take her eyes off the two beautiful babies gurgling in the pram.

Martha made Violet laugh and that evening, as she prepared tea, she happily told Aspen about the encounter. Soon, a regular washday routine was established and the two women became good friends. Once Violet fully regained her strength, she helped Martha with her confinement and also the care of Mrs Sale. When Baby Maisie was born, Martha seemed to recover in no time and it wasn't long before their Monday washdays and Thursday trips to town to get a few pounds of best tripe from Mr Fletcher at the market were re-established.

As Joe grew older, he loved the company of Lizzy and Anne, and the three of them were always getting up to some mischief in the back street, along with Maisie who toddled after them, not wanting to be left out.

The two women took it in turns with childcare until Joseph was old enough to go off on his own when he turned eight.

Violet didn't care much for Martha's husband, Cedric, who seemed gruff and was always grumbling about Sage Williams, the overseer at Barron & Cloughs. But Martha made her laugh, especially with her impersonation of Sage and his funny way of caressing the cotton bales and speaking as though they were alive. Both women shared a better sense of fun than their husbands, and Martha looked forward to

their joint cooking days. Their men loved sheep's head broth with parched peas, and the woman cooked it in big iron pans that made a welcoming sight and smell for their hungry husbands when they arrived home.

Cedric was a proud and uncompromising man who took any situation to heart and overreacted at times, but he loved his family wholeheartedly. Martha kept him calm whenever he came home fuming about something Sage had said or done. The couple seemed so different in character but were devoted to each other and if anyone ever upset Martha, it was Cedric they had to deal with.

A while later, Martha told Violet that she had another little one on the way, and for once was frightened of what Cedric would say when he found out. She was pleased to be pregnant at first, but there was a rumour about the mills being put on part-time hours due to cotton shortages, and that Barron & Cloughs would shut down entirely. Aspen didn't say anything to Violet when she told him over supper that night, but from the beer house he knew Cedric was worried sick and certainly wouldn't be pleased with the news of another mouth to feed.

Aspen was relieved his own work seemed to be going well. He'd set on a new apprentice from the orphanage, a thin, stick-like lad of seven who almost got stuck up the chimney at a local bigwig's house. He came home one day, telling Violet all about it. She laughed out loud. 'Oh Aspen, that's a fair caper – whatever next!'

He admonished her. 'It's not funny, tha' knows – poor lad could've been stuck up yon fer good.' He joked that he hoped it wouldn't happen once their Joseph started in their family business, which he planned to do as soon as he was old enough. Violet didn't reply but looked solemnly down at the cast-iron pan before her, and continued stirring the simmering broth, deep in thought.

She had big plans for her only son and didn't want him sweeping chimneys for a living. She always called him Joseph – not Joe, like Aspen sometimes did – and she hoped

he would get a nice office job, or cushy work at a bank or something. Over the years, her parents had doted on Joseph. Her father said he'd ensure his grandson had every advantage when it came to learning and studying. Violet had already made enquiries at the local school and intended that he start as a part-timer as soon as possible, much to her husband's scorn.

Aspen brought the tin hip-bath in from where it usually hung on an iron peg in the back yard. A cold blast of evening air caught her ankles as he guided the bath through the open doorway.

'Summat smells good,' he said. 'Brrr... getting a bit cowd out theer toneet.'

'Supper time soon,' she replied, smoothing a newspaper on the table that dominated most of the room. 'This'll warm you up, love.'

He clunked the bath down on the flagstones and pulled it in front of the glowing fire-range, opening the dampers in the flue, allowing the fire to build and heat up water in the copper kettle standing on the trivet above.

'I'll be bankin' tha' fire up with coal slack again tonight. Rent collector's not due till Friday, but I've not paid the coalman from last week yet,' he remarked, amiably, tucking into his evening meal of sheep's head broth, oblivious to the gravy that dribbled down his chin.

'I'm starving, Ma!' Joseph said, dashing in through the back door and causing a draught again. 'You'll never guess! Anne got some creepy-crawlies from near the canal and they got out of the jar on to Maisie and made her scream!' he said, relishing his mother's shudders.

'Don't bring any in here, our Joseph, or there'll be trouble,' Violet said.

'Aye, now then eat yer supper up, lad. Tha mother's been working all afternoon to feed yer this good grub and yer need yer strength for tomorrow,' Aspen said, wiping his face at last.

Even though Violet was grateful for their happiness, she

secretly thought there must be more to life than this constant daily struggle. She vowed Joseph would one day get a chance to find it and get away from Aspen and his expectations of drudgery.

***

Joseph didn't like the job and displayed all the impatience of an eleven-year-old boy. He leaned idly against the dry stone wall and fidgeted with the sooty circular flat brush and collection of poles, as his father spoke to the vicarage housekeeper. Pa had forced him into helping with chimney sweeping shortly after his birthday last month, and he hated every second of it.

He'd been playing in the yard at home after morning school, messing about, finding out how the mangle worked with its wooden rollers, when Pa returned home at dinnertime and said, 'It's about time, our Joseph. I've got a big job tomorrow and you can come with me and start learning t'ropes.'

Joseph knew it was a bad thing Pa was doing, and that he planned to send him up the inside of a chimney one day, because he'd heard his mam shouting about it a lot recently. 'Our Joseph will be too refined for that sort of work,' she cried. 'He wants to be in't factory offices, writing or summat. He's got gentry-like qualities, has our Joseph, and sending 'im up chimneys will kill him!.'

Aspen assured her he wasn't going to work him as a climbing boy but she knew if they were stuck on a big job it would surely happen because Aspen never saw danger and did what had to be done.

Aspen was angry that she was filling the boy's head with daft notions above his station by teaching him to read and write. He knew that breaking in Joseph would cause trouble with her. Joseph sulked for the rest of the afternoon; frightened of the prospect of the confines of the chimney as he told his mam he didn't want to do it.

There was another row that evening over supper, as his father bellowed, 'He's coming with me – that's final. And I'm setting him on full time once he's seen the operation in action a few times.'

Pushing his chair angrily away from the table, Aspen stood up. 'What's the use of all that ruddy learnin' when theer's a living to earn around here, eh, woman?'

Joseph had never seen his father so livid and cried himself to sleep that night. He wanted a cuddle as he lay in the dark, but didn't dare risk being called 'soft' again by his pa. His father was tough man's man, but his mam was always kind. She made a point of sitting and reading books, making sure he understood all his lessons at morning school and the extra stuff his grandpa taught him.

He was keen to learn and exceptionally gifted at arithmetic. Violet was pleased to see her boy enjoyed reading, particularly stories about the engineer Isambard Kingdom Brunel who had died two years earlier. His grandpa gave him magazines called *The Engineer* and old copies of *The Penny Dreadful*, too. Although he struggled with understanding what all the words meant, he loved the line-drawings and learned many new words. His grandpa did much to eradicate his thick, twisted vowels too, smoothing out some of his hard northern accent – much to the annoyance of Aspen, who said he was turning the lad into a right sissy having him talking posh like that and giving him ideas above his station.

But Joseph was no sissy. He loved all aspects of mechanical engineering and, whenever possible, would slip away into the big cobbled yard at Spinnercheck Mill at the end of their street, seeking out the chief engineer Mr Markley, who was responsible for the tandem compound steam engine that powered the weaving shed.

Sometimes, if he hadn't got his friends Anne and Lizzy with him, Joseph was allowed inside the engine room to see its fly-wheel turning like a big beast, driving the machinery on all four floors of the mill. The kindly engineer saw the boy's quick ability to understand the principles of how the

engine worked, and showed him how to fill the little brass lubricator pots with oil and polish the maker's plate.

Joseph loved doing this and afterwards would wander off into the boiler room next door to speak with the two fire-beaters, Mal Kitson and George Palls, who were in charge of a row of boilers that powered the engine. One day, when George opened the door to turn the coals, Joseph saw the fire burning as hot as molten steel and stepped closer to see the long, white-hot fire bars. The heat seared him and made the hairs frizzle on the side of his arm. Mal grabbed him and said, 'Mind now, don't get any closer – it'll cook yer like a mutton chop, if tha' don't watch out.'

After that, the chief stoker and fire-beaters became something of heroes to Joseph. He was amazed at the way they expertly scooped up shovels of coal to feed the hungry boilers and they explained to him how the products of combustion went up the tall chimney outside from a flue system at the back of the boilers.

But the thing he loved most was watching the steeplejacks working on the industrial chimneys around the area. He would stand at the bottom, gazing upwards, seeing the men scampering up the side on ladders. Usually, there was a strange contraption tethered to the structure at the top that looked like a wooden frame, from which the men sometimes dangled on ropes. It looked daring and exciting, and when the men came down their ladders at dinnertime they always looked wide-eyed and wild, as though the dangerous work had invigorated them in some way.

He wished his pa was a steeplejack instead of a daft chimney sweep.

'Come on, son, get a move on, don't stand theer catchin' flies all day!' Aspen shouted from behind him, breaking his train of thought. Joseph immediately grabbed the bundle of brushes and tugged it down the vicarage path. They entered a parlour stuffed with bulky furniture covered in brown cloths. The room smelt of flowers. 'Mind you don't scratch the piano, now,' the vicar's wife admonished, as his pa nearly

caught one of the polished legs with the brass-threaded end of one of the poles.

Aspen bent in front of the ornate fire place and fed the round brush slowly up the chimney. Great clouds of billowing soot tumbled down into the grate, some escaping through the long hole in the cloth where the brush went through. The vicar's wife tut-tutted again and stepped back to avoid breathing it in, as the parlour maid came scurrying in with a broom. It was Joseph's job to shovel this muck up afterwards and pile it into thick, calico sacks that were waiting outside on their handcart. Then, once they'd collected enough soot from a few jobs, they'd push their handcart up near the outskirts of town on a Saturday afternoon and sell the soot to the local farmers for fertilizer.

At his father's signal, Joseph went outside to gaze up at the tall, twisted terracotta chimney pots of the vicarage. He was waiting for the brush to appear. After a few minutes he yelled out, 'That's it, Pa! It's done!' and dashed back indoors to begin the lengthy process of dismantling the poles and cleaning up. While he worked, his father usually had a cup of sweet, strong tea.

Joseph found the work tedious but not too hard. However, the next day Aspen had a special job on for the wealthy family who owned Dales Pit, a coal mine on the other side of town. Mr Dales and his large family lived in a forbidding house with tall, spindly towers bedecked with cast-iron balustrades. Joseph was curious to see the interior, thinking it might be dark like the disused works up near the mill-lodge where he and his friends went swimming in summer.

On the way back from the vicarage, Aspen mentioned that Joseph would climb inside part of the Dales' chimney with a hand-brush to free the soot, because it was far too wide for the circular brush to do the job. His pa said he wasn't employing a climbing boy when his wife had birthed one of their own. Joseph was in tears by the time he got home and got called sissy again as he buried his head in his mam's apron and wept, his little body heaving with sobs as

she gently smoothed his hair and scolded Aspen.

# *ACT 2*

*V*iolet's clogs clattered noisily over the wet cobblestones on the way to the tow-path down by the canal. She scurried over the bridge as fast as the slippery irons on the wooden soles would allow, almost coming a cropper several times on the shiny granite, sobbing hard as she ran. Stopping by the cast-iron gas lamp on the other side of the wide basin, she wrapped her hand around its cold post, desperately peering forward into the mist before deciding which way to go along the canal bank. Then she disappeared along the path back under the bridge, running towards the lock gates, searching for Aspen, her steamy breath billowing behind her like a railway locomotive as she ran.

It was Sunday morning. Aspen used to like going for a stroll by the canal before stopping off at the King's Head in town for a pint or two of porter and a word with the inn keeper before dinnertime. But for the past year or so, he and his friends had no longer been able to afford visits to the beer house, so the men folk gathered each Sunday around the canal locks instead. Most of the men had large families to support; they were weary and out of work, and this was their only pleasure. Aspen hadn't got much work to do either. People were not able to buy enough coal to keep warm these days, let alone have their chimneys swept.

The cotton famine which started a year previously had devastated the local community. Supplies of raw cotton from the United States were cut off because of the American

28

Civil War and that hit the industry hard. Owners of mills in Oldham and its surrounding districts who were dependent on the raw cotton had had to lay off operatives. Spinning frames, carding rooms, bleaching sheds throughout the industrial north all stood idle for part of the week, and sometimes didn't run at all. People were starving and dying of hunger.

There are plenty worse off than us, thought Aspen. At least his family wasn't starving. He still had a few savings put by. For once, Aspen was glad he had only three mouths to feed. It was the first time he felt happy about having only one son. He knew of a family of thirteen who had less than sixteen shillings a week to survive on, and that wasn't unusual. Aspen and Violet were lucky – at least he'd been able to get some work, breaking stones for road mending at the yard on the outskirts of town. It was hard, back-breaking labour for a scant few shillings but what with that and his meagre savings, at least they had food in their bellies each day.

Violet heard a loud cough and, almost out of breath, ran a little further down the tow path. Aspen was propped up against the steam crane talking to Mr Fletcher, the tripe-seller from the market. Both men heard her approach and stopped talking when they saw the state she was in.

'Our Joseph's just come home and said Cedric Crebbe's killed himself!' Violet blurted out, tears rolling down her face. 'And now they can't find Martha and the girls either.'

Aspen never normally swore in front of his missus but he forgot himself now. Throwing down his cigarette, he used words usually reserved for the beer house. 'You what?' he asked. 'Our Joe said this?'

Violet tugged at his damp coat, urging him to come back to Potts Street. By the time they got back, the neighbours were searching for Martha, who was last seen going past Mr Green's provision shop on the corner of Urmston Street. Her eyes had had a glazed, fixed stare, and she was slowly pulling her two girls on either side of her.

Two weeks earlier, the Crebbes had lost their youngest, Daisy, a baby girl of three months, to fever. The whole family had been devastated. Within days, Violet found a highly-distressed Cedric and the twins huddled together around a fireless grate and Martha lying on the tatted old sofa, panting for breath. Her complexion was sallow and her eyes shrunken and full of deathly languor. She lifted her head helplessly as Violet entered the fetid room.

'Our lass has it too,' said Cedric, pointing at Martha. 'And this one here's feverish with it as well.' He clutched Maisie tenderly to his chest; she flopped against him without even blinking.

Maisie suddenly gave a piercing shriek, which set off the twins, Lizzy and Anne, into a fierce crying fit. Cedric tried helplessly to soothe all three girls. Martha's head flopped back down on the striped flock pillow.

Violet set about making a pot of weak tea with twice-used tea leaves. Looking at the empty shelves, she saw that there weren't even any oats for gruel.

Leaving the tea to brew, she went home and returned within a few minutes, clutching a quart of milk, which the twins drank hungrily. Maisie wouldn't touch it.

Cedric hadn't let on they were so desperate for food, or Violet would have tried to help sooner. Now she saw why he was so angry the previous week when she'd called round with some lard she didn't want after buying a little too much. He'd swiped it from her hand.

'What do you think this is? Be damned with your charity!' he'd shouted. 'Stop swanking with all yer fuss, woman!'

Violet had fled the house in tears. When she told her husband, he merely said, 'What d'yer expect – the bloke is grievin' for his daughter.'

Aspen got on all right with Cedric. When Violet told him about their predicament, he said he'd take a few cobs of coal and some sticks of wood around. At least Cedric might be able to cook a pot of stew for them all, he said. 'But they have nowt in to cook,' Violet replied. 'Here, we'll

do without supper tonight – take this bit of rabbit and turnip as well.' She handed over the pan of warm stew, then found some potatoes and a hunk of dry bread; 'These might tide them through tomorrow, as well. Surely Cedric won't refuse help now?'

'I'll have a word with him again about going to see the Board o' Guardians at t'Town Hall for some help,' Aspen said. Cedric Crebbes was a proud man and didn't like handouts but Aspen was concerned that the man hadn't revealed just how bad the situation was. Aspen knew Cedric would struggle standing in front of gentleman committee members, telling them his personal business. No matter how skint he was, he still had his pride, he had told Aspen and the men down by the steam crane last Sunday.

The Board of Guardians and Relief Committee had set up a soup kitchen in Chalfont Road. Two days later, with Aspen's encouragement, Cedric queued up for over an hour with his soup tickets, given to him by the local Clergy on the Relief Committee, hoping to get enough food for all his family. But he was only handed out enough for himself and was told, 'No show, no food – only for those present.'

'Give over, yer daft buggers,' Cedric shouted. 'Ah've got a family to look after tha' knows, and mi' wife and nippers are poorly.'

'I've told you, my good man – no show no food.'

'What's a bloke to do, then, to look after his own?'

'Have you considered one of the industrial educational classes, Mr Crebbes? They teach useful skills such as cobbling. It is a fine example of—'

'Bloody cobbling? What kind of trade is THAT for a skilled man! I'm a bloody time-served cotton spinner, you fool!'

'It will provide a few pennies each week, Mr Crebbes.'

Cedric felt his cheeks flame red in humiliation and vowed never again to approach what he called 'toffs' for help after the way they had looked down on him. 'You know what you can do with your few pennies!' he shouted.

Three days later, little Maisie succumbed to the fever and it looked like Martha would die too. It had all been too much for Cedric.

'Where's our Joseph now?' asked Aspen, searching for him amidst the chaos, knowing his son would be devastated by the news.

'He's heartbroken, but he's off looking for them. I mean, they can't have gone far in Martha's state, can they?' replied Violet. She was distracted as two of the neighbours came dashing out of the Crebbes' house, spluttering and pushing aside Arthur Deans from next door who was standing on the backdoor step. Because he always seemed to know everyone's business, Aspen went over to the man to enquire what had happened.

Glad of an audience, Mr Deans told Aspen the story. Cedric had wrenched the gas bracket from the wall. He stood on a chair, placed his mouth over the broken pipe on the wall and inhaled deeply. As he fell unconscious, gas leaked further into the house. Sensing danger for her girls, Martha struggled to get them outside but hadn't been seen since. One of the neighbours had smelled gas as he walked past and run through the open door to investigate.

Mrs Deans came marching over. She was a wiry, formidable woman who always wore the same heavy bonnet and shawl whatever the weather. She told her husband to shape himself, stop gossiping and find a bobby instead of standing idle on the back step. He shrugged his shoulders meekly, replying, 'Lucky th'grate weren't lit or else there'd 'av been a ruddy great gas explosion down all th'street so th'bobbies would have had summat proper to look into!'

Mrs Deans clicked her tongue and said it was a rum do, before making a cross with her right hand across her chest. 'Eh, God rest his poor soul, that's all I can say. Who knows what went on in that house?'

A man standing next to her retorted, 'Nowt suspicious abaht it, yer daft lass. Cedric were at th'end of his tether, see, all of them fair clemmed like that, without a bite to eat

in th'house.'

Mr Faulks from further down the street agreed. 'Bobbies won't do owt, any road,' he said, then pursed his lips in thought. He'd worked with Cedric for over twenty years and liked him. 'But some bugger will have to do summat about him dead indoors though, poor devil,' he added.

Another man remarked dryly, 'Aye, well it's still thick with gas in theer, so a body can do owt for now, can they?'

'Have to leave th'back door open for a while longer before we pull him out. Can't breathe in theer!' agreed Mr Deans, rolling up his shirt sleeves readying himself for the task. His wife threw him a cross look again, tugged at her shawl then shuddered.

When the gas fumes cleared and the men went inside the house, Violet mentioned about laying the body out, volunteering with Mrs Deans to wash and bathe Cedric, since Martha wouldn't be up to it.

'Yer'll be lucky to find anybody wi' pennies fer his eyes,' replied Mr Deans. 'Whole street hasn't got tuppence between 'em all!'

'Oh, do be quiet, Arthur,' said his wife.

'Keep Martha and the girls with us when we find them,' Aspen suggested to Violet. 'I'm going to fetch Doctor Smythe to make the arrangements.' Glancing up and down the street, expecting Martha to appear at any moment, he set off towards the doctor's house.

But Martha and the girls were nowhere to be seen and were still missing when it grew dark. Like Mrs Deane said, it was a rum do all right.

***

Next day, Joseph was standing in the middle of the ironworks' yard. He'd been out again since breakfast searching for Mrs Crebbes and her daughters. Momentarily distracted by the scaffolding circling the top of the brick chimney,

he noticed a sign which said 'STAPES STEEPLEJACKS, OLDHAM.' The sign, belonging to the area's foremost firm of steeplejacks, was new; he was sure it wasn't there when he was working with his pa last week.

Joseph traced the fresh white script with his finger. The ironworks was one of the few places not directly affected by the cotton famine, and even from where he was standing on a cool late September day, he could feel the fierce heat coming out of the works. The dull repetitive thud of the gigantic steam hammer always made the ironworks yard an exciting place to be; Joseph sometimes crept up to the tiny square windows and peered inside the smudged and broken panes of glass, watching men working at the rolling mill with long lengths of mild steel, or pouring molten iron into sand box moulds to form shapes.

'Now then, are't goin' up ter top, eh?' a gravelly voice enquired.

Joseph turned to see a fearsome but mischievous-looking man, with a creased face bearing untidy white whiskers step out from the side of the chimney. He wasn't that old, but to Joseph he looked ancient. His worn jacket was nipped in with a broad leather belt and his moleskin trousers had big holes in them. A hammer and several other items used in his work as a steeplejack dangled from his waist. He reminded Joseph of a court jester, the way he ambled about on bowed legs. His shoulders were broad, his face dirty with grime, and he grinned manically in Joseph's direction with his yellow teeth, or the stubs of what was left of them.

'Seen yer 'ere before. Dost tha want t'have a climb up, then?' he teased, looking upwards and pointing.

Another man appeared, similarly dressed and slightly taller though less mad looking. He was carrying a great length of coiled rope over his shoulder. He began asking the first man about some nuts and bolts for the iron bands they were placing around the top of the chimney. 'Howdoo lad,' he said, noticing Joseph. 'Not off helping your pa today?' Ron Stape knew all about the local chimney sweep who was

34

here last week with his lad, clearing the flue of soot while the ironworks was closed on a Sunday.

'No, we've not got any work on, sir. Pa's down at the stone breakers' yard, but they won't let me help there,' Joseph said, kicking around a few iron nuggets lying on the cobblestones.

'Aye, tha's only got work for them with families to keep,' replied the first man thoughtfully, dropping his frenzied grin.

Joseph explained about what had happened to Cedric Crebbes, but the steeplejacks hadn't seen or heard anything of Martha or the girls.

Ron Stape spoke up again, breaking the sombre mood as he placed the rope coil down on the ground. 'This here's me younger brother, Les,' he said, acknowledging the first man then turning his attention back to Joseph. He bent forward. 'Now then lad, Tell yer father we're lookin out for a good bloke not frightened of hard work or heights. Tekk him on casually, mind, at first,' he said cautiously, tapping the side of his nose. 'And his young assistant, of course,' he winked. 'We've got a rush job on at th'owd works in Chaucer Street. That old weaving shed once owned by Rigbys & Co. Couple of learned blokes from Bury has gotten themselves going with some local bigwigs as a co-operative and rented two floors of the mill. They're goin' to be tekkin on some workers when it's up and running. But them stone chimneys are in a right state and the boilers need fettlin' too. Boiler inspector nearly had a fit when he saw the state er't rusty tubes inside it!' he added, chuckling to himself.

'It'll never work, tha' knows,' said Les gloomily, spitting out a wad of chewed tobacco. 'They're spinning that Indian stuff made from yams. Rough stuff that. Bloody rough and useless it is; stinks too.' He adjusted his cap and looked up at the staging around the chimney, momentarily distracted.

'Better than folk starvin' out on't streets wi' no work for 'em, though, eh?' Ron quizzed. 'A co-operative like that worked at Dodge's place and a few other outfits over Bolton way an' all, didn't it?' he said with authority.

'What? A fine mill with over seventy-five carding engines, and they be running about ten for full capacity on each floor?' Les replied, spitting out the remaining tobacco. 'Fat lot of good that lot did too; bloody dreamers, lot of 'em!'

Joseph didn't hear a word of their debate. He was still deep in thought about what Ron had said. His pa working as a steeplejack and him a steeplejack's apprentice! It would be a dream come true.

Slightly out of context as the conversation had moved on, he blurted out, 'Oh, that's right champion! Thanks mister!'

Ron ruffled his hair with a calloused hand. 'Now be along with thee! We've work to do!' he said.

Joseph ran off in the direction of the heavy wrought-iron gates with the works name stamped through. He'd had his eleventh birthday the previous week and he'd got an apple – but this news was the best-ever present he could wish for in all his life!

He slowed down as he heard something that sounded like a distressed cat. 'Here, kitty-kitty,' he coaxed, walking towards the works' office block near the tall gateposts. Mr Sykes, who wore a splendid gold watch chain dangling from a waistcoat pocket and high white collar, usually pushed him out of the works yard whenever he saw him hanging about. Joseph was careful to avoid the office window today. 'Here, kitty-kitty,' he whispered.

Creeping cautiously behind the single-storey building in search of the cat, Joseph made a shocking discovery: his two friends, Lizzy and Anne, and their dead mother, Mrs Crebbes.

Anne sobbed softly and clung to her sister. Martha Crebbes lay stiff on the ground, her eyes gazing unseeingly to the sky, silver slug trails across her face and matted hair. Despite two highly-coloured patches on each cheek, Lizzy looked blue around the lips; she held on to her sister Anne, whose head lay on her mother's flimsy wet dress.

Joseph recoiled in horror, unable to take in the scene. He'd never seen anyone dead. Mrs Crebbes didn't look real

and her pale skin reminded him of a wax candle.

Anne shrieked when she saw Joseph and put her arms out towards him.

Joseph didn't know what to do next. He ran off and banged hard on the office door to draw Mr Sykes' attention. By the time the man answered, Joseph was in a panic.

'Slow down lad – whatever's the matter?' Sykes enquired, flashing pale, fierce eyes, thinking this may be a prank but at once seeing it wasn't.

'Come! QUICK, sir!' Joseph urged. 'Mrs Crebbes and the girls!'

Both of them dashed around the back of the building with Joseph leading the way. On seeing Mrs Crebbes, Mr Sykes sucked in his breath, exclaimed 'Holy Mother of God' and quickly crossed his heart.

He instructed Joseph to step aside as he pulled the girls away from their mother. He tried to hold Lizzy up but she flopped from side to side like a rag doll. 'Go and get the doctor and look sharp about it!' he shouted at Joseph. 'Now do as I tell you – scoot, lad!'

Joseph's lungs burned raw as he ran as fast as he could to the doctor's house near the big fountain outside the new park. When he returned twenty minutes later with Doctor Smythe, Mr Sykes told him to go home at once. Joseph wanted to stay to see what Doctor Smythe would do and was curious about what was in the brown leather Gladstone bag the doctor carried, but both men were firm and told him to leave.

Ten minutes later, Violet felt physically sick when she learned what had happened. She stood in the back yard, with her red hands over her eyes for a moment or two before tears spilled down her cheeks. The grey soap suds settled undisturbed in the dolly tub and Aspen's blue shirts lay soaking as the tears came harder. 'Martha – and them poor mites – oh my lord, will this never end?' she cried.

Only this morning she'd been talking to old Mrs Meadows from the end of Arkwright Street, whose husband had sold

the family's clothing to the rag and bone man for five pennies. Bargemen working a canal boat under the bridge found Mr Meadows lying face down in the swirling canal the day after, clutching the rope he'd tied round his neck to hang himself from the structure. Little whirlpools formed around his shoulders as he bobbed up and down in the dark waters. On hearing the news, Violet had rushed off into the back yard and vomited down the grid.

Aspen came home at tea time and learned the sad news about Martha. Joseph was in shock, hunched forward at the table, fidgeting about with some glass marbles. He couldn't quite believe Maisie and Mr and Mrs Crebbes had died, and he prayed Anne and Lizzy would be all right.

After hugging his wife and soothing her tears, Aspen leaned forward in his chair by the fire to deliver the sad news he'd heard on the way home. Things had progressed since Joseph left the ironworks at dinnertime.

'Young Lizzy's dead as well now; there's only Anne left out of 'em all,' he whispered softly, as he dabbed at his eyes. Violet broke down again and Joseph studied the floor in greater detail, letting out a long sigh before breaking into huge wracking sobs.

No-one spoke for a while then Aspen broke the silence. 'Both girls would have died right away but for the fairly mild weather we're 'avin fer't time of year. Bein' out like that all night and them fair clemmed as well…' He let the words trail off then quietly added under his breath, 'And it might 'ave bin better that way as well.'

Joseph's eyes widened in shock at his father's words. 'What'll happen to her now, Pa? Anne, like?' he urged.

Violet hushed him but Aspen put up his hand and replied, 'Orphanage job, I suppose lad, or workhouse. May God help her, poor mite.'

Even though Aspen had done a hard day's graft, no-one had much appetite for their modest tea of bread and dripping and later that night, Joseph had nightmares of slugs and dead people toiling in dark mills.

***

Aspen pushed his way back through the crowds waiting outside the town hall in Union Street. Its Grecian structure, dominated by a handsome portico made of stone in the style of a temple, seemed to mock the starving, bedraggled people queuing to see the Board of Governors inside.

Someone grabbed his arm from the line. 'Not workin' down at yon stone yard today, lad?' a gruff voice enquired. Aspen turned to see his old drinking pal, Bob Wright. Bob was once a skilled weaver, the highest-paid position of blue collar workers in any weaving shed, and the most respected. He was much older than Aspen but they always got on well and met by the steam crane every Sunday morning for a smoke.

Bob lived in a house with a big bay window in a nicer part of town but he hadn't worked for the last twenty weeks, and his childless wife Enid was bed-ridden with dropsy this past year.

'Nah Bob – just got the shove.' Aspen pointed towards the town hall. 'Them daft beggers in theer reckoned I had too much already. That's a laugh, eh?' He snorted sarcastically.

'Aye, lad, tha'll be more of us lot bloody slavin' for nowt for that stuck-up lot to keep a few scraps on't table before we're through,' Bob said.

Aspen nodded in agreement and continued, 'I've enough to keep us fed fer three weeks – and then that's it. Just on't way back home to break news to our lass.' After further examination of Aspen's home situation, this morning the Board had decided he had enough savings to provide for his small family without additional work which should be going to someone worse off.

'Bloody rum caper this Civil War and no end in sight,' moaned Bob. 'I'm too old now for any other work. Weaver for most of mi' life.' The previous Monday, Bob had been

sent to work as a labourer at the new Alexandra Park being built by redundant factory workers in the middle of Oldham. The corporation was handing out a few shillings and meal tickets in return for heavy digging and landscaping work. Bob lasted half a day before his back gave out. He was sent home in agony and told to report back to the town hall for further assessment.

Aspen shook his head. 'Wouldn't 'appen to a bloody beast would it?'

'Bloody chicken feed for slave labour; got us o'er a barrel, them lot.'

'Now't we can do about it. I reckon we're worse than them for doin' it.'

Bob sneered, nodding toward the building again which had taken on the image of an enemy to the two men, with its grand and rather forbidding appearance. 'Posh lot in theer, going back home to a hot meal and warm bed – toffs, no bloody idea any of 'em!'

Aspen was just about to add that the gentry were indeed lucky bastards when a tough, angry-looking man poked Bob in the back. As Bob and Aspen looked round, the dishevelled man turned on them with vicious sunken eyes and told both men not to be too quick to judge or turn away chance to earn a few shillings and a hot meal. He swept his arm over the crowd to illustrate his point, defending the weary queuing line of men by saying, 'You'd be grabbin' owt you could as well if your family were clemmed enough – back ache or no bloody back ache! For pity's sake, bloody shut up, will you, man?'

A few men murmured and agreed, and buoyed up by this the man sneered at Bob. 'Bloody weavers always did think they were a cut above – stuck-up lot, any road!'

The crowd drew closer and the two friends saw serious trouble brewing. Everyone was tired, cold, hungry and frightened for their families' future. Scuffles in the street were commonplace, usually started over something small like this, and could quickly develop into fierce fights. There

had been two riots recently in meal ticket queues and one man had lost his life.

Aspen ignored the confrontation and said to his friend, 'I'll see you on Sunday, Bob.' He walked away, pushing gently through the agitated, milling crowd to avoid sparking any reaction.

\*\*\*

Joseph was still shocked by what had happened to the Crebbes family but he couldn't stop thinking of what the two steeplejacks had said. After supper the previous night, he'd waited until his ma was washing dishes in the scullery and told his father about the offer.

'Don't be soft in th'ead lad. Steeplejacks?'

'But Pa, they said they'd have work for you – us both.'

Aspen tutted and studied his tin mug. 'Any road, I'm looking at doin' graft on Alexandra Park with a bit o' landscaping an' all.' He swigging his hot tea, thinking the job might be easier than any steeplejacking work. 'Ave to see t'Board tomorrow, and they'll probably be settin' me on next week.'

But today the Board of Directors had told him he didn't qualify for that either. One of the fine gentleman, who smelled of lemony cologne and had smooth, clean hands, leaned forward and peered over his horn-rimmed eyeglasses. 'Mr Wragg, there is absolutely nothing we can do to offer assistance. There are men far worse off than you with many more dependents to support.'

For weeks now, chimney-sweeping work had been at best scant, at worst none-existent. There wasn't much demand from working folk, and the toffs' houses were usually too far out of town up the big hill towards the suburbs to be practical. Besides, Aspen had sold their handcart to buy extra coal to help Cedric. It meant the Wraggs would be starving too in a few weeks, if he didn't do something soon.

Aspen marched home through the grey drizzle, the streets devoid of the usual heavy smoke from factory chimneys. Gas lamps placed at intervals were doing their best to cheer the gloom, their weak, sickly light bouncing off the wet flagstones. He thought about what the angry man in the crowd had said: 'You'd be grabbin' owt you could too if your family were clemmed enough....'

Aspen shuddered at the thought, and turned up his collar against the weather.

# ACT 3

'See this 'ere lad? It's called a lashing,' said Les Stape, holding out a short length of hemp rope to Joseph, who was busy wrapping his arms around himself to keep out the biting Lancastrian wind. One end was spliced to form a big loop. Les expertly flipped the rope around in his stubby, calloused hands and studied it thoughtfully for a moment. 'Your life depends on this, lad,' he said, shaking the looped rope at Joseph, 'so always tie them proper like this when laddering a chimney, then test them.' He expertly worked the lashing in his hands and handed it over to the boy.

'It's called a clove-hitch knot and it holds th'ladder firm against th'wooden skids resting against th'chimney stack like this,' remarked his brother Ron, picking up a piece of wood with blocks of wood nailed to each end. 'And this 'ere is the skid,' he added. 'Skids are just packin' fitted to the ladder, about a foot long to keep the ladder away from the stack, so your feet fit in.' Joseph examined the artefacts of their trade, taking it all in.

'Aye, that's after you've hammered in th'first iron dog to loop the lashing round. You do this about four feet from the ground then rope lashings are tethered from th'dogs round both cheeks of the ladder, wi't skid at the back, and tightened up,' said Les. 'Reckon there'll be about twenty-six dogs in t'last chimney we did at yon ironworks. A two hundred-footer should take about thirteen ladders.'

'Aye, an' we use all sorts of different knots in different

43

situations, such as a reef knot on tha bosun's chair, but we'll come to that later,' said Ron.

Joseph's eyes darted eagerly backwards and forwards between the two brothers. He was keen to learn everything and listened without interrupting as they continued. 'These big hooks, or iron dogs, here see?' Les held up the metal peg about eight inches long, tapered to a wedge shape at one end with a hook at the other. 'We 'ave the blacksmith make dozens of 'em for us and in winter, like, always be sure to place 'em on top of th'works boiler before goin' home at night,' he advised. 'Warm 'em when you use 'em next morning; nowt worse than workin' with cold iron.' He laughed.

'Either that, or ask th'factory watchman to put 'em in his brazier. Warm as toast next morning!' Ron added for good measure.

Stapes Steeplejacks, based at Hanging Ditch Yard, Oldham, was the oldest and most successful family business in the area. It was started originally by their grandfather when many of the first tall industrial chimneys were built in the late 1700s. Chimneys were built from the inside upwards, by means of wooden pegs called putlogs that stuck out of the structure, but no-one gave much thought as to how the outside would be maintained afterwards.

Up until a few years ago, the usual method was hammering pieces of wood between the coursework and ascending them to mend the chimney, which resulted in a high mortality rate. But their father, Josiah Stape, developed the laddering method by using iron dogs and a staging around the structure. Most firms used that system now and that meant that Stapes Steeplejacks were always in demand. Les and Ron started working with their father when they were just tiny boys and had known nothing else.

They knew the trade inside out but were aware of the pitfalls. Their father and a part-time iron-moulder's labourer had been killed eight years ago at a chimney-demolition job when the whole structure collapsed on top of them.

Steeplejacking was very dangerous work, and no-one liked to undertake it; demolition work was only usually done when a chimney was leaning badly, on the verge of collapse and in danger of flattening the surrounding buildings. It usually entailed chiselling a bit of the base away and placing a wire rope around the chimney, then bringing a steam locomotive on site and tugging hard at the wire until the chimney eventually toppled.

The chimney didn't always collapse in the way planned – as in the case of the one that got their father. Frequently, the locomotive got buried as well as the engine driver, as had happened again the previous summer over in Bury, when a small firm of inexperienced jacks attempted to bring down a stack. Five were killed in that disaster and one lad was paralysed in both legs.

Les and Ron decided to remain quiet about the dangers for now; they might frighten off the new bloke and his young lad. They thought the lad seemed smart and keen, but his dad seemed a bit shiftless and wasn't really cut out for the work.

The four of them stood at the base of the 150-foot stone chimney at the Cromer weaving shed. Aspen drew heavily on his cigarette. He'd begun working with Les and Ron a fortnight before, and today he'd brought Joseph along for the first time. Aspen had already been up the chimney at the ironworks several times and helped disassemble the staging and ladders, but he didn't like it.

Joseph had barely slept the night before because of his excitement. He couldn't wait and was up at five o'clock, pestering his father to get up and get ready. Violet was already awake, terrified for Joseph.

'Keep yer eye on him, for the Lord's sake!' she advised Aspen when they left the house.

'Now then, lad, fetch that block and tackle from over theer near th'wall,' Ron instructed.

Les began thumping an iron dog with a lump hammer into the solid masonry of the chimney as Ron guided the end of a long rope through the pulley-wheel which would hoist

the second red ladder up into the air once the first was fixed in place. Two men could easily get all the ladders up in a day; one man working hard could achieve the same result.

Aspen felt that he was in the way; he didn't even like the ground part of the job, but he had no choice but to do the work for now. At least he was earning a few bob, unlike most of the men down their street. Some thought he was bloody crazy getting himself set on as a steeplejack helper, especially taking his lad as an apprentice. But he idled as much as he could get away with so most work was shared between the two brothers; and besides, it was easier than the stone-breaking yard.

'Now, look sharp!' shouted Les from the second ladder, the top of which quivered like an arrow as he struck another iron dog into the brickwork high above his head for the next ladder. He gestured to Aspen as he fed up another one by pulling a rope attached to the block and tackle looped around it. They continued until dinner time; by then, the chimney was half-laddered. When they clocked off for a bit of bread and dripping, Joseph ran home, bursting to tell his mam all about it all, taking along one of the iron dogs to show her.

She couldn't help but be happy that he'd found something he liked doing. He'd never enjoyed working as an apprentice chimney sweep, and this seemed to be his calling. 'You mind out and be careful now, our Joseph,' she admonished indulgently. Doing this job, he would meet educated men and gentrified folks who owned mills and works, she thought with a smile.

'You always hold tight on th'cheeks of the ladder like this, son, never the rungs,' Les advised Joseph, who was standing on a rung several feet below. 'That way, if th'rung gives way, like, you don't lose yer grip and fall to your death.' They were both about fifty feet up by now, and the wind had picked up speed and reddened Joseph's ears. This was a taster for the boy. When they put the staging around the top tomorrow, he'd finally get chance to go all the way up and walk around the chimney circumference, while the

men fixed a new copper lightning conductor in place.

Joseph grabbed tightly onto the ladder cheeks as instructed. He could see far beyond the works yard and over towards the back-to-backs on the other side and wished he could go higher than 120 feet. But the last few ladders hadn't been fixed in place yet; the men were working more slowly as they instructed Joseph. Aspen stood looking at his son climbing easily up the stack without any sign of fear.

When Joseph returned to the ground, his head felt light and the excitement made him giddy. 'I did it, Pa! I did it!' he roared, dashing around the chimney base with glee. 'I did it!' He couldn't wait until tomorrow.

Ron came over. 'You go home now lad, tha's had a busy day, and you'll need yer rest for tomorrow.' He laughed, warmed by the young boy's show of raw excitement.

Next day, it was raining hard and blowing a gale, not a day fit to be outside. A knock came at the back door shortly before eight o'clock and Aspen opened it. Les was standing with his shoulders hunched against the weather.

'Hey up, come in, you favvers a drowned scarecrow standing theer like that!' said Aspen, standing aside to let the man through into the back parlour. Violet appeared and placed a brown stoneware teapot on the table as Les flopped down in front of the fire, splaying his palms towards the flames. 'Nowt doin' today in this rain, we'll leave the job for the morrow. Putting stagin' up round t'top in this weather is no good!' Aspen rapidly nodded his agreement.

Joseph recognised Les's voice and came running downstairs barefoot, wrapped in a rough woollen blanket. He sat down at the table, greeting the steeplejack like an old friend.

'Can yer read?' Les asked the boy. ''Ah've brought yer summat.' He took part of an old tattered newspaper from his pocket and pushed it across to the boy.

'Me mam and granddad taught me and I went to school as well. I'm good at it!' replied Joseph proudly as he examined the paper. 'It's a Scottish one!'

'Turn to the middle,' said Les. 'I can't read, but theer's a champion likeness of the biggest chimney in the world standing at 435 feet, and known as Tenannt's Stalk, at a chemical works in Glasgow.'

Joseph quickly found it and scanned the page headlined, 'Steeplejack D. Wright.' He glanced at the etching of a tall, slender chimney and read on: 'James Duncan Wright was born in Dundee in 1829...'

There wasn't a peep out of him for the next ten minutes as he devoured the whole story about the steeplejack and the chimney. Then he exclaimed with astonishment, 'He mended it by using a kite to lay ropes across the top!'

'Aye lad, now, does't tha' know they did that a long time ago before folk first got agate ladderin' stacks and started mendin' them the way we do now.' Les went on to tell saucer-eyed Joseph how his father had invented the laddering method. 'Then theer's the Lancashire way and Yorkshire way of laddering ... but I'll tell yer all about that later, so as not to confuse yer.'

'Why don't you read it out for us, son?' said Violet tenderly. They all sat listening while Joseph explained the daring antics of this larger-than-life steeplejack and showman, who kept a monkey as a pet and was known the world over for his success at mending chimneys and church steeples.

Joseph vowed to be exactly like him one day; from that day, Steeplejack D. Wright was his hero.

***

The sky was still murky by the time Joseph arrived at the weaving shed but by dinner time most of the staging was in place around the top of the stone chimney. Due to inclement weather, they'd lost three days and the co-operative were getting anxious for their investment. The boiler had had a new crown-valve fitted and was ready to be stoked.

The Stapes brothers had urged Joseph to stay at home that morning, since his presence would only slow down work. Ron was at the top of the chimney, fixing a copper lightning conductor in position. Les was dangling from the delicate staging, swinging about on his bosun's chair, pointing a crack directly underneath the over-sailer. He spotted the boy below and waved.

Joseph noticed his father talking to master boilermaker Percy Hayes at the boiler-house door, who had stopped by to pick up the old crown valve. He ran over to where the two men were standing. Percy was the managing director and consultant engineer at Hayes and Sons Ltd, the biggest boilermaking works in the North West. He always had a soft spot for this keen lad who asked clever questions about engineering whenever they met, and had once thought to ask about taking him on as an apprentice but Aspen had started him in the family chimney-sweeping business by then. Percy only had a daughter and a son who wasn't interested in boilermaking. Impressed by Joseph's aptitude for maths, Percy had given the lad an ivory slide-rule with silver ends and hoped he'd have a chance one day to teach him how to use it properly.

'Hey up, young Joseph,' the kindly boilermaker said, stroking his white whiskers. 'Do you want to come and have a look inside while she's lying cold? You can see the tubes at the back of the firebox.'

Joseph loved the idea; he'd only ever seen boilers working when they were fiercely hot and never seen inside one. They frightened him a bit with their roaring noises. It would be interesting to touch the maker's plate and examine the brass temperature gauge and water injectors close up. He was about to agree when he noticed Les ascending the red ladders outside.

'Eee, thanks Mr Hayes, that'd be champion, but it'll have to be another time if you don't mind, sir!' he replied and scurried off back across the cobblestones in the direction of Les.

Joseph stood on the first ladder with Les below him and looked up. Aspen watched thoughtfully from a distance with Percy. 'That lad of yourn, he's got a knack for this steeplejack lark, hasn't he?' remarked the boilermaker.

'Aye, there'll be a right to-do, when th'economy improves and we start up wi' sweepin' jobs again,' Aspen joshed, before adding more soberly, 'He's grown too big fer a climbing boy now, any road.'

Percy chuckled, pushing his cap further up his forehead. 'Ha'penny says you've lost your apprentice, then!'

'Nah, never a betting man, especially when th'odds are stacked against me an' all!' retorted Aspen, grinning. In his heart, he knew their Joseph would never want to return to work as a chimney sweep. He was greatly saddened that all his hopes for a family empire had been dashed, but the lad had a true calling. Besides, it would have been a lot of hard graft starting a big firm of chimney sweeps.

Aspen had realised, while watching his son repeatedly devouring the old newspaper story about the Scottish steeplejack and practising clove-hitch knots over and over until bedtime, that their Joseph was made from different stuff. All he could hope for was that the lad kept his brains and didn't act gormless and do 'owt daft to bring grief to him and his mam when he was working at the top of some ruddy great factory chimney or steeple.

\*\*\*

Joseph was almost at the top of the chimney. He could see clearly over the horizon as far away as Rochdale. The view took his breath away. The wind was blowing faster up here, making him light-headed, the excitement sending him giddy. Now, the trick was getting off the ladder and onto the staging tethered around the circumference of the chimney. The wooden planks of the staging were parallel with his chest and his hands were grasping both cheeks of the ladder directly under them.

Les advised him, 'Now, place your hand carefully above the planks, lad. You'll 'av to sway back a bit, mind.'

Joseph did as he was told and ascended another rung, firmly grabbing the ladder above the horizontal planks.

'Now, pull yersen up until plank's level wi' tha' knees' said Les, battling against the wind, which was picking up.

Again, Joseph did as he was told, but found himself in an awkward position.

'The tricky bit now,' Les said. 'Take yer right foot off th'ladder, and swing yer leg o'er the plank and hoist yersen up. But be sharp about it, don't hang about, like, it's the most dangerous bit! '

Joseph did as he was instructed and Les looked relieved. Before standing upright, the boy swung there for a moment with his legs dangling free into space either side of the two planks, then waved at his father and Mr Hayes. He thought his heart would burst with the thrill. As he stood up carefully on top of a chimney for the first time, gripping tightly onto the scaffolding tubes then walking around the quivering staging, he felt like king of the entire world.

Ron edged over slowly and they both stood by the side of the shiny copper lightning conductor. 'See over theer, lad? That's Bolton far off in the distance.'

'By gum, is it honestly?' asked Joseph, astonished. He knew the town was many miles away. 'How can you tell, Mr Stape?'

'Tall bleach works chimney near Bury, and beyond that is Bolton. Ye can't normally see so far. But what wi' t'cotton famine on, there's hardly any smoke, all the cotton mills are quiet…' He let his words trail off.

Joseph peered up at the lightning conductor. It was taller than himself and looked unlike anything he had ever seen before. And below, there were three capital letters carved deeply into the heavy coping stones around the top of the twenty-foot diameter chimney.

'See them, lad?' said Ron, pointing at letters. 'That's th'initials of th'blokes who built it fifty years ago!'

Joseph examined them carefully and ran a finger across the cold stone, scratching at clumps of soot covering the inscribed letter 'H'.

'Not many folk get chance to leave their mark on the world like this, lad. You think on that. Not many men can even get up a factory chimney, never mind have the skill and pride it takes to do this lark as a living.'

When they climbed back down after what seemed like hours, Joseph knew he never wanted to do anything else but become a master steeplejack. Les handed him a little round brass badge to commemorate his first ever chimney climb. 'What's that little flower in the middle?' Joseph enquired, pointing to the stylized rose design almost covering the badge.

'That's the Red Rose of Lancashire,' said Ron.

Les added, 'Wear it with pride lad, and tha'll always go far…'

# ACT 4

*P*int-sized Joseph put down his spanner on top of the oak cross-beam of the church bell and stopped working. Now in his early twenties, he was good-natured, broad-shouldered and handsome, with a rugged countenance that would be called 'weathered' as he got older. Twinkly blue eyes, the same as Aspen's, danced with merriment and the joy he found in his daily work as a steeplejack. His energetic swaggering walk suggested a brusque sportsman; his charismatic personality made people feel at ease, and he loved to hold court and converse with people from all classes with a liveliness that inspired others.

And he was a perfectionist in everything he did.

Les shouted up, 'Can yer see anything yet, lad?'

Joseph stuck his head out of the belfry. 'Not yet,' he shouted, cupping his hands against the wind. 'Just give us another few minutes and I'll be down.'

Joseph wouldn't rest until he found out what the problem was. He stretched himself up to his full height of five feet five inches and brushed at his short jacket, pulling the edges together and tucking it into his belt to keep out the sharp wind that was forcing itself through the louvred lathes of the belfry, assaulting him like a weapon. He'd been checking the U-bolts were securely in place, puzzled at first that everything seemed to be in order. The simplicity of a hanging bell should mean that he could easily determine what was wrong. Edging around the other side of the church tower,

he bent under it to examine the long iron dinger as three pigeons fluttered off, startled at the invasion.

Usually a lover of all creatures great and small, Joseph hated pigeons. He considered them the curse of any belfry work, where they would lay eggs in their mess and he'd end up covered in the sticky stuff. He shooed several more perched nearby and the birds flapped off, clapping their wings together, which made Joseph shuffle back slightly.

He'd helped Ron and Les fix this new dinger in place last year, but the bronze bell still wasn't pealing clearly. He deftly checked the bell further, his fingers gradually revealing a hairline crack and a tiny chip on the smooth rim. Joseph pursed his lips in thought. Not good, not good at all. The vicar wouldn't get much sleep when he faced the Lancashire Diocese with this news. A crack and chip, no matter how small, were the worst things that could happen to any church bell.

He climbed out again onto the staging and scurried up the fixed ladder towards the apex of the steeple, whistling to himself and examining the lead work as he went about his task. Below him, the streets were almost empty at this time in the afternoon and he could hear the steam engine throbbing in the weaving shed across the road, beating like the determined iron heart of industry.

Joseph peered down to shout to Les again and noticed his friend was speaking to Violet. It didn't appear that she wanted her son's attention, so Joseph decided to crack on with the job; he had a new mill chimney to work on in the morning.

Bigger cotton mills were being built and Joseph had worked non-stop for the past year, earning a very good living because of the boom after the cotton famine. He could now ladder any chimney on his own and had devised a new breaking system for the rope work, enabling them to hoist the ladders up faster and more safely. He'd helped to make Stapes Steeplejacks a by-word for the best and most popular outfit in the area; they got all the principal jobs and

commanded the most money. They were even working with a London firm of architects the following week, helping to design a chimney and flue system for a brand new spinning mill.

Aspen was working again too – whenever he felt like it. Joseph had recently joined with his old Sunday school friend Will Croston in a new business. Until recently, ginger-haired William had been an apprentice engineer at the local brass foundry and, like Joseph, was good with his hands and quick with his brain. The two boys formed a partnership, with Joseph investing the money and Will carrying out most of the work. They'd rented a small disused ironworks down by the canal and taken on a few operatives to produce copper lightning conductors and lightning rods to meet the demand of the new mills being erected in the boom.

Aspen helped finish them to a high standard before they left the works – when he was sober enough to turn up. The venture was successful, partly due to Joseph coming up with the novel idea of giving the company a peculiar name which made it stand out against its competitors. They called their works, 'Messrs Wragg & Croston's Lightning Conductor Manufacturet'. Joseph liked the odd, jarring word 'Manufacturet' on the large, striking copperplate sign attached to the lintel above the works' entrance, but William wasn't so sure.

Recently, Joseph had started bending the Queen's English to suit himself by mixing up sentences and speaking in an affected, peculiar fashion. He was still trying to smooth out some of his rough, northern vowels to imitate the speaking style of mill owners and the gentry. The effect was rather charming, if bizarre. He was becoming known for other flamboyant eccentricities too, such as wearing colourful velvet jackets on the day of rest, instead of well-worn home-spun drab like everyone else from his background.

William, with his more conservative views, thought labelling the works a 'Manufacturet' was daft, but it worked and people would frequently stop and stare at the sign,

wondering if it was deliberate or a mistake by the sign-writer. It became the most talked-about sign in Lancashire, and eventually the name was on everyone's lips as the company moved into increasingly larger premises. Eventually, trade and industry coined the generic name 'WRAG-RODS' for lightning conductors as they became the biggest and most successful manufacturer of lightning conductors throughout the commonwealth.

Joseph quickly descended the ladder, jumped down the last three rungs and faced Les, who looked grim. 'Lead work's got nowt wrong with it, but the bell is damaged with a hairline crack,' Joseph said, wiping his face. 'What did Ma want?'

'She wouldn't say, lad –but she seemed in a bit of a state and you have to get over to see William at yon Manufacturet as soon as you can.'

Joseph looked puzzled. 'Didn't you ask, then?'

'Of course I did, yer soft beggar. But she said she just wanted you to see William and he'd explain what's been going on.'

Joseph was still puzzled. Why hadn't William come over himself if it was important enough to disturb him at work? What did his ma have to do with anything and why was she upset? It must be to do with Pa, but it couldn't be anything serious or she would have shouted for him to come down the ladder.

'Look, you get off and I'll finish up here,' Les said.

William looked up from his powerful lathe as Joseph strutted into the Manufacturet. This wasn't going to be pleasant. 'Hey up Joseph!' he greeted his lifelong friend above the noise, easing Joseph's worry that something was seriously wrong. The lathe stopped turning and William stepped back. 'Fancy a stroll? I'm about to stop for mi' dinner, any road,' he said, removing his thick gloves.

Joseph usually grinned whenever he saw William, but today he remained stony-faced. 'Ma rushed over to the church an hour ago and told Les I'd better find out what's

been going on at the Manufacturet, but she wouldn't elaborate further,' he said. 'Is there a problem then, eh?'

'Aye, I reckon you could say that,' replied William. 'Come on, let's step outside for a minute or two.' He took his friend's arm. Joseph stopped after several steps and studied a large pile of green copper rods waiting to be fashioned into conductors.

'So what is it then?' he asked.

William took his arm again. 'Not here, my friend. We can't talk over this din. Let's go outside.'

They made their way across the works' floor, bending as they walked to avoid a crane driven by rope gearing, and then cutting through the moulding shop to reach the back entrance near the dispatch area. They walked into the yard and towards the gate.

'It's not good. I've had to send your pa home,' William said.

'He's poorly is he? What's the trouble, William?'

His friend looked uncomfortable. 'Did yer mam not say owt, then?'

'She said to ask you instead.'

William stared at his friend, still not knowing how to tell him the truth.

'He's been boozin' again, is that it?' asked Joseph.

William nodded, glad the matter was out in the open. 'Aye, that's it, but you see, I had to let him go, Joseph.'

Joseph let out a long sigh and looked angry. It wasn't difficult to guess why William had sent his father home and Joseph couldn't blame him. But like everyone who knew the steeplejack, William was wary of his temper at times and so he said gently, 'It's not the first time, but I've said nowt about it before.'

'So what's different this time?' asked Joseph. 'We all know he likes a tipple or two, for Chris'sakes'

'Aye, but as I say, Joseph, I've had to let him go.'

'With all this palaver, I thought it was something serious. I'm losing work here, man. Couldn't this have waited until

clocking-off time or tomorrow?'

William felt a flicker of annoyance. Joseph was inferring that drunken behaviour was just an everyday hazard to be endured. 'What's *different* is that I found him trying to work machinery in the pattern shop, *drunk* out of his empty skull. Could have had his hand off if I'd been a minute later.'

Joseph let out a long sigh and looked upwards. William spoke up again 'We're going to have to let him go for good this time, Joseph. Factory inspector finds him like that, they'll shut us down for good. Or he'll kill himself.'

Joseph said, 'Perhaps if I have a word or two with him?'

William shook his head assertively. 'You just don't get this, do you, Joseph? I don't want him here any more. He's a useless old soak and that's about the size of it.'

The day had started so well, but finding the crack in the bell followed by the news of his pa in drink at the Manufacturet was almost too much to bear. Joseph stormed off without speaking and felt resentful as he made his way back to Potts Street. He was going to have it out with his father when he got home.

\*\*\*

'You addled heathens, keep away from here. I want NONE of you or your stinkin' lot in my house!' Violet screeched at the top of her voice, wielding a brush-steel. Joseph could hear her halfway down the road.

Two neighbours stood outside, gossiping on their doorsteps, speculating about the disturbance at the Wraggs' house. They moved as they saw Joseph approach and began whispering about the young steeplejack who always thought he was a cut above and his drink-sodden, boorish father. How did Violet put up with them both, they wondered, as they went indoors to continue their tittle-tattle.

Joseph saw two of his scruffy uncles, Charlie and Isaac, his father's brothers, scurrying like rats along the street as

Violet chased after them with the broom. 'Yer not coming back in – now push off and get LOST!' she wailed, trying to hit them.

Generally, his uncles were never allowed indoors and had to wait for Aspen in the street but today they'd carried him back from the Manufacturet and placed him on the couch in the best parlour. Charlie kept trying to skirt around Violet so he could get back in to see if Aspen was breathing because he'd drunk so much gin they were worried about him.

Aspen had been out all night with his unruly brothers and the three intoxicated men had let themselves into the Manufacturet and continued drinking in the pattern shop until William came in at seven in the morning. Charlie and Isaac tried hiding in a pile of cotton waste used to polish the conductors, and Aspen tried to look busy working at a lathe. But he could hardly stand and William immediately saw he was drunk, pulling him back just in time before he lurched forward into the heavy spinning machinery. William sent the three men packing. The workforce grinned and smirked as they began their shifts, watching the spectacle of Aspen being dragged across the machine shop by his brothers.

Violet was inconsolable after giving Charlie and Isaac the dressing-down of their lives. 'Whatever are we going to do? This daft, drunken lummox will have me homeless!' she cried. 'And now he's no job to speak of!'

Joseph looked angrily at his father on their best parlour couch, still snoring, his chest covered with dried vomit. He placed a protective arm around his mother and pulled her close. 'Don't worry, Mam – I'll always take care of you, you know that.'

He shook his head at the state of his father who didn't deserve this wonderful woman. Violet snuggled up to Joseph and slid her hand up to his chest, cupping his left shoulder as she held on tight, returning the love that came from her son. He was the one good thing that made her marriage bearable.

'I know you will, son, I know you will,' she crooned, feeling much calmer now he was here to take care of her.

Aspen continued snoring, oblivious to the subtle changes taking place in front of him. He would never feel like master of his own home again.

# ACT 5

Septimus Stark loved the hymn 'There Is a Green Hill Far Away' and sang it with gusto from the family pew each Sunday in church.

As a light breeze fluttered his grey frock-coat tails, the wealthy, spindle-thin industrialist smoothed a stray greenfly off his silk lapel and mentally sang the words again as he waited for his carriage. The hymn always made him feel as though he was somehow related to God and above the common rabble. A respected magistrate, as well as a prominent figure amongst Lancashire's best families, the name Septimus Stark was always connected with charitable movements in Oldham. He gave the impression of being someone who could walk on water with his frequent acts of benevolence in the community.

He adjusted his stove-pipe hat with a gloved hand, the other brandishing a silver-encrusted ebony cane which he tapped impatiently while waiting at the front gate. Within the leafy suburbs of Chadderton, this overbearing villa of dark, Yorkshire stone, known locally as 'The Fens', had been his home since childhood. Now he lived there with his wife Winifred, five sons and their sixteen-year-old daughter, Tabitha. Set within stylized green lawns, flower beds and shrubs that were tended by two gardeners, it was a place of opulent rural tranquillity at odds with the town on the horizon.

From his own green hill far away, Septimus Stark

observed the sunlight occasionally pressing sharp-edged through the thickening discs of grey smoke hanging over Oldham. The smog shrouded the workers below, toiling away in his lucrative empire of three weaving sheds, a bleach works and the finest drapers in town, Messrs Stark & Sons on Union Street.

And, of course, the Stark Orphanage for Young Girls of which he was founder.

Septimus Stark was a highly-respected figure and a keen capitalist.

Today he was meeting with an architect and a steeplejack, together with his business partner, Richard Elm, to examine plans for his new venture. Messrs Stark & Elm Spinning & Manufactures Limited would be the biggest factory in the north west of England.

The partners and gentlemen of the board gathered, along with Joshua Stubbs, the architect from Stubbs, Entwistle & Grays and steeplejack Joseph Wragg, in the imposing boardroom of the bleach works owned by Stark & Sons.

'Well, it is indeed impressive,' remarked Loftus Elm. He leaned further over the architect's plans spread across the table in the mahogany-clad boardroom, pushing his portly frame against the edge for a better view of the mule-spinning areas. His red neck looked like it would billow forth from its constricting starched collar at any moment and explode over the table like an overripe fruit. He favoured his right leg slightly because of a recent painful attack of gout; he leaned to the left to take the pressure off his foot, then leaned back to adjust his waistcoat again.

'The internal boiler house will contain two rows of six boilers,' said Stubbs, pointing with his pencil. The concept of incorporating the boiler and engine houses to economise on space and give a squarer footprint to the huge mill had never been done before. 'These Lancashire boilers are a fairly new design. They have a larger diameter and two furnaces that will improve steam production significantly; they will improve production to a standard never before achievable.'

'What is the benefit in terms of economy? I dare say larger engines mean greater consumption of coal, hmm?' queried Edmund Floris, one of the senior directors, keenly aware of the need to keep the firm's investment budget to a minimum.

'Sir, because of the incorporation of the engine and boiler houses, this will save money immediately in terms of building costs. It also frees up land for an independent on-site foundry.' Stubbs did a little drawing illustrating how it would work.

Septimus nodded slowly, stroking his chin and taking in the added power needed for the extra capacity of the new double mill and foundry. They examined additional drawings of the improved 1,500 horse-power triple-expansion steam engine and a massive twenty-four-foot diameter flywheel with grooves for seventy-five ropes to run the mill machinery, wondering about the additional cost of installing all this. The board of directors pondered the drawings and, after a while, seemed as impressed as the corpulent Mr Elm, who shifted again in his seat to relieve the pressure on his foot.

Joseph looked up from studying the plans for the chimney and frowned as he addressed the room. 'The ratio of height to chimney draught needs a little work, though,' he advised. 'The pull needs to be far greater, with a much taller chimney, and I'm not sure the water-feed system is sufficient for twelve boilers working at full power. This may result in overheating of the furnace tube crowns, which could potentially be disastrous.' He was familiar with the finer points of boiler engineering due to his long-standing friendship with Percy Hayes and he had one or two concerns about this new steam plant.

Joseph asked for a pad and pencils, picked up a slide-rule and said, 'There, see, gentlemen, there may be a fault because of this equation.'

The four men gasped at how quickly he pointed out the flaw in the original design and devised a better system by incorporating an economiser to pre-heat water with hot

flue gases. Septimus shook his head and pursed his lips, concerned at the lack of budgeting sense and annoyed by Joseph's savoir-faire. What the steeplejack was suggesting would add another £2,000 in costs at least. Although Wragg was gaining recognition and a brilliant reputation, the industrialist had some doubts about the flamboyant nature of his words and the recklessness of his personality, which at times drew comments such as *'It's that idiot Wragg'* when Joseph undertook a daring chimney-straightening job that no one else would touch.

Septimus spoke out. 'This is not necessary, gentlemen. Are we to take the scribblings of a *steeplejack*, against those of a qualified and time-served *architect* such as Mr Stubbs here?' he declared, raising his voice almost an octave higher.

In response, Joseph nodded briskly then stood up again to give a detailed lecture on the problems they faced if they didn't alter their plans. The directors listened with interest, all except Septimus Stark.

'Well, I'll be damned! What do you know about pressurized steam then, Wragg?' the industrialist challenged. 'Nothing, I'll wager—'

Septimus was just about to launch into a further personal attack when Loftus Elm removed his monocle, polishing it as he spoke. 'Gentlemen, we must not let personal issues get in the way here. Let us consider for a moment what Mr Wragg is saying.'

'Thank you, gentlemen,' said Joseph. He sat down, pleased to see at least some of the men took him seriously although Stubbs shot him a look of pure annoyance and shook his head in disagreement.

'We should at least consider these plans for the economiser,' said Mr Elm. 'Anything which saves us money must be considered after we have gone so far over our intended budget, and this will save on coal. Perhaps there may be other cut-backs we can consider too, gentleman?'

\*\*\*

As expected, the immense, nine-floor, red-brick, double mill was the talk of Lancashire and beyond. Boasting a state-of-the-art steam engine, vast spinning rooms, great weaving sheds, carding rooms, cloth warehouses, it even had its own machine-shops and foundry. The mill was also talked about because it boasted a gymnasium for the 4,000 operatives and slipper-baths for them and their families. It took the cotton industry forward in gigantic strides, its huge chimney casting a long shadow over the rest of the Lancashire textile trade.

It had been a good year for Joseph and he'd just celebrated his twenty- fifth birthday. His shares in the lightning conductor Manufacturet were paying handsome dividends. He'd recently invested in a small engineering works that was doing well and a chemical company owned by his friend, William Edge of Bolton, that was developing a new blue dye known as 'Dolly Blue' for use in the bleaching industry. If this patented formula took off and woven cloth could be given a whiter appearance like never before, Joseph would become a very wealthy man.

Before the inauguration ceremony for the new mill, Joseph finished applying a coat of raw linseed to the brickwork on the tall, hexagonal chimney. Then he, Les and Ron removed the ladders in preparation for the opening ceremony the next day.

As he came down, he stopped halfway when he saw Septimus Stark and his graceful daughter, Tabitha, alighting from their carriage outside the mill gates. He watched and felt his heart lift. How beautiful she was. She always seemed subdued, reminding him of the fine pink crinoline lady on a milk jug his mother once had. Tabitha's movements were graceful and, with her slim body, she seemed to skim above the ground as she walked. Usually she blushed attractively whenever she saw Joseph, her features becoming more animated. They were aware of each other, even though they had never spoken.

He watched her teeter demurely across the cobblestones, her lace petticoats visible above her dainty buttoned boots,

her fair hair plaited across the crown of her head. Her father took her arm and guided her through the doorway that boasted a copperplate plaque engraved with the company name. Just before she entered, she looked up at Joseph and lingered for a moment or two, her rosebud mouth gently curling upwards at the corners.

That shy smile again.

He would have her as his own one day.

\*\*\*

'Over my dead body!' Septimus Stark cried, when he learned that Joseph had been secretly courting his daughter for the past few months. Now the young man was asking for her hand in marriage. 'I will die before you have any further contact with her,' he fumed.

All those weeks ago, at the inaugural ceremony on the day the mill opened, all classes of the community joined in a splendid promenade through the streets. Fine refreshments and entertainment were available to everyone, courtesy of the company.

Joseph saw his opportunity and spoke freely to Tabitha as she enjoyed the brass band, sipping lemonade and timidly giggling as though it were the finest champagne. She fluttered her eyelashes and looked coyly at him over the rim of her glass. His heart melted and he leaned forward, smelling the lilac-scented sweetness of her smooth skin.

'I need to see you again,' Joseph whispered, his voice laden with a raw, male need that came from somewhere deep inside him. Something in Tabitha responded immediately to that need and she felt her body flush with an unfamiliar longing.

'But Papa will never allow it,' she lamented, aghast at the thought of not seeing Joseph again.

'You must find a way; we cannot allow any slight provocation of paternal anger to scare away our hopes

and dreams,' he said, charming her with his unique way of speaking. 'There's a bond between us. I know there is.'

Tabitha was a dutiful daughter, easily scared by her draconian father, who often made her mama cry. She was surprised that Joseph had been so bold as to try and court her. But daydreams of him made her lie awake at night, exploring sensitive parts of her body, imagining his rough masculine hand arousing her before she was carried away on a wave of ecstasy.

A brief courtship developed. Hundreds of notes passed between the pair, and occasionally they managed a few moments together in the churchyard, chaste meetings that only served to intensify their desire. His longing to be with her every second of the day was like a sickness and Tabitha felt the same; she was certain their bodies would melt into each other when they kissed.

When he'd proposed, she thought she would faint. *To be his in every way!*

Finally Joseph approached her father, ready to declare his intentions. He wanted this rare, delicate creature for his wife. Nervously, he faced Tabitha's parents to ask for her hand.

'Tha' nothing but an upstart, lad!' fumed Septimus. 'How *dare* you!'

'But papa, we are in love!' protested Tabitha.

Her mother was weeping into her handkerchief, delicately dabbing her eyes at the ruination of her daughter. The thought of Tabitha even kissing a rough labourer made her wince.

Joseph turned to face the three of them in their elegant drawing room. 'I can assure you, sir, I have means to provide a standard—'

'Now look here young Wragg, I don't want to hear another word about this – this – FARCE!' Septimus shouted, searching for polite words in front of his wife and daughter, his hooked nose more predatory than ever. 'Get out of my sight, you imbecile. And if you ever come near my daughter again, ye gods, sir, I'll have you *flogged* within an inch of your miserable life!'

Tabitha sank to her knees sobbing and Septimus rang for his servant. 'See this – this – jumped-up *street Arab* off the premises. You are NOT to let him into MY house again, is that clear, Walton?' he demanded of the man.

'Please, father—we *love* each other!' Tabitha begged.

'For pity's sake, man – hear me out at least!' declared Joseph.

'Walton, remove this parasite at once,' Septimus exploded.

'Very good, sir,' replied Walton, looking as though nothing untoward was happening, ignoring Tabitha the tense atmosphere.

'We'll be ruined! Tabitha, how could you meet him unchaperoned?' moaned Mrs Stark. 'What will our friends think? Oh, we are ruined!'

'Perhaps if you would be good enough to follow me, sir,' Walton said.

'You can go to the blazes and the very devil himself!' shouted Joseph, pointing his finger at the industrialist. 'This is not over yet!'

'Wragg, I'll have you shot if you don't leave my house this minute!' fumed Septimus, whose face was now the deep purple colour of a plum.

There was nothing Joseph could do but go, leaving Stark ranting about finding his brace of pistols. His face burned with humiliation; he'd been treated like a common guttersnipe. He vowed one day to show Septimus Stark what a crass little man he was. Joseph would amass his own fortune and return to give *Septimus* a good whipping!

Of that he was certain.

Joseph waited patiently for many days in their meeting place by the churchyard gate, but Tabitha never came. He left passionate letters for her under their secret stone but they were still there the next day, smudged and ruined with the early morning dew.

He could never approach her again. She was immediately sent away to stay with an aunt in the Cheshire countryside

until she 'came to her senses'. As Joseph pointed a church steeple, the frosty weather matched the coldness inside him. How dare Septimus Stark treat him like an impecunious peasant!

\*\*\*

Joseph had become increasingly cultured by emulating the gentlemen industrialists he encountered during in his work. By cultivating similar interests in classical music, literature, arts and science, he had succeeded in grinding away his rough working-class edges. Violet was keen to help him, tirelessly supplying him with the works of the greatest philosophers and thinkers, which he read almost obsessively. It was her ambition to see him accepted by polite society. He could hold intelligent conversations on a whole variety of topics with mill and factory owners, as well as expertly swinging heavy lump hammers around in his work as a steeplejack.

Violet frowned as Joseph removed his braces and sat down for his tea of black pudding and mustard. She knew why he sighed so loudly. 'Come on, our Joseph, you'll meet other nice lasses,' she coaxed gently. 'You've a lot of time to find the right one yet, love.'

Aspen spoke up from his seat by the fire. 'No use sniffin' around that Stark lass, any road. That's not fer th'likes of us, lad, them lot. Thought tha' knew that by now! Tha' shouldn't always be getting' ideas above yer station, lad.'

Joseph was angry. 'What?' He slammed down his knife and fork. 'Their family wealth came from Australian gold and British industry. Hardly aristocracy, now, are they?' he fumed, dropping his usual, slightly affected way of speaking. 'Not for the likes of us? Good God, Pa!' He snorted in disgust.

The two men locked stares over the table.

'Yer nobbut a dreamer, lad,' challenged Aspen.

'I could kill you for saying that, you drunkard!' Joseph retorted.

'Yer a bloody milksop, always have bin, always will be!'

'Keep yer hair on, please!' Violet shouted. 'Both of you.'

Aspen stood up, ignoring Violet. 'Tha's not too big for a thick ear yet, lad, fer all yer bloody pomp and swank!'

'Oh! You'd know all about that, Pa, wouldn't you? Answers in the bottom of a gin bottle, are they?' Joseph mocked. 'Try working hard like I do for a change.'

'Stop it, Joseph, please,' urged Violet. She didn't want trouble, and this lad had a temper on him now he was grown. It was high time he was wed, but setting his sights on local gentry – well, it wasn't the done thing. Not with Aspen the way he was, showing them all up.

More and more these days her menfolk were at each other's throats; they didn't understand each other at all. Joseph considered his father lazy and Aspen thought his son jumped up and above his station. If only they'd get on, life could be so good. They now lived in a smart part of town near the park, thanks to their Joseph looking out for them. He'd bought them a nice house after the episode at the Manufacturet – even if it did make Aspen feel like a failure.

When Joseph was dressed to up to the nines in his posh frock coat, ready for church on Sunday, he looked like a regular toff instead of a steeplejack. The neighbours were starting to click their tongues at his swank, with his fine lacy cravats and gold watch chain. In a rare sober episode, Aspen had noticed it too and his resentment of his son grew

'I'll not have the name of the Lord taken in vain in this house, lad,' Aspen admonished at the top of his voice, swaying slightly on his feet. 'Tha'll watch tha' tongue while yer under my roof.'

Joseph stood up to meet his wrath and harshly kicked his chair back. 'Your house, is it now, Pa? You want me to leave, do you? Take the money that provides you with all this and the *booze?* Shall I then? Shall I really?' He swept his arm around the room, pointing at the mantelpiece adorned with a beautiful ebonized timepiece sitting on a lacy runner. 'Aye then, I will if yer like – I'll take that bloody thing back as

well!' He stabbed a finger at the fine Westminster clock that Aspen took pride in winding up each evening.

Aspen leaned towards Joseph and squared his shoulders. 'Get out of mi' sight, lad, before you regret it. So help me God, I've had enough of yer gibberin' rubbish an' fancy talk.'

Joseph stared up at the blazing eyes and saw the bitterness there. He knew that his pa didn't really like him.

Aspen carried on. 'Yer a bloody disgrace to this family. Any proper son would be wed by now wi' a nipper on't way; aye, what's wrong wi' that lass Nellie from th'cobblers at end er't road? She likes yer. Not good enough, I suppose, eh?' He spat in the fire as if to prove a point.

'You have no idea what you are TALKING about!'

'You mean like you, yer daft bugger, spoutin' all that claptrap to Stark?'

Joseph roared in frustration, and swept his arm across the table. There was a clattering of crockery as it hit the polished parquet flooring, and he noticed from his reflection in the over-mantle mirror how enraged and desperate he looked. Storming from the room, he dashed upstairs leaving Violet to retrieve the broken Wedgwood teapot and delicate saucers while Aspen shouted more home truths upstairs after him.

# *ACT 6*

'*E*ee, come on, Joseph. Give us another kiss then,' said Nellie, giggling.

Her mouth was hot and she wrapped her tongue around his, pulling him closer. He felt her stubby warm hand searching for his flaccid penis under his nightshirt. He gave out a low groan and pushed her aside gently.

'Nellie, it's been a busy day, love,' he said. 'Not tonight, eh?'

He could feel her heart beating in her ample breast as she wrapped herself around him again and heaved and sighed in the candlelight, finding his mouth once more and working him hard under the lace-edged sheets.

'Aw, come on, it won't harm the baby, tha' knows,' she said.

Joseph groaned and felt himself stiffen involuntarily. Nellie pushed harder against him and guided his hand under her nightgown before he gave into her and mounted her for several minutes, then rolled away.

As they lay in their matrimonial bed afterwards, a hideous iron thing Nellie had chosen, with a huge half-tester and clumpy ornamentation resembling mating garden slugs, he contemplated his future. Since the night of his humiliation at the Starks' house and the falling out with his father, Joseph had done as his mother suggested and kept the peace. Courting and wedding Nellie was done solely to appease her. His mother was sad at him leaving home, but he could

stand his lazy, drunken father no longer.

Nellie was an uncomplicated, voluptuous girl with flowing dark hair and eyes to match, who came from a family of ruddy-faced, hard-living cobblers. She looked like she'd do anything for a dirty shilling, but was actually innocent when he'd married her. But once she'd discovered sex, there was no stopping her – and the pregnancy hadn't seemed to slow her down, either.

Her father ran the clog shop not far away and was known as 'Rough Harry' on account of his love of distilled alcohol and a good game of cock-fighting behind the weaving sheds. As they'd courted near those sheds each evening, smooching under the soft green-yellow glow of the gas lamps at the factory gate, Nellie always smelt of fish-glue and leather. Joseph liked her well enough; she had certain attractiveness even if she was a bit lacking in refinement, and of course Violet wholeheartedly approved of his submissive wife who wouldn't try to compete with her. Joseph was glad he'd proposed and had been accepted; it made his mother happy – but he still felt something was missing.

The middle-terraced house he'd bought on smart York Street after their wedding was the grandest on the row. Recently Violet had been fussing with Nellie to get it prepared for a new addition to the Wragg family.

In acknowledgement of their new social standing, Violet cajoled Nellie into several dress fittings for more lady-like clothes, but the girl struggled against the restricting stays of the garments as her stomach grew with her child. Violet was busy giving lessons in etiquette too, to help Nellie become more socially acceptable. Violet's manipulative charm seemed somewhat at odds with her expectations of marriage for Joseph, but she knew he needed a good, solid dutiful wife who would provide a large family in which Violet could play a major part. In any case, Joseph would no doubt take a mistress one day to provide the fun and passion he needed for a man of his social standing.

Had he married the Stark girl, that might have been

problematic, thought Violet. In her own way, Violet was just as ambitious as Joseph.

As well as a loving, devoted mother with cat-like instincts.

If only he could forget the dewy-eyed Tabitha with her natural hauteur, finely-chiselled features and wide-spaced eyes, which had attracted him far more than Nellie's raw earthiness and lust for physical love.

Nellie was insatiable and began toying with him again. 'Come on, lass, let off now,' Joseph said. 'I've got an early start on laddering a spire tomorrow and you need your sleep too.' He rolled further over to his side of the feather mattress, tucking his flaccid manhood away and extinguishing the candle flame.

At seven month pregnant, Nellie looked like a haystack boiler about to explode. Joseph was ashamed to feel the way he did whenever he held her in his arms. He often fantasised about the cool, silky feel of Tabitha's sweet rosebud mouth, of chastely kissing her and holding her tiny gloved hand as he probed deeper into his willing, naive wife as he had done tonight.

*\*\**

Joseph climbed over the mountain of sooty bricks. Les and Ron followed him.

'Another close one, that!' Les said to the younger steeplejack, extracting the bent copper lightning conductor from the rubble. He turned to find his brother running over with the mill owner, both men looking ashen. Part of the weaving shed roof and end wall was demolished and in tatters; twisted metal that had once been looms spilled out like iron guts onto brick, slate and stonework from the top of the chimney that now lay on the ground.

That morning, the crumbling factory chimney had been felled. It should have fallen the right way to make way for a new one but it hadn't. Fortunately no one was killed – or

they hoped not.

Ron scratched his head, turning to Joseph then back to the mill owner. 'How is the poor devil now?' he asked, enquiring about a young apprentice engineer who was hit with flying bricks.

'Poor bugger, lucky to be alive. Three clobbered him, eh?' said Les. The head injuries he'd sustained meant the lad would never be an engineer again.

The mill owner said, 'I expect he'll live but he's lost a lot of blood. He was almost buried under the rubble as he tripped.'

The incident brought back thoughts of their father, old Steeplejack Stape, who had been buried under rubble when a chimney fell the wrong way.

'He has some broken ribs as well,' the mill owner continued.

'There has got to be a more controlled method of undertaking a chimney felling operation other than relying on sheer brute strength and damned good luck!' Joseph exclaimed.

The young engineer was a nice lad with glowing prospects before the accident. He'd come along with his father to watch the felling operation from what he thought was a safe distance. But the impact had launched hundreds of bricks into the air as the weaving shed crumbled under the falling weight of the chimney. As he ran away, he lost his footing and a shower of bricks rained down on him. The lad had lost an eye, had a strange lopsided look to his mouth and couldn't speak right. They could only wait to see if he'd mend.

Ron and Les shrugged, remembering again the time they were lucky enough to run faster than their father, when that fatal felling operation killed him. This chimney had been felled in a similar way: the bottom weakened by the removal of a few bricks, then a railway loco brought on site to tug at the chimney using a wire rope until the structure fell. It was always by luck more than good management if no one got

killed.

Joseph felt edgy for the rest of the day and returned home to rank odours of stale urine and a screaming child. Nellie came wobbling over, unrestricted by corsets, holding baby Rudy to one exposed, pendulous breast; the ten-month old sucked wetly on her nipple in between screams. Nellie had put on a few stone since giving birth and it didn't suit her. Joseph noticed her flabby chin as she looked down at the child, who balled up his fists and beat against her dimpled cheeks.

Violet came in, carrying a pail full of soiled grey nappies. Passing Joseph on the way to the scullery maid, she greeted him by saying, 'He's got the squits again, poor mite.'

Joseph wrinkled his nose and turned to his wife. 'Where's the nurse I provided?' he demanded.

Nellie looked blank, then said, 'Oh her? I sent her home. What does she know about th'baby and what's wrong with it?' She snuffled her nose into the child's damp head.

'How much laudanum have you given him, any road?' he asked.

Nellie looked blank again and he wondered if she'd taken it instead.

Joseph let out a long sigh. 'What in pity's sake is the use of me sending proper help if you're going to turn it away, Nellie?'

Rudy was a sickly child and Joseph considered what might have happened had he not been able to afford the services of a doctor and nurse. How the boy might not have survived. But right now, he wanted some peace and quiet to mull over the day's disastrous chimney-felling operation. He went into the orderly front parlour, leaving Nellie shaking her head at Violet who looked at Joseph in a knowing way.

'I'll have a word with him,' Violet said, and left Nellie struggling with Rudy, who had filled another nappy with foul-smelling, yellow liquid.

'What is it? Something isn't right?' Violet urged. Her son, who was sitting on the chaise-longue under the bay window,

buried his head in his hands. He pulled a sour grin and let out a snort. Baby Rudy screamed again from next door, and Nellie's high-pitched voice grated on him still further. He impulsively grabbed an aspidistra leaf from a nearby plant as though it was the most important thing in the world and held onto it, stroking the green veins, still not speaking.

Violet sat next to him and placed a maternal hand on his stocky shoulder as he examined the leaf. Even though he was a man, he was still her baby and she knew he was deeply unhappy.

As he told her about the chimney felling disaster and the badly-injured boy, Violet knew there was something else too. He was bright, making a name for himself, doing well in business. He had every reason to be happy about his success and this wasn't the first time a felling had demolished a weaving shed or maimed someone. Each month you read about something like this happening to lesser steeplejacking outfits in the area. Her grey eyes scanned his face and she could see torment below the frustration of a job gone awry. 'What is it son?' she gently coaxed again. 'What's wrong?'

Joseph looked directly into his mother's eyes but stopped short of telling her. Ever since he was a boy, she could read him as easily and naturally as he could fathom out complex engineering formulas. 'Ee lad, yer not too happy, are yer, son?' she soothed again. 'Pray tell, what is it?'

But deep down Violet knew what it was.

Tabitha Stark.

And that afternoon, Nellie had shared news with her mother-in-law that would ensure Joseph would feel even more trapped and distressed.

Violet wondered how Joseph would take the news.

Nellie was pregnant again.

***

Joseph double-checked the mathematical formulae over and over as he did with most things these days, before leaning

back and placing his hands behind his head.

He sat at his desk in the study in York Street. The room reflected his elegant but masculine tastes, with its arsenic-green wallpaper and ornate gas brackets bearing etched cranberry glass shades above the heavy mahogany desk. A cupboard on the wall contained an arrangement of guns, swords, china, tobacco artefacts and pipes. Joseph didn't smoke but these harmonized with his ideas of living like a gentleman. The orderly atmosphere contrived to give the appearance of wealth and prosperity.

The padded green Windsor chair creaked as he stretched out his short legs and crossed his ankles as he spoke to the Stapes. 'The sums are precise and, according to all the figures, these are simple mathematical equations and should work.' He pointed out that they wouldn't know until he tested his theory; now he intended to take that chance, come what may.

'I don't know much about arithmetic, our lad, but I hope yer right,' said Ron. 'For all our sakes.'

A telegraph had arrived a few days earlier from a premier Bolton spinning co-operative that was building a new chimney. Stapes Steeplejacks had been commissioned to fell the old one at a site surrounded my hundreds of houses in what promised to be a high-profile job. But there was a catch: the chimney was highly unstable and the only way it could fall without disaster meant bringing it down accurately within three feet either side of a gap between the mill yard and the timber merchants and the steam saw mill next door.

And Joseph had accepted the job on that basis.

'It's a tall order, lad,' said Les, who looked as worried as his brother.

'You say you want to do this one on your own, though?' asked Ron.

'If it goes wrong, I don't want you or Les near it,' Joseph said, leaning forward again to study his equations. 'I'll take full responsibility.'

The chimney was sinking due to insufficient foundations

and it leaned away from the direction it needed to fall. Two major steeplejacking outfits had already refused the job, saying it couldn't be felled in the way required. Les and Ron also insisted it couldn't be felled without damage to property and loss of life unless it was dismantled brick by brick. But Joseph insisted it could be done successfully by dropping it with great precision.

The local journal, the *Bolton Evening Standard,* ran the controversial story for a few weeks and journalists from far and wide had picked up on it, calling Joseph a madman or a genius for attempting to fell it.

This would be the most daring move of his career ... or the most stupid.

'Saw them up at intervals like this,' Joseph instructed the Bolton timber merchant adjacent to the doomed chimney. 'They have to be exactly the same length,' he advised, pointing to the wooden pit props the merchant was holding. Using his flowery way of speaking, he continued, 'Then I need several dozen wedges to this exact specification, my good man, and lots of lovely waste timber to adorn my beautiful creation.'

The merchant brushed his leather apron, scratched his head and listened to this outlandish young man intent on flattening his works next week and killing half the neighbourhood in their own homes into the bargain.

A gang of wild-looking local drunkards recruited by Joseph, bearing heavy hammers, pickaxes and a promise of free beer, started to hammer fiercely at the face of the chimney facing the direction of the fall. No sober man would go anywhere near a dangerous chimney such as this. And now it was being weakened further by being propped entirely on wooden stilts. Joseph turned up with Les and Ron as work progressed and the two brothers stood by, watching glumly as Joseph marked out in chalk where a lip would be cut into the base of the chimney.

Les remarked, 'Hope you've checked them sums right, young Wragg – tha's got us all of a dither.'

'You'll collapse the base if you start opposite the flue,' Ron advised.

'This'll never work – the weight of the thing will crush the wood with a gap that wide!' cried Les.

But Joseph ignored them and carried on instructing his staggering, swivel-eyed operatives, who had more interest in the opening time of the pub opposite than their mortal danger.

This continued all week long and, come Saturday, the chimney had a long, horizontal cut as its base was removed by a third and its weight was supported entirely on pit props. The gash gaped wide like a hellish smile bearing healthy wooden teeth, ready to sing its own death knell.

Around the back, Joseph measured between the two intervals marked out in paint where several cracks had already appeared in the brickwork. His set of brass trammels and measuring rod showed the chimney leaned over slightly towards the cut, but was in no great danger of collapsing as long as the pit props were securely in place. Each would hold over fifty tons. Working with his mathematics, he'd projected the line of fall would definitely be within two feet each side, once a fire was set at the base to burn the wood away.

Les and Ron had never seen anything like this set-up before, and arranged for a man with a camera to take shots of it. The photographer turned up toting his box camera, and looked terrified. 'Exactly, *how* close did you say you want me to stand?' he asked, as Joseph walked around the opening, hitting the props with a lump-hammer to test their stability. The photographer shuddered and wished the steeplejack didn't hit the props so hard.

'Next to the pit props, and take an image of the gap,' said Les.

Joseph saw the man's pallor. 'What's the matter with you?' he asked. 'It's perfectly safe – or else I wouldn't be standing here, would I?'

'You get paid for being a bloody madman and I don't!'

exclaimed the photographer, quickly grabbing his apparatus and retreating to a safer distance. Despite their worry, Les and Ron gave out huge belly laughs. Joseph joined in, too.

\*\*\*

The morning of the chimney felling arrived and a vast crowd gathered to watch. Joseph felt sick with worry. People peered from bedroom windows and the rooftops of surrounding houses; some stood at factory windows or climbed up onto the engine room roof for a better view.

They knew their lives could be in peril but everyone wanted to see this steeplejack who ludicrously claimed he could guarantee an accurate line of fall within a few feet for the demolition of a tall factory chimney.

Joseph was the centre of attention. 'Here, will you put your mark on this paper for my son? He collects people's signatures,' one man said. That started a trend: 'Me too – can I have one as well?' someone else asked.

People came to shake his hand and wish him luck.

A brass band played and several vendors selling penny tin-whistles, chestnuts, cockles, whelks and refreshments set up at the side of the wrought-iron gates at the entrance to the yard. Children wrapped in thick scarves and bonnets cheered and shouted, some waving flags bearing pictures of Joseph and the mill. Dogs ran around yapping and a strange man had a chimpanzee tethered on a long chain, which screeched and yelled, frightened by the swarming crowds. Some of the braver men and boys pushed their tricycles and bicycles through the streets to gain a better vantage point nearer the chimney base. Several journalists jostled together, waiting to speak to Joseph afterwards – if he wasn't killed.

Les and Ron felt sick, too. They had never seen anything like this audacious felling job. 'This is more like a carnival day,' said Les.

'Aye – there must be at least a thousand people here, probably some from as far away as Manchester!' Ron

remarked, full of enthusiasm. Then the smile left his face and he said he hoped half of them weren't killed.

The mill owners gathered more soberly at a safe distance, wondering what today would bring. 'Who instigated this damned foolery?' remarked a caustic old gentleman with a walking stick, whose father had built the mill. 'In my day this would never have happened.'

'I'll wager it cannot be done,' said his companion, shaking his head.

Violet sat at home knitting and, as usual, Aspen got drunk. He called his son mad and a bloody fool. Nellie shrugged her shoulders, uninterested, attending to the children and simply adding, 'Oh well, he picked the job, didn't he? I'm sure he knows what he's doing.'

Septimus Stark blew out a fine line of smoke across his table at the Breechland Gentleman's Club in town, as he discussed the event with several business partners and members of the board. 'I've told you, that idiot Wragg is far too big for his boots,' he remarked. 'This escapade will be the ruination of him, I hope!'

'Nonsense, my dear chap! Wragg does seem to be making rather a name for himself, not to mention a tidy fortune as well,' Edmund Floris said with a grin, relishing the flicker of irritation that crossed Stark's face. The other men smiled slyly at his comment.

The sour industrialist quickly composed himself, aware of his companions' reactions, and relished the thought of reading about this young pretender's misfortune in the papers tomorrow. He cared not a jot about the innocent people who might be killed or injured as well. He only wanted this upstart to fail; it was his mission in life to see he did just that.

Tabitha stared at the fire screen in the drawing room of her comfortable home in Royton, where she'd lived since her society wedding to Captain James Herrick ten months ago. She felt twisted with fear for Joseph.

The dutiful parlour-maid entered the room with a pail of coal.

'What is it, Lawson?'

'Please madam, I've come to set the fire early, seeing how you've been feeling unwell lately an' all,' she said. Lawson liked her kind mistress and was concerned about her. The previous day Tabitha had been confined to her room with a headache and her supper tray had been left untouched.

'Yes, thank you, Lawson, that would be nice,' Tabitha said, smiling warmly at the thoughtful girl.

Joseph planned to light his own fire at 11.30am and worked out it would take almost thirty minutes for wood soaked in lamp oil to burn, leaving the chimney with no support and with no alternative but to fall. He hadn't slept the previous night, partly because of Logan's crying and partly because of gut-wrenching fear. His new baby son seemed much sturdier than Rudy but, as usual, Nellie was restless; her bulky frame took up most of the small double bed as she snored throughout the long, lonely night.

At 11.29am, Joseph held a flaming rag torch to the paraffin-soaked scrap timber piled up against the pit props at the base of the chimney. A rich whoosh of orange and blue flames immediately consumed the wood. The crowd roared in anticipation. The draught caused by the fire sent smoke curling up the two-hundred-foot stack, where it spewed weakly out of the top, like a sickly parody of the hearty belting industrial fumes of its former life.

Each second seemed like a century to Joseph as the moments ticked by on his open half-hunter gold watch. In his other hand, he held a large hand bell to signal the fall of the chimney.

Despite the cold November day, beads of perspiration dotted his forehead, not from the heat of the flames but from adrenaline which pumped like liquid silver through his terrified body.

The crowd was restless and its noise distorted in his ears; they sounded like wolves baying for blood. After ten minutes he bent to examine what was happening, and could see the red glow of the wooden props in the roaring flames;

sparks flailed off in all directions. Going around the other side of the structure, he measured again with his trammels. The chimney had developed a rather frightening vertical crack and he could hear it creaking and groaning in its death knoll. It leaned over further as the props weakened.

It could collapse at any moment; the stress on the masonry must be tremendous at this point, thought Joseph. The props must burn clearly and evenly away for the chimney to fall in the right direction.

The crowd was murmuring. They could also see the props starting to burn fiercely by now. Joseph checked the time on his pocket watch again; another four minutes and it would hopefully fall.

The point of no return

He backed away and stood at the side of the timber yard wall with Les and Ron to see what would happen next. He saw it going before anyone else and rang the bell as hard as he could as several vertical gashes split open the brickwork, exposing the internal lining of soot. If it fell just three feet over the predicted line of fall on either side, houses and people would be crushed and Stapes Steeplejacks reputation would be in ruins.

Seconds ticked by.

Any time now…

It *should* be falling…

Tick-tick-tick…

Suddenly, another thundering crack rent the brickwork from top to bottom down one side. There was a great roar as three thousand tons of masonry kicked slightly back on itself and imploded to the right, giving Joseph an immense feeling of terror. For a moment it looked like the chimney would envelop him and the crowd in a terracotta tomb. Then it gracefully moved forward, gathering momentum as it traced a path like a fine pencil, drawing a straight line and landing quickly and safely exactly as Joseph predicted, without any damage to life or limb.

The crowd roared with joy. Joseph had accomplished

the impossible and invented a new way to fell an industrial chimney. People cheered and threw their hats in the air. Joseph was the centre of all this attention as they rushed forward to pat him on the back. The man with the magic lantern appeared and took several likenesses for the Sunday periodicals as Joseph climbed on top of the pile of rubble, found the lightning conductor and waved it at the crowd.

Joseph had achieved the height of his success and was the most celebrated steeplejack in the land.

***

Next afternoon, after another sleepless night, Tabitha said a silent thank you in her prayers and dabbed a fine lace handkerchief to her eyes as her husband James read the story out loud from the *Sunday Times* at her parents' house after lunch. 'I say, wasn't that the ridiculous chap who your father banished from the house, dear?' he said, smoothing his tidy waxed moustache.

Stark sniggered. 'The cur should certainly have been felled with it. '

James, amused at the joke, laughed along with everyone else as they sat around after lunch. 'Quite a strange little fellow, by all accounts, but a brave one I dare say,' he added, reading the article in full, as his father-in-law quaffed his port and lit another cigar, reflecting on Wragg's audacity.

Tabitha let her own thoughts wander free.

Later that night, she fantasised as she lay still under her husband. How might it have been to feel the heat of a million fires burning in her belly, stoked by the thrusting engine of her Joseph, instead of the perfunctory fumbling of a limp, public-school educated husband who had never made her feel anything but cold with his graceful, wraith-like body?

***

Over the next several weeks, companies manufactured pottery novelties depicting pictures of falling chimneys, and pictures of Joseph appeared in shop windows. Several more chimneys in Lancashire and three in Yorkshire were felled successfully using Joseph's method, and newspapers followed him everywhere. In Oldham, there was a big advertising placard outside the railway station. Joseph's sooty face smiled out from the picture, recommending Sunlight Soap, the best and most powerful washing medium in the world. People shook his hand everywhere he went and letters flooded into Stapes Steeplejacks with more work than they could possibly cope with.

Whenever Joseph worked on a chimney or steeple crowds gathered below, and children drew pictures of the working hero who had invented a method of felling a chimney known as a 'WRAGGFELL'. It would be used by steeplejacks for the next hundred years. Companies listened to his advice, considering him to be not only the greatest living steeplejack but one of the most knowledgeable men about steam engineering too.

The spinning industry was a much safer place now that Joseph and his old friend Percy Hayes acted as part-time consultant boiler engineers. The exception to this was Messrs Stark & Elm Spinning Co and their board of directors, influenced by Septimus Stark, who thought their grand factory was without fault.

It was an error of judgment that would cost the industrialist his life.

# *ACT* 7

*V*iolet sat beside Nellie on the couch with Aspen on the other side. The two women watched Rudy and Logan crawling around, playing with a toy steam locomotive on the parlour floor of their York Street home. Nellie bent down to pick up Logan who protested, waking up Aspen.

'Choooo ... chuff-chuff!' gurgled Rudy, pushing the tiny locomotive to and fro as Logan tried to join in the game. He shrieked as his mother grabbed him.

'Hush, it's time for a feed and nap, now,' Nellie soothed.

Aspen looked irritated. 'What time is it? I'm hungry.'

'Joseph will be along shortly. There are cold cuts for supper,' Violet said. 'If Les and Ron wish to stay, there's plenty to go round.'

'It's Sunday, does the lad never rest?' grumbled Aspen.

'It's the only time he's got free,' replied Nellie.

Joseph was busy working with the Stape brothers, designing and building a huge brick monstrosity of a clock tower and several turrets and castellations for the top floor of their terraced home and the rented properties each side, which the Wraggs also owned. Nellie seemed unconcerned about Joseph's unique home improvements. As always, Violet was indulgent towards her son, labelling them 'tasteful', and Aspen passed his usual disparaging comments about his son's sanity.

Since his rise to public notice, and at the advice of his industrialist friend William Edge, who was doing

exceptionally well with his bleachers' blue, Joseph had successfully invested in two other businesses in Bolton: Hanley Ironworks, the biggest firm of its kind in the North West, and Messrs Dobson & Barlow Ltd leading manufacturers of cotton-spinning machinery. Joseph could have easily retired on his investments and lived as a gentleman in the suburbs, but he still loved steeplejacking and was fiercely loyal to Les and Ron Stape.

Joseph was in much demand throughout Lancashire and beyond by the nouveau-riche and people with pretensions to grandeur. He was a prize at any supper event and was frequently invited to social functions and family gatherings.

Two weeks previously, he had seen Tabitha with her husband James at a Christmas gathering in a country house near Cheshire. It was the first time Joseph hadn't been overjoyed at receiving an invitation to such a splendid social event. As Henry Edwards-Bradley Junior, whose family owned a company manufacturing spindles and flyers, leaned gracefully against the mantelpiece addressing his audience of industrialists and cotton barons, Joseph found it hard to concentrate and join in the heated debate about the pros and cons of having oneself 'done in marble'.

Edwards-Bradley Junior said, 'It's up to us fellows to set a good example to the working classes. What better way for them to look up to us than by having a full-sized likeness in marble?'

'But the lower classes do not have the intelligence to appreciate art, surely?' replied Mr Dobson, a kitchen range manufacturer.

'I think several strategically placed marble statues of their betters are of great significance to them,' said Victor Simpkins, owner of a saddlery warehouse. 'It reassures them of their place in the general plan of things.'

'Quite right, my dear fellow. I say, hasn't Ponsonby-Smythe just had one done too?' exclaimed Mr Tomkins, a spinning mill owner from Bury, talking about a fellow mill owner in the district.

'It's just gone on display at the Manchester Exhibition, or so I believe,' replied Charles Entwistle a fat, squat man whose family owned a large brass foundry. He didn't mention that he was in the process of commissioning one for himself.

'What about you, my dear fellow? Any thoughts on the matter?' Edwards-Bradley Junior asked Joseph.

Joseph looked blank for a moment and, for want of anything better, said, 'Yes, I agree with you.'

Nellie sat silently in the withdrawing room, listening to the polite, idle chatter of refined ladies, and was glad when the men came back from their cigars and port for the musical recitals and tableaux entertainment. She was alert for once that evening, and noticed how her husband looked with hunger and longing at a lithesome, corseted figure in a beaded dress gliding past. Their eyes met briefly and Tabitha saw understanding and jealousy in Nellie's eyes.

Joseph was uncommonly quiet for the rest of the evening and Nellie feigned a headache so they could leave early, just as Tabitha did with her husband, James.

Joseph was a complex individual, motivated not only by money but driven by an almost obsessive need to be accepted by society after what had happened with Tabitha. Since his humiliation at the hands of Septimus Stark, Joseph vowed that one day he would be richer and more influential than that mean-spirited man could ever dream of being.

Recently a lot of Joseph's time had been spent travelling, giving reports on chimneys and boilers and he seemed tireless as he undertook each job with great determination. The Stape brothers had taken on four young apprentice steeplejacks and Joseph was enjoying training them up.

Each Sunday, as he strutted around Alexander Park and the finest streets of Oldham with Nellie on his arm, dressed in her rather vulgar finery, he cut a fine – if slightly odd – figure with his tall stove-pipe hat, three-inch stand-up collar and flashing diamond cravat pin. He wore lavender-scented cologne and high patent leather boots; the only things that gave him away as a manual worker were his ruddy

complexion, rough fingernails and highly-painted wife.

His voice was a complex mixture of northern dialect and refined words, sometimes used back to front for effect. Even Joseph himself didn't know why he did this. He had an extraordinary presence and, although only five feet five and a half inches in height, his striking personality immediately captured attention. 'There goes a man who would tackle the very Devil himself,' people thought as he passed them in the street.

Joseph never used tobacco and abstained from alcohol because of his father. But when asked about his abstemiousness, Joseph would simply say, 'A man that has to do the jobs that I do cannot drink and be successful.'

His latest idea of adding a clock tower and crenulations to his home was the result of a trip to Lancaster where he saw the splendid castle. He thought it was the most beautiful building in the world. Since then, he'd dreamed frequently of owning his own castle.

It was then he'd had the idea of building one.

'Dearest, you recall I told you about my trip to Lancaster recently?'

'Yes?' Nellie listened and pursed her lips as he told her of his plan; she seemed more interested in the gossip she'd heard about their neighbour's daughter.

'I thought you'd be pleased that we would have our own castle to live in,' Joseph said, puzzled by her lack of enthusiasm.

His wife shrugged her shoulders. Sometimes she didn't understand what compelled him to do such things. She only wanted a simple life.

Yet again, Joseph realised he had nothing in common with the girl he'd married. Only once had he asked her to host a dinner party for some of his business friends, and it had been a disaster. Crudely presented courses consisting of boiled pig's trotters and chunky-cut onions, served with thick doorsteps of bread, and cheap dessert wine served throughout the meal. The men were slightly amused; their

wives smiled demurely, glancing knowingly at one another over the encrusted pickle bottle on the table. Joseph was mortified, and Violet said that in future she would oversee social occasions herself. She had promptly engaged a rather ferocious but able cook on Nellie's behalf, a woman who had once worked in Manchester for the gentry, until they found she was too fond of cook's-nips, that is.

Nellie, with her lack of etiquette and awareness of 'correct form', was the reason he'd not bought a finer house in the Lancashire countryside. She wasn't capable of managing servants; it was a good job he had his mother. Joseph realised that he'd never make a silk purse out of a pig's ear, not recognising the irony of his own predicament as he strutted around the table, with his cut-glass decanter of costly port, serving friends in his finery after their repast of pig's feet.

\*\*\*

Joseph's eldest son, three-year old Rudy, beamed as his father walked in covered with dust and mortar from setting the chimneypots on their turreted roof. The job was nearly complete and Joseph referred to his recent creation as 'York Castle' on account of the street name.

'Cup of tea, our Joseph?' asked his mother. Joseph accepted and sat on floor with his son, who was playing with his steam loco in front of the polished Davenport desk. The little boy chuckled and baby Logan joined in. Although Joseph was unhappy and felt trapped in his marriage to Nellie, he loved his sons with all his heart.

'Aye, ma – but I'm going to scrub up first,' he said, rising from the floor.

'Don't be long, son,' said Aspen, knowing how frequently Joseph liked to bathe and how long it took. 'We've got to get off now, any road.'

As usual, there was tension between the two men.

Aspen's idea of fun was sitting idly playing dominoes and cards with his pals at the beer-house, trips for which Joseph always picked up the tab.

Nellie bent down and picked up Rudy, who cried as his father left the room. She felt worn out but the laudanum was helping settle her and the terrible arguments with Joseph were now a thing of the past. The laudanum was something else for which he picked up the tab, but in this case he didn't mind. Tiny doses of it kept her docile and she always went to bed shortly after the children, giving Joseph plenty of quiet time to study and make his plans late into the night.

Recently he'd been reading about the talented architect Pugin, who designed Westminster Palace in London. The gothic-style parliament building had a huge clock tower named 'Big Ben'. Pugin had died six months before it was completed. Joseph was touched and saddened by this. One day he hoped to see London; it was a place that attracted him more than anywhere else. He'd followed with interest a steeplejacking company called Mansells which had recently worked on Nelson's Column, and he wondered what it might be like to swing about on a bosun's chair amidst the fine cathedrals and grand structures of the capital city of England.

Violet stood up and adjusted her velvet bonnet.

'Listen, son, if you need my help with Nellie, just ask,' she said. 'The lass don't look too well at present.'

Aspen shrugged. 'Come on, old girl, let them be. We've got our own life to bother about,' he said.

Violet ignored him and hugged her son. 'Remember where I am if you need me,' she said.

The evenings were drawing in again and their maid would have lit the fire in the front drawing room, ready for their arrival home. Joseph's parents now lived in a detached stone house near Alexandra Park, next door to Dr Smythe. Kitted out with the finest furnishings and textiles, with artwork on the walls and beautiful furniture, Joseph didn't resent for a moment the money he'd spent on his parents' beautiful home. He was happy to see his mother busy overseeing the running

of her new house. To stop his father squandering their money and getting them into bother with the bailiffs, Joseph had put the house solely in Violet's name. Since her own parents had died the previous year and Aspen spent most of his time in the beer-house, Violet took comfort in looking after Rudy and Logan. They'd been with her since last weekend. During their absence, Nellie spent her time lying in bed until noon and eating biscuits and cake throughout the rest of the day. She hardly noticed her children were missing.

Violet kissed her son's warm cheeks, cupping his head with her hands as though he were still a child. Setting out with Aspen along the stony path to a carriage that waited for them, she wished she lived here with her son. No matter how beautiful her new home was, her heart was always here with him. That fool Nellie had no idea how to behave with a man of his station now that he was doing so well. *Pig's trotters indeed!*

Poor Joseph, it's a good job his mother can take charge when necessary, thought Violet, as she stepped into the waiting carriage. She was helped up the step by Aspen, another complete waste of time!

# $\mathcal{ACT}$ 8

Oliver Dobbs struggled continually with boiler Number Five. It became his nemesis.

As chief boiler-man, Oliver Dobbs handled the huge boiler-house with pride, watching water levels on all twelve boilers and keeping steam production at a premium throughout his nine-hour shifts. It was the first of its kind in Lancashire and Dobbs ran the steam plant like a military operation. Never once since being a young fire beater had he lost boiler function because of negligence, but he now felt he was being unfairly judged. It was as though the Board of Directors blamed him for loss of production as the steam engine continually slowed and looms were disabled to cope with loss of power.

That day was the third time in the week that the fire had gone out and caused the boiler to fail. He was called before his bosses.

Septimus Stark clicked his tongue in disgust. The nearest he ever got to getting dirty fingernails was examining his prized petunias each summer. Dobbs liked him no more than the Board of Directors did, or the other workers at the gigantic mill. 'You are clearly not in a position to speculate what the exact problem is then, my man?' he said pompously, tapping his pen impatiently. Dobbs shifted uncomfortably from foot to foot. One of the directors coughed and several others shifted in their seats, waiting to hear the chief stoker's response.

'Boiler Five seems to be causin' the trouble, sir, but I can't fathom out why,' replied Dobbs, hanging his head almost in shame. 'I respectfully suggest getting th'services of th'boiler engineer who installed her to prepare proper reports, sir. There's summat not right with her and that's a fact.'

The men murmured between themselves and peered over their half-moon spectacles. Loftus Elm removed his monocle. 'I take it this is an ongoing problem, Dobbs? Well, prepare to take the boiler out of service again for today and we will have a decision tomorrow on how to proceed.' He dismissed Dobbs back to his duties.

After the man left, Mr Elm addressed the other directors. 'Gentlemen, I suggest closing production down for several days while we ascertain the exact problems connected to the steam plant.'

Septimus made a sucking noise with his mouth again and wiped his beaky nose in a gesture of irritation. They had lost three days' production the previous week at his other factory through boiler problems and now this as well. 'I pass the motion that production must continue at full capacity for the foreseeable future. We are simply not in any position to close the mill for a full week,' he replied.

'As a compromise, may I suggest continuing working at fifty per cent capacity on three days for investigation and reports? That won't make any real indent to our investment, surely?' countered Richard Flanders, a senior director. 'I recall having a discussion with that steeplejack fellow Wragg about potential difficulties such as this with the steam plant.'

Septimus bristled at the mention of the name and the inference that this was his own fault in some way. Because of economy and his reluctance to spend further capital, they had ignored Wragg's suggestions and gone along with the architect's original plans for the flue system. But now, if there was a problem caused by ignoring the steeplejack's advice, then the embarrassment would be all his.

He covered his tracks, ignoring Flanders' pointed

remarks. 'Gentlemen, need I remind you of your current commitment to further capital investment over in Bolton?' he said, drawing attention to the fine-spinning mill being built by their company, which would eventually command the market in that area. The men murmured again uncertainly. Septimus continued, sure of his authority over them. 'I propose that we run at full capacity until the new Bolton factory goes into full production. We can dispense with costly engineering reports and the modification of the boiler plant.'

The board was in full agreement and the matter was closed for now.

Septimus sighed in relief as he sat in his carriage returning home to The Fens. Modification for factory power could run into several thousands of pounds. And what did one lame boiler matter? It was that fool Dobbs' problem – *not his!* By the time the new Bolton mill was in production, he was certain the slight trouble with the flue system – if indeed that is what it was – wouldn't seem as problematic to his personal finances as it did at this stage. He'd recently suffered the expense of sending a young girl off to the Lake District to avoid scandal where she could have their illegitimate child in secrecy. His floating capital was tied up in hush money for her greedy family and the new Bolton mill. He didn't want any spotlight on his finances right now.

\*\*\*

Joseph entered the boiler house and was met by ferocious heat. It was always a comforting place to be, if at times unbearably hot. Dobbs was busy shovelling coal and grumbling to Cyril Urmston, a spinner, who leaned against the door jamb, passing dinnertime by talking to his friend. Cyril was dressed in the usual spinner's garb of a collarless shirt and thin white drawers that reached to his ankles. His feet were dirty, calloused from years of running barefoot through muck and filth as he worked the mule frame.

Dobbs stopped shovelling; he liked young Wragg, who frequently called for a cup of strong tea and a chat. He wiped his face free of greasy sweat. 'Hey up, if it ain't the celebrated face of bloody Oldham itself!' he joked.

Joseph chuckled and replied, 'Would you like to arrange a likeness, sir? One can recommend a good artist if you like!' All three men laughed.

Joseph noticed the front plate had been removed from one of the boilers and the furnace tubes were exposed. 'Having trouble here then?' he enquired.

'Aye, bloody thing's givin' grief and goin' out all the time,' replied Dobbs, frowning. 'Never bin right since t'mill opened and that's a fact!'

A young fire-beater at the end of the room shouted to make himself heard over the roar of the furnace. 'Needs fettling, like – but t'big-wigs upstairs said they leavin' it fer now.'

Cyril smiled and pushed himself away from the door jamb. 'Septimus Stark, tight old git. I'm no engineer, but that's your ruddy trouble, right theer – *him!*' He emulated Starks' long, beaky nose and thin, bandy legs as he strutted around like a cockerel.

'Somebody should stick a steam injector up his arse, see how it feels to have a bit of life in his dry soul!' joked the fire beater. Everyone laughed heartily at Stark's expense.

Dropping his smile slightly, Joseph walked over to where the dismantled front plate of boiler number 5 lay, sticking his head inside the cold furnace. He immediately saw the problem: there was a huge steam pap, which meant there was a bulge in the roof of the furnace tube. 'Steam keeps putting out the fire, I take it?' he said.

'Aye lad! How the blinkin' 'eck do you know that?' asked Dobbs, astonished.

Joseph pointed out several tiny, almost invisible hairline cracks in the roof of the furnace tube. 'You see, this boiler is different from the others. It's made of wrought-iron instead of steel,' he explained. 'Not as robust as the others and it's

a weak link.' From his close friendship with boiler-maker Percy Hayes, Joseph knew all about recent design and what to look for.

'The boiler is well over twenty years old and although it's new, it's been in storage all that time,' said Joseph. 'I recognize the design and materials it's fashioned from. They are obsolete now.'

'Why the blinkin' 'eck would it be installed here now with the others, then, if she's an old one?' asked Dobbs, scratching his head. 'A mistake, surely?'

'No. Very likely the manufacturer has struck a deal with the mill company to provide a cheaper set-up by using an old boiler left over from old stock,' Joseph said. 'I've seen it done many times. It's not unusual.'

Dobbs let out a long sigh and propped himself against his shovel.

Joseph continued, 'It isn't usually dangerous but the capacity of this great mill running continually at the super-heated high steam pressure required by the new powerful engine is potentially serious.' He paused for a moment, and then added, 'Something I certainly would not have advised.'

'So what can be done?' asked Dobbs, shocked at what he'd been told.

'You'd better tell the board what I've said,' Joseph urged, frowning. 'This could mean serious trouble in the long run if it's not rectified. This boiler needs replacing right away. You should inform the directors without delay.'

Later on that day, Dobbs stood in front of the Board of Directors and did exactly that. Once again, Joseph Wragg was considered a young upstart and his advice was dismissed as poppycock by an irate Septimus Stark, who vetoed the idea and insisted that the steam plant run at full pressure as always.

*\*\*\**

Les commiserated with Joseph, who felt like he had a great

jubilee clip tightening around his brain, so intense was his headache.

'We've only just found out the news, lad,' said Les, looking sad.

Ron was also glum-faced as he stood clutching his cap in the doorway of York Castle and, like Les, sounded awkward and forlorn. 'Aye, came over as soon as we heard, like,' he said, referring to Aspen's sudden death.

The two men followed Joseph indoors. Violet looked up, her eyes watery and swollen from crying. Joseph went to hug her while Nellie comforted the children. 'Look, you stay with yer family the rest of the week,' suggested Ron to Joseph. It was only routine stuff they had on and the four operatives they'd taken on were busy straightening a chimney over in Rochdale.

Les agreed. 'Aye, we're only replacing t'lightning conductor at yon plumbing works over towards Stark & Elms mill. Stay with yer mam and look after her, son.'

Joseph didn't know what to do. He never usually took days off and the thought of sitting around all day made him uneasy. He wanted to go to work but knew it wasn't the right thing to do under the circumstances and would set tongues wagging.

Even though most of her life with Aspen had been drudgery and disappointment, Violet felt surprisingly empty now he was gone. She'd found him last night, keeled over in the kitchen, surrounded by gin bottles. Thinking he was drunk again, she was sharp with him. But he was as stone cold as the floor when she turned him over on his back.

Nellie spoke. 'I'll look after you, Violet, and you can go to work, Joseph.'

Violet completely ignored Nellie as Joseph hugged her protectively. 'No, Mam, I'll stay with you. It's all right. You'll be all right now,' he whispered.

There was much to do organising the funeral and Nellie would be of no use. Joseph was surprised how sad he felt now his father was gone and he forgot about work and his

ambitious projects for a whole two days. As Joseph had become a man of substance, Aspen had slowly sunk into a pool of self-pity and bitterness. He took every opportunity to bemoan his fate to anyone who would listen. Twice last month, the bobbies had brought him back home during the early hours of the morning, drunk as a lord.

The maid brought in a silver spirit kettle and set it down on the table in front of Violet. She thanked the girl, who left in respectful silence.

'Tea perhaps then, gentlemen?' Violet enquired. It was characteristic of her that she made a point of offering tea whenever there was trouble. The two older steeplejacks looked awkward, not used to sitting in best parlours or using small cups with delicate handles and roses on the side. Joseph nodded his head, giving a signal that it was acceptable to leave.

Les replied respectfully, 'Erm, tha'rs allreet, Mrs Wragg. We'd best be on our way. If that's all reet with you, like?'

Violet made a dismissive gesture with her hand. 'But of course, gentlemen. Thank you kindly for stopping to offer your condolences,' she said in rather an affected manner, and bade the two steeplejacks good day.

Once the brothers were back in the street, Les lit his cigarette. 'You can see where our young Joseph gets all his swank and pomp from an' all, can't yer our Ron?' he observed wryly.

'Aye, tha's not wrong theer,' agreed his brother, and they both chuckled.

He wasn't wrong. Joseph was determined to succeed at everything he did and Violet validated him. Joseph wanted to be the biggest and best, and the money he was making allowed him to be just that. Only last week, Joseph had another quarrel with Aspen who said Joseph was 'putting the show on' and 'throwing money away' – as though he earned it himself!

At great cost, Joseph was having a handsome Pullman coach built for towing behind a railway locomotive whenever

he travelled the country to give engineering consultations and advice on building chimneys. He was sick of staying in damp beds and questionable hotels, and the food was sometimes risky too. The coach contained specially designed furniture: sliding tables and richly-upholstered seats, ornamental mirrors and highly-polished mahogany fittings. The coach also had a separate sleeping section with a brass bed and thick feather mattress. There were separate quarters for two man-servants adjacent to a small kitchen so that he could be served in his own personal dining section. Joseph had designed most of it himself and felt proud of it. His father thought he was mad but it made Violet proud and that was all Joseph wanted.

Since moving into their new, grander house near Alexander Park, Violet had encountered difficulties. She had been snubbed by their middle- class neighbours on account of Aspen lurching around making guttural noises and singing in the street on his way back from the beer house. Nothing she or Joseph could do prevented Aspen from becoming a drunkard, so they just put up with it. He had wheezed and belched continually through baby Logan's christening, reeking of stale booze; the vicar gave him and the family stern looks. As Violet strolled in the park, pushing the perambulator and enjoying sunny days with her grandchildren, people avoided her and women gossiped behind lace-covered hands whenever she walked by.

Joseph was livid that his father was compromising his attempts to break into upper-middle class society. Aspen was the subject of continual gossip and scorn and the newspapers frequently carried obliquely-disguised snippets such as:

*'Surely a person's taste for the high life is at risk when the sobriety of fatherhood is exchanged for the recklessly intoxicating life of bachelorhood, as regularly seen in certain circles these days. Someone with tall ambitions may not be happy at*

*this lack of paternal decorum...* '

And now, as expected, the morning's papers were full of news and speculation about his father's death.

# ACT 9

Septimus Stark licked his dry lips in anticipation.

Walking through the noisy carding room of the mill the previous week, he'd spotted two young female spinners at a machine showing a new recruit how to piece cotton. The mill regularly recruited girls of fourteen provided by the workhouse and also the Stark Orphanage for Girls. This girl was no exception but her lean, angular frame, made tough since childhood by years of work, particularly caught his eye.

He'd suggested to the Board of Guardians he should set the girl on as a winder at his mill. She was pretty and pale, just his type, and her milky-white complexion reminded him of his last conquest, Loma, a daughter of one of the mill operatives. But unlike Loma, whose confrontational family was now blackmailing him, there was something not right about this one. Her flaxen hair framing high cheekbones and large blue eyes, belied the fact she was simple and perhaps not even up to mill work. No matter; if she didn't last long, it was enough for his purpose before he dumped her back at the workhouse or some place else. Perhaps he would pass her on to Mrs Gaskell, who ran the discreet brothel he used whenever he couldn't find a suitable fresh, young girl. But he was more careful these days after Loma, and usually looked towards the workhouse or orphanage for girls without families.

The darkness at the bottom of the empty stairwell towards the engine room was a place he'd often use to seduce them.

he cruelly inserted a finger hard into her vagina. He placed his mouth over hers to shut her up as he probed deeper and deeper. Her eyes bulged with pain and fright.

'Now, you will become a woman,' he said pulling away, removing his wet finger, ready to enter her.

\*\*\*

Les and Ron hauled the new lightning conductor up the stone chimney of the plumbers' merchants backing on to the mill yard.

'Should be done early today. This won't take too long,' said Ron.

'Rum do that, y'know, with Aspen. Suppin' gin like water all day and night,' said Les, holding the conductor as Ron fixed the sturdy bracket to the top of the chimney. They'd spoken about it earlier on their way over after picking up the conductor from the Manufacturet.

'Aye, he's never worked since getting' push from't Manufacturet, lazy bugger!' Ron replied, hammering the heavy conductor into place.

Les grabbed hold of the copper strip to attach it to the base, which would run down the side of the chimney. 'It would've done young Joe good to work on this lot today, but folks gossip enough about him as it is.'

Ron disagreed. 'Aye that's as may be, but yer don't want to be climbing or fixing chimney tackle in place when yer mind's not on t'job, like.'

By lunchtime the two steeplejacks were done and slowly came down the ladder, feeling their years. 'Gettin' too owd for this caper now,' joked Les, as he flopped on the ground with his back against the chimney. 'Let's 'ave us dinner.'

As usual, Les produced his snuff tin and Ron offered him a thick slice of pork pie with pickled onions, remarking they may as well remove the ladders tomorrow instead. No point in killing themselves. They opened a bottle of milk stout each, chomping food, sitting in the warm sun with

their backs against the stonework, as they'd often done since being apprenticed by their father.

Conversation got back round to Joseph. 'Eee, do yer remember when he nubbut a scrap of a lad we took on? Kept coming gawping at yon ladders, and then shot up before we knew it,' laughed Les, fondly recalling the excitement of the boy's first chimney climb.

'Aye, he were all bloody eyes and legs when he saw that rusty ironwork on top of t'stack, and that's a fact!'

'He went up theer brisk as a body louse!'

'Never had much time fer t'lazy cur of a father though. Never make a climber out of yon mon as long as he had a hole in his arse!' chuckled Ron, and Les agreed. The two men nodded, contemplating their hard, but contented lives.

'Pass us another bottle, might as well make a day of it.'

***

Mr Dobbs was in a foul mood again at work, furrowing his eyebrows and continually wiping sweat off his face as he coped as usual with boiler Number Five. All morning he'd struggled to keep the steam up to full pressure. Bill Sherwood, the mill engine driver, was complaining about fluctuations in power to the steam engine driving the mill. The fire went out twice and, when he opened the fire-hole door to investigate, he almost got scalded by steam escaping through a crack in the top of the firebox as it violently extinguished the roaring furnace. That idiot Stark insisted he keep it stoked 'to use what power he could', he reflected angrily; bloody stuck-up toff had no idea what he was on about. But it was more that Mr Dobbs' job was worth to disagree. 'Yes sir,' he'd said mildly.

He'd struggled re-firing it again about an hour ago. As the kindling and oily rags took light, he'd shovelled on more coal than usual, thinking to himself, 'Let's see how long it bloody lasts THIS time!'

Every floor of the mill was running full-pelt an hour later,

and boiler Five stayed at optimum power for precisely forty-three minutes and eleven seconds as it reached maximum temperature. White-hot flames roared over glowing fire bars towards the tubes at the back of the firebox, heating water to produce deadly, pressurized power. Mr Dobbs went over and injected some more water; that brass gauge was the last thing he ever saw before his eyes vaporized into steam as his head exploded along with boiler Number Five.

The three fire beaters died instantly, smashed against the roof and wall by the force. A huge rush of scalding steam, ash and white-hot coals filled the air, projecting several lumps of thick, exploding boilerplate against the wall, thrusting masonry through into the engine room next door. The force of the explosion damaged the boilers on either side and they exploded in tandem, adding to the might of the blast. Bricks and twisted iron landed on the lengthy connecting rods of the working steam engine, an iron girder jamming it violently to a standstill. The momentum of the iron flywheel continued, wrenching it free from its moorings, crashing through the huge engine room window, then hurling across the yard, like a hideous wheel from hell.

The back mill wall imploded; workers were thrown several feet into the air and killed instantly as parts of the disintegrated heavy scutching engines and huge bales of cotton landed on them then fell through into the storage room below. The side of the mill opened up like a cavernous mouth. The pump feeding water to the boilers burst. Pressurized steam filled the engine room and the chief engineer Bill Sherwood staggered out, dazed and knee deep in boiling water and metal, the skin from his neck and face peeled off and hanging like a gauzy scarf on his chest.

Septimus Stark was just about to explode himself when a huge piece of sharp iron upright from the mill floor above speared his neck like a javelin and took his head clean off. It dropped several feet from his body, eyes still staring and wide, before being crushed flat by a falling iron door. The girl screamed in terror as tons of concrete and brick rained

down, snuffing out her short wretched life for good. Several operatives tumbled through the gaping hole in the roof and smashed their heads and bodies open as they landed on top of the bloodied debris. They were quickly followed by parts of a destroyed bundling press and its operatives.

Les and Ron watched with horror as the giant flywheel, as tall as a house, crashed through the thin wooden fence opposite and continued its deadly trajectory, tossing tons of masonry through the air like confetti. The blast stunned them both and, as Les held his half-eaten pie to his mouth, he saw the front of the boiler house explode. There was just time to register that he should run before the terrifying wheel thundered and pinned him against the chimney, demolishing its base completely. Ron was slightly quicker and managed to rise, but the dreadful shock rendered him unable to move quickly enough; his last thoughts were of the pain it may cause, but he didn't feel a thing as his body merged into his brother's then slid down stonework of the disintegrating chimney in a mix of blood and soot.

The gigantic wheel fractured into several pieces on impact; its pent-up kinetic energy sent chunks of iron in all directions, slewing into people and horses who sustained terrible injuries. The remaining force effectively demolished the chimney which toppled and crashed to one side through the bedding manufacturer's roof, killing twenty workers below and blinding others. Two died after the lightning conductor shot through the air at great height and speared a carriage. Within seconds, escaping steam cooked several people where they stood and flying masonry and machinery killed more than two hundred in the blink of an eye.

The boiler house disintegrated as part of the wall caved in and metal twisted in the heat, affecting the iron roof supports holding the mill above. Workers of Messrs Stark & Elm Spinning Co, the pride of Lancashire, staggered around the yard and into the surrounding streets, injured, moaning, blinded, dying and pleading for help.

*\*\*\**

Joseph was helping his mother into a carriage outside her home by the park.

'Good grief, what in hell's name was that?' he said, hearing the commotion.

Violet would usually admonish him for using language, but on this occasion she looked in the same direction as her son. 'Sounded like an explosion,' she said.

For a moment Joseph mentally ran through the works in the area. Then, a second later, he registered what he'd discussed recently with Mr Dobbs at Stark & Elm. Boiler explosions were not a rare occurrence but in a factory that large, with a newly-designed internal boiler and engine houses, the death toll would be unbelievable should it happen.

Violet ushered him off and he ran down the road through the terraced streets, coming out at the corner near the mill. Before he arrived, he knew what he would find. The streets were littered with iron and rubble and some of the houses nearer the blast had broken windows. People were staggering out of their homes, faces cut open by flying glass.

Turning the corner, he saw the carnage. A dead horse lay on the ground, a deep wound in its side; an injured man trapped underneath his carriage writhed in the oozing, thick blood of the animal. An old woman tugged feebly at his shoulder trying to free him, her eyes bleeding, and Joseph saw the left side of her face had been gashed open, her cheekbone exposed and glistening white. Groups of men scurried past pushing handcarts, loading the injured and dying. One man was crying wildly for his missing wife. A few of the dazed and shocked but uninjured mill workers stumbled about trying to help the injured. They were lucky; they'd been working on the unaffected upper floors.

Joseph reached into his waistcoat pocket and pulled out his silk handkerchief, handing it to the old woman. 'I can't

SEE!' she wailed. 'My eyes, I can't see!'

He pushed deeper into the crowd. Someone tugged at his arm. It was Samuel Ormrod from the bakery and he wouldn't let go. The fire brigade was pumping water, attempting to put out a fire. Everywhere was thick with dust and smoke and the sound of hysterical screams rent the air. Joseph pulled away in confusion but the man insisted. 'Leave it alone, lad. You don't want to go that way.' He nodded towards where the plumber's merchant's chimney had been standing and Joseph understood at once.

'For mercy's sake – NO!' Joseph yelled at the top of his voice. He tore his arm away from Ormrod's firm grasp, ruining the delicate fabric of his coat sleeve. He lumbered forward several yards before three men held him back.

'It's not going to help them now, lad,' Samuel advised. 'Leave it for th'authorities to deal with.'

Joseph fell to his knees, his body crumbling under its own weight. He shook his head and wailed in despair. The two men helped him to towards a low wall; one had a small flask of whisky in his pocket and he pulled the stopper out with his teeth before offering it to Joseph.

***

It was days before everyone was accounted for. A horrible mixture of blood and soot marked the spot where parts of Ron and Les lay smeared into brickwork. Joseph had to be guarded all day as he continually tried to return to the rubble of the chimney collapsed by the fly-wheel. His mind whirred like hot, oily spindles as he pieced together the catastrophic chain of events.

But for the death of his father, it would now be Joseph's remains they were scraping up. But if that silly fool Stark hadn't taken everything so personally and replaced boiler Number Five, then hundreds of people would have surely lived.

The three funerals later that week were almost too

much for Joseph to bear. It was like losing three fathers. He felt bereft, numb with shock. Piles of unopened letters accumulated on his desk at York Castle. Only one caught his eye. A slight backward slant on fine quality vellum made the tiny, neat handwriting appear almost apologetic. He opened it, knowing who it was from.

*My Dearest Joseph,*

*Perhaps it is wrong of me to correspond. However, I was greatly shocked this morning at seeing the announcement in the paper of your father's death and that of your closest friends the Brothers Stape. I feel most deeply for you and yours in these melancholy circumstances. Pray accept expression of my heartfelt sympathy and regret for your loss. These are no mere formal words of sorrow, since my dear papa was also lost in the terrible events at the mill. I will pray that your grief may be lightened as soon as possible.*

*Yours very truly,*

*Tabitha Anne Horrocks (nee Stark)*

Joseph held the letter to his face and inhaled deeply; vivid images of the beautiful wraith-like creature captured his heart. The immediate rush of emotion was replaced by bitterness as he thought about Septimus Stark and the way he'd affected both their lives and those of strangers now dead or maimed. To see his death validated like this, alongside those of Ron and Les, aroused Joseph's anger. He was certain that this was a tragedy born out of that tyrannical man's negligence. He balled up the letter, casting it aside, and stood up. Her signature, her married name, seemed to mock him cruelly; a great wail leapt from his lips. He was wounded deeper than any man could ever know. Love found, love lost … and death of those he loved.

The hopelessness of it all

Violet came running into the room and threw her arms around him. 'Oh son, it's a right tragedy, it is, but be thankful they didn't suffer,' she said, knowing instinctively he was more heartbroken about the death of the Stapes brothers than his father.

He was a little boy again, crying at the unknown, just as he'd done when his father said he had to become an apprentice sweep.

'It should have been me on that chimney, Ma, not them!'

She comforted her son more as the tears came faster. 'There, there,' she murmured. 'Be still, lad. I'm here.'

The loving solicitude of his mother was all he had left now; Nellie was forgotten by both of them. But as she stood behind mother and son and watched with sad eyes, feeling more than ever an outsider in her own home, she knew that her husband had never really been hers.

# ACT 10

'Put it down there, young man!' Violet told the delivery boy and gave him a farthing for his trouble.

She pulled the provisions from the basket, placing them alongside a pheasant – Joseph's favourite – and examined the remaining groceries in the bottom. The cook would be along shortly to prepare the meal and dinner would be served at 8pm as usual, after the children were upstairs with their nanny. It was important to stick to routine, and today was no exception.

Violet now lived full time at York Castle and took it upon herself to oversee the running of the house, gradually swapping the role of mother for that of wife. Nellie didn't seem to care and usually stayed in her room or sat in the parlour window, simmering with repressed hysteria, staring out over the garden. That's when she wasn't mooning around searching for food and fancies.

Violet couldn't face the Alexander Park house alone and had been with Joseph and Nellie for the past three months. She sat at Joseph's desk and sifted through the steeplejacking and business accounts. Over the past weeks, she'd been helping Joseph run the business as well as the house.

She finished off a letter by writing:

*'The representative of Mr Joseph Wragg of Oldham, chimney repairer, shall wait on the board requesting payment of his account for pointing and sundry work at Messrs Terrance & Briggs Chimney*

*amounting to £122-1-3.'*

She smiled slightly to herself and was glad her schoolteacher father had insisted on teaching her to read and write to a good standard. Perhaps when she was feeling better, Nellie would allow her mother-in-law to teach her a better appreciation of the written word. Violet smiled again at her cleverness. Everything was calm and quiet now that Aspen was gone; Joseph didn't use alcohol so there would be no more drink-induced scenes. Violet was happy and contented and had everything she wanted, even if it meant sharing her son with that great lump of a backward girl he'd married.

But Nellie wasn't backward, just a simple soul who wanted a simple family life. After the night when she had witnessed how close Violet was to her son, she'd decided to be a little more assertive in her own way. And the laudanum was a thing of the past now that she was pregnant again.

Joseph had assumed Nellie was just putting on more weight from her hours of eating. He sat slumped over the mahogany Davenport in the drawing room, his back to Nellie after she told him about the pregnancy. 'Oh you silly little FOOL! How could you DO this to me right now!' he fumed. 'Good grief, woman, how COULD you?' He spat the words out cruelly, and his eyes bulged as he turned to face her. Tightness gripped his stomach and he felt he would stop breathing. He loosened his smoking jacket and cravat as his mind spun. 'Have you never thought to be careful? Are you really that foolish? We already have two children to care for.'

Nellie stared at him, eyes wide in shock. She'd waited until the omnipresent Violet was out at Variety Hall before telling him about expecting another baby. She didn't know that that morning he'd heard the final engineer's reports about the boiler at Stark & Elm Spinning Co. His fears had been right. The boiler failed as the steam pap grew larger, then completely fractured the furnace tube and caused an explosion. The death of his friends and many others could

have been easily prevented by replacing boiler Number Five.

The news had put him into a dark mood all day. What if he had gone to the board of directors himself – could the explosion have been avoided? He felt a terrible sense of guilt.

Nellie began crying, crestfallen. 'I'm so sorry, Joseph. I thought you'd be happy an' all,' she wept. 'I really did.' She thought they were becoming close again now she was not as distracted with laudanum, especially that time he'd taken her in his arms and made eager, passionate love to her shortly after Aspen died. She could never know the reason was more to do with a letter bearing neat back-slanted handwriting.

He was immediately contrite and rubbed his face, almost as shocked as she was by his own outburst. 'Nellie, do please forgive me, I'm behaving like an animal,' he soothed. 'Of course I'm happy.'

But the damage was done.

Violet took the news of the pregnancy well. She saw it as another way to become indispensable. She knew Nellie, with her flaky grasp on life, could never cope through the confinement and the birth alone and, although Joseph was unhappy, it meant that the decision to sell the Alexandra Park house would be a certainty.

Joseph busied himself with work and going to see his new Pullman coach. He would travel to Liverpool next week to price a job and liked the idea of being away from Oldham for a while. The grime and filth had been eating at his soul since Les and Ron died, and for once he felt no joy in his steeplejacking work. He stuck mainly to running his other enterprises, apart from the prestigious job on a new bleach works' chimney.

His first – and only – row with his mother occurred when Violet suggested dropping the name 'Stape' and changing the business name to Wraggs Steeplejacks. He was amazed at the power of his own feelings as he lost his temper violently and shattered an oil lamp against the wall. Violet felt wretched as paraffin seeped into the rich green and gold

brocade wallpaper and tried her best to calm him. She should have known how he would react. He was sorry afterwards, of course. He'd recently invested in shares for a small weaving shed being built in Royton and he paid handsomely to have the name around the mill chimney top amended from 'The Lilac Mill' to 'The Violet Mill' to say sorry for upsetting her.

The only blight in Violet's life was a growing worry that something was amiss with her son. His grief over the loss of the Stape brothers wasn't mending. Recently, she'd found him cowering under the stairs with Logan in his arms. 'You mustn't let him out of the house,' Joseph insisted, clutching his son tightly so he could hardly move.

Logan screamed and bawled. Violet approached Joseph gently as he sank to the floor, his eyes darting fearfully from side to side as he held the struggling boy. 'NO! He shall be killed! Danger lurks at every source … why, anything may happen!'

'Easy now son, easy—'

'NO! We are all DOOMED!'

Yet the day before, he'd told Violet and Nellie he intended the boy should climb his first chimney on his seventh birthday the following month. There were other things, too. She'd called down to the Stapes' yard to take some food and he said he'd made some wooden skids with Robert Quigley, a younger apprentice steeplejack. As she waited for him to clear away, he counted and recounted the iron dogs while the younger operative insisted he'd already done so. Joseph still needed to count them once more before he left and wouldn't leave until he'd done so three times.

Violet was the one person Joseph would take advice from.

'You need to see old Doctor Smythe. I insist you do, son,' she said, after another sleepless night. She'd heard him rise several times and go downstairs to check the door was locked and the gas brackets turned off. He wound the grandfather clock until the spring gave out and it had to be repaired several times. His jumbled-up way of speaking was becoming worse; he used nonsensical sentences back to

front and didn't seem to realise how bizarre it sounded.

'It came from bright to dark then back again,' he mumbled. 'Cross the skies in light .... tell you, me and us ... we are in the skies ... bright then dark.'

Nellie said uneasily, 'What's wrong with him, Ma?' as Joseph continued speaking at breakneck speed one evening after supper, reading from a newspaper about the threat to monuments and buildings as new railways lines were laid. He muttered, 'Succeeding memorials? The Vannals triumphed by their ubiquitous wildness. Be dammed, the very zenith of progress!'

Violet knew that his guilt over the death of the Stape brothers and those innocent souls at the mill was eating away at her son.

He was anxious about making mistakes at work and instructed his seven steeplejacking operatives to tie and re-tie clove-hitch knots several times whenever he was on site at a job. He became convinced the ladders would randomly rip from any steeple or chimney; one day he manhandled his workman, Terrance Cottrell, to prevent him climbing, saying the lad would die. 'You silly fool – *stop!* Do you not see that last night I had an omen you would be killed?' he shouted. 'Do you wish to *die?*'

The next day, Cottrell told Joseph he was going to work for a rival firm.

Joseph had always handled his business dealings with fairness and trust. But now, many firms that Stapes Steeplejacks had dealt with for years were amazed to get arrogant demands from him. Before Violet started handling all his correspondence, Kirkham's brass founders in Bolton were sent a huge bill in error. Joseph wouldn't budge or listen to reason.

He'd written:


*Dear Sirs,*

*Although I consider my bill entirely free from*

*anything in the shape of an overcharge, I am nevertheless willing to allow you in this instance 25% off for cash in good faith. But I cannot on any future occasion make a similar allowance; otherwise your account would be a source of loss instead of profit to me. My collector will call upon you tomorrow noon for your outstanding payment of Seven Thousand Pounds and Twenty Shillings and Sixpence*

*I am, Sir,*

*Your obedient servant*

*Steeplejack J. Wragg*

On receiving this letter about the account, which should have been for a nominal sum of two pounds for some trivial lead work, the manager decided to tackle Joseph in person. He received a good thumping for his trouble and had part of his walrus moustache ripped out. The police were summoned as three men struggled to pull Joseph back from the startled man.

The employees at The Lightning Conductor Manufacturet dreaded hearing the clatter of hooves announcing the arrival of his carriage each day at 12.13pm precisely. One person had been sacked on the spot for suggesting in jest that Joseph was losing his mind. He was overheard saying his employer would be better off changing his new mill name to 'BEDLAM' instead of 'THE VIOLET', referring to Bethlehem Hospital the notorious lunatic asylum in London. The previously affable and good-natured steeplejack was becoming a dark, cologne-scented spectre, dressed in elaborate frock coats and high collars, lurking around the board rooms and workshops of his various enterprises.

He would often rise at dawn and call for his carriage so he could visit as many chimneys as possible in the area before noon, checking they were sound and no one had been killed in the night by one falling. If any were found to be in slight

disrepair, he would use a telescope to examine the trouble. Fiddling with the eyepiece, he would shout out to his startled coachman, 'Who owns that manufacturing company there? The chimney is in much disarray!'

His unbearable grief of losing three people he loved within a very short time, and learning he was going to be a father again by a woman he now despised, completely unhinged his mind. Violet worried he would have to be sent to the lunatic asylum if it continued much longer.

Then a dreadful situation occurred with one of the steeplejack operatives, a new lad called Jasper Higgins. He came from a rival firm which had fired him for allegedly thieving lead off church steeples. Joseph, who would help anyone in need, didn't agree that the boy was at fault. He might be a bit simple, thought Joseph, but he considered him to be a good steeplejack and gave him a chance.

One of the operatives came over before a chimney climb. 'Forgive me for saying this, Mr Wragg, but you'll want to know that yon Higgins lad is not only uncouth and vicious but quite mad, too.'

'What?' Joseph demanded. 'Is that all you have to say, Foster?'

'I know a bloke who worked with him over at Faulkner's outfit in Manchester. He's as mad as a bag of cats and once tried to throttle a mill owner.'

'Speculative hearsay!' said Joseph, pompously. 'Get about your own work, man – and stop gossiping like an ugly fishwife on washday.'

Several months after the Stark & Elm incident, the scrawny lad and Joseph were working together fixing a lightning conductor at the top of Oldham's new flagship bleach-works chimney. Joseph immersed himself in this work wholeheartedly and tried to blot out his continuing pain, despite Violet suggesting he now gave up steeplejacking work for good and enjoy his considerable wealth.

Higgins was acting very strangely, becoming giddy and not applying himself, then dancing around on the high

scaffolding like a mad man. Suddenly, he went berserk, and said he could fly off the top of the 280-foot structure.

*'Ye Gods!'* shouted Joseph, immediately dropping his hammer and struggling to catch the man's ankle before he leapt from the staging. He pulled Higgins back at great danger to himself, lying on his stomach along the planks.

'Stop struggling, will you lad, for pity's sake!' Joseph held onto him tightly and tried pulling him backwards.

Higgins howled and thrashed about like a lunatic, trying to kick out and shake himself. Joseph took a blow to the head and momentarily saw stars. He screamed again but held firmly onto Higgins. 'Be *still*, I tell you – you'll have us both over the edge.'

Joseph was perilously close to the edge as he slid further along on his belly, still holding the boy by the shins. The weight of the boy was almost unbearable, as his top half dropped further over the planks. Joseph felt his muscles pulling tight under the strain. The ground below seemed to loom upwards and, had he let go, Higgins would have been killed instantly in the fall.

Joseph fought with superhuman strength. His shoulder felt as though it would wrench from the socket at any moment, but the boy wouldn't be still. Spotting an iron crowbar on top of the coping stones, Joseph grabbed it with his left hand, and cracked the boy hard across the head, knocking him out cold. Joseph almost fell over the edge of the narrow staging as he prevented Higgins from toppling off, the dead weight dragging him further forward.

After struggling for ten more minutes, holding onto Higgins and not knowing what to do as his arms went numb, two of his operatives came onto the staging and helped Joseph hoist the boy safety back onto the planks. Tying a rope around Higgins' waist, they lowered him safely to the ground with a block and tackle, but it took every ounce of their strength to stop the lad from banging against the face of the chimney as they did so. As a shocked Joseph wearily descended the ladder, Higgins was still out cold. Someone

put a stone bottle of brandy to his lips as a restorative; as he came to, he bit the neck clean off with his teeth and started thrashing about again.

The incident made Joseph doubt his own judgment about people and he became even more fearful. He hadn't noticed the boy had serious mental issues and should never have been allowed up a ladder. The other steeplejacks had been right; the boy was unstable; although Higgins recovered fully from the ordeal, he had to be committed to the mental asylum in Manchester. Joseph suffered terrible guilt, as though somehow he'd contributed to the lad's problems and nearly killed himself into the bargain.

After that incident, Joseph mostly stayed away from the steeplejacking side of his business and looked around for new ventures to satisfy his ambitious nature. During one of his early morning forays to check the town's industrial chimneys, he asked his coachman to drive past Stark's villa, The Fens, in nearby Chadderton. He sat for an hour in the quiet lane peering through the darkness towards the large circular bay window of the drawing room where he was crushed by the venomous industrialist. Joseph was indeed richer than Septimus Stark could have ever dreamed, but the gnawing pain of losing Tabitha, the love of his life, couldn't make the victory worthwhile.

He tapped on the roof of his cab with his cane, and the horses continued back down the long road back towards Oldham. Then he tapped again for the coachman to slow down. 'Stop here for a moment, will you?'

To his left were two huge stone gateposts flanking a driveway leading to a handsome house: the vacant and stately Chadderton Hall. Until recently the mansion had been used as a school but now Joseph was intrigued to see a 'For Sale' notice plastered to one of the gateposts.

Walking up to the large house with its impressive portico bearing tall stone pillars, the vacant dark sash windows stirred something inside him. As he came to the back elevation, he saw an overgrown boating pool and extensive gardens as far

as the eye could see in the dim light.

He placed a gloved hand to a window; the huge ornamental fireplaces and oak ceiling beams inside the room made his heart leap. Through an open doorway leading into the vast hallway, he could just make out thick, twisted mahogany balustrades leading to the upstairs rooms. 'You are beautiful,' he said to himself. 'Quite beautiful. And this time beauty will be mine.'

\*\*\*

'Are you certain about this, Mr Wragg?' asked Mr Lomax, senior partner of the Veritis, Stottard & Oldham Bank Ltd. He leaned ominously towards Joseph over the reams of paper that illustrated the steeplejack's enormous wealth, placed both elbows on the leather-topped desk and clasped his hands together. 'I can assure you, sir, that my partners and I can meet your requirements in relation to disposal of certain stocks and shares.'

'Exactly, my dear fellow! I feel now is the time to move forward into other business ventures. I'm certain you will agree that the construction of a menageriet in England is quite a novel idea,' Joseph said.

'A menageriet, Mr Wragg?'

'A menagerie; indeed, a pleasure park with wild animals, Mr Lomax – *open to the public!* I shall use the word with a pronounced *'t'* on the end as before with the Manufacturet.'

'Quite, Mr Wragg.'

Joseph leaned back patently while a junior clerk entered, placed more paperwork on the desk and whispered something to Mr Lomax, who crossly flipped his hand and said the matter could wait. Joseph examined the office with its tall windows and mahogany panels set off by a handsome clock, noticing the fine plasterwork of egg and dart cornice.

The banker waited until the clerk left before speaking again. 'A-hem, now then, my dear Mr Wragg, it is rather

a large outlay of capital. Having examined your business accounts in some detail I can see that there will be no difficulty in ensuring you meet the repayment schedule of a substantial mortgage. Or, as you suggest, you could float shares to raise capital to buy outright.'

Joseph didn't mind what it cost. He wanted the house.

And he got it.

Violet clapped her hands with glee. *Their very own mansion!*

The small family moved in after several weeks of consultation with designers, upholsters and decorators who came to see Violet with the latest designs and samples of fabric. Nellie was allowed to give instruction on the nursery, since she was due to give birth in a few weeks.

Joseph quickly found a buyer for York Castle. Its provenance ensured that people flocked to view the property once it went on the market and there was almost a war over who would eventually buy it.

The newspapers showed pictures of the new house and several carried stories of the intended menageriet that would bring tourists to Chadderton, Lancashire.

Rudy and Logan loved Chadderton Hall and quickly established their claim on the plentiful ducks on the lake, running outside to feed them each day.

'Be careful near the water!' shouted their mother. She enjoyed watching them play and often strolled alone contemplating the beauty of the tranquil boating lake. But there was something empty about the idyllic scene, as though it lacked a soul.

Joseph laughed indulgently as his mother swept around the vast interior, her arms splayed wide, eyes shining brightly, taking in the exquisite furnishings she'd ordered with Joseph's blessing.

'We must throw an elaborate ball at the first opportunity, son,' she said.

'That would be perfect, Mother. To show society we have arrived, so to speak,' replied Joseph. 'Yes, a grand ball for

us, indeed. Quite the thing.'

Violet clapped her hands. 'Then I shall set about organising it at once!'

She now ran all Joseph's accounts and businesses and anyone who wanted Joseph to do work of any kind had to go through her.

Nellie looked worn out with all the fuss and sat silently through dinner. 'Why don't you go to your quarters and rest, dear?' instructed Violet, wishing the girl would leave the room. Her demeanour was affecting the atmosphere and she would not have her Joseph upset.

Nellie did as she was told, resignedly ascending the staircase to her own room, feeling more alone than ever before.

Joseph now insisted on his own sleeping quarters and adjoining dressing room, much in the way any gentleman of his standing would do. Recently, Nellie's mother hadn't been well with pleurisy, but the carriage never seemed to be available whenever Nellie wanted to visit her. Violet always said that Joseph might need it. Now they were living in Chadderton, there was barely any chance for her to return to Oldham to see her parents and she wasn't allowed alone on the omnibus that ran past the end of the road in case she got lost. She felt trapped, lonely and confused, and she hated Violet even more than she loved Joseph.

Joseph was enjoying being lord of the manor. He set about researching the dietary requirements of lions, tigers, chimpanzees, elephants and all manner of exotic birds and fowl. All the joy of steeplejacking work had left him now, although he still regularly oversaw the efforts of Stapes Steeplejacks, where he employed twenty men who secured the bulk of work in Lancashire and beyond. Inventing the 'WRAGGFELL' was a byword for safety so they got all the important jobs, even through many other smaller outfits had adopted the method, too.

Rudy and Logan had made their first climb months earlier and continued to pester him to teach them the trade.

He could see the enthusiasm that had sparked him as a child reflected in their bright eyes as they climbed and felt no fear. They would be the next generation and he would continue to expand this business empire for his boys. Joseph was pleased to see his other business ventures thriving; he went from strength to strength and was soon the richest man in Lancashire.

Violet was happy that her son's more peculiar habits of spending time washing himself for hours, and riding around in the middle of the night looking for falling chimneys, had abated. She supposed it was only right that he would want to be fastidious about his person after spending so many years working in a grimy environment. And now he had the money, why shouldn't he have the best it could buy? Joseph left a trail of fine cologne wherever he went, Violet dripped in diamonds and fur – and Nellie dripped in misery.

Joseph had secured animals from all corners of the globe for his menageriet. Lions, tigers, monkeys, giraffes and elephants were caged in the grounds or allowed to roam free. Exotic peacocks woke the family each morning with their shrill cries. Soon, people flocked from far and wide not only to see the menageriet and pleasure park or to use the boating lake, but to meet Joseph and get his signature on a printed picture or a likeness as he posed, leaning against the polished twisted mahogany balustrade under glittering crystal chandlers in the impressive hallway.

A rare and beautiful black lion named Chang, imported from India and displayed in a specially made brass cage, seemed to be the main attraction. Pictures of the impressive big cat appeared in daily and weekend journals, with Joseph holding its paw. Its handsome head held high, its emerald eyes defied people to approach as it roared. Joseph was often seen strolling through the fifteen acres of grounds with the cat plodding at the side of him wearing a red jewelled collar. There was a bond between man and beast, since the lion was ferocious with everyone else; recently it had mauled its feeder to the point of death. Rudy and Logan were not

allowed out when the lion roamed free with Joseph.

Joseph was particularly fond of the chimpanzees since his boyhood hero, steeplejack D. Wright, had had one of his own. The animals were more to him than prized exhibits; he treated them well and loved each and every one of them. Exotic birds and vivid parakeets flew wild in the denuded trees, shivering as the uncompromising Lancashire seasons changed. Elephants observed the scene as tigers and deer were kept apart, and giraffes strolled gracefully through the woods to drink from the boating lake where hippopotamus wallowed in the late autumn sun then laid on their bellies as night fell.

The menageriet was the only part of Joseph's life which struck a genuine chord and fulfilled a need in him; he loved the rareness and beauty of its livestock. Journalists from all over England flocked to see it, and before long Steeplejack Joseph Wragg's Pleasure Park & Menageriet was the most talked about place in Britain.

Joseph strutted through the streets of Oldham and people of all trades came to greet him. He'd brought many people to the grimy town who otherwise might never have visited but for the menageriet. Oldham was becoming a tourist spot as well as a mill town. Posters of the menageriet appeared in railway stations and on the side of omnibuses throughout Lancashire and beyond.

\*\*\*

Joseph sat at the breakfast table in the sunny morning room and put down his knife and fork. 'It is inevitable that I should be invited to work on the greater edifices of the nation in the capital city,' he announced after he read a letter from London brought in by a servant on a silver platter.

'Aye? What is it, son?' Violet enquired.

He examined the elaborate green copperplate scrawl entwined with a set-square and tools of his profession on the ornate letterhead. 'Steeplejacks by appointment to HRH

Queen Victoria,' he read aloud, examining the royal seal of approval through his gold glasses. 'Mansell & Co, Ltd.'

Joseph had heard all about Mansell Steeplejacks. It was a southern outfit recognised throughout the land for excellence, second only to Joseph, whose face was known everywhere from the tiniest village to the biggest city.

'Does that mean they are friends of the Queen? Shall we have her to tea, then?' enquired Nellie, slurring and leaning slightly to one side, her eyes widely dilated as usual. 'Whatever shall I wear? The new crimson silk, perhaps – or the velvet blue with the lace collar, hmm?'

Joseph looked up above his glasses and wondered if she'd started taking nips of laudanum again. He gave a long sigh. 'No dear, this letter simply means I shall be going away to London for a short while,' he said gently.

Violet flashed him a look of understanding, shaking her head at Nellie in dismay. 'Why don't you see if the baby is settled?' she soothed.

Nellie stood up at once, setting her dull eyes on the mahogany door and walking towards it. 'Yes, I must. Dear Gilby will need me. You are right, of course, Mama,' she said carefully.

Violet insisted that the girl try and speak properly and was giving her vigorous instruction each day. Baby Gabrielle had been born last spring and was a difficult child who cried all the time; she seemed sickly, just like Rudy had been.

Joseph didn't look up but continued reading the letter. It was signed by Rufus Mansell, the senior partner of the firm, and requested that Joseph attend celebrations next spring and undertake some light gold-leaf work on Big Ben, the huge clock tower on the Palace of Westminster. It was to be a prestigious occasion, the letter explained, with the purpose of uniting two of the greatest steeplejack firms in the north and south of England in a celebration of industry.

Joseph was overwhelmed with pride that he should be asked to represent Lancashire in this way and he threw back his head and laughed. It had all been worth it.

'Mother, we made it. We have arrived at our destiny,' he said proudly. Joseph was now a man of substance, the 'Gentleman Steeplejack of Oldham'.

'Eeeeh, by 'eck, our Joseph, that's reet champion, like!' his mother exclaimed, momentarily forgetting her refined manners. 'Whatever next!' she said, before getting up to hug her son.

PART TWO


LAND OF HOPE & GLORY

# ACT 11

Chang's sad death triggered a series of events at Chadderton Hall.

As the sleek animal lay sickly and panting for more than a month before going to sleep at the hands of a veterinary surgeon, Joseph slipped further into guilt and depression. So distraught was he at the animal's suffering, he cancelled his plans to go to London. The work with steeplejack Rufus Mansell seemed insignificant.

'What do you suppose is the matter with it, then?' asked Nellie, coming outside to find Joseph kneeling next to the sick black lion.

'It?' Joseph huffed indignantly, scowling at his wife. 'The blessed creature has a name, you know!'

Nellie turned on her heels and fled back to the house in tears. Everything seemed to be going wrong. She could never say a right word these days. Joseph only paid attention to his mother and this treasured big cat.

Joseph couldn't face any kind of merrymaking or celebration and lovingly nursed Chang through the long, cold November nights. Stroking the lion's head and running fingers through its glossy mane as the beautiful creature looked beseechingly into his eyes wrenched his guts. There was a special bond between man and beast, two brave souls fighting against all odds in artificial surroundings, recognizing each other's courage and loyalty, that made them kings of their own kind.

Ironically, after cancelling his plans to visit London, at Joseph's request the Lancashire and Yorkshire railway made arrangements for his luxury Pullman coach to visit the capital and bring a distinguished visitor to Chadderton Hall.

Veterinary surgeon Sir Reginald Ediss-Carr MRCVS of the celebrated zoological gardens in Regent's Park arrived three days after receiving Joseph's desperate telegraph, sure of what he would find as he arrived in freezing conditions at Oldham's congested, smoggy Central Station.

'You must be aware of the climatic stresses these poor animals are subjected to, Mr Wragg?' enquired Ediss-Carr as he strolled across the icy pathway towards the lion house, his educated accent rounding each vowel perfectly as he spoke.

'I'm sorry, what do you mean exactly, sir?' asked Joseph, caught off guard, assuming a disease would be diagnosed.

'The cold, damp northern climate is alien to these rare creatures, my good fellow,' the vet said as Joseph opened the gate to the lion's cage.

Chang didn't stir; his tongue was hanging out as he lay panting, the ferociously long fangs now as harmless as a kitten's. Joseph knelt down and rubbed the animal's head in greeting. It made a mewling sound, attempting to respond, as Joseph stepped back to allow access for Sir Ediss-Carr.

The vet could tell immediately the lion would not survive long, despite the gentle care it was receiving from the man who obviously loved it above all else. Chang's heart was scarcely beating and he hadn't eaten in three weeks. Ediss-Carr poked its prominent rib-cage gently, finding its liver swollen. It let out another weak mewling sound but apart from that did not respond, and its green eyes were glazed.

'This, and others of its kind, cannot survive the harsh climate.'

'But the cages are heated throughout the colder months,' said Joseph. 'I don't see why Chang should be so ill?'

'I'm afraid it is not enough. These animals need exercise and stimulation. A lot of the hunting instinct is repressed in caged wild animals, therefore boredom sets in quickly,' the

vet remarked. 'I assume you had him captured and brought from India?'

'Well, yes – but as a cub. I have personally undertaken his care – and that of all my animals – with utmost attention to detail,' Joseph replied, feeling rather guilty now it was dawning on him that he might be the cause of the poor creature's suffering.

The vet continued his diagnosis. 'Big game also require many pounds of fresh, lean red flesh – not just cooked meat or a variety of fats and hides from the horse-breaker's yard or tanneries.'

Joseph was wretched as he watched the vet put the lion to sleep with a hypodermic needle. He wasn't ashamed to let his tears fall.

The celebrated vet seemed to be a harbinger of several unsettling events during his overnight stay at Chadderton Hall. Two tigers fell ill, and almost all the exotic birds died the following night; the remaining ten plucked continually at their feathers, squabbling and miserable in their cages. Oldham was facing the fiercest winter in a decade, with temperatures below freezing point most of the day. Snow billowed like grey, fallen clouds along the path to the monkey house and sugar-frosted the land as far as the eye could see. Colourful birds could not tolerate sharp frost that stuck their feet to perches. Their sweet daytime song was no more.

The vet sniffed the crisp, sulphurous air suspiciously next morning before returning to the capital, his bulbous red nose unaccustomed to the industrial north. The toxic properties of mill town air were familiar to those used to living within the continuous smog, but exotic animals and old Oxford dons were a different matter. Even though Chadderton was a quieter suburb of Oldham, it still had many industrial chimneys issuing forth black smoke. The vet thought the Wragg chap a fool to even consider keeping such a variety of rare animals in the menageriet.

'I'm afraid their lungs are badly congested with fluid and the more exotic creatures cannot survive because of that

alone,' Ediss-Carr said, after placing a stethoscope to one of the male chimpanzees lying flat on its side.

Joseph lashed back. 'But the air is cleaner here than in Oldham – why, that's a preposterous assumption!' he said.

Sir Ediss-Carr shook his head in dismay, placing his stethoscope back inside his leather Gladstone bag. 'The kindest thing would be to put all the animals to sleep, Mr Wragg. You must understand that there is no other option. Unless you do this, they will suffer greatly before they die. These creatures are not native to Lancashire soil and cannot survive here.'

The camel and the rest of the birds died later that morning. The only species that remained healthy was the plentiful deer, which seemed unaffected and teetered on delicate hooves, leaving tracks through the snow as they gambolled through the woods.

Silence fell across the menageriet as the vet did his terrible rounds, trudging through the snow in his stove-pipe hat and caped coat, clutching his bag, visiting each group of sickly animals and putting them to sleep. Joseph felt sick with grief.

Six labourers were brought in to create a burial site and Joseph commissioned a spectacular black marble monument in the shape of an obelisk, set with engraved ladders and a block and tackle, simply inscribed 'CHANG'.

Within days of the vet leaving, the family physician attended Joseph, prescribing rest, calming medication and a sleeping draught for his patient's 'shattered nerves'.

The following night, Joseph woke the household with his agonizing screams. He had nightmares of finding Chang half dead with silver slug trails across his black fur as they spilled from a cavernous mouth encrusted with slime. When Joseph was awake, he was haunted by the feelings he had at the time of the boiler explosion, his thoughts jangling and whirling as he tried to determine what he could have done to prevent the catastrophe. He felt useless and fearful, yet hyperactive and restless at the same time.

By late December, Joseph was confined mostly to his quarters. Regular doses of strong opiate drugs had calmed the terrible rages and violent nightmares. Nellie and Violet worried constantly about him as he ranted in gobbledygook, sometimes frightening them to the point of terror before the medication took hold. The physician increased the dosage.

Rudy and Logan were allowed to see their father for an hour a day, and that seemed to be the only time he showed any sign of life as they spoke of steeplejacking to him. Baby Gabrielle was brought in only occasionally as she disturbed Joseph with her crying and made him fractious. Nellie sat alone with him for hours reading from periodicals and books, now she'd learned how, as Joseph gazed mournfully out of the window.

Nellie spent New Year's Eve quietly nursing her husband. She didn't mind as the seconds counted down and she bade farewell to the old year. Even though Joseph was poorly, there was a certain intimacy between the two that even Violet couldn't breach. Nellie finally knew that her husband loved her.

She stood at the marble-topped washstand, pouring water into the bowl, returning to Joseph's bedside to cool his forehead. She turned down bedclothes and wiped gently around his neck, drying him before looking for medication in the bedside cabinet. Not seeing it, Nellie entered his dressing room, finding it nestled behind hair brushes. She held up the tiny blue hexagonal bottle and extracted the cork as she returned to Joseph, offering a spoon of the bitter liquid to his lips, before settling again to hold his hand.

Drugged with the heavy medication that made him all hers, half-awake in his dream-like state, he whispered, 'I love you, my own true darling. I shall always love you, my beautiful one.'

More than anything, this was what Nellie wanted; she had always known deep down that he cared for her, despite what her father and others suggested. When she'd last returned home to the modest rooms above the clog shop

to see her long-suffering mother, Pa accused her of being 'stuck up'. The rest of the family sneered at her fine silk and lace garments, gauzy red bonnet and the marzipan fancies she'd taken as a gift.

'Buy us a week's grub wi' what that little lot cost, mi' lass,' Pa admonished. 'And what's that fancy reek yer 'ave on yer? Lavender water, I'll wager!' He wrinkled his nose.

Nellie didn't intend to be a lady; she only wanted to please Joseph – and he only wanted to please Violet. So she primped and preened and altered the way she spoke and dressed until she never knew who she was.

Joseph's business success seemed to be the criterion for entering a grotesque, cynical world of sophistication that Nellie despised. Before his illness, when Joseph took her to visit their pompous neighbours the Bickshaws, who owned an aerated water manufacturing plant, she was so ill-at-ease that she felt quite unwell.

Her head spun as she listened to Mrs Bickershaw, a crushing snob. 'One understands that the working classes are emotionally stunted, dear, but one so abhors having to deal with them... Of course, when one has £5,000 a year income, one has *such* expectations of the servants, don't you think?'

Nellie made an excuse, saying she needed to use the water closet, which brought a look of horror to her hostesses face. 'Well, REALLY!' she remarked to her husband later. 'That girl is *so* common, *no* shame – poor Mr Wragg!'

The day ended in absolute disgrace. No one could find Nellie and the house had to be searched from top to bottom. She was finally discovered hiding in the nursery, chatting to the governess. Joseph nearly blew his top, storming out and leaving his mother to deal with the situation.

*'Nellie!'* scolded Violet, forgetting she was very nearly a governess herself at one time. 'Come out of there at once, you silly girl!'

The Wraggs left under a black cloud. And Joseph was furious.

'Oh but my dear, how amusing the afternoon has been!' Mrs Bickershaw said later to her husband Godfrey over dinner, gleefully recalling the reddened cheeks of both women and their complete humiliation.

After that embarrassing faux-pas, Nellie filled her room with books and magazines about how she should behave in polite society, all provided by Violet, who took it as a personal crusade to educate her daughter-in-law in the ways of a lady. A piano was installed for her to practise on after breakfast each day; it was hoped that Nellie would eventually play recitals at the frequent social gatherings at Chadderton Hall.

Violet successfully broke through the barriers with some of the more prosperous members of the Lancashire middle classes, hoping that Joseph could buy himself into country society. It seemed to be working. But sometimes the Wraggs were patronized and lampooned with amused tolerance.

Nellie wasn't exactly sure where she fitted into this comedy of manners. All she knew was that she loved her husband and would do anything for him – or Violet, for that matter.

But now Joseph wasn't well and Nellie was beside herself with worry. She nursed him as only a loving wife could.

'I love you more than life itself. I can never be complete without this love! Nobody can come between us!' Joseph rambled incoherently, as if reading her thoughts. Nellie was beside herself with happiness; he had finally realised that Violet often came between them with her meddling! Oh joy! He *would* get better and she *would* assume her rightful place as his loving wife, queen of his heart – but on their terms and not Violet's.

'Oh, Joseph – you've been away from me for so long but now we are together again,' she soothed.

There was a knock at the door and the chambermaid came in with a stone hot water bottle for Joseph.

'Thank you, Ivy. You may retire for the evening now and leave us undisturbed,' Nellie instructed. When Joseph was better, they'd forget all this nonsense with staff now the

menageriet was closed. They could move back to Oldham into a nice modest house and she'd rid herself of all this troublesome etiquette that left her afraid to speak whenever they had guests to dinner.

The click of the closing door roused Joseph again. He rolled his head towards his wife and whispered hoarsely, 'We should never have been apart – never, never, never...'

'It couldn't be helped, my dearest Joseph.'

'Yes, my sweet, circumstances and people prevented our love...'

Nellie decided to be bold. 'One must surely love a parent dearly, but they can be destructive with their interference. '

Joseph shifted slightly on the pillow, sighing loudly. She clasped his hand hard to her breast and kissed his cheek. 'Yes, my sweet, my darling, that is exactly what happened, why we have been so far apart...'

He sighed heavily again as his eyes flickered closed for a moment.

'Oh Joseph, we are here, in this room together properly at last!' Overcome with emotion and relief, Nellie buried her head into his chest and sobbed.

In her elation, she didn't catch the long, barely audible whisper leaving his lips: *'Tabitha... Tabitha.'*

# ACT 12

*I*t had been a long, uneventful summer dedicated to nursing Joseph. Now the wind blew in cool gusts again from the north. It would be winter soon.

Autumn leaves were scattered across the abandoned grounds of Chadderton Hall, their rich colours bringing joy to the otherwise neglected tapestry of parkland and the forbidding appearance of the shadowy house surrounded by tall trees. Squirrels ran amid rusting cages, burying nuts, climbing trees and scampering up wooden structures once used as sign-markers, their sharp black claws digging into the rotting wood, disturbing scurrying insects that lived unseen within flaky crevices.

Throughout the year and beyond, Joseph was lost somewhere inside himself, struggling as the seasons changed but eventually coming back to face reality as the frost arrived. It had been a hard climb. The demons subsided on their own; the doses of potent drugs were reduced and eventually replaced with beef tea.

Joseph sat muffled in a quilted satin dressing gown, waiting for his valet to lay out clothes and help him dress before joining the family for breakfast. He still felt weak but his mind was calm as a mill pond now.

In the morning room, Nellie played with the children and Gabby cradled her doll as Violet spoke. 'Now, gal, we must be very careful to keep a calm and tranquil atmosphere at all times. There must be no discord, none whatsoever. Do you

understand?'

'I know, Mama. I shall do nothing to cause it,' Nellie said, not bothering to look up. It would only be a matter of time before Joseph tackled his mother and stopped her being so haughty. Nellie decided to let matters rest until Joseph regained his strength.

Violet eyed her daughter-in-law suspiciously; there was a new confidence about this girl and it had been difficult to control her since last winter. She'd even started going out alone on the omnibus to Oldham twice a week! Joseph wasn't well enough to participate in disciplining his wife; the fight for supremacy had been between the two women and the balance of power was shifting.

Violet had noticed an oblique hostility peppering her conversations with Nellie. Last night over dinner, Nellie had said, 'I'm certain that when my husband is well, he will make radical changes for the better.'

What on earth did that mean? Violet wondered.

Perhaps when Joseph was better, he needed a long break to regain strength and get away from his wife for a while. The last thing Violet wanted was her daughter-in-law imposing her will on her vulnerable son before he was strong enough to cope. The consequences might be disastrous. It was no secret that Joseph was grief-stricken after losing the menageriet and that Nellie hated Chadderton Hall. Violet needed to bear this in mind; nothing was going to put her second place in her son's life, or take away her beautiful home.

Joseph came into the room looking well-rested, if a little thin and pale.

'My darling!' said Nellie, leaping up to greet him. 'Here, come and sit with us by the fire.' She guided him to his favourite chair. The room was warm and Joseph said he felt rather faint; he adjusted his collar before Nellie took charge and helped unfasten the gold stud. She reached behind the glass-domed clock on the mantelpiece, offering him a bottle of smelling salts. He smiled tenderly. She had become a

dutiful and loving wife during his long illness, and he was fonder of her than ever.

Violet rustled her skirts in irritation as she watched this display of wifely devotion; if she wasn't careful, the wretched girl would succeed in making him dependent on her.

\*\*\*

A fortnight later, a letter arrived. Joseph set aside his newspaper and studied it over breakfast. It bore a London postmark and was from Rufus Mansell. The southern steeplejack had been greatly saddened to learn of Joseph's long illness and by his absence from the royal celebrations at Crystal Palace. As Joseph had improved over the months, the men started to correspond regularly – slowly at first, but with Nellie's help a firm friendship had been forged, and Joseph enjoyed reading the detailed descriptions of how some of London's fine edifices were repaired.

'Good Lord! He's working on the St Pancras Station as we speak,' said Joseph, removing his reading spectacles. 'It's a splendid example of Gothic Revival.' Then he winced as he recalled his lost chance to work with Mansell on Pugin's masterpiece at the Palace of Westminster.

Joseph continued reading the letter. The London steeplejack described in fine detail the modifications he'd carried out on the clock tower of St Pancras, and Joseph could visualise the work. His expression lightened and he nodded his head in eagerness, scanning the words.

Violet poured tea and spied her chance. 'Have you ever thought of visiting your friend in the capital, son? You could write to Mr Mansell and ask if he would accommodate you – or stay in the Pullman or at a good hotel.'

Nellie stopped nibbling her toast to protest. 'I couldn't possibly think of leaving the children, Mama. Rudy has been unwell with the measles and there wouldn't be enough room

for all of them on the Pullman.'

Joseph looked up. 'I think Mama means I should go to London alone, dear. As a recuperative measure of course,' he said, reflecting on the suggestion for a minute. 'By Jove, you know, it may be just the ticket to aid my recovery and to get me busy again.'

Violet smirked and looked down at her plate. Her plan was working. 'Yes, it would be a splendid chance to see all those wonderful monuments and structures you've often spoken of, son. Perhaps even chance to climb St Pancreas clock tower if you feel well enough?' She sipped her tea, knowing this suggestion would whet his appetite. Then she pushed ahead, sure of her position. 'And there's nothing to worry about with your business. I have everything under control, as always, my dearest.'

Joseph became animated the more he considered the idea. 'You are right, Ma! Visiting London – what a splendid idea! I've never found time before and it's always been something I meant to do.'

By evening, Joseph seemed full of life and sat busily writing in his study, replying to Rufus Mansell, saying he would arrange for his Pullman coach to be towed to London at the earliest opportunity.

\*\*\*

The manservant was pushing a stout wooden trolley with iron wheels along the platform at Oldham Central as Joseph lagged behind. The platform was congested with luggage and bustled with people waiting for the 8.45am to Manchester. An unruly squabble was breaking out between passengers boarding a third-class coach and a vendor selling mutton pies and ginger beer.

Two ladies stepped back to allow a policeman to pass. He and the station master calmed the disturbance at once, taking hold of a man who was threatening to kick the vendor.

'Come on now, lads, if you don't want draggin' down

t'police station, pack it in pair of yer and give that pie back,' the sergeant said, removing a black truncheon from his belt.

'Oi! Give us that pie back, yer thievin' begger!' demanded the vendor.

The offender lashed out again and said, 'I paid and he's a swindler!'

''E's right – he did. I saw him give him sixpence!' said his accomplice.

'Right then, come on lads – tha'll be gettin' a spell in't cells if tha don't give up and hand it over,' shouted the policeman.

As his manservant skilfully skirted around the edge of the skirmish, the stationmaster caught Joseph's eye and doffed his hat. Joseph remembered the fun he used to have dashing into Mr Sparks' provision shop before the cotton famine and pinching an apple or pear, knowing the old man couldn't catch him.

As Joseph walked alongside the packed train towards First Class, another locomotive came into view on the opposite platform, filling the station with black smoke. Minutes later, a whistle shrieked and great woofs of black smoke issued forth from the funnel as the regulator opened. The engine gradually pulled away from the platform and the noise from its clattering, crimson-red rolling stock, followed by several modest wagons, ricocheted off the leaded glass canopies above.

Once the smoke cleared, Joseph could see his own Pullman coach, with its red rose emblem entwined with stylized ladders, hooked up immediately behind a gleaming black locomotive engine. He was pleased to discover a brass nameplate on the engine's side, seeing it as a good omen that the locomotive was called 'The Lion'. The driver and stoker stood talking idly, one man leaning down from the footplate, his face and blue jacket covered in coal dust, the other leaning against its iron wheel.

They had ten minutes left before their train pulled out of the station. Inside Joseph's carriage, two servants set

about making his journey comfortable. It smelled of polish and cleanliness and Joseph stroked the varnished oak of the carriage. They had toured many places together during his life as a steeplejack.

He had needed to get regain his fitness to climb St Pancras. Joseph began helping his own operatives for a few hours whenever they were working on a chimney or steeple near Chadderton. A horse-drawn carriage would arrive at noon with Joseph, Ruddy and Logan dressed ready for action. His two sons climbed with him and Joseph explained the job, allowing the boys to undertake some tasks with a trowel or hammer. Joseph loved his sons beyond all measure and thought his heart would burst with pride as he watched them try their best; they had as much enthusiasm as he'd once had for the job. It was the only thing he disagreed with Violet about – but he insisted the boys be allowed to climb and try the work. There would be plenty of time later for him to pass his business empire on and then they could live a life of luxury, but Joseph knew the tough work would make them into strong men.

The stationmaster blew his whistle and, as pressure coursed through the valves and chambers of the locomotive engine, they picked up speed after leaving Oldham. Mansell would meet him at Paddington and accompany him to The Ritz Hotel where Joseph had booked a suite for the duration of his stay. It seemed to be the talk of London that 'The Gentleman Steeplejack of Lancashire' was visiting, and Mansell told his friend to expect several journalists at the station.

Joseph intended to sleep for most of the journey so that he would be fresh for dinner with Mansell that evening and he had told his manservant not to disturb him. As the wheels took up monotony of the journey with their repetitious chorus, Joseph slipped into a dreamless, heavy sleep.

# ACT 13

Rufus Mansell was taller and far more rugged than Joseph had expected. He wore a curious hat with two flaps tied across the top, the likes of which Joseph had never seen before. It drew attention to the broken-veined features of a man who enjoyed a drink. His tweedy jacket was made from coarse, woollen material more suited to the country.

Joseph felt slightly overdressed in his elegant, silk-edged frock coat, tall hat and cane as he stepped down from his Pullman coach.

'Good to see you at last, my son,' said Mansell, eyeing Joseph's smart attire and poking him in the ribs. 'For a minute there I thought the bleedin' Prince of Wales his very self had turned up!' The man threw a heavy arm around Joseph's shoulder, almost dislodging his top hat before crushing his hand in the vice-like grip of thick, scaly fingers.

Joseph grimaced and recoiled slightly from the fellow's beery breath.

Mansell didn't wait for a response. 'Look, I'm sorry about the lack of a welcoming committee as it were. It's just you and me, son.' His bovine features were full of delight at meeting his friend at last.

Joseph glanced around to find no-one but Mansell there to greet him. Where were the crowds? He had expected several journalists and perhaps one or two civic representatives from London Corporation. Did they not realise that Joseph Wragg, the gentleman steeplejack of Chadderton Hall, was

coming to town? He felt slightly disappointed but greeted Mansell enthusiastically to save face.

'Good journey, I take it, eh?'

'As expected.'

'Look, truth is, Wragg, I got to thinkin' about it … and I weren't sure if you'd be bone tired after your long journey from the dark, satanic mills, so I figured I'd cancel the pomp and ceremony stuff,' Mansell said. He tried to gauge whether a formal civic reception was important to Joseph or not, and decided that it was. 'Ain't no bloody use floggin' a dead horse – or even an iron horse, come to think of it,' he said, laughing at his own quip about the railway. 'I should be on the bleedin' music halls, you know, not running up steeples for a bloody lark.'

Mansell had been amused by all the tittle-tattle he'd heard about Joseph's flamboyant nature and his pretensions of being a gentleman. Judging by the man's appearance, it wasn't wrong. He intended to loosen him up a bit during this trip; heavens above, the man were a bloody steeplejack for gawd's sake – not some bleedin' dandy!

They strolled along the platform pushing against jostling passengers, porters, costermongers and brassy street musicians. Mansell pointed to the noisy one-man band, saying to Joseph, 'Watch out for pick-pockets – thievin' bastards make a bee-line for any travellers, and what with you dressed up like a toff as well…'

A tiny, barefoot flower girl came bounding up the platform and tried to sell Joseph some wilted posies. 'Go on clear off, yer little bleeder, or I'll 'ave yer nibbed by the coppers!' shouted Mansell, angrily pushing her away.

She flinched back, in case he lashed out with his hand. Joseph was annoyed by Mansell's aggression, beckoned the little girl closer and gave her a half-sovereign from his pocket. She bit at it, testing its validity, ignoring Mansell's rant. 'Blimey! Thanks mister,' she said, her eyes shining on discovering the coin was gold. She offered Joseph all her flowers, but he said, 'No, you keep those to sell to someone

else, my dear.'

'Blimey,' she exclaimed again, still not believing her luck. 'I ain't never seen a real gold sov before, yer lordship. Thank you kindly, sir.'

Joseph noticed she was barefoot. He reached into his waistcoat again and retrieved another half-sovereign. 'Buy some warm shoes too, mi'dear,' he said, doubting she would. But at least it would put some food in her belly today.

She looked at him as though he'd gone mad. Lost for words, conditioned to a harsh life where people were never kind, she viewed him suspiciously at the offer of more brass.

'Do you want more than flowers, guv'nor? I can give you a feel, if you like?' She clutched the two half-sovereigns tightly, looked at them again, then dashed off before he could reply, afraid that the gentleman might change his mind and want them back.

'Bleedin' little whores learn early round 'ere,' said Mansell, who had watched the exchange with puzzlement. 'Now wotcha gone and done a thing like that for, mate? Whole bleedin' tribe will be around beggin' soon. Come on, let's bugger off art of it.' He tugged rudely at Joseph's arm.

Seeing the girl reminded Joseph of when he'd come across his mother's friend Mrs Crebbes lying dead in the ironworks, her daughters Lizzy and Anne starving and cold, huddled against her rigid body. He had often wondered what became of little Anne Crebbes; seeing the flower girl so worldly-wise at such a tender age upset him greatly but he said nothing to Mansell.

As they left the station entrance, Mansell put two fingers in his mouth and whistled for a hansom cab to take them to The Ritz. Joseph cringed at the coarseness of the man. In the cab, Mansell used colourful language better suited to tap rooms and told Joseph where to find a woman who would do things he couldn't imagine for only a few bob. 'Might as well enjoy yerself, and a few jars at the music rooms later will revive your flaggin' spirit a treat, guv!'

Dinner with Mansell was in seedy eating rooms where

warm, cloudy beer was served to a noisy crowd. The rabbit pie was sinewy and of indistinct origins, and he felt sure the bread had mould on it, but could not see properly in the dim gas light.

Although Mansell commanded good money as a top steeplejack, he was never one to waste it on 'fancies', but didn't mind squandering it on a good time. He was a larger-than-life character, just like Joseph, but he lacked his northern contemporary's finesse.

They met up with a group of Mansell's operatives in Whitechapel. There were foul-smelling rows of dimly-lit beer-houses, tap-rooms and brothels, reached by pushing through crowds of street urchins, drunken men and prostitutes with brightly-painted faces.

The air in each establishment was ripe with the smell of tobacco, beer and unwashed flesh. The filth made Joseph's stomach heave as he struggled to digest the gristly dinner they'd eaten. Mansell seemed to be enjoying himself and was determined his visitor would do the same. They entered a gin palace and pushed through crowds towards the bar.

'Mansell! Over here, guv'nor!' a man shouted over the din of an accordion and someone singing bawdy songs. Joseph turned to see the ruddy face of an inebriated man with his arm around a buxom woman of the night, swinging a glass of ale in drunken salutation. Another man sat at the table with four similar women. Mansell acknowledged him, and shouted back, 'Faddon, we'll be there in a jiffy. Fancy another bevy, mi' son?'

He explained to Joseph the operatives had just got paid for work on a tower over by the docks. 'Then they'll wake up still stinking of the cork and wonder why they've got less than a bloody florin left in their pockets.'

Joseph didn't feel comfortable. He saw a few more men eyeing him up as he followed Mansell to the table.

'Hey then, mi' old geezer!' said one of the seated men, nodding towards Joseph in acknowledgement. 'Boss tells us you are into this steeplejacking caper like us, eh?'

'Yes, though mostly industrial chimneys up north. I dare say there aren't many of those around here?' said Joseph, wondering whether to sit or stand. In the end, he fanned his coat tails and took a seat next to the man.

'Too bleedin' right, guv. We've just done a grain stack over by the docks. Builder won't touch it, too damned big—'

The man stopped mid-sentence, threw his head back in a manic laugh then took a long sup of ale. Any chance of a decent conversation was lost because the women to his left kept groping him and making high-pitched giggles. Joseph felt a hand caressing his crotch and a painted whore with yellow teeth smiled in a parody of seductiveness. 'Fancy a rush up the straight, dearie – two bob, that's all?' she asked, fumbling for his penis. Joseph pushed away her hand and she pulled a face, her thick powder cracking off in flakes as she scowled. 'Suit yourself, I'm sure,' she sneered back.

Mansell chugged several pints of ale then sat, openly groping two drunken whores. 'Oh, you are a one, Rufus!' said a rouged woman with half her considerable bosom hanging out. The steeplejack fondled and slowly stroked her erect nipple then bent to suck at it hard, making animal grunts as his rubbery lips assaulted her breast. Her friend tried climbing on Joseph's knee, lifting her own pendulous breast to his mouth but he pushed her harshly aside.

'Well pardon *me*, your honour,' she quipped, leaning back then bursting into harsh peals of laughter. Mansell and the other girl joined in.

One of the women noticed Joseph was sitting stony-faced and unmoved by the offer of sex. She made graphic promises about what she could do to him and he shook his head in disgust. A younger, less repulsive whore leaned forward and whispered, 'You can watch me with my friend instead if you like, mister ... two bob is all.'

Mansell mistook Joseph's uneasiness for shyness. 'Daisy don't mind it, do yer, mi' love?' he said, and bent to work her mouth roughly with a wet, loud noise. The women threw their heads back and shrieked again as the other steeplejacks

gawped and made comments about what they would do to them later. At the promise of a half-crown, one of the older hags with a pock-marked face covered with dark moles suddenly dropped to her knees under the table. Joe was disgusted as he watched the man's face twist and turn for a minute of two as she earned her money, then got up wiping her mouth.

Astonished at what he'd just seen taking place in a public bar, Joseph turned away in revulsion and happened to fix his eyes on a burly man with tattoos making his way towards the bar. He fleetingly thought the man looked rough, maybe a stevedore or certainly someone who worked with ships.

The man caught Joseph's lingering expression of disgust, stopped with his glass halfway to his mouth and sneered. He ambled towards their table, summing Joseph up. 'So what 'ave we here then? The Prince of Wales his bleedin' self staring down on us all? he slurred, echoing Mansell's words at the station and laughing at his own joke. 'Oooh, I've had the devil's own business finding my way here, I'm sure, my good man!' he mocked in a fake upper-class accent, baiting Joseph whom he assumed was a toff out for a good time with the local whores.

Joseph remained seated and silently glared at the man. The burly stevedore loomed over the table, addressing him menacingly, mistaking his silence for fear. 'So, whatcha starin' at then, Lord Muck? Cat gotcha tongue has it?' he challenged.

Mansell stopped what he was doing, dropping his smile and false geniality. 'Push off back to your own sort, there's a good boy,' he snapped, assuming a mock upper-class accent himself for the insult.

The man turned on him. 'Look matey – why don't ya just mum ya' dubber and keep out of it? In other words, keep ya trap shut, eh?'

The stevedore baited Joseph again, enjoying the sport and sure of his position. 'A cut above dining at the Palace, is it, your lordship?'

Mansell extracted himself from the grip of his female companion, narrowed his eyes and glared at the man a few seconds before everything kicked off. Joseph didn't want trouble, he knew his temper would be uncontrollable if he got going, but he could feel the pent-up frustration of the evening welling up. He glanced at Mansell, ready to take his cue.

Before the burly man realised it, Joseph was out of his seat, grabbing him with such brute force around his neck that he began to splutter and turn redder than he was already from the drink. His delayed reaction gave Joseph and Mansell an advantage as they dragged him to the floor and punched him and several of his friends who had come to join in.

Tables turned over, glasses smashed and women screamed. Joseph took a punch on the chin from his left, but returned a heavier one before launching himself bodily and straddling the stevedore on the floor. The man was shocked by Joseph's brute strength and fighting ability and struggled to get up, but Joseph punched him hard and loosened several of his teeth.

Fighting continued all around them. Mansell and his operatives seemed to be having a good time, shrieking as they lashed out and climbed on tables to launch into the swarming rabble of men.

Joseph pinned the man's arms to the floor with his knees and held a broken bottle inches above his opponent's face. 'Nah sithee, lad. Seeing you're so bloody keen on toffs an' all, like. The Marquis of Queensbury invented boxing rules a few years ago but since I'm no gentleman, they don't bloody apply. So what's it to be, lad? Dus'tha wanna leave us alone before I make a reet bonny dent in yon ugly fizzog of yorn?' He moved the glass closer and the man's eyes pleaded for mercy – even if he didn't understand the thick Lancashire dialect he knew what Joseph intended to do.

The bar owner and several of his men stopped the fight. The women huddled together in a far corner with the trembling accordion player. They all watched Joseph, his

ripped tailcoat covered in blood, fighting like a seasoned docker, wondering if he would carve up the thick-set man beneath him. Mansell and his men were wiping blood off their own faces. Joseph continued staring into the prostrate man's face, before his victim finally shook his head in submission. 'Hey, sorry, mate!'

Joseph slowly got off him and dusted down his sleeves. Everyone relaxed as the man stood up, looking bashful. Joseph moved forward, glad to see the man flinching and said again in thick Lancashire dialect, 'Come in here again with yer bloody feightin' talk, yer mardy bastard, an' I'll 'ave yer. Now get lost.'

Everyone cheered and patted Joseph on the back as the man slunk out of the door, mumbling under his breath.

By the time Joseph headed back to The Ritz, he was shocked and sickened by the debauchery he'd witnessed and become a part of that night. He couldn't believe such things happened in full view of everyone, and was astonished when Mansell later told him there were regularly kick-offs like that at the drinking houses.

It was a steep learning curve and one he didn't really care to be a part of. Joseph dreaded meeting Mansell the next day, but couldn't find any excuse not to. Mansell's social circle revolved around his wild operatives, gin-palaces, singing rooms and shady establishments around Whitechapel.

Now that Joseph had shown what he was really made of, Mansell and his men thought he was the best thing from Lancashire since spun cotton. But their coarse behaviour reminded Joseph of Aspen, though even his father would never have become embroiled in such lewd behaviour as that. Joseph had seen no sign of Mansell's true nature during his correspondence with the man; topics were usually only to do with the steeplejack trade and engineering matters. He was very disappointed.

Over the next few days, he met with Mansell and enjoyed some of his conversation when they stayed on that common ground. He found Mansell highly intelligent and

well-informed about current issues. In the evenings, however Joseph felt isolated as they mixed with Mansell's cronies in seedy bars and vulgar music halls.

One night someone even threw a dead cat on the stage during a performance! 'Gerroff, ya bleedin' nonce,' Mansell roared at the hapless act, then threw his hands up in the air and bellowed like a tribal warrior.

Joseph wished he'd brought Nellie along for at least they could have enjoyed some theatre or light operetta. He wasn't even sure he wanted to climb up St Pancreas; the London trip seemed a waste of time.

He planned to send a telegram inviting Nellie to join him. Mansell's company was insufferable and to be avoided at all cost. Then fate intervened when he learned that Mansell's daughter had contracted typhoid fever and was gravely ill. Joseph felt sorry for him, of course, but it was a welcome relief to get away from the constant ribald jokes, drinking and coarseness. Joseph decided to have a few days alone in the capital to recuperate before sending for Nellie.

*But London!* Oh, his heart leapt as he viewed the monuments he'd only seen pictures of; what ordinary mortals could ever build such beauty! Used to the oppressive grimy fog that settled each day back home, he hardly noticed the London smog as he admired the exquisiteness of Buckingham Palace and St Paul's Cathedral. Walking the streets of Westminster and Kensington was a joy, as was strolling around Hyde Park and listening to the speakers on the corner at noon each day. Each night he dined alone on lobster and oysters at The Ritz, sipping fine wines and wishing for further tastes of fine culture that the great city could offer the lone traveller.

# $\mathcal{ACT}$ 14

*L*ady Olivia Blenheim glanced into the embellished, silvered mirrors flanking the dining room. She'd been living at the hotel since her husband Augustus died two years ago. She seldom felt like returning to their country seat in Buckinghamshire after the season finished, but one must, she supposed, if only to see the family now and then. But it was always such a dreary affair. Really it was.

She loved the great noisy, smoky city and had many friends in town. The Ritz felt like home and she relished the freedom that widowhood brought. Her favourite occupations were matchmaking and causing mischief; she had nearly caused a scandal with her last protégée, a convent-educated lady who had fallen for the rather masculine charms of a married duke.

Olivia thought back to the days of her youth at Brampton Hall; all that tedious sitting around waiting to be asked to dance, wearing virginal white. Then being courted by a dreary beau picked by Papa and the great wedding to solidify the land ownership of two long-established families.

She was offered up as a chaste, virgin bride.

But she wasn't. The stable boy had seen to that.

And now she was bored again.

The man at the other side of the room didn't appear to be the most joyous of creatures, but he looked strong. Perhaps his conversation might extend to matters that would amuse her?

Joseph dipped into his bouillabaisse. Tomorrow he would make a decision to either telegraph for Nellie or remain alone a few more days. He thought his wife would like London and he owed her that after the dutiful way she'd cared for him through his long illness. But he hadn't seen all of Crystal Palace yet and it was doubtful Nellie would want to do much sightseeing.

A waiter arrived with a note. 'From the lady in the corner of the room, sir,' he said, offering a silver platter. Joseph opened the note and read it, then looked towards Lady Blenheim. The widow smiled, lowered her feathered head and tipped her champagne glass to acknowledge him.

'Please tell the lady I shall be happy to accept,' he replied.

The waiter bowed and stepped back discreetly.

'Mr Wragg, do please join me,' Olivia purred as the waiter pulled the chair back for him. 'I am delighted to make your acquaintance having read about you in the newspapers.'

Joseph kissed her gloved hand, and flailed his coat tails before sitting and accepting a champagne flute. 'I am honoured to be your guest, madam. I have noticed you dining alone several evenings this week,' he said cautiously. His ear was highly attuned to the slight difference between the affected speech of rich industrialists and old nobility. He sensed that she came from the latter.

'I do fear this is my lot in life now that I am left all alone.' Olivia gave a theatrical sigh.

'You live alone?' enquired Joseph. 'At the hotel, I mean?'

'I have a number of properties but I feel my heart and soul are here in London – and the hotel is *so* convenient. Fortunately, I am able to keep a suite of rooms at my disposal when life is … shall we say, *less* than amusing.'

Joseph wasn't used to upper-class games and sensed he was being toyed with, but he was confident he could extract the meaning of the curious exchange and deal with it. 'You seem to know me, madam?' he asked.

She took a long draught of champagne. The waiter immediately appeared and poured some more. 'Yes, you

are a rather a colourful tradesman from Oldham, which is in Lancashire, I gather? Am I correct?'

Joseph felt slightly wounded by the mention of his humble background, but to be defensive would ruin the opportunity to see what this woman wanted. 'Chadderton actually, which is a suburb of Oldham,' he replied evenly. 'Chadderton Hall, to be precise'

'Trade, nevertheless,' she sighed, gauging his reaction. 'But you are rather an oddity, for it seems you've made quite a little empire in the northern provinces, have you not?'

Joseph was trying to think of something suitable to say when she spoke again. 'Would you be so kind as to accompany me tomorrow? My friend, the Marchioness of St Chepe, is having an informal "at home" and I have no-one to go with.' She smiled, noticing him flinch slightly at the grand title.

Joseph was flattered to be asked. At last, a stimulating occasion and chance to meet people more akin to his way of thinking. He experienced a flicker of gladness that he hadn't already invited Nellie to join him. She was never any good in social circles where she felt belittled and uneasy.

'Madam—'

'Oh, do call me either Olivia or Lady Blenheim, please,' she purred.

'I would be delighted to accept your kind invitation. Thank you.'

\*\*\*

The manservant dressed Joseph in finery next day, polishing his top hat then handing over his kid gloves. Joseph was grateful that he'd consulted his tailor in Manchester before leaving Oldham and had several new outfits made. He surveyed himself in the mirror and pulled at a sleeve, pleased that his hands no longer seemed rough after months of recuperation at Chadderton Hall.

Lady Blenheim arrived shortly after he went down into the hotel lobby and smiled when she saw him coming down the steps to her carriage. Quite the handsome man about town, she chuckled to herself, and admired his fine manners as he raised his top hat in acknowledgement.

The Portland stone townhouse in the centre of fashionable Belgravia was smaller than he'd imagined, but in one of the best parts of London. Lady Blenheim stepped down from the carriage and waited for a servant to appear with an umbrella. Joseph didn't expect to feel nervous but he did.

'The marchioness has a taste for *amusing people,*' explained Lady Blenheim. 'It is a trend started by the Prince of Wales who flits between the demi-monde – actresses, artists and poets who would not normally be acceptable at court or in high society. And, of course, members of the preposterous nouveau-riche,' she said. The remark was aimed at Joseph but he missed it.

She enjoyed the steeplejack; he'd turned out to be an excellent dinner companion and a good conversationalist, but unfortunately had rather grand ideas of his own position in life. It would be interesting to see how he conducted himself among the aristocracy. If it went well, she would have someone to amuse her while she was in town.

A stern, unsmiling footman welcomed them at the door, taking Joseph's hat and cape before announcing them. The drawing room was darker and far stuffier than Joseph had anticipated, perhaps because of the heavy green drapes and people gathered amidst the potted palms and heavy furniture. The air was highly-scented with incense and a crystal chandelier caught the fine jewellery of the guests, flashing rainbows of colours as they moved about.

The marchioness came forward with a smile to greet them. Joseph bowed to their hostess and was introduced to some of the other guests, until the marchioness excused herself to attend to a new arrival.

Lady Blenheim took her seat, ready for the entertainment to begin.

'What's your position on colonial expansion into Africa, Mr Wragg?' asked Cuthbert Brookfield, who bore a striking resemblance to one of the baboons at Chadderton Hall with his deep-set, closely-spaced brown eyes. Before Joseph could respond that he hadn't got a position, a feathered fan waved in his direction and a thin, diamond-covered claw plucked delicately his sleeve. 'Nonsense, Cuthbert! You mustn't monopolize our Mr Wragg.'

Joseph turned to see an imposing woman of similar age to Lady Blenheim, dressed entirely in black. She spoke with beautiful clarity. 'You simply *must* meet our delightful artist, Saseng Denbar. A foreign individual, I'm afraid, but quite a rare talent. And he has the most *exquisite* brown eyes!' she said, scrunching her own as if in pain. She guided Joseph towards the piano where the brooding young artist observed the scene intensely.

They were stopped by another man. 'Wasps' nest or beehives, eh?' he enquired.

Joseph was caught off-guard. 'Sorry, what?' '

'Well, aren't you the brave fellow who removes things from high structures or something?' the man asked gruffly. 'Rather an inconvenience which, I dare say, happens as frequently in Lancashire as it does in Surrey!'

'A *steeplejack*, Robert dearest,' whispered the woman at his side. 'A man who climbs industrial chimneys for a living.'

'Why on earth would anyone climb a chimney? Don't they have boys for that kind of thing?' the bantam of a man replied, genuinely puzzled.

'They tell me you are quite famous where you hail from in the provinces of Lancashire,' said another woman. 'Do you find it tedious at all?'

'Tedious?' asked Joseph, unsure what to say.

'Now then, my dear fellow, hmmm … yes, we have a second-cousin in Lancashire and I must enquire if you are known to us. The Wraggs, eh? Yes, indeed …Chadderton Hall? That Capability Brown chap rings a bell … gardens by

any chance, dear chap?'

Others came forward and inspected Joseph curiously.

'You are from Lancashire? Oh, isn't that simply too wonderful!'

'Are you glad you came to London? Awfully chilly though…'

'Mr Wragg, may I present myself, I am Sir Thomas Moresque…'

Joseph's head swam with the questions. He overheard random snatches of several conversations as the man bored him silly about cricket and politics in which he had no real interest.

A gauche looking man and his friend strolled past. 'One never misses a spot of filly hunting, what?'

A fine-looking older lady announced to her younger companion: 'Oh, it shuts the door on the pretentious and vulgar, but opens it very wide for exceptional merit…'

Two gentleman walked in heated debate about a naval career: 'Arctic explorations? Not much in your line, surely, old boy!'

A peal of laughter caught his attention and he excused himself from Sir Thomas, who had just got started on the first international game of cricket played in the state of New York. Joseph turned to find two pretty young ladies tittering behind fans. Composing herself, one of the girls patted an empty seat at the side of her. 'Please, do join us, Mr Wragg, we've all heard so *much* about you.' The other girl giggled again and coyly hid her smile behind her fan.

Joseph was relieved to sit down and spoke to the two girls, who bubbled and fluttered throughout the entire exchange. The room felt like a battlefield and he wasn't expecting the rudeness, the gratuitous insults, disguised as acerbic wit. His face was hot.

Lady Blenheim extracted him from the giggling young women. 'You mustn't mind Beranl too much,' she said, referring to a crusty man who had very nearly felt the full force of Joseph's fist earlier as he mocked his trade and

humble Lancashire background. 'He is one of the approved parasites of the aristocracy and many people live in a state of terror of his sharp tongue and criticisms.'

Joseph felt his cheeks redden in humiliation but kept his thoughts to himself. As long as Beranl had a hole in his lardy backside, he could never accomplish all that he or Les and Ron had done in one lifetime.

Lady Blenheim moved closer and explained with relish, 'You see, Mr Wragg, we are a very civilized lot who play by certain rules. And you must *learn* the rules of the game, dear boy. To survive you must learn.'

Joseph narrowed his eyes and, taking her words to heart, nodded slightly. Lady Blenheim looked pleased. 'Now, do come along and observe our Mr Wilde at play.'

Joseph had heard about the celebrated Oscar Wilde, his extreme cleverness and accurate, perceptive wit. Wilde was the darling of London society with his dazzling humour and keen observations.

He caught the end of Wilde's exchange as they moved into his circle. 'But my dear Mrs Radley-Jones, life is *much* too important ever to talk seriously about!' he lamented, pausing for effect. Everyone laughed politely.

Holding court, his bulky frame fascinated Joseph, not because of his studied pose of nonchalance but because of what he was wearing. Wilde's six-foot figure was clad in a striking purple velvet jacket of the most vibrant hue, set off with a bright pink neck-tie. He leaned back slightly and ran pale, tapering fingers through the longest hair Joseph had ever seen on a man. But it was his voice that mesmerised: chocolate-rich, the mellifluous tones enunciating each word to perfection. He delivered lines in the way of a trained actor.

'Don't you think that art is a sign of decadence in any country?' Wilde announced to no one in particular. 'And of course the proper school in which to learn art is not life, but decadence!'

'Oh Oscar, there's no-one quite like you!' replied Mrs Radley-Jones, fluttering her fan. Wilde gave her a sweeping

bow.

Joseph had no idea what he was talking about, but everyone seemed to like it. Personally he thought it was a load of old gas and gaiters.

'I say, Oscar, there was a fellow named Tristan Trollope down from Oxford for the shooting last season. Claims you know him from Trinity College? Rather a stuffy sort of chap, though.'

'I fear your Mr. Trollope is gravely mistaken, dear boy. You see, I am the *only* person in the world I should like to know thoroughly well … but I don't see any chance of it happening just at present,' he replied. The crowd roared merrily. Unlike Joseph, Wilde never allowed anyone to needle or embarrass him before he parried words and demolished the speaker in a skilful way that commanded laughter.

Lady Blenheim stepped close to Joseph, cautioning, 'The unwritten rule for newcomers is never attempt to be amusing and never venture into an anecdote, Mr Wragg. If he catches your eye, you must allow him to lead the conversation. Do not compete.'

Joseph kept his eyes on Wilde. It was nothing like his soirées back home, where he felt sure of his place with Violet at his side. He thought he knew how polite society behaved, but now he saw was wrong. He stepped back a little, feeling intimidated and on uncertain ground as he sipped his soft drink.

'The *nouveau-riche* has rather a disturbing inclination to drink everything on sight – except that which is actually *worth* drinking,' Wilde teased as his eyes met Joseph's. The steeplejack wondered briefly if Wilde had somehow overheard Lady Blenheim or possessed a skill in reading lips, for the comment seemed to be aimed at him. Wilde nodded his head at Joseph and waited for a response as the crowd laughed again.

Joseph remained silent, but raised his glass to toast Wilde. Wilde acknowledged it with a slight tilt of his head.

'Do not be afraid, Mr Wragg,' Lady Blenheim whispered. 'Wilde belongs here no more than you do. It is just that he knows the rules … and you must always obey the rules in society until you are allowed to break them a little.'

# ACT 15

*I*f the game was to succeed, thought Lady Blenheim, it would mean investing far more time than she'd originally planned. But she had plenty of time to spare.

Wragg was successful in *appearing* as a gentleman, that much was true, but he wasn't one. Like other pretenders of his humble class who made a lot of money from commerce, Wragg equated wealth with social standing; he believed it gave him the power to ape his betters. The best thing about him was that he could afford to buy huge diamonds!

She could see no hope of forging a romantic alliance for him with an aristocrat. No lady of breeding would embark on a romantic liaison with a tradesman. Besides, there would be no fun for her, since everything would be kept secret. What a deadly bore *that* would be! And if he *were* to meet a titled lady who fell for his charms, Wragg wouldn't understand how to conduct the affair.

No, it had to be someone from a similar background who would capture his heart, another great pretender. A famous actress perhaps? One accustomed to the ways of the high society which Joseph aspired to, with his delusions of grandeur and carefully cultivated manners.

Lady Blenheim tapped her index finger thoughtfully against her lips and gazed out of the window towards Piccadilly, letting her mind wander free as she waited for her afternoon guest to arrive.

The thrill of plotting the best way forward for her new

protégé had kept her awake until the small hours. She knew he'd be susceptible once she'd decided how to proceed with her scheme; look how easily she'd persuaded him to stay in London for another month. Joseph had confided about the difficult time he'd been having with Rufus Mansell, and his reluctance to return home to Lancashire. He'd seen no harm in revealing his troubles with Nellie and his guilt because he didn't love her.

He did not resist Lady Blenheim's suggestion that he should delay sending for his wife and welcomed her proposal that they spend time together sightseeing in the capital. Lady Blenheim knew that her role as confidante was taking good effect; the steeplejack's trusting nature tempted her to meddle and cause further disarray. Now it was time to push the game further.

Disorder was her speciality since her late husband's parliamentary career, had been ruined by an alliance with Kingsley Petro, a provincial who had bought his way into society in much the same way as Wragg. Petro had earned himself a baronetcy and quickly gained Augustus's confidence. Having persuaded her husband to invest overseas, Petro had landed him with debts of £1,000,000 and destroyed his political career. Poor, dear Augustus committed suicide – and left Lady Blenheim with a loathing for anyone who had pretensions to her own class. Although Wragg seemed an amiable chap, he was hewn from the same rough cloth as Petro, and he had to be taught his place in life.

Finally, she had come up with a plan.

At first she'd thought of Fanny Kemble but she was a little too old. She also had a scathing tongue and could be wickedly cruel; Lady Blenheim realised that Joseph would soon become Fanny's victim – and that wasn't the game at all.

Her maid Ruth came into the sitting room. 'Mr Wragg is here to see you, ma'am,' she announced.

Joseph entered, extending both arms. *'Olivia!'* he said, feeling as though he'd known her forever, such was her

warmth. Like a second mother, she wanted to take him under her wing and for that he was grateful. He kissed her cheek, pleased that she'd summoned him this afternoon.

The 'at home' with the Marchioness of St Chepe had been full of unanticipated pitfalls, but with Lady Blenheim's help during the days that followed Joseph felt sure of his future position in society. Yesterday, as he escorted Lady Blenheim in her carriage around Regent's Park, he felt he'd finally found his place in life. He even wondered out loud about moving his family to the capital city.

'You have much to discover yet, my darling boy,' Lady Blenheim replied cryptically, turning her head away towards the carriage window, leaving him puzzled at her sudden aloofness.

Today, she was all smiles again. 'Joseph, we still have many things to speak of, my dearest,' she said, dismissing Ruth with a quick flick of her wrist. 'And I hope you will forgive me for being candid, for I only wish to help,'

'But of course, my dear Olivia,' he replied with a boyish grin.

As they sipped tea, Lady Blenheim gave him the full benefit of her wisdom. He learned of people from the highest echelons of society, determined to preserve their status no matter what, with whom he could never associate. These members of aristocracy would not tolerate outsiders and their ranks remained closed to the likes of Joseph. But some, like the Marchioness of St Chepe, were more progressive and welcomed amusing characters. And that was where Joseph's appeal lay.

'But I am very happy with my lot here in London, now we are good friends,' replied Joseph, flattered that she'd taken pains to explain how London society worked. 'Indeed, I would like to meet more new acquaintances.'

She returned his smile, pleased that she hadn't dampened his enthusiasm with her cautionary tales. It was a fine line between nurturing his spirit and breaking it. 'Well, in that case, my dear Joseph, I have an excellent idea! There is

someone that I would like you to meet,' she said. 'There is to be a late supper at the home of my good friends Lord and Lady Granville after the opera this weekend. But in the meantime, my dear, we still have a *lot* of work to do…'

She took his hand and stroked the back of it in a motherly fashion.

***

Joseph loathed the opera. He'd expected something like the pleasant musical interludes at the Alhambra Grand Theatre he'd visited in Bradford before he was ill. Bellini's complex production didn't make sense and it was several moments before Joseph realised that the prima donna was singing in Italian.

What a disappointment. As they'd travelled to Covent Garden he had been as excited as a child; when they took their seats in a box overlooking the stage in the Royal Opera House, he had caught his breath in wonder. But he'd lowered his head during the shrill performance and closed his eyes as if lost in the music so that Lady Blenheim wouldn't register his displeasure and think him provincial.

By the time they left the Opera House and pushed through bustling crowds of people waiting for carriages, Joseph felt a headache coming on. But as their hansom cab rattled through the darkened streets towards Mayfair, he was determined not to allow it to spoil the rest of the evening.

Approaching Berkley Square, Lady Blenheim was aware that something was the matter. Wragg seemed uncharacteristically glum and quiet and she guessed he was worrying about the social codes of the evening ahead. She patted his hand. 'Don't worry, my dear Joseph. You shall have many contemporaries here tonight. I am told the Brasseys are in town. Sir Thomas Brassey is the son of a farmer and made his fortune on the railways.'

Joseph felt better.

The French-inspired drawing room at Lord and Lady Granville's town house was tasteful and lacking in ostentation. Seeing the beautiful gilt furniture, Joseph pondered for a moment on Chadderton Hall and wondered about replacing some of the heavier carved items his mother had picked out.

Lady Blenheim pulled at his arm. 'Come along, Joseph, we have people to meet!'

Joseph smiled at a few guests glancing in their direction as they made their way across the drawing room. Lady Blenheim introduced him to someone with a name he immediately recognised: Linley Sambourne, the celebrated illustrator and cartoonist for the satirical magazine *Punch*.

'Why, dear fellow, you must come along to supper one evening at Stafford Terrace,' said Linley amiably. 'My wife Marion and I would be delighted to have you!' He pumped Joseph's hand in an unguarded display of enthusiasm. The steeplejack was warmed by the gesture; he'd been reading *Punch* while in London, and enjoyed its stance on current affairs.

'Yes Mr Wragg, do please come along,' echoed his wife. 'We had a very jolly dinner with Oscar last week. He spilled claret all over my dress!'

'And what about that old gentleman to your left, mi' dear, who came along with poor Mrs Grossmith?' remarked Linley. They both laughed, lost for a moment in their memories. Joseph liked the married couple; they seemed sincere and lacked the snobbishness he'd encountered among some of Lancashire's land-owning families. He was happy to accept their invitation for supper the following Tuesday.

'Oscar not here tonight?' enquired a tall, fish-eyed man decked in medals who'd wandered up to join them. He was introduced as Major Hareman-Twiss. He bowed and took hold of Joseph's hand, saying he was delighted to make his acquaintance.

'I have it on rather good authority you are an uncommonly brave man, sir?' he quizzed.

Joseph smiled back and started to describe some of his experiences as a working steeplejack.

'Jolly good show,' the major said, becoming rather distracted. He shuffled away towards another group, then embarked immediately on a debate about politics, twitching his fine set of silver whiskers.

Joseph turned to the Sambournes for reassurance. He raised an eyebrow at Marion, wondering if he'd said something to upset the Major. Marion shrugged as if to appease him. 'Our dearest friend, the Pre-Raphaelite artist Mr Dantini, passed away suddenly last year and the Major became quite distraught. I would never have guessed those two would be close companions. I fear he's rather been in the doldrums since…' She looked tearfully at the floor.

Linley took his wife's hand and gently patted it. 'There now, dearest. We mustn't embarrass Mr Wragg by becoming maudlin,' he muttered.

Marion composed herself, apologising that she had also been overcome with grief about the demise of poor Mr Dantini. Despite the awkwardness of the past few moments, Joseph felt confident with the Sambournes and chatted a little longer about art and politics. When he moved away to talk to other guests, he was flattered to discover that many people knew who he was and were curious about scaling the great heights of an industrial chimney.

At the advice of Lady Blenheim, he broke his golden rule about not drinking alcohol. 'It would look curious for a sophisticated gentleman-about-town not to be seen with a small glass of something in his hand,' she advised. After several dry sherries he felt warm and relaxed.

A ripple of excitement surged through the group of people closest to him. 'She's *here*!' someone whispered. Voices lowered to murmurs but a few of the ladies present became animated, jostling for a better view across the crowded room.

Lady Blenheim straightened her beads and feathers and protectively linked Joseph's arm as the double doors opened. At first Joseph saw no more than another group of people

dressed in evening wear. Then a slim woman of similar age to himself in a delicate pink taffeta dress came into view.

The butler announced their arrival. 'Mrs Lillie Langtry and Sir Montague Lowther-Simpkins.'

'Come Joseph, you must meet my dearest friend, the celebrated actress Lillie Langtry,' Lady Blenheim said. 'She'll be curious to meet you.'

Captivated by her large blue eyes, the glow of the enigmatic smile on her proud, classical features and her fine deportment, Joseph took hold of Lillie's gloved hand. He stood speechless for a moment or two, drinking in her loveliness before he felt all eyes were on him.

'I am very pleased to meet you, Mr Wragg. I have heard so much about you,' Mrs Langtry said, in a low but playful voice.

Joseph bent to kiss her hand, keeping his eyes locked firmly on hers. She smiled graciously, her cheeks dimpling in the process. His mind was jumbled; he couldn't think what to say or do but felt certain this woman was his destiny. The woman was a gift from God. For how else could she so closely resemble his one true love, Tabitha Stark?

His inability to say anything was not missed by Lillie, who gave him the benefit of another dazzling smile. She was lovely but in a natural way like Tabitha – not rouged like some of the painted beauties he'd met during his stay in London. She was truly exquisite.

There was a magical spark; he adored her on sight.

He would become her suitor, no matter what.

Lillie cast a shrewd eye over the smitten steeplejack knowing that, like many others, he had been captivated immediately by her considerable feminine charms. Sadly however, she already knew Wragg was useless to her; he was from the provinces, a man of commerce and perhaps of limited means.

Her good-hearted but wicked friend, Lady Blenheim, of whom she was fond, had spoken highly of the steeplejack. Apart from a little fun and distraction, nothing could come

of a dalliance with him. Both women had known this as they gossiped and plotted over luncheon last week. But that was where the fun lay, in the baiting and capturing of an admirer.

Lillie knew that Lady Blenheim wanted her to break the steeplejack's heart. 'Love is like poetry when it's sublime. The tending of a bleeding heart requires great skill, which you have in abundance, my dear,' said the manipulative older woman. 'We must ensure Mr Wragg is completely beside himself!'

'You are simply too much, Olivia,' Lillie admonished, and they'd toasted their new challenge, Joseph Wragg, who now stood before her.

Lillie smiled as Lowther-Simpkins introduced himself to Joseph. She thought of her many suitors queuing up to deliver flowers and jewels, their pledges of devotion, the unrequited love that led one hapless beau to give up his life at the hands of his own dagger! This game must be short and brutal, for Wragg would soon return to his industrial empire. Time was of the essence. But seducing him would amuse her before she sailed off to the United States of America next spring.

Had Wragg been as uncouth as his grimy trade suggested, then the idea would have been preposterous! She had expected rather a dull sheen to the man but he exuded a certain charm. She took in his gentle smile and rather touching openness. The actress knew that the steeplejack was trapped in a loveless marriage, but she wasn't too concerned about that. Neither did she care about the gossip should their little romantic tryst be discovered among her set. She'd sacrificed her reputation long ago.

And, he *was* handsome as Lady Blenheim had suggested – if rather stocky and short. There was something of the rough, northern industrialist about him; something she liked in spite of herself. He was like a large uncut emerald once given to her by darling Bertie, her beloved Prince of Wales, before it was shaped into a rare gem and revealed its beauty and fire.

'I trust you are enjoying your free time in London, Mr Wragg?' Lillie enquired. 'I understand you have seen many of our beautiful monuments.'

Joseph snapped his attention away from the simpering Lowther-Simpkins. His cheeks were slightly flushed. 'Yes, indeed, Mrs Langtry!' he enthused. 'I recently enjoyed a stroll along the new Embankment to admire the many statues of distinguished men concealed among the trees.'

Lady Blenheim was amused by the raw hunger in Joseph's eyes as he gazed at Lillie. The beautiful actress was still charming and graceful but in many ways even more of an outsider than Wragg now that the Prince had abandoned her.

\*\*\*

The actress, once toasted by high society as *'The Jersey Lillie'* was the daughter of a clergyman in Jersey before she came to London. She made her name as a professional beauty and as the mistress of Albert Edward, Prince of Wales for four years, despite being a married woman herself. She was highly celebrated, received by the aristocracy and was even presented at Court on one occasion.

Lillie was gossiped about, admired, hated and adored. The Prince had been passionately in love with her, despite having a beautiful young wife, Alexandra. He built a house for Lillie in Bournemouth and set up a love nest for them – until she embarrassed him by placing ice cubes down his collar after drinking too much wine at dinner. The Prince was outraged and ended the relationship, although they remained friends.

Shunned by high-society once her royal lover had abandoned her, no aristocratic hostess worth her salt would invite Lillie to a dinner, ball or reception where her presence might cause embarrassment to the Prince of Wales. She now lurked among the shadowy demi-monde with her close friend Oscar Wilde and the celebrated artists Millias and Whistler.

At Wilde's insistence, she had embarked on a stage career.

Lillie became the toast of America with her considerable skills, both on stage and off. She resurfaced in England after giving birth to a daughter rumoured to be fathered not by her husband, Ned, but a lover, Prince Louis of Battenberg.

Joseph learned all this by reading as much literature as he could find about her – much of it provided by Lady Blenheim, who seemed willing to help him woo this social butterfly.

'All men of standing have a beautiful mistress, Joseph,' Lady Blenheim declared. 'Why, just look at his Royal Highness!'

She clapped her hands gleefully as he proclaimed his growing affection for Mrs Langtry, confiding that he'd fallen helplessly in love.

Lillie was amused by his courtship. Even if the flowers were not *quite* the same quality of those she received from other admirers – particularly the American cosmetics heir who was also hotly pursuing her – she laughed gently to herself and contemplated her good fortune.

# ACT 16

$\mathcal{N}$ ellie was beside herself with grief. It was unthinkable: Christmas spent alone with Violet and the children in gloomy Chadderton Hall.

What a tedious, thoughtless chap this Mansell character was! Nellie wanted to scream and throw things. It was regrettable that the man's daughter had succumbed to typhus fever and it was unfortunate for *anyone* to be alone at this time of year. But did he not realise that Joseph had a family of his own to look after? She sighed and handed the telegram back to Violet, who read it again, wondering aloud if she should wire Joseph and ask him to invite Mansell back to Oldham instead.

'Oh, I don't know, mama. He will be cross with me if I fuss,' Nellie said. 'You know he dislikes me interfering in his affairs.' She sighed; she missed him so much. In one respect she was happy that her husband was loyal to his friend Mansell, but it hurt that he'd chose to remain in London for the festivities.

Nellie opened the tiny gold locket he'd given her as a birthday gift and gazed lovingly at the lock of his dark hair. Once he was home for good, she thought, they might have another child for her to cherish. It would be their fourth. Their marriage was happy now; after all, he'd revealed that she was his one true love when he lay poorly. Nellie smiled at the prospect. She would speak to him about it.

'A gentleman has to be free to make his own arrangements,

I suppose,' advised Violet, but something about the telegram disturbed her. It was written by someone intoxicated by life, not someone concerned for a bereaved friend. Her shrewd antenna picked up its tone, as though it were written as an afterthought; something needing to be done, then dispatched quickly without further ado. She wondered what exactly was going on in London.

\*\*\*

Joseph was ecstatic as he read the telegram he'd received that morning. The Sambournes had invited him and Lady Blenheim to share Christmas Day at their home at Stafford Terrace in Kensington. The couple were horrified to discover their dear friends, Joseph and Olivia, would be spending the day alone at The Ritz. Marion said she'd already invited several other people for Christmas dinner, including Oscar Wilde and his friend Lillie Langtry. Joseph smiled at the hand of fate putting Lillie in his path again.

Since meeting her, Joseph had attended the aptly-named Prince of Wales Theatre each evening to see her play Rosalind in Shakespeare's *As You Like It*, then filled her dressing room with two dozen pink roses, the exact same shade as the dress she wore when they first met. *'Bravo! Bravo!'* he bellowed from his box, whenever she came back on stage at the end of the performance. Then, after their late-night suppers at The Café Royal or Connaught Rooms in Berkley Square, they returned to her house in Eaton Place to make love.

Joseph was anxious about returning to Oldham for the New Year celebrations. How long would it be before he saw Lillie again? His heart was wrenched in two with the very thought of it. But due to fate intervening, he would see her again over Christmas.

Lady Blenheim said she found the idea of returning to Buckinghamshire for Christmas preposterous; she would remain at The Ritz during the festive period. She'd been so

174

kind to him, Joseph thought; he couldn't leave her in the impersonal hotel dining room eating Christmas dinner alone. He had decided to stay in London to keep her company.

He didn't know that her family had politely requested that she did not return to the family seat after her sinful game on Christmas Eve the previous year, when she'd manipulated an inebriated parlour-maid into having sex with the chauffeur in the dining room, with several other drunken guests cheering them on. It had nearly caused a scandal when the shocked butler reported the matter to the rest of the family. Since then, Lady Blenheim had been disowned and left to fend for herself.

*** 

The Sambournes' cluttered, cosy house was full of children's laughter. Joseph stepped inside on Christmas Day and was immediately comfortable. He'd eaten supper here twice in the last week, entertained by Linley's stories as they shared a cigar and a brandy together in his study afterwards. Hundreds of objets d'art competed for space with books, sketchpads and photographs in the masculine room. The cartoonist had a keen interest in photography and Joseph laughed when he was shown pictures of his amiable host posing in army uniform in some ridiculous stance or other. Linley was coy about his antics: 'For the magazine, dear chap, one has to reflect the body in the right position, see.'

The couple's children, Roy and Maud, bustled past with several others of a similar age, thundering along the narrow hallway to view the new rocking horse in the nursery. Joseph was amazed by the freedom they enjoyed. He thought sadly for a moment of his own children at Chadderton Hall but reflected on how happy they'd be with their own presents that he'd sent by parcel post the previous week.

'Would you like a mince pie, Joseph?' Marion offered as her parlourmaid Kitty walked by with a sliver platter. 'Rather odd shapes I'm afraid. Young Maud would insist on

helping Cook with them!'

Joseph acknowledged several people he knew and accepted a lopsided mince pie and small glass of sherry. He walked over to the group standing under a large stained glass window at the back of the drawing room and was immediately welcomed. They were discussing their host's latest offerings in *Punch*.

'I say, Lin has done rather a marvellous drawing of a seamstress, don't you think?' one guest remarked. 'Had poor Marion all togged up in costume for it though.' They laughed at Marion's willingness to help her husband with his career as an illustrator.

'By the way, Wragg, did *you* see it in the latest edition, then?' The man speaking looked as bohemian as their host with his russet-coloured jacket and billowing cream cravat. He was introduced to Joseph as the celebrated royal painter, George Wyndham. The two men chatted for a while – then all heads turned towards the door.

Oscar Wilde made his entrance in a flowing opera cape lined with red silk, which he removed to reveal an emerald-green quilted smoking jacket with gold lapels, set off with a bright red necktie bearing a large diamond pin. He posed for a while, holding out both arms while people admired him and applauded.

'What on *earth* is dear Oscar wearing, today?' said Marion to Linley, laughing. Wilde bowed formally to his hostess and exclaimed, 'Madam, there shall be no mourners today, for I have revived the spirit of Christmas by coming as a tree!'

Joseph didn't care much for Wilde or the attention he commanded, and let out a thin snort as he observed the celebrated playwright perform in front of his small, captive audience. The rumours about him buggering young boys made his stomach heave. Although the man was married with two children, he seemed always to have an entourage of young men trailing in his wake, gazing at him with sad, doleful expressions.

Wilde caught Joseph's judgmental eye and shrewdly summed up the steeplejack. He smiled, knowing the only reason Wragg was here was because of Lillie. He approached him. 'Good Lord, man. You go everywhere, I notice.'

Joseph stood his ground, but could feel the heat rising underneath his collar. He did not reply.

'The ubiquitous Steeplejack Wragg! You must surely like society as much I do,' Wilde challenged, waiting for a response from his quarry so he could parry further words.

Joseph remained silent as Wilde continued. 'But I forgive you and wish you a merry Christmas, my dearest boy.'

Joseph didn't feel comfortable at being called a dear boy by the wordsmith. He merely nodded his head in Wilde's direction then made small talk about Lady Blenheim to a man standing at his side. He used none of his usual florid language to avoid drawing further attention from the overbearing Wilde, who grinned knowingly.

'And where *is* the dear old trout?' enquired Wilde, glancing around.

Linley came over and slapped him heartily on the back. 'Good to see you again, dear Oscar,' he said. 'You're an inspiration to all poets,' he added, bemused at his friend's outlandish garments.

'One should either be a work of art, or wear a work of art,' Wilde quipped. At that moment, Lillie entered and everything else was forgotten.

Joseph took a sharp intake of breath on seeing her willowy frame enclosed in a gauzy dress of the palest gold thread. Marion went to greet her guest, extending both arms in warm welcome. 'My dearest Lillie, what an absolute picture you are as always!'

Lillie smiled warmly at her hostess and glanced across the room towards Joseph, but didn't approach him. He felt slighted but then realised Wilde was waiting for an opening to draw attention to them both. It was difficult to get her alone; she was surrounded constantly by a crowd who danced attendance on her.

'Sin is a thing that writes itself across a man's face. It cannot be concealed,' said Wilde to an elderly man who was staring in open admiration at Lillie as she expertly worked the floor. Wilde grinned and motioned towards Joseph. The elderly man followed the playwright's gaze and registered his meaning. 'Ah, yes, the northern industrialist fellow thinks our beautiful Jersey bloom is ready to be plucked, I'll wager,' he chuckled.

'We shall see, my good fellow. A woman will flirt with anybody in the world as long as other people are looking on.'

'Damned fine woman still, for her years,' exclaimed the man, adjusting his monocle for a better view. 'No harm in looking, surely?'

'Indeed, for 'tis a far better thing to take pleasure in an exotic bloom in an exquisite setting than to put its roots under a microscope and see its ordinary structure,' retorted Wilde, mindful of Lillie's humble beginnings as the daughter of a clergyman. 'She had nothing at all to her name – but looks delightful. What more can one possibly desire?'

Linley sat next to Joseph throughout dinner. They discussed Pugin's widow Jane, who lived near their second home in Margate; Linley knew how much Joseph appreciated her late husband's architecture at Westminster Palace. The conversation continued about art during the long meal then turned to music through dessert and coffee. Joseph felt the room becoming stuffy and had difficulty paying attention to what was being said. He failed to laugh at several anecdotes from other guests and remained out of sorts. He pushed plum duff around his bowl; the room seemed to be getting hotter as he forced down some of the heavy pudding. His mind was constantly distracted not only by Lillie, seated next to a stout old ram ponderously telling everyone about the time he was accosted by a policeman, but by the contrived tones of Oscar Wilde, which carried across the table. The dratted man had an opinion on everything!

Wilde was holding court. Pulling his large features into a parody of bliss and majestically announcing to the world, 'I

like Wagner's music far better than anybody's. It is *so* loud that one can *talk* the whole time without people hearing what one *says*,' splaying slender, artistic fingers to enhance his point. The effect was suffocating.

Lady Blenheim was seated at the far end of the table and seemed to be enjoying herself. There was a deaf lady to his left, who was having trouble understanding him and insisted on using an old-fashioned ear trumpet that poked him in the face each time she raised it.

He felt a dull headache coming on and made excuses to leave as the grandfather clock stuck six. Marion was concerned, noticing his lack of enthusiasm. 'You do look a little peaky, Joseph. Would you care for some tea or to lie down for a while?' she asked, genuinely anxious. She had noticed that he was uncharacteristically quiet all day.

'I'm fine Marion, my dearest. Just missing my family and feeling a little tired, I think. Perhaps I have been away from home too long after all.'

Just as he was about to leave, Lillie stopped him and whispered, 'My dearest Joseph, I must beg your forgiveness for I have not had chance to speak with you alone.' She leant forward and placed a lingering kiss on his mouth, touching his lips with her wet tongue. He inhaled and then opened his eyes, taking in the warm muskiness of her breath. He wanted to pin her to the wall, crush his mouth on hers, devour her until there was nothing left but a single molecule.

Lillie swept her lips lightly across his cheek, breathing in his ear and whispering, 'I must see you alone before you leave for Oldham.'

His head felt tighter and he thought he might faint. A steel trap closed somewhere deep in his brain, its claws digging deeper until he could almost bear it no more. He had to have her, hold her, possess her.

'Oh, my darling Lillie, I must see you again,' he whispered.

He had promised Nellie that he would return to Chadderton Hall for New Year's Eve. His departure from

London couldn't be delayed without causing suspicion, although he had considered making another lame excuse about poor Mansell. Joseph explained his position to Lillie and felt the weight of the jeweller's box heavy in his pocket. He'd meant to give it to her today before lunch, a festive token of his undying love. It would have to wait a little while longer.

'We cannot talk here, not now. Come to tea at my house at 5pm tomorrow evening. I shall await you then, my darling,' Lillie said, kissing his lips lightly before breaking away from him and re-entering the drawing room without looking back or waiting for a reply.

***

Lillie bathed in perfumed water then summoned her maid to help her dress after her bath. She wanted to look her best when Joseph arrived. The blue tea-dress revealed just enough décolletage and accentuated the colour of her large blue eyes. His devotion would need to be curbed this evening, for though she liked admiration she found worship somewhat suffocating. And Lillie was determined to return to America to continue her acting career. She had reciprocated his love in full over the past few weeks, knowing their fate was always to be apart. She thought that he had understood this, but found she was mistaken. Now she was growing slightly tired of the game but worried about how he would take the news.

As with all her lovers, she had made Joseph feel special but it was becoming difficult to see her other admirers because of his possessiveness. She was afraid of his temper too, which seemed to lurk beneath the surface when he saw other men looking at her.

As planned, and much to the joy of Lady Blenheim, she'd undoubtedly captured and won Joseph's heart. Caution advised against breaking it though, and she did not want to humiliate the steeplejack publicly. He was a sensitive

lover and came alive whenever they were alone together. Something inside her warmed to him. Finding none of the boorishness she had experienced in the company of other entrepreneurs in less intimate situations, she was more than a little fond of Joseph. His manners were impeccable, even if his attitude was quite provincial.

Lillie decided to be gentle. He was unaccustomed to the foibles of high society, and had read too much into their liaison. Like her, he should have taken it lightly as nothing more than sexual fulfilment dressed up as a love affair. She was a passionate, lusty woman and here was a man who took her body to exciting places some finer gentleman could never imagine. But most of her previous conquests played to stricter rules. She hoped it wasn't going to be another case of blood on her hands as it had been with the young suitor who had taken his own life.

She voiced her opinion to her friend, the actor George Miles, who had stopped by on his way to see Oscar for tea at The Grosvenor Hotel.

'You realise what you are letting yourself in for, don't you?' he remarked. 'You will have to be straight with him, dear girl.'

She knew he was right about the legendary steeplejack.

George left eventually and Lillie thought more about Joseph until the maid came into the drawing room and announced his arrival. He did look handsome, she thought, and he swept her into his arms, kissing her with a greedy passion to which she wasn't unresponsive. He sat next to her on the couch, eyes shining with love.

'I have something for you, my darling Lillie.' He handed over a flat leather box bearing the name of a prestigious Bond Street jeweller. She lifted the lid. Inside blazed a diamond bracelet set with tiny ruby hearts; one larger ruby on the clasp was surrounded by several smaller ones in the shape of a red rose. It was exquisite.

'Allow me,' he said, fastening it around her tiny wrist. 'I am having earrings made to match, once suitable stones

have been sourced.'

Flustered, she exclaimed, 'Oh Joseph, really, it's too much!'

'Why, my precious darling?' chuckled Joseph, indulgently. 'It's Christmas after all, is it not? And perhaps a necklace too for Easter to accentuate your fine long neck?' He traced his forefinger across her face and leaned forward to kiss her just below the ear.

Lillie pulled back slightly and studied the thick snow falling outside for a moment or two.

'What is it?' he asked, puzzled. Was she melancholy because he was returning to Oldham within the next few days? 'Please, don't fret, my sweetest. I shall see you again soon. Why, we can rent a villa for the whole summer on the coast, if you like.'

Lillie stood up, and turned her back to him, lost for the right approach. Finally she said, 'We need to talk, Joseph. That is why I have asked you here this afternoon.'

'I can see you are upset. But we will be together again soon,' he repeated. 'I promise my Lillie, my dear beloved...'

'Joseph, I can hardly bear to say this but I am returning to America.'

He blinked, then shook his head as if he'd misheard. She repeated her statement with more force.

'No! What are you talking about, Lillie?' he demanded. 'You cannot be serious.'

'I am to return to my stage career in America.'

'Why America, for pity's sake? What wrong with bloody London?'

She winced at his unexpected coarseness and anger, but remained resolute. 'When you have finished using the language of the servant's hall, Joseph, I trust you will not adopt its manners, too,' she said, haughtily.

'Look, I'm sorry Lillie, but leaving England is totally out of the question. Surely you must see this? I simply cannot allow it!'

'You seem to forget, sir, I have a career to pursue in order

to support myself and my daughter Jeanne,' Lillie replied defensively. She wished she hadn't said anything and just left for America instead. Perhaps the kindest thing would have been to allow him to dream that she might return to his arms one day. George had said Joseph would not take rejection as a gentleman, remarking *'silk purse, sow's ear, that sort of thing, old girl'*.

'I can provide you with an income,' he fumed. 'Why on earth would you leave England now, when we have so much to look forward to?'

'Please don't make this any worse for us both. I must remind you that you have a *wife*, Joseph, and I have a husband.'

'Nellie? Oh, what of it?' he spat. 'I love her as much as you love Ned.'

Lillie pursed her lips and wondered what to say next. They took a seat opposite each other while she rang for tea and sat in awkward silence while the maid brought it in then stoked the fire, giving Joseph time to think and alter his tactics. His mother was a strong woman like Lillie and he knew that any amount of dictating to her would never work. He had to use subterfuge, ideas that would bloom slowly and develop.

As the maid closed the door, he said, 'I'm sorry, Lillie. Please, let's not quarrel on our last afternoon together for some while.'

'I'm sorry too, Joseph. But I feel I really *must* return your gift.'

'Keep it, Lillie. It was my intention to give you my heart and this will suffice until our paths cross once more, my darling.'

He sat beside Lillie on the couch and kissed her hard. The bitter-sweet pleasure of her warm mouth soothed the turmoil inside him, if only for a few short moments.

'While I am away, we shall correspond regularly, dear heart,' she promised, knowing that would be difficult.

It was the least she could do.

# ACT 17

'What does verisimilitude, mean?' asked Nellie.

Violet looked up from her desk and stopped writing. 'Oh, I think it means something which has the appearance of truth,' she replied. 'What on earth are you reading now, you silly girl?'

'It says the play lacked verisimilitude,' said Nellie, tapping at the page of her new lady's magazine. She'd been reading the section about London's West End theatres in a bid to have something to talk to Joseph about when he returned home.

She couldn't wait to see him and had been to town to buy new clothes and fake pearls to impress him. She thought she looked much slimmer now when she wore her corset from Paris Fashions in the centre of Oldham. It was rather daring, blue with bright pink ribbons, but Nellie thought her husband would appreciate it, having been away from her bed for so long. She relished the thought of many lusty romps now he was well again.

Violet was concerned about Joseph. His latest telegram sounded strange. The words were jumbled up: '*Celebration Year Back New Monday Mother Sorry. This is now that is what counts and I bid you good day.*' She hadn't shown it to Nellie because it made no sense.

She checked with the stationmaster at Oldham Central and he confirmed that Joseph's Pullman would arrive at five o'clock today, the 30th December. Violet arranged for

his carriage to meet him there and the house was now busy preparing to welcome him back home.

When they heard the carriage pull up, Rudy and Logan ran into the courtyard shouting, 'Father! Father!' Gabrielle followed behind, not wanting to be left out of the fun. One of the boys had drawn a picture of a tall factory chimney bearing the Union Jack as a welcome home gift, and smacked his sister hard about the ear as she tried to grab it and rip the corner off. She screamed and twisted her pretty features into a grimace.

'Behave, you little lot,' scolded Violet. 'Or I'll clip your ears.'

Nellie smoothed her new dress and pinched her cheeks to give them colour. Her stomach leapt when she saw her husband. He had put on weight after looking so wan when he left two months ago and he was dressed beautifully. He wore a well-cut black frock coat with an unusual chequered blue and green silk waistcoat set off by a heavy gold Albert which bore his elegant, jewel-set timepiece. He handed his stove-pipe hat, silver-topped cane and gloves to his manservant before flinging his arms open to hug his children. Afterwards, he kissed Nellie first instead of his mother, which didn't go unnoticed by either woman.

'They've missed you so much, my darling – we all have!' Nellie said as she held him tightly, smothering his face in kisses.

Joseph laughed and twirled his wife off her feet. 'I've missed you all! By golly, I really have!'

'Come inside before we all catch our deaths,' said Violet, taking charge of the children who were still clamouring around Joseph.

Over tea in the front parlour, Joseph talked about Rufus Mansell, leaving out some of their more colourful escapades around Whitechapel. He said he felt relaxed and rested after his break. He told them about the Sambournes, his good friend Lady Blenheim and Oscar Wilde's outlandish outfit on Christmas Day. 'And he gave me this as a souvenir of my

visit to the capital city!' he said, extracting a slim volume of poems signed by the author from his travelling bag.

Nellie was surprised; she'd read all about Wilde in her latest copy of *Vanity Fair*. 'He looks rather dashing I must say!'

Violet pulled a face. 'Dashing? A sodomite they say...'

Nellie let out a shocked gasp, 'Oh, Mama!'

'Mother, please, not in front of the children—' urged Joseph crossly.

'What's a sodden-mite, Papa?' quizzed Gabrielle. 'Is it a foreign insect?'

'Just someone who is not acceptable in polite circles like ours, dear,' her father replied, flashing his mother another look of annoyance.

Nellie forgot her careful manners in all the excitement and rushed on, the slight on the playwright's character forgotten. 'Oh, but such fun! Fancy having Mr Wilde as an associate; why, I were reading, that he—'

Violet stopped her in her tracks. '*Was,* dear – I *was* reading, not *were,*' she corrected.

'Yes, sorry, Mama,' replied Nellie, examining her fingernails in shame.

Violet was full of pride as Joseph told them about meeting members of the aristocracy and being invited to their homes. She decided to assert her authority over their household. 'Of course, we'll invite the Sambournes and Lady Blenheim to Chadderton Hall, but I'm certainly not having anyone like *that* one under my roof,' she remarked, referring to Oscar Wilde. Her caustic tone reminding Joseph of his bombastic father, he simply replied, 'We'll see mother; we'll see.'

His wife had recovered her brio and wanted to hear more of the theatre trips he'd mentioned. 'What about the actress Lillie Langtry? Did you meet *her*?' she asked. 'She's a good friend of Oscar Wilde's, so they say, and very beautiful. I've been reading all about her and Ellen Terry. They also say—'

Joseph was alarmed. Would there be any oblique reference to his intimate relationship with Lillie in any of

Nellie's publications? He hadn't thought about that until now.

He clicked his tongue irritably. 'I'm sorry Nellie, but I really must insist you stop reading those frivolous periodicals. They are full of rubbish. I *forbid* you to receive further editions. Is that clear?' he said a little too forcefully. They all stared at him. 'Your mind seems to be fettered with idle gossip. It dominates your entire conversation,' he admonished.

Nellie looked down, sticking out her trembling bottom lip. Joseph turned to his mother and, by way of apology for his unexpected outburst, said, 'I'm so tired after my journey. Would you excuse me if I rest a while before dinner, Mother?'

Violet took the slim volume of Wilde's poems from Joseph and threw it into an empty chair opposite like a piece of rubbish. 'You go upstairs son. I'll have a tray sent up with refreshments.'

\*\*\*

Joseph missed dinner that evening and slept a full twelve hours. It was six o'clock on New Year's Eve when he awoke to hear voices downstairs. He swung his legs from the high bed, pulled down his nightshirt then padded towards the door and opened it slightly. It sounded like his friend and business partner William Croston speaking to his mother in the hallway.

William had called round to see Joseph and his family to wish them glad tidings for the year ahead. The rather perplexing letter he'd received recently from Joseph would have to wait. He couldn't make any sense of it and, with his friend unaccustomed to drink, wondered if he'd imbibed a festive tipple or two before writing it. Violet was acting on her son's behalf as managing director of the firm but obviously had absolutely no idea that Joseph had written to him from London regarding the Manufacturet.

'*Joseph!*' William declared, surprised at seeing his friend standing at the top of the stairs in his dressing gown at this time of day. Joseph slowly descended to greet him. William grinned but he noticed the dark circles and hollow look on Joseph's face as he came into clearer view. He knew Joseph had been very poorly but had assumed he was now fully recovered but he looked terrible and had put on weight around his face, which didn't suit him.

'Eee, by 'eck our Joseph, Happy New Year to you,' said William.

Joseph nodded weakly. 'Greetings of the season to you too, my dear fellow,' he replied.

'Me and yer mam, we were just saying it's come round quick again, like,' said William. 'Another good year for us all ahead, I hope,' he added, then bit his lip. He'd forgotten that this time last year Joseph lay gravely ill.

'No matter, my friend,' Joseph said breezily, noticing William's discomfort. 'The worst is over now, thank goodness!'

'Reckon it is,' replied William, relieved. 'And it's blummin' good to see yer back in Oldham again. But I'll best be off now or t'missus will be wondering where I've beggered off to.' He still felt awkward; it was like talking to one of them life-sized dummies clad in garments in the big store on Union Street, not his life-long friend, someone he'd known since they went to Sunday school together.

The steeplejack's stilted response worried him; where had all the flamboyance gone, the enthusiasm they once shared when making plans for the future? Joseph seemed to have changed, as though part of him was missing. And that odd letter he'd sent, what was all that about?

Joseph turned to Violet and Nellie. 'Please excuse me while I see William on his way,' he said.

'Don't be standing outside in the cold too long dressed like that, son,' replied his mother. 'We don't want you poorly again, do we now? Good evening to you, William, and please give your family our fondest wishes for the new year.'

'Aye, I'll do that all reet. Thanks, Violet. Same to you as well. Bye, Nellie luv.'

As soon as the two men were out of earshot, Joseph pulled the front door closed behind him and said to his friend, 'Look William, I know now is perhaps not the right time to address this but I'm serious about what I said in the letter. And I shall need to know your position early in the new year, certainly by the third week in January and no later.'

'Joseph, I can't discuss this right now. We have to leave it and do summat in't New Year when all't businesses are up an' runnin' again and I can talk to our accountants. Give yersen more time to think as well, my friend.'

'There is nothing to think about. I have made my decision,' Joseph replied.

'You're not talking sense, lad. After all we've been through...'

'William, I'm deadly serious about selling all my shares in the Manufacturet to release capital. I have another venture planned that will put Oldham firmly on the map as a centre of entertainment to rival even Manchester! As I said in the letter, I am offering you first refusal on my fifty-one per cent of the Manufacturet shares.'

'So, yer talkin' about a major capital investment for this new place – this theatre, I gather?' asked William.

'I prefer to think of it as an entertainment centre, where people from all classes will gather under one roof.'

William furrowed his brow, brushing away a few stray snowflakes that had landed on his shoulder. 'Aye lad, but that'll cost a pretty penny. 'Ave you any idea what the Manufacturet shares are worth now, what with the price of copper? The takings are down and you might not get their proper value if you liquidate now.'

Joseph shrugged his shoulders as if his friend's cautionary words were of no consequence. ''Tis my decision and will be taken care of on that basis alone.'

'Well, you might as well know here and now I can't get mi' hands on the sort of brass you're looking at to buy you

out,' said William. 'So, where does that leave *me* then, eh?'

'Oh, come on, my dear fellow – since when did *you* ever worry about starving or ending up in the poor house?'

William snorted, angered by the selfishness of the exchange and added, 'That's all well and good, but I don't 'ave to tell you this serious investment in't other venture – which might or might not work – could lose you the bloody lot if yer not careful, lad!'

'I have always been one to take risks, William. You should know that,' Joseph reprimanded. 'You will find another business partner, of that I'm certain.'

'Aye, well, that's as mebbe man, but what about them lot in there?' William stabbed his finger over the steeplejack's shoulder towards the closed front door. 'Yer family is trusting you to do the right thing for them; this is *their* future you are risking, and on what – bloody *entertainment*?'

'I have other investments, William; you seem to forget the Edge's Blue manufactures and my boiler works,' Joseph replied, jutting out his chin. 'Though why I should need to explain to you...'

'Cut the bloody horseshit with me, will you, man! In yer letter, yer were on about selling them shares too, as I recall,' interjected William. 'What the bloody 'ell are you hell-bent on building – the soddin' London Palladium or *what?*'

'If necessary – yes!'

William frowned and threw down the stub of his cigarette. 'Well, a happy and a very prosperous new year to you, Joseph – you'll bloody need it, cock!' he huffed, leaving his friend standing alone on the cold doorstep.

Joseph watched William trudge away into the night and gazed across the snow covered grounds of Chadderton Hall to where his Menageriet used to be; his business investment that went wrong.

'Happy New Year to you, William,' Joseph said quietly to himself. 'And it will be, by God, it will...'

# ACT 18

*V*anna Boston pursed her luscious lips in exasperation and listened.

The young ticket box attendant stood in front of her, wringing his cloth cap as hard as he could, anxious to make things right. 'But you see, ma'am, I have six mouths to feed!' he explained to the manageress inside the draughty office, its walls lined with faded theatre posters bearing the names of long dead music-hall acts. He gazed above her head. The theatrical comedy-tragedy masks depicted in the stained-glass window seemed to mock him. He identified with the downturned mouth of the tragic one on the right of the glass etchings.

Vanna wasn't interested. She clicked her tongue irritably and leaned back. 'You've been late seven times this month, Wilfred, and absent for a whole evening last week.' She tapped a pen on the blotter before her. 'I need someone I can depend on at each performance.'

'It won't 'appen again, thanking you missus, thanking you very much, I'm sure,' he offered, mindful of his predicament. 'The young un's bin poorly for the past month wi' some coughin' sickness, see,' he added. Wilfred knew it wasn't looking good for his baby daughter and what with his wife expecting again, he couldn't cope with the brood they had already, let alone another mouth to feed. He couldn't afford the services of a doctor or any proper medicine, not with his meagre earnings.

She replied, 'Do not thank me, Wilfred. I am letting you go. I have already filled your post.' She dismissed his worries with a flourish of her hand.

His pleas came with more excuses and promises to do better in future as he appealed to her better nature and begged for his job back. But she remained aloof, her eyes as cold as steel. He knew the outcome and dread gripped his stomach.

Vanna never took any prisoners and ran her theatre staff with an iron rod. The broken man left the room weeping but she didn't bat an eyelid.

Until she was seven, Vanna Boston's name was Valentina Janecki. Her mother was British and her foul-tongued father was a Polish immigrant who worked in Billingsgate Docks, unloading fish. Her surname was changed to Boston shortly after he swindled his brutal employer out of ten crates of fish to sell for his own gain. The family went into hiding to avoid the wrath of the fishmonger, and was swallowed up by London's East End slums. Her mother suffered poor health and had ten children so she expected Vanna to help raise her siblings. The girl developed a hard shell as she begged daily for food.

As they endured their squalid life and her weak, dishonest father struggled to feed his starving children, Vanna grew up thirsting for better things and looked for a way to find them.

The glittering music halls and claustrophobic singing rooms, with their bawdy patrons who never realised they were being robbed, soon provided rich pickings. She changed her name to Vanna and her bonny face and buxom figure as she grew into her teens led her to tread the boards herself as a singer. What she lacked in talent she made up for with business acumen in a man's world.

Now there was nothing Vanna Boston didn't know about running a theatre.

Or causing trouble.

Vanna was an unusual woman for her time. She had the passion and drive of any man and the softness and allure of a beauty. Her dark, glossy hair and smouldering black

eyes sucked men deep into the well of her mysterious aura. And there they burned. A longing for better things powered her ambitions and the refined theatregoers of better establishments were her focus. They were easy prey once she'd crawled up from the gutter, helped by a placid, silver-haired lover thirty years her senior.

By the time she was twenty-five, she was manageress of her own West End theatre. Thriving in a tough, male-dominated business environment, she used her charms to disarm her opponents.

But she had her weaknesses. She had fallen for a cultured patron of the arts, the owner of a chemical works in the north of England, who sent his sons to Cambridge University and regularly visited London on business. They'd met when he attended an evening performance at the theatre where she worked front of house. A disturbance in the stalls needed her attention; walking past his box she caught his eye. What started with a sultry look moved on to supper – then bed. She was smitten; he was lustful and married and *rich*.

He was also kind and thoughtful and made her feel special, something no other human being had ever done. He courted her with lavish gifts of flowers and chocolates, said he adored her uniqueness, gave her the nickname 'Albertine' after a mistress in an Alexandra Dumas novel, which he read aloud in French when they sipped champagne in bed after making love.

For once, Vanna Boston was lost in something more powerful than hate.

At her request, he established her in a theatre in Manchester and in a tiny flat above an ironmonger's shop in the next road. She had everything she wanted, provided by an educated, distinguished man who regularly gave her sex, if not love. He said he would take care of her, that she didn't need to work – but Vanna loved her work. She had power over staff, if not her lover. She'd learned as a girl of fifteen to keep her options open and this way she was independent. She desperately tried to prevent herself from loving him but

couldn't stop him stealing her heart. His visits became less frequent when she screamed at him to leave his wife.

All toys that become old and worn lose their appeal and are discarded when their flaws are discovered. Soon, the owner of the theatre – a friend of her patron – was hot on her tail, trying to prise away the managerial job she loved. The struggle went on for ten months; her work record was faultless and her attitude was ferocious. Discovering a plot to frame her in a scam to 'rob' the box office, have her arrested and sent to prison, she took radical action as soon as she had the information she needed.

She wrote a letter to her patron's wife, describing in detail the raspberry-shaped birthmark near the base of his penis.

Buying a can of paraffin from the ironmonger's was her next plan.

As she stood watching the flames lick the great copper dome, melting lead and shattering windows, she laughed out loud as the theatre collapsed to the ground. It was her parting gift. Then she left town on the first train out of Manchester, heading to Oldham.

Union Street, in the centre of Oldham, had two theatres; one was without a manager when Vanna arrived. At first the owner was reluctant to give her a start but she used her acting skills and he soon relented. Within weeks he could see she was an excellent choice, if rather harsh on the staff. She'd now been there for three years as general manageress.

Vanna was in a bad mood. She looked around her dilapidated office, picked up the leather blotter and hurled it across the room. The Lyceum Hall was shabby and old with its long, narrow auditorium and rickety seats. It had none of the embellishments and comfort of her last theatre in Manchester. Box office takings were low and recently a leaking roof had made the place smell of rot and damp. The seats were covered in mould and occasionally the performance would be interrupted as large rats skittered across the floor and alarmed members of the audience.

Then part of the ceiling collapsed.

The condemnation notice had been served the previous month by clerks from Oldham Corporation; tonight's performance would be the last. The brightest part of her day had been watching Wilfred, that little fool from the box office, squirm, not realising that the theatre was due to close.

But Vanna was a woman of formidable strength and intellect; she knew it was only a matter of time before a new opportunity would present itself. If the rumours were correct, it wouldn't be long either. Half of the street on either side of the Lyceum was being sought by a local industrialist who was intent on building the largest and grandest theatre complex in northern England, right here in the centre of Oldham. If that was true, she'd be the one to manage it. Of that she'd make certain.

\*\*\*

Joseph studied a letter from Oldham Corporation, which owned the land he wanted on Union Street that was currently occupied by the Lyceum Theatre. It was a prime site and the project would cost more than he could afford by liquidating the Manufacturet shares alone, so he had recently disposed of his holdings in Edge's Blue Works too. He had other assets to sell beside these. He had in mind a two-tiered business plan, if only he could get things moving. First, he would secure the prime spot by buying it from the corporation; the Edge's capital would be used to secure the shops either side from private landlords. Secondly, he would find the finest architect in London and build his Palace of Entertainment with his remaining capital and loans.

It was taking far longer than he'd anticipated and the months dragged slowly by without any sign of his dreams being realised.

He discarded the letter and plucked a slightly crumpled one from a stack at the back of a locked drawer, searching the elegant copperplate for hidden meaning, reading it over and over. The ink threatened to fade under his kisses.

It read:

*My own darling Joseph,*

*I was so furious with myself for forgetting about that stupid early post which left by five. Please forgive me taking so long to write, my darling. I am beside myself with longing for time stands still as my heart beats each second, marking the dark hours now you are gone. London is so miserable without you. I shall leave again for America soon, as rehearsals start in New York and Boston early springtime, but my soul will remain forever with you in England. Lady Olivia sends all good wishes too, my darling.*

*Your very loving and devoted Lillie,*

For a time after his return home, almost two years ago, he was miserable, sure that he would lose her for good. But his spirit soared once Lillie decided to remain in England and take a lead role at the Imperial Theatre in a production of *An Unequal Match*. He thought it an excellent choice for her but the reviews of the play had not been good. The theatre pulled it after a week, saying box-office sales were poor.

Lillie was struggling to understand why her roles were failing. She was heartbroken to read in one publication: *'Mrs Langtry is of far too solid a physique for any light skittish movement; her laugh not being under control appears forced and painful...'* Her stage career wasn't bouncing back. Her only hope was to return to America for good, although she withheld this information from Joseph, afraid he would return to the capital and refuse to leave her alone for a single moment. She realised that his love knew no bounds and it frightened and confused her.

At the country mansion in Hertfordshire, which Joseph had rented for her and her daughter Jeanne, she'd hinted that she would travel to America to start her career afresh on

Broadway. Joseph initially saw her acceptance of the house as a sign that she would remain indefinitely in Britain; later he realised that he was wrong.

Early in 1886, he secured a first-class passage to New York for her on the *S.S. Arizona*. He went to Liverpool himself to purchase the tickets and then travelled to London to present them, along with a diamond and ruby necklace that matched the bracelet he'd given her.

The couple spent idyllic nights together; for Joseph the liaison was as intoxicating as the finest Perrier-Jouet champagne they drank after making love in their four-poster bed. But they had broken one golden rule this time: they were shamelessly indiscreet in public. And now the shocking rumour that Lillie Langtry had taken a lover, a man of commerce, was the talk of society. Some clicked their evil tongues at how low she'd fallen after being a royal mistress.

\*\*\*

The future King of England threw down the copy of *Vanity Fair* in disgust after reading insinuations about his former mistress being linked with Wragg. It resulted in terrible indigestion after his breakfast at Marlborough House.

'Confound that bloody man, the very devil himself knows no limits!' the prince fumed, rubbing his chest to relieve the discomfort. He normally didn't read such inferior publications but his faithful butler, Soames, had whispered about a picture of a Lancastrian steeplejack on the same page as himself and Lillie. The Prince of Wales was livid to see Lillie on the arm of the chap. 'In commerce and trade!' he blustered to Soames. His mother, the Queen, would be livid! While she always turned a blind eye to his predilection for actresses, poets, artists and other lowly species, she didn't want people across the Commonwealth reading about his extra-marital follies. And his wife, Princess Alexandra, would be compromised since at one time she'd graciously

accepted Lillie and acknowledged her as his official mistress.

The Prince felt humiliated on a personal level that Lillie could be susceptible to the charms of such an insignificant man. He thought she had more style than that. He'd truly loved her once – before she became an embarrassment. Her morals had finally been swept away, he thought angrily. And where previously Lillie's estranged husband Ned was cowed into silence by the Prince's status as Lillie and her royal lover conducted their affair, this was different. Living openly with a common labourer was another thing altogether!

Ned was now a drunken, jealous husband who was increasingly making a spectacle of himself by insulting his wife's reputation to anyone who would listen. He was talking about this steeplejack Wragg. If he spoke to the newspapers, well…

That could only mean one thing for the monarchy: scandal.

The Prince knew what he must do but regretted Lillie's fall from grace. Roles in good plays were increasingly denied her after his representatives discreetly put the word out to discredit her. A great pity, he sighed, thinking of her talent. She was very talented in the bedroom too, as he recalled, and he was genuinely fond of the woman. Yes, a great pity – but the Crown must always come first.

The Prince read the article once more. The bounder Wragg was openly parading her around London! It was not the done thing at all; Wragg was, after all, a married man himself. The man must be ostracized from polite society and Lillie must be prevented from acting in theatres of any standing. Doors must be closed. She would soon fall from public notice. Wragg would return to the provinces where he belonged and remain among his own middle-class, industrialist set in Lancashire.

As a consequence of their indiscretion, Lillie and Joseph fell from favour; even the Sambournes didn't seem to welcome them with quite as much enthusiasm. Soon no one would receive them. Only Oscar Wilde stubbornly refused

to bend to the whims of society, being used to gossip about his own affairs. He turned out to be a far better person that Joseph had imagined, and even defended Joseph's honour at a social function shortly before Joseph returned home and Lillie left for America.

The Dowager Lady Frances Holland had a reputation for offending her guests and was notoriously cruel to anyone she considered socially inferior, but she tolerated Lillie because of her royal connection. Joseph Wragg, however, was quite a different matter. The dowager coolly observed Lillie and Joseph dancing together at a ball held by her friends the Radley-Thompson's, then she waited until the pair were enjoying their champagne before strolling over to them.

They were chatting with Oscar Wilde. Lady Frances began fanning herself vigorously and put her hand to her head. She made a great fuss, threatening to faint and requiring smelling salts from the hostess. She addressed Mrs Radley-Thompson: 'Oh! It is so warm, my dear, I feel so faint!' Placing a gloved hand on her hostess's wrist and hiding behind her large feather fan, she continued, 'One simply cannot breathe properly or see across the room for coal dust!'

A polite titter went around several people observing the exchange.

Wilde stepped forward, bowing politely. 'But my dear Lady Holland, how very charming you look this evening as always. And it is only very *ugly* or very *beautiful* woman that hide their faces in public. Fortunately, madam, you leave me in no doubt of your position.' He smiled charmingly and kissed the back of her hand then backed away.

'*Well, really*!' she huffed at Wilde's thinly-veiled insult, and marched off, her paid companion following in her wake like a trained puppy.

A low snigger went around the room again. Joseph stormed off angrily. Wilde whispered to Lillie, 'My dear, you must teach our precious Mr Wragg that to be perfect in society at all times is indeed a very difficult pose to maintain.'

***

On the way back from London next day, Joseph sulked in his Pullman coach as the towns and cities flew past. His mind was conflicted as he reflected on his troubled life. All the things he'd strived for and expected from a better class of people – was it worth it? During his time with his beloved Lillie, he'd discovered an ugly side to human nature. There were layers of society where an individual would never be accepted, no matter what they achieved. He'd toiled hard, achieved his dreams, fulfilled his ambitions and built a business empire. Was it worth it?

Lillie made it so.

Joseph kissed her likeness again, which he always carried hidden in his pocket. She was due to sail for America the following week. He had contemplated throwing caution to the wind and going with her but that was impossible. The scandal would be immense and his family and business would flounder without him.

As the train rattled through Crewe then on towards Oldham Central, he stretched back in the leather seat and extracted his pocket watch. This time tomorrow, he would have only an hour or so left before meeting an important representative from Oldham Corporation, with his accountant and stockbroker. Soon, he would have some good news for Lillie.

# ACT 19

*V*iolet twitched the thick green velvet drape and pulled it aside. She peered through the sash window then returned to her seat opposite Joseph. 'She's gone, son,' she said. 'So now you'd better explain what all this palaver is about before they all get back.'

Joseph looked sheepish for a moment or two, not knowing how to begin.

Earlier that day, as Nellie busied herself getting the children ready to take the carriage to visit her family, he'd whispered to his mother: 'I have something important to tell you that will affect all our lives, but Nellie can only ever know part of the story.'

Violet was beside herself with worry. Perhaps he was ill again and this time it was much worse? Joseph was always acting odd, fluctuating between melancholy where he would take to his room for days and not eat, and boundless happiness when he hardly slept and was full of grandiose plans. He'd never seemed right since that London trip to see Mansell. Perhaps his long illness and love of London had something to do with his mysterious comments today; lately he'd been talking incessantly about his time in the capital.

Now, facing his mother in the parlour, he toyed with the most recent copy of *Vanity Fair*. Violet was surprised to see the periodical, since he'd banned Nellie from buying it. In the end, he decided to let the pictures speak for themselves and handed the magazine to his mother, instructing her to

look at page twelve. Violet narrowed her eyes and did as suggested.

She found the page and scanned it. 'Lillie Langtry?'

He explained as best he could, telling her about his love for Lillie; he didn't mention liquidating certain business assets to provide diamonds, furs and a handsome house for Lillie to live in. Finally, however, seeing her bewilderment, he told her the full story.

'But how?' said Violet. 'I wasn't aware of this and I ran all your accounts.'

'I was a sleeping partner in several firms. And don't you recall I asked that you allow me to do certain accounts myself?' he reminded her. 'I needed to show her I loved her, that is all.'

Violet was indignant. 'Yes, a mistress is a very expensive business, I grant you that, son. And one you can easily do without!' She was more hurt that she'd been kept in the dark than that he'd been unfaithful to Nellie. 'And I understand Mrs Langtry is an actress?'

'I intend to marry her one day, mother.' Looking bashful, he muttered, 'I love her…'

Violet held up a hand in protest and interrupted him. 'Do I understand this right, son? You mean to move to London, to live in sin with a *stage* actress, a married one at that?'

Joseph remained silent, afraid of what she might say next.

Violet nodded her head towards the window where she'd observed Nellie and the children walking down the path a few minutes before. 'What about your *own* wife? And me and the children, for that matter?'

'No! That's just it, Mother! I cannot live in the capital with Lillie; there are forces at play in London which prevent us from being together!'

'*Together?*' she exclaimed. 'For pity's sake lad, you are already *married*, or had you forgotten that? Have you lost all reason? You'll ruin us with your folly. A mistress is one thing – but openly going about in public with a royal mistress?'

Joseph winced at her harsh words. 'We love each other

mother and besides, that business with His Royal Highness is over.'

'So why has she gone off to America and left you here then, if not to escape her shame?'

'Lillie is driven, like me, to achieve great things.'

'Great things as an actress? Pah, I have never heard such nonsense! Great things, is it? Have you lost all gumption when it comes to this woman who's no better than a whore? Are you completely off your hinge?'

Joseph was taken aback at her uncharacteristic attack. 'I've never gone against your wishes before, Mother, but this is something I intend to do and no-one will stop me. And there is more…' Joseph explained about his plans to sell his shares in the Manufacturet and build a huge theatre.

Violet couldn't believe what she was hearing. 'But *why?* How can you risk everything you have built up for this woman?' She was beside herself now, frantic and feeling challenged. 'And where will she live, this – this *actress?* Here, with us in Chadderton Hall?'

'As I've already explained, I shall build the theatre for my Lillie. It will be her home in the centre of her own empire, where she will dazzle everyone with her beauty and charm. A fine setting for an exquisite, rare gem of talent, the likes of which the provinces have never seen before. People will flock from far and wide, not only to see my beautiful Lillie but many other fine London actresses too. And there will be grand rooms and conservatories with fine refreshments and other forms of entertainment, all under one roof!'

Violet sighed and looked up at the ceiling. 'This can only end in tears. You did not answer my question – where will she live, son?'

Joseph looked flustered and had no ready answer. 'That is not important at this stage, mother. I have Nellie to consider---'

*'Ha!'* exclaimed Violet. 'So you do see at least one of the problems? And what of the scandal caused by your indiscretions? Getting yourself into magazines such as

*this*—' She threw it at his chest. 'You think no-one will see what you are about? Or do you expect Nellie and me to be subservient to the point where we ignore gossip-mongering among decent friends when they discover you have squandered your children's inheritance on a jumped-up painted *harlot!*'

Joseph was livid. 'Now look here, mother! I fear you forget yourself. I am master in this house and under no obligation to explain my actions or make excuses for my business decisions. I shall liquidate all assets as necessary to build a unique theatre complex that will put Oldham on the map as a centre of entertainment – not just cotton.'

Violet saw that her son was quaking with anger and she decided to be silent for now. After he left the room, she remained deep in thought. This wasn't like her Joseph. She knew him better than anyone. And at no point during the ugly quarrel had he mentioned what that damned upstart Lillie Langtry thought of coming to live in grimy Lancashire.

Piecing together the exchange and recalling how irrational he'd been, Violet could see her son had lost himself to passion. During his outburst, he referred several times to Septimus Stark and his atrocious treatment which resulted in Joseph losing his true love, Tabitha. Joseph insisted that Lillie was sent to him by God to make up for losing Tabitha. 'You do see it, don't you mother? I am finally to find happiness with the woman of my dreams.'

Violet shook her head slowly. Her comment, 'You cannot turn back the clock, son, nor recapture a lost love,' resulted in Joseph overturning a chair then storming from the room, vowing he would prove her wrong.

Joseph wasn't in love—he was *obsessed.*

***

Nellie seemed to be the only adult family member thrilled with Joseph's idea of building a theatre in their home town. 'Oh, my darling husband … why, this means I can attend the

theatre any time I like. We shall have our very own box and invite famous actors and actresses here to tea!'

Nellie loved all aspects of the music hall and theatre. Since Joseph had forbidden her to receive the London theatre magazines, saying they were *'too racy'*, she followed the provincial newspapers instead, poring over them for news of new shows in Manchester or beyond. Now, with their own theatre in Oldham, London would come to them!

Nellie hoped it might also stop Joseph from being so intent on her boys learning the dangerous steeplejack trade. She had tried many times to dissuade him from taking them to see his operatives at Stapes Steeplejacks, and spending afternoons at the top of some lofty structure while she sat biting her nails and worrying if they would return home safely. But at least he did not want to send them away to boarding school in Northampton like Violet did.

Her husband had been in good spirits since he decided to build the theatre. Nellie knew that running all his businesses was stressful, and she was relieved when he sold his shares in the Edge's Blue Works, the small boiler-works and iron-founders. After that, he seemed more settled – if a tad too keen to spend time alone in his study.

\*\*\*

Joseph leaned against the disused chimney base, waiting for Rudy and Logan to descend to chimney. Stapes Steeplejacks were clearing the site ready for a new mill and the square chimney was due to be demolished stone by stone. Joseph didn't bother with climbing now but he knew he needed to start building his strength up again soon. In Lancashire he commanded public attention because of his trade and he'd been asked to participate in Queen Victoria's Golden Jubilee celebrations by placing fireworks on the top of a chimney. He'd met recently with architects designing a new mill for Messrs Longhorn & Co Spinning Mill, advising them about a new chimney and flue design system. The architects wanted

it to be the tallest chimney in the county, and the mill owners felt it only right that Joseph should carry out the topping-out ceremony to correspond with the Jubilee celebrations.

Logan came scurrying down the ladder as fast as he could. 'Papa! There's a falcon's nest at the top and it's got four eggs!' he called.

Joseph ruffled his hair; the boy had inherited his love of nature and kept an aviary of birds at Chadderton Hall. Joseph insisted that they were of a species native to Lancashire.

Rudy soon followed down the ladder. 'Can we take one of the eggs, Papa?' he asked. 'Can we?'

'No, we mustn't remove them,' Joseph replied. 'The mother bird will be very upset, and she will attack if she sees anyone disturbing the nest. Come on now, boys, we must return home. I have work to do.'

On the way home, all three Wraggs sat in silence. Joseph had stopped by to pick up the boys after a meeting with William Croston and a stockbroker at their accountants' offices. William was sharp with Joseph before they'd entered the meeting, calling him an indulgent, selfish fool. It upset Joseph, who wished William could have a bigger vision and be more supportive. He had even offered his friend free shares in the new theatre venture, to which William remarked caustically, 'One percent of nothing is nothing, Joseph!'

The stockbroker Bernard Stebbings shook his head and looked up from the papers he'd extracted from his briefcase. He peered at his famous client over his half-moon glasses. 'Now is rather a bad time to liquidate your assets fully, Mr Wragg, as I explained when you consulted me over the boiler works and your holdings in Edge's Blue.' The stockbroker coughed then carried on. 'Since the boom in lightning conductors at the end of the cotton famine is now at an end, turnover has steadily dropped over the years.'

The accountant, Mr Evans, consulted his copy of the company returns and looked a little awkward. 'I agree, Mr Wragg. But perhaps if you can hold off, say another twelve months or so, we shall see an increased interest in these

shares. But taking into account the raw materials, the current low price of raw copper continues and tin, of course—'

'Let me stop you for a moment, gentlemen,' interrupted Joseph. 'I am not here to debate the issue, but rather to find an immediate buyer for my shares.' He scowled at both men.

'Mr Wragg, I urge you to reconsider your position,' offered Mr Evans. ' We are advised by Mr Stebbings here that in Colebrookdale in Shropshire, the very seat of the iron industry, there are indications of strong growth which I am assured may impact your copper—'

'Enough, I say!' the steeplejack shouted. *'Enough!'*

William Croston let out a slow, exasperated sigh as his irate partner banged a fist down hard on the desk. 'It seems like Joseph – sorry, our *Mr Wragg* here – is hell-bent on a meltdown of his own.'

Joseph pulled a sour face then turned on him. 'Well, perhaps you should realise it is my keen brain and business sense that put the Manufacturet where it is today – and not the coarse pair of hands that simply ran it,' he said, arrogantly. 'A little more faith in my abilities might not go amiss, my friend.'

William, hurt by the harsh rebuke, decided to keep quiet. He was angry that he'd been unable to raise sufficient capital to buy out Joseph's fifty-one per cent share of the Manufacturet. Now he would have to deal with a new partner with a casting vote. William had assumed that Logan and Rudy would one day run the Manufacturet with his own two sons, Duncan and Victor.

Wanting no further outbursts from his client, Mr Stebbings announced, 'I can have the necessary papers drawn up to broker the shares on your behalf immediately, Mr Wragg. But I have to warn you that the price of the shares has plummeted and you will be lucky to receive forty to fifty per cent of their value based on current calculations of the stock market. But if this is acceptable…?'

'Gentleman, I think this concludes our business today,' replied Joseph. He signed the paperwork and rose from his

chair, taking hold of his top hat and cane. 'I shall instruct my solicitor to contact you.'

Joseph briefly shook hands with Mr Stebbings and Mr Evans then left the room with William. His disgruntled friend and business partner shot him a filthy look then pushed past him without speaking, not bothering to hold open the heavy mahogany door. Its full force swung back on the steeplejack.

*** 

Life at home with Violet was strained. Nellie noticed that Joseph was uncharacteristically quiet in her presence and the atmosphere between them was cool. She was beside herself with glee. It could only mean one thing: Joseph must have stood up to his mother and made Nellie's position as his wife clear. Although Violet still took charge of everything in the house, Nellie knew by the demanding and almost brutal way Joseph took her body each night that her husband was working through deep emotions. This was a form of rebellion. As he rode her body in the dark, making her faint with pleasure, proclaiming his love and telling her he was intoxicated by her, she knew she'd finally won.

Sometimes, he lay with his back to her afterwards and she could hear him weeping into the pillow. But that wasn't surprising either, for how could the tension between him and his mother not destroy his sensitive soul? Kissing him gently between the shoulders as she stroked his back, noticing the strength of the muscles beneath his skin, she knew their life would be wonderful when he was happy again.

Her happiness was almost more than she could bear. If only he wouldn't be so quick to pull away as he reached his climax, then they could have another child. There would be time, once the new theatre was built. There was time for anything now that he was hers for good.

Joseph missed Lillie beyond measure and was tormented by thoughts of her in America. As he made love to his wife,

he imagined Lillie beneath him, taking his soul. He threw himself into plans for the theatre and in the evenings sat reading with his three children until their bedtime. Nellie loved watching him; he was an unusual father in this way. Most of their friends never saw their children, passing their care on to nannies and governesses.

During the bad days, Joseph thought incessantly about the times he'd shared with Lillie, and when he'd lain miserably at her side, unable to function as a man after she'd spoken of leaving for America. It was becoming difficult to blot out vivid images of her as he toiled over mathematical formulae, working on the complex flue system for Longhorn & Co Spinning Mill. At the last meeting, when he was explaining the need to paint the brickwork with double-boiled linseed oil to prevent frost damage, his mind suddenly went blank. When one of the architects asked about the built-in stresses of the chimney and what magnified them, or if iron bands were the answer, Joseph stared blankly at them, and muttered, 'What?'

He took his stress out on Nellie. He ravished her each night, his excitement ignited by images of a lithe, naked Lillie, who transformed into Tabitha. Later he would fall into a disturbed sleep, sometimes dreaming that he was stranded on the top of a chimney and unable to get down because the ladders had been removed, while below him Oldham froze into a dying city of closed factories.

He was exhausted, physically and mentally; the only thing going well was the plans for the new theatre.

He'd recently met the Corporation representative, who named a price for the land that was rather higher than Joseph had anticipated. But the agent assured him the price was fair for a prime spot in the middle of town. A surveyor would be engaged once the old Lyceum was demolished and by then Joseph would have found a suitable firm of London architects to design his theatre complex.

He was impressed with the manageress of the old Lyceum. Vanna Boston was her name. 'How do you do, Mr Wragg,'

she said, greeting him formally and rising from her desk to accept his handshake. Joseph wasn't fooled; he could tell by her rather masculine grip that she was tough as well as beautiful.

'Miss Boston, it is a pleasure to meet you. I hear many compliments about your fine work,' he said.

'Thank you sir, although I fear I will not have my current position for much longer in on account of the theatre closure,' she replied without any note of self-pity.

The drawback to owning a theatre complex would be management issues and booking productions, for Joseph had no idea how these establishments were run. The leaseholder of the Lyceum was complimentary about Vanna Boston's managerial skills, so Joseph said on impulse, 'I shall require a general manager when my new complex is completed. Would you care to consider the position – on a provisional basis, of course, Miss Boston?'

Vanna smiled. After a moment, she said, 'Why yes, that would be most acceptable, sir. Thank you. I accept your kind offer.'

'Good – that's all settled then! We can discuss salary nearer the time. It will reflect your experience in running the Lyceum and additional responsibilities in my own theatre,' said Joseph. He rather liked the prospect of a female manager running the place. And for the venture to succeed, he needed someone whom he could trust.

# ACT 20

*L*illie took her final bow, looking more radiant than ever. The flushed actress took another step towards the footlights, avoiding slipping on the sea of flowers strewn at her feet. She stepped back again as the heavy curtain fell. As usual, the audience roared and cheered for her. The stage-manger shouted to the stagehand, 'Again!' and Lillie graced the noisy crowd with another curtain call. She blew kisses to her adoring fans and the curtain fell again.

She ran back to her dressing room along a darkened corridor teeming with supporting and bit-part players. Bursting through the door, she recognised the middle-aged man with the bedraggled moustache sitting in an easy chair, smiling. He leaned forward as she entered and raised a bottle of vintage champagne to his star. 'Nathaniel not here this afternoon, I take it?' he asked. Sitting down in front of the long mirror, she accepted the tall glass of fizz and began scrubbing the greasepaint from her face. 'He's overseeing the delivery of all my possessions, Anton. I don't suppose he'll mind not seeing me until after the evening show. Or at least until we've enjoyed a late luncheon,' she said, leaning sideways to kiss the man's cheek. 'Cheers, my darling. I'm absolutely starving!'

'I expect it will be good to settle down after the extensive touring, Lillie,' he said, basking in the warmth of their close friendship. The playwright was fond of his new protégée and had written the lead role of Esther in his new play *Without a*

*Reason* especially for her. It had opened to critical acclaim the previous week on Broadway.

Since her arrival in America, Lillie had enjoyed success in Chicago and San Francisco and many of provinces with the flamboyant Anton Bluesquith's plays. He'd always adored Lillie. She was a natural actress and he was a celebrated, original playwright.

'I do hope Henrietta packed away all the crystal and porcelain in cardboard as instructed,' Lillie said, still scrubbing at her face. 'The north Atlantic crossing can be very rough at this time of year.'

Anton poured more champagne. 'Sending for one's belongings is never easy,' he said. 'I gave my own collection of crystal to my dear friend Theo before I left France.'

Lillie turned to face Anton. 'Listen, darling, you mustn't mind Nathaniel. He can be a little … *possessive* at times. I'm sure he didn't mean to cause offence. It's just that you and I have been spending so much time together for rewrites and rehearsals – goodness knows what goes though that boy's mind!'

The playwright shrugged as if the comment were of no consequence, and pointed to the diamond and pearl bracelet Lillie was adjusting around her slender wrist. 'I expect this sort of thing is to be expected if you have a torrid affair with a young millionaire playboy who has never fallen in love before.'

'He is jealous of any man. He loves me so much,' she sighed.

'Announcing my own fascination with his exquisite blue eyes and fine physique would injure him more, I suspect!' the playwright joked. 'Surely he realises by now that you're just not my type, Lillie darling?'

Lillie giggled. 'Well, I hope he's careful with my precious crystal while we are out enjoying luncheon! Broken hearts are one thing – broken crystal is quite another!'

Nathaniel Wallis was the sole heir to a huge cosmetics dynasty. He was used to getting his own way because of

his family wealth and his good looks. His social position in New York and Baltimore was unquestionable and his $250,000-a-year allowance allowed him to indulge in things lesser men could only dream of. His main interests lay in wooing pretty women, yachting, gambling and horse racing. He was also academically gifted and fond of the arts and culture.

The handsome, Oxford-educated American, who carried himself with an air of quiet superiority, showered Lillie with extravagances and amusements. In the past, Nathaniel had found female theatricals easy. But Lillie was different – and she was fifteen years older than him. Nathaniel had a list of broken hearts to his discredit but Lillie had successfully tamed his playboy ways. He worshipped her and she adored him. It was the first time he felt truly loved for himself and not simply for what he could provide.

But it hadn't stopped him from providing generously as only he knew how. Nathaniel had recently bought her a mansion in Manhattan and she was moving into the property the following day. Of course, with his social position it was out of the question that he would ever marry an actress, even if Lillie had been free to do so, but here he could spend time with her and make her happy. As long as he was discreet, his family turned a blind eye to his dalliance with an older married woman.

To celebrate his victory in capturing her, he had given her a matched diamond and pearl bracelet set ordered from Tiffany's and had it delivered to the stage door in a brown paper bag by a bell- hop. Nathaniel liked the idea of exquisite gems being almost dismissed as cheap trinkets, and it always made Lillie take notice.

At their first meeting more than a year ago in London, she was at the buffet table eating caviare with an older female companion, Lady Blenheim. Lillie felt unwell as the evening progressed and left the ball early, but her friend remained. The older lady was charming and spoke to him at length, insisting he woo Lillie, despite the actress being on the arm

of some industrialist chap from the north of England.

Lillie seemed agitated by Nathaniel's ardent attention at first. She avoided him when they met at another gathering, even though she was without her beau. Nathaniel sent two dozen red roses to the theatre after each performance with a request that she have dinner with him at Claridges. When the roses didn't work, he sent expensive baubles from Asprey's; they arrived back at his apartment in the hotel with a polite note of refusal. He had never known a woman return jewels before.

By the time he left London for the States two months later, he was beside himself with frustration. Nathaniel couldn't understand why he had failed to win her as a lover.

On his return to Philadelphia, the playboy kept close tabs on Lillie's stage career. A year later, when he learned of her arrival in New York by sea, he was waiting. He stepped forward as she came down the gangplank of the *S.S. Dolores.* Crowds cheered at the sight of her. The pier was jammed with hundreds of people vying for a better view of the famous actress. Nathaniel pushed through to get to the gangplank. He bowed formally and put out a hand to her as she stepped onto the pier. 'Welcome to America, Lillie,' he said. 'I have my carriage at your disposal to take you to your hotel.'

Lillie was charmed by her handsome young escort, whom she recalled meeting several times in London. She remembered the expensive gifts; Joseph would have killed him on the spot, so returning the gifts had been essential to prevent trouble between the two men, or any hint of scandal that might hinder her career. But now she was in America, alone. Her relationship with Joseph was something she'd left behind in England with the rest of her unwanted baggage.

When they eventually arrived at her Madison Square hotel, Nathaniel immediately prepared to leave. 'But at least stay for refreshments while the porter brings up my luggage, Mr Wallis,' Lillie offered, puzzled at his eagerness to depart so soon.

Nathaniel refused and replied, 'I am certain our paths will cross again one day, Mrs Langtry.' He kissed her hand and gave no indication whenever that might be. Lillie felt bewildered by the whole exchange.

The pair met again a month later at a function in Philadelphia, where she was appearing in theatre. Nathaniel had used his family contacts to allow her entry into an elite world that would otherwise have been closed to her. She was not aware of this when the invitation to the illustrious Easter ball arrived. Now, dressed in a gown of kingfisher-blue shot-silk, she stood talking to Theodore Roosevelt about his political ambitions. He was explaining his keen interest in exploring and psychology when she saw Nathaniel staring at her from the door.

Nathaniel acknowledged her with a slight smile and then approached them. Roosevelt spotted the young man and smiled in recognition. 'Ah, Mrs Langtry,' he remarked. 'Allow me to introduce my very good friend Mr Nathaniel Wallis.'

Nathanial kissed her hand and bowed. 'I am charmed to make your acquaintance,' he said, making no reference to the fact that they already knew each other.

Roosevelt went on, 'We were at Harvard together studying biology, and our families have been acquainted since our grandfathers were small boys.'

'I believe you are smitten with our theatres in New York, Mrs Langtry?' Nathaniel quizzed. 'Much more exciting than anything one finds in London, no doubt.'

Since that night, the pair had been inseparable when Lillie was not rehearsing with Anton Bluesquith, of whom Nathaniel was insanely jealous.

Lillie was happier than she'd ever been. She had finally escaped the harsh rebukes of her drunken husband, Ned, and his constant demands on her money. She looked forward to the arrival of her daughter Jeanne from England the following month, then her life would be complete. She knew that Nathaniel would never marry her but she now

had a beautiful home and the future looked good. She was successful, her talent applauded by American audiences. It would be a long time – if ever – before she set foot on British soil again.

Lillie regretted her treatment of Joseph Wragg. She had never really loved him but she had been attracted by his strong muscles, grown tough with years of hard manual work. It was an infatuation which had died, as she had known it would. They continued to correspond and she could see that he still loved her passionately, but she hoped his feelings would fade now that they were apart. She wanted to let him down gently, a tactic that had worked successfully with many other lovers in the past.

She did not mention that she intended to remain in New York or that she had a new lover, for that would break his heart. But, she reasoned, once the steeplejack's ardour had cooled she would tell him their affair was finally over and the reason why.

Joseph's intensity worried her at times. He appeared – possessed. His letters often troubled her; they were morose and full of longing. Especially when she'd written and told him she would not be able to write for a month because she was so busy with rehearsals. His reply was curt:

> ...*Since I received your letter, I have been unable to eat and sleep. All reason has left me. I could never explain to you the shock it gave me, nor would you understand it. How can a woman in love so callously sever the lifeline which binds us together, even for a short while? I am wretched and miserable without you in my arms. Must I bid you farewell for four long weeks? Must I really? For in my dreams you return with sweet kisses each night. I pray you will find time to write...*

And so the letter rambled on for ten long pages. Towards the end, the words had become incoherent ramblings:

*'I am anything but strong, who ordained it? Lately
in our midst unwilling victims of fate be gone! An
auditorium without sad faces if my accomplishments
pass without a hitch but are sure it is only a matter
of time!!*

Lillie had no idea what Joseph meant and destroyed the
letter, not because she feared Nathaniel might discover it,
but because she found it chilling and rather disturbing.

Hopefully Joseph would eventually come to his senses. If
she stopped writing altogether, he might come to America to
find her and that would never do: there would be bloodshed
between the two hot-blooded men and a public scandal. Her
career would be in tatters.

Now she looked at her own letter again, written in the
dressing room before the evening's performance.

*My dearest Joseph,*

*You will by now have read that I was successful
in the new play written for me by Anton. I was so
nervous in case I didn't hear any applause from
the audience. I have engagements all through next
month and beyond, so shall be working dreadfully
hard. I fear I shouldn't see much of you even if you
were here with me in New York, my darling. But I
do miss you and pray that you are well. I am just
going to be photographed in my dressing room, so
I must finish this in haste.*

*Your ever loving Lillie*

A rap at the door distracted her. Thinking it would be
Nathaniel, or Anton returning for the ebony cane he'd left
behind last night, she hurriedly placed the letter under a pile
of telegrams and cards near the mirror.

A young bell-hop held out a crumpled brown paper bag from a penny and dime store. 'Delivery for Mrs Langtry!' he trilled cheerfully, handing it over.

She searched around for a few cents on top of the cluttered table. 'Thank you,' she said handing over the coins. The boy smiled, happy with his tip, then ran off.

Lillie opened the bag and extracted two plain boxes wrapped in cheap, brown paper. The contents took her breath away: the most beautiful opal and diamond ring and matching bracelet she had ever seen! Opal was her birthstone. The enclosed card simply stated: 'For my darling Lillie, these simple trinkets can never reflect the rainbows in your eyes.'

# ACT 21

*J*oseph left the solicitors' office in Oldham with mixed feelings of elation and sadness. A buyer had finally been found for his shares in the Manufacturet. It felt like the end of an era – but it was also the beginning of his new life.

He'd been growing impatient and knew the only way for a quick sale was floating the shares on the stock market at a much reduced price. It wasn't important that he would only get thirty per cent of their real net worth, only that he released sufficient capital to buy town centre land and the money he needed to build his theatre complex. The rest he would raise by disposing of several smaller holdings in companies around Oldham and with a mortgage secured against Chadderton Hall.

William Croston was devastated. The buyer of the shares was based in Sheffield and owned a steelworks that manufactured cutlery. There was rumour the new partner intended to diversify and put the Manufacturet to other uses besides producing copper conductors. Without a casting vote, William knew he faced serious problems. He didn't speak to Joseph after the paperwork was exchanged; he felt that their lifelong friendship had been of no consequence. The pain it caused was far worse than the distressing situation he now faced with the Manufacturet.

Joseph felt at times that he was wading through treacle. There were constant arguments between his mother and wife, who seemed to be getting more self-assured by the day

and asserting her authority over the household. Everything seemed to move in slow motion as he struggled through each day, pining for Lillie. Occasionally he would wake up and feel power surge through his soul. He wondered if this had something to do with the new electric lighting he'd been examining in Manchester, where civic buildings and certain main streets were brightly illuminated by little orbs of shining glass. His theatre would boast these light bulbs and be lit entirely by electricity.

The partners of the London architects Simmons & Wright were meeting him today, together with local surveyors, on the site in Oldham town centre that Joseph planned to develop. As he waited outside the town hall on the same spot where Aspen once stood all those years ago, talking to the starving men during the cotton famine, Joseph considered his vast wealth. He looked across the road and visualized his theatre complex. If only Aspen were alive to see it, he thought sadly, even though memories of his father often brought much sadness.

Four properties stood in ruins either side of the now-flattened Lyceum; the derelict church at the back was also being demolished as he watched. The brick-dust reminded him of his chimney demolition jobs in the past. The gap left by the old theatre revealed just how large the theatre frontage would be. Joseph envisioned a gleaming placard, lit with electricity, bearing Lillie's name. He had no worries about placing all his golden eggs in this particular basket, because the beautiful goose would thrive. And he would not only be one of the wealthiest men in the country, he would have Lillie at his side as his wife.

Joseph had already discussed instigating divorce proceedings with a solicitor other than their usual family one. Although the generally placid Mr Studley raised his bushy eyebrows in surprise, he remained professional and explained the complicated grounds that would be needed to support such an action. Joseph decided to wait until Lillie was back in England to discuss it further; the last thing he wanted

was a scandal with the public naming of co-respondents. Her reputation as an actress must not be tarnished if they were to eventually marry and successfully run the theatre together.

He was *so* excited! Lillie would be astonished and delighted at having her very own theatre. It would be the finest in England – the whole of London would be envious. Why, not even the very Prince of Wales himself could prevent Lillie from performing at Wragg-owned premises! She knew nothing of Joseph's plans of course; he would wait until the complex was finished before wiring her to return from America and travel to Oldham for rehearsals for the opening night.

Joseph planned to commission the most talented playwrights to produce quality productions suitable for all tastes. In the smaller variety hall, there would be singing and light-hearted gaiety from popular acts of the day. But the jewel in the crown would be his Lillie in her many starring roles.

'Mr Wragg I presume? How do you do, sir?' announced the architect Julian Wright, proffering his hand and breaking into Joseph's daydreams. The architect was accompanied by his partner, Thomas Simmons, a stout man with a set of large, even teeth and an oversized top-hat. The three men toured the demolition site as local surveyors busied themselves taking notes and measurements for water mains and sewage outlets.

Joseph handed over several large pictures of Buckingham Palace. 'I have a very definite design I wish to adhere to, gentlemen. I require a similar frontage to that of Buckingham Palace.'

The two architects studied the pictures for a moment, surprised at the lavish requirements. This was going to be no ordinary theatre design. Simmons replied calmly, 'Yes, quite, Mr Wragg. The new east frontage of the Palace conceals, in my opinion, the rather more splendid original one with its colonnades and porticos designed by Mr Thomas Nash. Perhaps an amalgamation of the two would suit your

purpose?'

Joseph contemplated the comment then ignored it. 'This will be a grand palace of entertainment. I have the idea of an auditorium to seat more than three thousand people, based on the design of the state ballroom. Here, like this—' He showed them a picture of the inside of the palace and several of his own drawings. 'And for the smaller music hall, perhaps a copy of Queen Charlotte's Salon in gold and red, here, see— '

The architects exchanged a worried glance. Simmons, clearing his throat said, 'To achieve this look will be prohibitively expensive, I fear.'

A flicker of mild irritation crossed Joseph's face, 'Poppycock! It must replicate the palace. The complex must be fit for my *own* queen! I want the detail to be correct, irrespective of worry about expenditure. Is that clear, my good fellow?'

'Quite, sir. We are certain that Mrs Wragg will not be disappointed,' said Wright, naturally assuming his client was referring to his wife.

'Good, I think we all understand each other, then.'

'Will you be requiring a central balcony too, sir?' asked Simmons.

'No, we shall be installing electrocuted signage on the front,' replied Joseph.

'You refer to electricity then, sir?' responded Wright. 'Throughout I take it?'

'Yes indeed, I require the finest and most advanced technology.'

Simmons spoke this time, sensing a lucrative deal. 'Then we must endeavour to produce designs to your own specification, sir, regardless of cost.'

'Yes!' Joseph looked at the two men as though they were stupid. 'Indeed!'

'Although it will not be possible for us to employ the services of Ludwig Gruner, Prince Albert's adviser on decorating of palace, since he passed away several years

ago,' added Simmons.

Joseph flapped his hand impatiently as if to hurry the conversation along. 'I want no one associated with the Prince of Wales involved at any level. All I want is Buckingham Palace replicated here in my home town of Oldham. And it must be fit for a queen.'

The architects exchanged bemused glances again.

'Very good, sir. When we are assured of your complete satisfaction with our designs and specification, we can apply for council approval,' Wright said. The fact that no expense would be spared in the creation of a theatrical paradise would make their job a lot easier and more profitable. The architects excused themselves to consult with local surveyors, leaving Joseph gazing into space, lost in his reverie.

***

Another letter was waiting from Lillie when he arrived home at Chadderton Hall that evening. He sat in his study after dinner. At first his stomach knotted but gradually he relaxed. Perhaps it was a good thing she was so wrapped up in her acting in America. It would stop her from pining for him too much and getting lonely.

She'd written: ...*so we are busy bringing* She Stoops to Conquer *before an American audience and I am obliged to work very hard. I am in a nervous state about everything. Oh dear, I fear I shall be ill if I do not rest. The criticisms in the weekly papers were very good for the play in Boston, and I must admit it is one of my favourites....*

The letter ended in the usual way with kisses and declarations of love, but Joseph thought they now appeared almost as an afterthought. Tapping the letter against his chin, deep in thought, he worried about her working too hard.

He heard raised voices from another part of the house. He didn't know what had got into his silly wife these days. She had always been so submissive and now she seemed to challenge his mother at every opportunity. At her request,

he'd recently allowed her to organise several dinner parties. In the past, Violet had always taken charge of the details. Now Nellie was in control, invitations were sent out for wrong dates, menus included inappropriate food and the children were never in bed by the time guests arrived. He had intended to speak to her about her incompetence, but he had so much to do.

He allowed the voices to fade into the background as he thought more about Lillie and opened a desk drawer to retrieve her bundle of letters. He held them to his nose in the hope of smelling her perfume, before adding the latest to the growing pile. Then he searched for his fountain pen; he would compose an affectionate reply and maybe hint at greater things to come once she'd returned to England.

Life in Oldham seemed shallow and empty and he was growing weary of trying to live up to his mother's expectations. After London's high society, he realised how gauche the county set in Lancashire was. Besides, when his theatre complex opened, he would be deemed 'unsuitable' to those parochial snobs who tried so hard to emulate the aristocracy.

He laughed out loud at the thought of that silly fool Stark with his absurd pretensions which excluded Joseph. He didn't fit into the glittering world he once craved to be a part of. He would show them all; he would be king of his own empire one day and rule the world!

He was just about to start writing to Lillie when Nellie burst angrily into the study. 'Joseph, will you please instruct your mother that *I* am redesigning the drawing room this time. We are *not* having pale green and primrose again!' she shouted.

Violet followed, hot on her daughter-in-law's tail. 'I am in charge of the household, lady. What do *you* know about colour design, any road? Look at the way you are dressed, you ridiculous girl – you can't even get *that* right!'

'I am *not* ridiculous – you are! Why, the time you bought a hamper from Stones & Co and said it contained mouldy

cheese and it was Stilton! *Ha!* '

'You little minx! What about the time you poured sherry instead of claret?'

'And you thought a mantle was a something for a gas lamp instead of a fashionable item of ladieswear!' taunted Nellie.

Violet shrieked, 'Why, you – you. . .! How dare you speak to me like this!'

Gabrielle ran through the door, clinging to her mother's skirts, crying loudly and adding to the discord. Violet lashed out with her tongue again, pointing to the child and addressing her son: 'Do you want your daughter to grow up under the influence of nothing but a common, working-class mother who knows nothing about polite society – not even a sherry glass from a burgundy one?'

Joseph threw down his fountain pen, which bounced off the desk and splattered black ink on the Turkey red rug in front of the brass fender. 'That is *enough*!' he fumed. 'Damn it, I have had quite enough of this silly nonsense!' He turned on both women in a flash of pure temper. 'You seem to forget where we came from, Mother. Potts Street, may I remind you? May I also remind you what I have done to elevate you all from that dire existence and put food in all our mouths? We are not gentry, nor are we going to act like it from now on. I have had quite enough of this – this damned *charade*!'

Nellie and Violet stood wide-eyed and speechless as he continued his tirade. 'I have provided for us all handsomely, but I shall not be subjected to any more demands from either of you. Do I make myself clear?'

Logan and Rudy, attracted by the loud altercation, stood open-mouthed in the doorway of the study. They were shocked by their father's uncharacteristic outburst and watched him repeatedly thump the desk.

Gabrielle pulled closer to Nellie and bit her thumbnail, noticing how her father's face reddened as he continued shouting. None of the family had seen him as angry as this before. He thumped his fist on the desk once more and kicked

back the buttoned leather chair which toppled on its side, crashing into a low table. 'There will be serious changes made here when the theatre opens. In the meantime, I ask you all to consider the immense pressure I am under. Do not upset me with your petty selfishness.'

Violet was just about to assert herself again, when Joseph raised his hand to silence her. 'Enough, Mother! Nellie is my *wife*. If she wants to redecorate rooms in whatever colour scheme she chooses, then she can do so.'

Nellie looked smug and smiled – but then Joseph turned on her too. 'And you will act with decorum in future and not run around the house screaming like a fishwife and setting a bad example to the children.'

Gabrielle was shrieking and sobbing into her mother's dress folds again, which seemed to break the spell. Joseph twitched his head as though correcting himself on something, then knelt down beside the girl, taking her into his arms. Her little body shook with sobs as he cuddled her for several moments. Joseph didn't say anything as his family quietly left the room, but each member knew something had changed. And each one wondered exactly what he meant when he said, *'There will be serious changes made here when the theatre opens.'*

The terrible argument opened up another raft of problems for Joseph as he closed the door and flopped wearily down in his chair. Where would they all live once Lillie and he were married? He couldn't see Violet remaining at Chadderton Hall with him, Lillie and the children. And what would become of Nellie? He hadn't given the matter much thought until now. What if he and Lillie wanted their own child? If he were to sell Chadderton Hall, how would he provide three sets of suitable accommodation for everyone – especially Lillie, who was used to a high standard of living? Even building a dowager house for his mother in the grounds of the Hall wouldn't work – assuming he could afford to do so once the theatre was completed – and it still didn't solve the problem of what to do with Nellie and the children.

He rubbed his head. Pain was shooting up the front of his face and he felt quite sick; he would need to take something in order to relax. He would have to write to Lillie, tell her about his plans and ask that she return to London immediately so they could discuss the best way to proceed.

That night he had the recurring nightmare about being stranded on top of a chimney while Oldham froze over.

\*\*\*

There were many problems to overcome before the theatre complex was ready to be opened to the public, and it cost double what Joseph had originally budgeted for. The venture was a drain on his resources right from the start, from the time when Simmons and Wright sent in their final account, including a bill for several sets of modified plans that had been required before Joseph was happy.

The building process was besieged with difficulty. The builders said they couldn't get delivery of a vital cantilever girder for three months so they couldn't start on the main proscenium arch. Joseph had to pay almost double to secure the services of a rival company so that work could start.

Problems occurred with the elaborate plasterwork Joseph insisted on. It added too much weight to some areas of the upper circle, part of which crashed down onto the dress-circle below, ruining several rows of seats.

The red plush seats cost twice as much as anticipated because Joseph decided he wanted them to have an embroidered tapestry design after they had been installed. The red cloth was removed and a team of thirty seamstresses was employed to sew a design of a golden lily on each of the three thousand seats.

Joseph was preoccupied by the fact that he'd heard little from Lillie. His request that she return to England at once to discuss their respective divorces and their forthcoming marriage had not brought any response at all. He believed

what he needed to believe, saw what he wanted to see. He put lack of communication down to the fact that she was busy touring America; his letters and telegraphs probably hadn't caught up with her yet.

No one could doubt that the impressive Red Rose Palace of Entertainment in Union Street was being built by a very wealthy man, a true patron of the arts. But as Joseph fumbled through the mounting invoices from iron merchants and glaziers and specially commissioned artists, he began to feel his investment was taking charge of him. His headaches grew worse and he felt achy and tired all the time. The tincture he took helped, but it didn't allay his fears about Lillie not returning in time for the opening night.

At times he thought he heard her speaking to him as he lay awake at night. He clutched a small love token she'd once given him to his breast, a Lancashire rose carved in red soapstone; he held it as though it was her body. And everywhere he looked, he saw and tasted her.

He installed a telephone at Chadderton Hall at great expense – a folly much disparaged by Nellie and Violet who were frightened of the apparatus. He sat by it patiently before he left for the building site each day.

When it rang one day during breakfast, Nellie almost dropped her cup of tea in surprise. 'Good grief! Does it have to make so much noise?' she grumbled to Joseph.

For once Violet agreed with her daughter-in-law. 'Work of the devil, son – it's not natural to speak to someone miles away like that, is it?'

Joseph looked irritated and shot back, 'For pity's sake! I have a theatre complex to build and cannot be there at all times therefore I must make myself available to discuss business as needed. Can you not see that?'

Violet said nothing, just raised her eyebrows slightly and kept her thoughts to herself. It was just another abnormality to cope with. Joseph instructed the household staff to be alert in case it rang. His intensity over the new telephone drew idle speculation from his servants as he repeatedly asked if it

had rung; sometimes he shushed his valet mid-conversation so he could stare at it and listen. He sent a number of letters to America with the new phone number and he sat in his study each night, waiting, waiting, waiting.

He started to doubt his own judgment. Changing his mind at the drop of a hat, he began to worry his builders and designers. The colour of the silk wasn't right for the huge stage curtains, they had to be remade in gold lame... A staircase balustrade wasn't an exact copy of Nash's original for the grand staircase at Buckingham Palace and had to be ripped out... Later he was unable to sleep because of the stupidity of his request. But it had to be right for Lillie...

Then he got angry. While the family celebrated Easter, gave each other chocolate eggs and listened to psalms at church, Joseph paced his study, refusing to speak to or see anyone. Lillie had gone – left him! He fired off rapid letters to America, sometimes up to twenty a day, using all his pent-up emotion to tear apart the woman he loved, to destroy her, bring her to her knees – anything to make her respond. But nothing came back.

He stalked the grounds of Chadderton Hall each night before bedtime, looking at the rusted empty cages of his menagerie and repeating over and over again, 'Sorry, sorry, sorry.'

Violet was increasingly worried about her son but he refused to see the doctor, saying it was a complete waste of time. When she challenged him and insisted, he became angry and bellowed at her, 'And just *who* do you suppose will oversee getting the theatre completed on time? Don't be absurd, mother!'

He never seemed to sleep or eat. His movements were jerky and he'd lost more weight; his eyes looked black and dead, and his features were lifeless. Sometimes when people came to Chadderton Hall, he'd cower like a small child in the front parlour, begging the servants to dismiss them and say he wasn't home. Even the children had grown wary of him; Gabrielle told her mother he smelt like old Mr Bannerman

who came to clean out the drains.

Rudy, who once casually told his father about a chimney repairing job in Rochdale that Stapes operatives were working on, was stunned to hear his father retort, 'You cannot see it, son – it will blind you to all else!' Joseph grabbed his son's arm, hurting him and causing bruises. Rudy didn't know what to say as his father shook him and continued shouting, 'You must not go to see it, son – you mustn't. *Do you understand me?!*'

Violet thought her son was slowly going mad and wondered what to do. But in truth Joseph was locked in a personal battle, fighting poisonous addictions and black demons that gradually stole his sanity. What if Lillie didn't turn up in time for the opening night? What then?

# ACT 22

Vanna Boston removed her new bonnet, carefully untying the satin ribbon under her chin. Not used to spending large amounts of money on such fine millinery, she hoped it would be a worthwhile investment. Studying her pretty face in the mirror, she was pleased to notice that the subtle green shades in the trimmings brought out the hazel in her eyes.

Perhaps he'd noticed too? But then again, he'd looked too distracted to care. And Vanna knew why. She searched through her cloth bag, retrieving a letter with an American stamp addressed to *Mr Joseph Wragg, Chadderton Hall, Chadderton, Near Oldham, England.* It bore an unusual postmark and Vanna recognised the handwriting immediately. The letter was unopened when she came across it earlier, lying on a silver platter in the hallway of Chadderton Hall, as she waited for Joseph.

She'd just found time to hide it in her bag when her employer came out to greet her. 'Miss Boston, please come through to the drawing room. I shall send for some tea if you like,' he offered. He was snivelling and shaking as usual. 'Or perhaps we can go through to my study if it's theatre business you have come to discuss?'

'Are you feeling well enough, Mr Wragg? You do seem to be a trifle indisposed, if you don't mind me saying so?' Vanna asked, noticing his stumbling gait and unshaven face. She stifled the urge to wrinkle her nose at the stale body

odour that always marked his presence. .

'I shall be fine after some tea, Miss Boston.'

'Perhaps the study is best, sir. You will need to consult your paperwork,' she said. 'I have successfully completed our opening-night programme and need you to agree the details.'

Joseph edged behind his desk and she took a seat opposite, noticing the mustiness of the room. He leaned to accept the list of shows and variety acts for the music hall opening night. Aware that it was one of Lillie's favourite roles, Joseph had decided to stage a performance of *She Stoops to Conquer* in the main auditorium

'I'm still waiting to see if Oscar Wilde will be joining us for this auspicious occasion,' Joseph mused, while scanning the list. 'I realise his time is at a premium, so I have offered him the Pullman Coach. He can dress for the event on the way to Lancashire and return to London overnight if he so wishes. But I rather hope he decides to stay with us at Chadderton Hall for a couple of days at least.'

'I have heard much of Oscar Wilde. It will be good to meet him, sir.'

'Yes, indeed. I imagine he'll entertain my wife who is keen to know about such follies as the latest London fashions. Did I tell you about the time he dressed as a Christmas tree at the Sambournes' house, Miss Boston?'

'No sir,' Vanna said.

He failed to explain his odd comment, and for a moment was lost in thought. 'I wonder what the weather is like today in London. Warm, I expect?' he mumbled, with his head down.

Vanna pressed on with arrangements for the opening night, 'I have followed your instructions and contacted Miss Ellen Terry's representatives. They say she is free and will be happy to accept the leading role of Kate Hardcastle, subject to a suitable fee, of course. '

'Good, good,' Joseph said vaguely. 'It is regrettable we have not been able to secure Mrs Langtry for the lead part but

I gather she is still away touring America. My sources say it is uncertain when she intends to return to England.' Joseph felt the strain of maintaining an air of casual indifference in front of his manageress and busied himself shuffling through more artistes' contracts. Once Ellen Terry had signed for the part, he knew Lillie would definitely not be coming home in time to star in the first production at his theatre.

'Perhaps we can look at numbers for the opening night party, sir?' Vanna offered. 'I understand this will be held in the eating salon on the first floor once the performances in the main theatre and the music hall are finished.'

Joseph glanced up from the papers and blinked, speaking clearly for once. 'There will be two parties and a pre-show reception for the mayor and civic dignitaries and my personal guests in the music room, Miss Boston,' he replied. 'One party shall be for the main theatre company and their invited guests, and another for the variety acts and their guests. The first in the eating salon and the second to be held in the music hall tavern or the beer rooms at the back of the hall, once patrons have left.'

'Very good, Mr Wragg,' Vanna said, making notes on a small pad. Joseph studied Vanna with interest; she was indeed a peculiar woman. Never before had he come across a female who understood complex business matters so easily. The only parts of his enterprise that seemed to be going right were the areas where Vanna was in charge. Organising future employees, booking acts and taking away much of the daily strain, she left him free to deal with building contractor and suppliers' issues.

Vanna appraised the situation as he absent-mindedly produced a grubby handkerchief and blew his nose. He muttered then handed her a set of accounts she'd left for approval last week. 'These all seem to be in order, Miss Boston. Perhaps you can attend to these matters without consulting me until we are up and running. I am, as you see, feeling slightly unwell at present, due to my recent period of influenza,' he said. 'And I see that you are doing a

remarkable job.'

Vanna smiled and lowered her gaze modestly. 'Thank you very much, sir.'

He returned her smile. 'I have every confidence in you, my dear.'

She feigned slight bashfulness as though taken aback by his bold comment. 'Why, thank you again, Mr Wragg. I have every intention of becoming an asset to your company. I am certain that once we open and you see how lucrative the business is, as well as being such a splendid addition to Lancashire, you will feel much better, sir.'

Joseph was charmed by her manner and her beautiful face, which made an agreeable diversion from his otherwise gloomy existence and continuously troubled thoughts. She got up to leave and firmly shook his hand, bending her head again slightly in deference. 'Thank you sir, I shall attend to the matters we discussed and take charge of staffing and the wages' accounts when the time comes. I am currently interviewing people for various positions.'

'May I send for a carriage to take you home, Miss Boston?' he offered.

'Thank you sir, but no. I would rather take the omnibus. I have errands to do on the way home.' Joseph opened the study door and allowed her to pass. 'Don't worry, sir, I can see myself out; I have no wish to take up any more of your time, Mr Wragg.' She noticed again the untidy slew of paperwork on his desk and the smell of his unwashed body. Vanna was determined that he see how thoughtful as well as efficient she was. This was only the first stage of her plan.

'Well, goodbye for now, Miss Boston,' he said, closing the door gently behind her with a smile that fell away within seconds.

As Vanna was about to leave through the front door, Nellie descended the staircase and spotted her. 'Oh Vanna – how exciting it all is. Only months away from the opening party! What fun, eh?'

The manageress turned around. 'Hello madam. Why, yes,

indeed – I shall look forward to it myself.'

'Have you decided what to wear? I'm beside itself with worry. I wanted to wear an evening gown but it may be too formal. What do you think, Vanna?' Nellie asked. She rather liked Vanna but found her a little too serious at times, perhaps because she had so much on her mind about the theatre, or maybe because the woman, like herself, seemed to have few friends.

'I don't know, madam. Perhaps that is something you can discuss with your dressmaker?' Vanna replied, uninterested and keen to be off.

'But Joseph has forbidden me to order a new dress because he says we must make economies after redecorating the drawing room.' Nellie pouted. 'I shall have to make do with what I have already. Would you care to see it – the drawing room, I mean? I have chosen the most exquisite shades of orange and lilac.'

'I'm sure you will think of something to wear and you will look wonderful. But you must excuse me, madam, I have errands to run before it gets too late.'

'Yes, of course,' said Nellie, who had been hoping for some female company. 'I shall see you at the opening night party, unless you have cause to visit us before then to see Mr Wragg. Perhaps I can show you the drawing room then?'

'That would be lovely, Mrs Wragg, and thank you.'

'Please call me Nellie. I insist!'

'Goodbye for now then, Nellie.'

Vanna walked up the driveway to the omnibus stop and smiled to herself. One of her errands was to visit the post office and pick up her copy of *Vanity Fair.* She'd subscribed to the London publication several months ago, anxious to know more about current trends which would be useful to her position as theatre manager. Only a few weeks ago, when the magazine featured an article entitled '*Where are they now?*' she'd spotted a picture of her employer with his arm around the tiny waist of actress Lillie Langtry. 'Well, I'll be dammed!' she'd mused, reading the few lines

about their alleged affair. There was also a signed picture of Lillie in a stage production role and today she'd spotted the same handwriting on the letter waiting in the hallway at Chadderton Hall for Joseph. If there was one thing Vanna had discovered since childhood, one should never miss an opportunity that comes one's way.

In her humble room Vanna settled in a chair, carefully opened the envelope and extracted a sheet of white flimsy paper. It read:

*My darling Joseph, my own love,*

*I fretted about writing, knowing how dearly you love me. But I must speak from my heart, my dearest, and try to free yours – for anything less would be an act of cruelty. We have been locked in many passionate embraces, known each other as intimately as a man can ever know a woman. But two souls beating as one cannot survive when parted this way. Fate works mysteriously for you see, my darling, I am to remain in America indefinitely. I have met someone. I so regret breaking your heart, but we can never be together. Hemispheres and circumstances prevent that. I know you are unhappy with your life and detest being married to a woman you despise and have never loved, but you must remain strong, for you are a good man.*

*Goodbye my darling, from your ever loving Lillie*

So, that's it, thought Vanna, carefully folding the letter and replacing it in the envelope. She opened a corner cupboard and put the letter behind a jumble of detritus on the top shelf. She was pleased for two reasons: by intercepting the letter she'd prevented Joseph being heartbroken and distracted from promoting the theatre, and now she knew his guilty secret!

Vanna recognised that her employer wasn't emotionally

strong and something like this could jeopardise the theatre complex and her own position. Now she had the ammunition to protect herself, a form of security that could be far more useful and damaging than a mere bargaining tool of careless, extramarital sex.

But most of all, the letter would guarantee her own stage career as a reputable actress. Ever since she'd performed in the seedy London music halls and singing rooms, she'd wanted to become an actress like one of the greats such as Sarah Bernhardt. But she knew that to do so she needed to be smart and secure the attention of a refined, wealthy patron; after all, look what had happened to Lillie Langtry after the Prince of Wales took an interest in her!

Vanna had intended to seduce Joseph into a love affair which she could threaten to expose if ever he decided to dismiss her from her position at the theatre. After the business was established, he would launch her on the stage as his protégée. With his status as a theatre owner and famous steeplejack, together with her contacts in the entertainment business, there would be no stopping her from becoming wealthy and famous herself! Then he would see she was the woman for him, instead of his simpering wife Nellie.

This new development would require careful handling. She hadn't realised the extent of his involvement with the Langtry woman before reading the letter. She would need to get far closer to him, in order to transfer his affections to herself. At least she knew that Nellie in his life would not be any kind of threat after reading Langtry's cool observations on the state of his marriage.

Then Vanna had an idea about the lonely, vulnerable Nellie sitting at home alone each day with only her children and that overbearing harridan of a mother-in-law for company.

'Perhaps I *should* like to see this orange and lilac drawing room after all,' she said to herself, smiling.

\*\*\*

The situation had become intolerable. Such was Lillie's fame across the ocean, Joseph's many fevered letters still found her despite being addressed simply to *'Mrs Lillie Langtry, United States of America.'* The last one was the most disturbing of all. It appeared Joseph wanted her to return to England to discuss marriage!

At the risk of upsetting Nathaniel, she had no choice but to tell him of the situation; it was feasible that Joseph's letters could be handed to him inadvertently, given the random way Joseph was addressing them and the frequency of their arrival. Lillie fretted constantly, and at every theatre venue or hotel her heart leapt when Nathaniel said he'd received mail for her in her absence.

Nathaniel was outraged at her disclosure. Oh, how she wished she'd been honest with him from the start! 'Good grief – you mean to tell me you've been corresponding with this Wragg chap behind my back all along?' he stormed.

'No, not exactly – well, just to appease him,' Lillie stammered back. 'I was afraid he'd come overseas and seek me out.'

*'Seek you out*? I must be missing something here. You encourage this rough fellow, but you say you are *afraid* he'll travel to America to find you?'

'I've been an utter fool! Do forgive me, Nathy, please say that you will.'

'I have given you everything, including my heart, and yet you continue to send love letters to another man?' He was looking angrier by the second. 'Is this because we cannot marry? Is it a subtle form of punishment, perhaps?'

*'No!'* shouted Lillie, in tears. 'Not that! I'm confused and afraid, that is all.'

Nathaniel acted as expected, throwing things to the floor, punching a ragged hole through a window pane with his fist, protesting his undying love but then moodily refusing to speak to her for six weeks. He left her life – and she feared it was for good.

She saw pictures of him in newspapers with young society

beauties, at the races or aboard opulent sailing vessels. They made her feel old and abandoned; the creases on her face were multiplying and her waistline was not as trim as it used to be. She cancelled several shows because her face was raw and puffy from crying; her heart was breaking and she thought the pain of longing for Nathaniel might kill her.

She was sitting in the garden contemplating her bleak future. Perhaps the best thing would be to return to London and keep a low profile. In the warm sunshine, reading with her daughter on the lawn, tears were never far away. A bluebird flew past and, as she watched it land on a bush, she saw the familiar black carriage coming up the driveway. Nathaniel! She threw down her parasol, and ran towards it, all poise and decorum gone as she waved her arms and shouted, '*Nathy! Nathy!*'

Nathaniel jumped down from the carriage; he looked thinner and had shaved off his thick moustache. But his feelings had not changed. He spun her around and kissed her passionately. Her hair escaped from the confines of its ivory pins and flowed around her face in bouncing curls.

They fell to the ground and held each other tight, smothering each other in kisses.

'My darling, I could never leave you. My beautiful Jersey Lillie, I can never escape from your arms,' Nathan said. 'I need you! Please forgive me and stay mine forever, my darling.'

'Oh *Nathy* – my darling boy. I have missed you so dreadfully,' Lillie cried, cupping his face in her hands. 'Never leave me again.'

Later that evening, between passionate lovemaking and tender endearments, they discussed their future together. Nathaniel was brutally honest about his position: his family would never accept her as his wife. But he vowed he would never leave her again. If that was enough for Lillie, then they would be together always. But there was one condition. She must write to the British steeplejack fellow and tell him she had someone new. Nathaniel would not compromise on this.

'It would not matter if he sent dozens of letters a day, as long as he knows the score,' he said.

'He probably will write again, even if I tell him not to. He's possessed and doomed to love me always, I fear. I have had a letter from England that says he means to marry me!'

'Show me,' he demanded.

'I am a little afraid of him.' His letters seemed full of discord and anger. Nathaniel had some difficulty reading the untidy scrawl and jumbled words, but the steeplejack's intention was clear.

*My dearest most beloved Lillie,*

*Transformation complete! Your very own theatre my darling, here in England! We must lose no ground, plans are afoot, must insist you return, arrangements to be married can make for surprise of life. Now where to live? Ha – problems interchangeable necessary grief for Nellie and Ned but no love can flourish where none. I long you see what plans have been born out of this divine love we have. Exaggeration? No! The dragging days are over for we are to be together you my queen with her very own palace. You'll see!*

*When this letter finds you, dearest, reply post haste for the night is close when all revealed is not far away. Retrospective fears largely fictitious but transformation in any capacity godly as is our love. Love adoring, yes ADORING!*

*Your beloved soon-to-be-husband, Joseph*

*(PS – your pet role awaits you!)*

Nathaniel handed it back with a frown. 'Lillie, the guy is crazy,' he said, shaking his head in disbelief. 'What the devil is he on about?'

'I am afraid he shall come for me if I don't return.' She

pulled her arms tightly across her bosom, as it to ward off attack. 'What happens if he *does* come? We cannot afford a public scandal.'

'You must write back at once. Brook no further correspondence about marriage plans; just tell him it's over and that you have met someone else.'

'What does he mean I wonder - my *own* theatre?'

'I guess he's rented premises. Or perhaps he means you will be the lady of the household. Who knows – but this guy is completely nuts, that's for sure,' said Nathan as he stared at the letter.

'I shall write at once, just this one time, my darling.'

Nathaniel put his arm protectively around Lillie, glad that there was the Atlantic Ocean between them and this raving madman.

So her reply was written next day and sealed in a blue airmail envelope. As Lillie handed it over to the clerk, knowing she would never see its recipient again, she was calm. 'Goodbye Joseph,' she said out loud. 'Our paths will never cross again.'

# ACT 23

*A*n excited crowd gathered on the wide pavement outside The Red Rose Palace of Varieties in Oldham; some people were seeing electric lighting on a grand scale for the first time. It was a formidable, colourful sight in contrast with the weak green glow from the row of gas lamps in front of the granite steps.

Feelings were mixed as labourers shoved forward and rubbed shoulders with the gentry, businessmen, bank clerks, nursery maids and tradesman who queued for tickets to see *She Stoops to Conquer*.

Some people thought the venue vulgar but still wanted to be seen at this major event in the social calendar. Certain local land-owning families refused to have anything to do with such an outlandish enterprise. They discussed it over elaborate breakfasts where sideboards were laden with enough food to feed a family of mill-workers for a week. They clicked their tongues, mumbling that the garish frontage looked like a fairground. Others, cut from the same fabric as Septimus Stark, remarked that a park full of animals at Chadderton Hall had been quite enough to blight the area; when would this bloody fool cease making a spectacle of their town?

The working classes hadn't seen anything like it. As they stood outside the complex, ready to enter the music hall for a few pennies, they gasped as fancy carriages arrived and dropped off bejewelled toffs who wanted to be seen at the

opening night. Some spotted their employers, dressed in smart evening wear, the women draped in furs. The children of spectators who couldn't afford the entrance fee clambered on walls for a better view, some sitting high on their fathers' shoulders, waving flags. Workers from neighbouring mill towns as far away as Halifax treated it like a national holiday, and had spoken about nothing else for weeks.

Civic dignitaries, invited to a banquet before the performances began, were gathering on the first floor of the building, drinking champagne, nibbling fancies and speaking with Vanna Boston, who left periodically to oversee the staff in the ticket office.

Invitations had been sent to anyone and everyone who mattered, although Tabitha Stark never received one, nor would she and her husband James have agreed to attend. One sent to William Croston by mistake was ripped up and thrown into the fire. Joseph's former friend spat out a curse before trying to get drown his sorrows. 'Go to hell, you selfish swine,' he hollered, watching the pieces of gold and cream card burn to ash.

The massive Portland stone fascia, a replica of Buckingham Palace, revealed the main entrance to the foyer. Huge, brightly-lit signage adorned the splendid frontage. The building was split into three halves for plays, music hall acts and light orchestral entertainment. The steps leading down to the street were black, polished granite, and flecks of twinkling mica caught the lights on either side of the thick red carpet that had been laid for the opening night.

The more cynical observers said the steps resembled those at a mausoleum, and joked that each one should be engraved with 'Finis' in gold lettering since the complex was surely doomed to failure.

Joseph knew none of this as he stood in his evening suit with bright red cravat, welcoming his guests. A short, pre-show tour had been arranged for newspaper journalists. As they walked, he expanded on his grandiose ideas. 'The whole complex easily caters for more than five thousand

people per night, and I expect it to be full for most of the time,' he said, missing one or two raised eyebrows at his great expectations. 'To accommodate the main auditorium at the back, the grand foyer is a smaller replica of the one at Buckingham Palace. But more than 150 tons of Italian white marble were used for the white columns.'

Patrons strolled around; some glamorously dressed in evening gowns and formal dress-suits, quaffing champagne offered by liveried servants with powdered wigs. Others wore their Sunday best, clothes usually reserved for church; they pointed at the imposing spectacle from a roped-off area while they waited to go through to the music hall foyer and beer rooms beyond.

Several men with crooked teeth and threadbare jackets surged forward towards the barrier for a better look; it suddenly toppled under the pressure. As a member of the liveried staff rectified the problem a small elderly woman, dressed in rags and a shawl, stepped over the flattened barrier and approached Joseph. One of the staff tried to block her but Joseph gestured to allow her through. She held out a gnarled hand; her lipless mouth gave a wide, toothless smile which exposed dark gums. He held her gaze for a few moments.

She touched the fine fabric of his coat, then ran a dirty finger along his jawbone and mumbled, 'Eee, by 'eck little Joe, yer did yer mam and dad reet proud, lad. That's a fact!' Her words touched him, and for a moment he thought back to Potts Street and how hard he'd strived to get away from people just like her. He smiled fondly and patted her frail hand, instructing one of the livered staff to allow her free access to the music hall and see that she got something to eat and drink.

Joseph's group continued upstairs. Either side of the foyer encompassed a leg of the grand staircase with its magnificent gold balustrade. It was lit from overhead by a shallow dome of leaded glass depicting colourful designs of birds, harps and flutes. The new electrical lighting gave it a dream-like quality.

Joseph pointed forward as they ascended the staircase and the journalists followed the direction his finger. Hanging from the ceiling in the foyer were huge crystal chandeliers, imported from Italy, set amidst ornate ceiling roses and elaborate plasterwork. They highlighted friezes of thousands of lilies painted in oils by eminent artists – and at more than twice the cost Joseph had anticipated. 'These chandeliers are the only ones in England made to such exacting specifications, so they are quite unique,' he remarked proudly. 'There are none like these, other than in Venice.'

One of the journalists asked with genuine curiosity, 'You mention Italy, Mr Wragg. Do you feel your theatre venture will become known throughout the Continent and attract attention from overseas?'

'But of course!' Joseph huffed defensively. 'We are talking about the best theatre in the whole of the British Commonwealth – let alone Europe! This theatre will rival London and take Lancashire's fame into a new dimension!' The journalists looked uncomfortable, not knowing what to make of his bold statement, and asked no further questions.

A heavy bronze-coloured doorway to the left of the main foyer led to a smaller, more modest one which belonged to the music hall. To the right, a doorway led to the mahogany-clad box offices, flanked by marble statues, and a manager's room. Hidden from view were vast storage and office facilities and corridors which ran around the side of the building to the stage door area and dressing rooms.

The building had a full set of dressing rooms that were accessed separately, so Thespians and variety artistes could remain apart. Dressing Room One in the main complex was reserved exclusively for Lillie; it was styled like a miniature version of the gold and red throne room in Buckingham Palace, complete with replica gilt furniture modelled on two sumptuous throne chairs made for Queen Victoria by Thomas Dowbiggin in 1837.

Joseph descended the stairs, leaving the journalists on the wide landing outside one of the music chambers. Soft music

wafted across to the patrons admiring the view from the balcony overlooking the foyer. Another group of journalists and photographers continued across the foyer below, and Joseph joined them. Entering the main auditorium, they gasped.

'I once travelled to London and saw The Palladium when Ellen Terry was there. But I've never seen anything on the same scale as this, Mr Wragg,' said Peter Urmston, a reporter from Oldham who had covered the story about the opening of the Menageriet and its eventual demise.

'Quite so, Mr Urmston, but the general idea is not to replicate the Palladium here in Oldham, but rather, create a brand new concept in theatre design. That is why I call it a *palace* rather than simply a *place* of entertainment,' Joseph said proudly, his eyes shining in the reflected light from the crystal chandeliers. He waved his hands about excitedly, urging the journalists note down every detail.

Peter Urmston liked the steeplejack but considered him quite mad and had recently heard several rumours about him buying large quantities of laudanum.

The two auditoriums were similar in design but the one where Lillie would perform was magnificent; no expense had been spared. It represented the love Joseph felt for his queen. Its vast proscenium arch, the largest in Europe, boasted raised fibrous plaster enrichments of huge lilies gilded in gold-leaf. The design was echoed on the fronts of the circles and upper galleries. The private boxes bore heavier designs of lilies entwined in elegant vines, with the red rose of Lancashire standing proud.

The music hall was smaller and narrower and did not boast the same opulent richness. Instead of lilies, around its proscenium arch was the stylized red rose of Lancashire entwined in vines. The light fittings were of deeply-etched cranberry glass and not crystal. The only reason Joseph had not furnished it like the main auditorium was because he had to economize a little by the time it was fitted out.

Joseph looked at his pocket watch and adjusted his red

cravat causing the huge square diamond ring on his little finger to flash like fire in the reflected light. He felt hot in his constricting evening wear and a little fatigued by all the fuss. 'Now, you really must excuse me, gentlemen. I have the Mayor and other guests to meet before the performances,' he told the reporters. 'Miss Boston has arranged for a box in the main auditorium for tonight's performance. I would be delighted if you would all be my guests.'

The men murmured agreement then thanked him and wished him luck.

Joseph set off to join his family and the civic dignities upstairs in the music room. He could hear another loud cheer from the crowd outside as he cut through the congested foyer. He had not been able to sleep for days before the opening night. He was sad that he'd still not been able to locate Lillie. But Joseph knew that his enterprise would be a commercial success and one day she would be the jewel in his northern crown. He had spent thousands of pounds on posters, handbills and programmes and, although most of tonight's guests for the main play were here by invitation only, he knew it would only be a matter of time before word spread and all the world came to see his theatre – and watch his darling Lillie perform...

***

Oscar Wilde smiled as he stepped down from the carriage, holding an oblong package tied with string. He waved at the cheering crowd and gathered his red-lined opera cape to avoid dragging it through a puddle on the pavement.

Several of the keener reporters heard the commotion outside and knew someone important had arrived. They pushed their way through the foyer and into the heaving crowd, eager to speak with the celebrated London intellectual, sensing another dimension to their stories.

*''Ere, Mr Wilde, sir!'* shouted one, waving his pencil and advancing, regardless of the irate comments from

theatregoers whom he shoved aside. He wanted to be the first to interview the London playwright and get an exclusive story. Pushing his dark brown bowler hat back, he stood in front of his quarry and enquired, 'Is this yer first visit up north, then, Mr Wilde? If so, what do you think of it, sir?'

'It is, my good fellow, and it's extraordinary to see how one can forgo such places without out feeling compromised,' said Wilde, looking amused. He continued, almost savouring the words as he spoke, 'Quite intriguing to see it all first hand having heard so *much* from Mr Wragg about the industrial north.'

'Did you come up alone in Mr Wragg's Pullman coach, sir?'

'Indeed, I did. I think generosity is the essence of friendship, don't you?'

'Are you staying in Oldham or Manchester, sir?'

'No, I shall be staying with my good friends the Wraggs at Chadderton Hall.'

'And what's your personal view on the sanctity of marriage, Mr Wilde?'

Wilde faltered for a second or two, surprised by the insensitive remark. He furrowed his brow, cocking his head to one side, buying time. 'I'm not sure I understand the question, my good man,' he replied. 'This is no time to discuss such serious matters as matrimony, surely? The evening is purely for fun, I believe!' The reply lacked his usual aplomb and Wilde knew if he wasn't careful, this would turn into a witch-hunt; he'd heard a few jeers in the crowd as he delivered his delayed response.

'And, what's *your* idea of having fun, then, matey?' someone snickered.

The playwright faltered again. He was in the middle of a long and difficult libel case against the Marquess of Queensbury who had publicly accused him of homosexuality. Wilde's legal advisors had urged him not to attend this opening night in Oldham, but he wanted to support his friend. Someone in the crowd shouted an obscenity and

others joined in, jeering with the man who had started to harangue the playwright about unnatural practices.

A cheerless representative of the theatre bustled forward to help Wilde into the building. He addressed the loud man and the avid reporters surrounding the playwright: 'No more indiscreet questions, gentlemen. I'm sure Mr Wilde has had a tiring journey, so if you don't mind stepping right back and allowing us passage,' he said, pushing them all aside and guiding his vulnerable charge through the milling crowds towards the theatre doors.

'Indiscreet questions? Indiscreet *buggery,* more like!' a foul-mouthed man hollered. 'That's *his* idea of fun!'

A collective jeer went up.

'The dirty bastard,' continued the drunken man, staggering closer to block his victim's path. 'Answer the question, you ruddy great queer!'

The celebrated playwright felt affronted; he should have remained silent, but his pride was injured. 'Questions are never indiscreet but answers sometimes are,' he shot back, pulling himself up to his full height before continuing and addressing the onlookers. 'I shall illustrate my point. I once told a very dear painter friend that *work* is the curse of the *drinking* classes, and so I have made an important discovery – that *alcohol, taken in sufficient quantities,* produces *all the effects of* intoxication!' He arched his arm towards the bad-tempered drunk as if to illustrate his point before the theatre representative shoved the man aside. 'As this pitiful fellow demonstrates, the theory is proven accurate time and time again...' Wilde knew the comment lacked his usual sharp wit, but it was the best he could do under the circumstances.

One wily reporter had been busy researching the case with the Marquess of Queensbury. He pushed past the theatre representative and stuck his pen in front of Oscar's face, asking about an associate in London who had recently suffered scandal after being arrested for homosexuality. He caught Wilde off-guard. 'But what are your thoughts about the shaming of your good friend Lord Constantine and recent

allegations about his character, sir?' he challenged. 'Is there any truth in it?'

Wilde stopped in his tracks and held his hand high to silence the reporter. 'I never speak disrespectfully of society, my good man – only people who can't get into it do that,' he replied cryptically. He locked eyes with the reporter and said much too brightly, 'Now, if you'll kindly allow me to pass...?'

There were more boos from the crowd and someone threw a rotten cabbage. Wilde entered the foyer and breathed a sigh of relief. A slender boy dressed in the gold and red livery of a footman took his cape and hat. Wilde stood with his parcel, glancing briefly around for a moment or two before moving towards the grand staircase to join Joseph and the civic dignitaries upstairs. He contemplated the vast expense his friend had gone to in building this incredible theatre. He knew it would cost Joseph dearly in many ways; he was aware of Lillie's new career in America and her love affair with Nathaniel Wallis. Oscar wouldn't say anything to Joseph just yet, but he knew that even if Lillie were to return to England, a provincial theatre could not possibly sustain enough interest to be successful long-term. The venture was doomed to failure.

Joseph spotted Wilde and rushed over to greet his flamboyant friend, throwing an arm around his shoulder. The pair had become firm friends by telephone since Lillie had left. Joseph knew Oscar was his only means of finding out about her, so had cultivated the friendship despite loathing Wilde's private life. To his surprise, the more he spoke to him, the more he liked the playwright. He saw that beneath Wilde's mask lay a genuinely caring person.

'Oscar, dear fellow! You found us all right, then, I see?' he announced. 'Come, let me introduce you to my wife Nellie, my mother and my other honoured guests.'

Wilde bowed charmingly before Nellie and Violet, kissing each slowly on the back of the hand. He turned to Joseph and said, 'I have brought you a small token to mark

this glorious theatrical occasion, my friend,' and handed over the parcel. 'Please, do open it now.'

Joseph examined it, surprised by the gesture. Pulling off the string and paper and peering at the contents of the oblong box, he exclaimed with joy, 'Why Oscar, I don't know how to thank you! It's truly magnificent.' Inside the parcel was a small frame containing a beautiful mounted silver trowel. The ornate, ivory-handled object was inscribed, *'To Joseph, for each artist is a creator of beautiful things. With fondness, Oscar Wilde.'*

Wilde looked pleased with Joseph's reaction. 'I thought it would make rather a charming addition to your manager's office. After all, one has to find relief from the dreariness of looking at official papers all day long, I imagine?'

Wilde was distracted by the mayor of Oldham and several local councillors who wanted to shake his hand and welcome him to Lancashire. 'So, what do you think of our new addition to the borough of Oldham, my good fellow?' asked the mayor, pulling himself up to his full height to match that of the tall playwright. 'Quite the thing to bring in tourists, I dare say?'

'But of course, Lord Mayor, how right you are. For myself, as a humble Irishman, I am always a man of most simple tastes,' said Wilde, pausing for effect. 'You see, I am *always* satisfied with the best!'

Everyone laughed, Nellie a bit too loudly. She felt a little nervous with all the fuss and slightly light-headed with champagne. Nellie looked around for support from Vanna but instead noticed Violet scowling. Her mother-in-law reached across and took the glass from her hand. 'Be careful' she hissed. 'This is an important night for our Joseph and you need to watch what you are drinking, you foolish girl.'

Nellie pouted and stormed off towards the table bearing drinks and defiantly grabbed another flute. Violet marched after her and tried to block her route back to Joseph. Nellie made a small moue with her mouth then hiccupped loudly. 'I shall have as much as I like. As the *prime* Mrs Wragg, it is

my prerogative!' she slurred.

Joseph was speaking with the town planner and his assistant, but noticed the altercation between the two women as Violet tried to remove the second glass from her daughter-in-law's hand. 'Excuse me for a moment,' he said, and quickly walked over to his wife and mother. 'What on earth is going on here? Pray, keep your voices down.'

'It's her, the dry old hag; she won't let me have *any* enjoyment at all!' Nellie challenged. 'It's not FAIR!'

Violet looked astonished and remarked, 'You'll apologise for that at once, my girl. Who do you suppose you are addressing in public like that?' Joseph blew air through pursed lips, ignoring his mother and taking his wife's arm by the elbow. 'You will not do this tonight, Nellie, or I shall order you a cab now and you will go home. Do I make myself clear?'

Nellie's lip trembled but she started to insult Violet again, just as Vanna came back to the group. 'Is everything all right, Mr Wragg?' she enquired, scanning the faces of the group.

'I would like you to order a cab for my wife please, Miss Boston.'

Nellie stamped her foot and scowled. 'It's not *fair*! Why should I have to leave?'

Violet looked pleased, but the manageress said, 'Sir, you can leave Nellie with me if you like. I'll look after her. I would not like to see her miss tonight's grand performance.'

'Thank you, Vanna, but I'm sure you have a lot to take care of already.'

'Not at all sir, it is no trouble at all.'

'I am *not* going home – you can't *make* me!' stormed Nellie.

'Be quiet, Nellie! You are in danger of making a dreadful scene,' hissed Violet, looking around, not quite knowing how to handle the situation.

Vanna turned to Nellie and placed her index finger to her own lips and shook her head slightly. Joseph was surprised to see Nellie calm down at once. Vanna said to her: 'Nellie,

please don't allow the night to be spoiled for everyone and make your husband angry. He has worked very hard for this evening, and we owe him our allegiance.'

Despite being tipsy, Nellie took her cue and apologised to Joseph.

Violet still insisted it would be better to send his wife home but Vanna spoke up again, addressing Violet directly. 'But Nellie is his *wife*, madam, and it would not be right to deny her – or her husband – her rightful place at his side on this auspicious night.' She turned to Joseph, adopting a studied, coy look. 'Besides, it would look odd, Mr Wragg, what with all the papers here to report on the night's events.'

'Yes, you are right, Miss Boston,' Joseph agreed, and thanked Vanna for her help. 'Now, you really must excuse me. And mother, perhaps you would care to join the ladies over by the window for refreshments and allow me to meet my honoured guests in peace?'

Vanna smiled. She knew she'd scored a point and made a friend of Nellie, which was far more important than making an enemy of Violet. The two woman locked eyes before Violet realised she'd met her match, picked up her glass and stormed off. Nellie giggled, repressing a loud belch with her hand.

'No more champagne for you tonight, my dear,' said Vanna lightly.

'But my, what fun!' replied Nellie and burst into another fit of giggles.

The performances were received with enthusiasm and deemed a complete success. Joseph flitted between the after-show parties, speaking to the principal players of both productions. Everyone stopped to congratulate him and he knew the glamour of the evening would remain in people's minds indefinitely.

In the early hours of the morning, Joseph and his family dropped Vanna at Lever Road near the market place. Nellie hugged her new friend tightly before Joseph escorted Vanna upstairs to her room and thanked her for taking good care

of Nellie. The belligerent landlady came into the hall and shouted upstairs, 'Oi, you, lady! No gentleman callers allowed at this time of night – this is a respectable single ladies' lodging house!'

Joseph tried reassuring the woman his intentions were honourable.

*'Humph!'* She said, ignoring him, seeing his nocturnal appearance as a local toff looking for a bit of late-night fun. 'You think on now, gal, I'll be listening out with my ear to the ceiling!' she shouted. Vanna giggled as the landlady slammed her door shut and the hallway fell silent. She smiled at Joseph, sharing their brief moment of fun, imagining the landlady trying to climb tall ladders to plaster her ear against the ceiling.

'A sterling effort tonight, Miss Boston. I am indebted to your skill and dedication in making this a night to remember. For myself and my wife too, of course,' he said, making oblique reference to the incident with Nellie earlier. 'I can see we shall make an extraordinary team, you and I.'

Vanna was ecstatic and allowed Joseph to kiss her gloved hand. As he looked deep into her eyes, he thought of Lillie. 'Good night, Miss Boston. I shall see you at the theatre tomorrow afternoon, for I am certain we each deserve a morning of leisure.'

As the carriage rattled on back towards Chadderton Hall, Nellie fell asleep in her husband's arms. Joseph wasn't tired and his mind raced like a mainline railway locomotive. Nor was Oscar Wilde, and the two men sat drinking and smoking cigars into the early hours in Joseph's study.

'Hats off to you, my dear boy. You sowed the seeds of success this evening in Lancashire's grimy soil and shall grow very rich!'

'Thank you, Oscar. But I'm afraid tonight applies only to the music hall and beer rooms, my dear fellow. Did you see it? The place was populated mostly by intoxicated mill workers and miners,' said Joseph. 'Tickets for the principle production were by invitation only, so we cannot know if it

was successful or not.'

Oscar took another sip of his cognac and let the liquid warm his throat. 'The working classes will always spend more that way. A man is made for something better than disturbing dirt. All that kind of thing should be done by a machine, for industry is the root of all ugliness. Is it any wonder they drink so?'

'But the working classes are changing, Oscar! And I intend to educate them into appreciating the finer things in life.'

'But of course, my dear fellow. For example, the Cabinet has absorbed its first radical working man. I believe John Bright is the son of a Rochdale mill worker,' said Oscar, swirling his glass. 'But he is debarred from Court. It's a closed society that can never be breached, dear boy. One can only ever be a whimsical fancy of London's high society – but a very amusing one I hope.'

'We shall see,' Joseph reflected. 'I feel sure that once ordinary people see quality productions on their own doorstep, they'll become aware of things other than getting drunk all the time.' He drew on his Cuban cigar, adding almost as an afterthought as he blew out the smoke, 'Speaking of whimsical favourites of society, I'm sad that our delightful Lillie didn't show up for tonight's opening ceremony.'

The playwright let out a long sigh. 'You mustn't be too hard on her, for she is a peacock and must forever display her talent on stage. So she may come round, who knows...?' He shrugged his shoulders. 'But I gather she is doing well in America,' he added.

'Have you heard from her, Oscar?' asked Joseph suspiciously. 'Has she corresponded with you?'

Wilde swirled his glass for a moment before lifting it to his lips. Oh, what torture it is trying to protect a good friend from hurt, he thought. How could he tell Joseph that Lillie was nothing more than a bolter; a woman who loved wholeheartedly but for a brief spell – then ran? After speaking with the most *sinful* Lady Blenheim, he knew that

in Lillie's eyes Joseph was merely an interlude before she discovered true love in another distant land. He could not refer to his own recent trip to America, where he spent a lot of time with Lillie and Nathaniel. Seeing the couple's dance of intimacy left no doubt that this was a deep and abiding love. He didn't want to spoil this special evening, so he resorted to gentle subterfuge.

'I cannot tell a lie, my dearest friend. I have had so many of those lately with my own troubles. You must understand a woman's mind works around curves of emotion, dear boy. Who are we as men to understand? You must give her time to explain her thoughts,' he said gently.

'You didn't answer my question, Oscar.'

'For once, my friend, I do not have an answer,' he replied.

\*\*\*

Vanna was exhausted by the time she went to bed at two a.m. The night had been successful and she dreamed of her own fulfilment as she watched Ellen Terry play Kate Hardcastle in *She Stoops to Conquer*. At the reception afterwards, Vanna thought the actress wan and lacking in presence as she spoke to admirers and accepted compliments. When her own turn came, she would dazzle at all times – particularly in bed when she entertained Joseph.

She pulled the thin curtains closed, shutting out the factory wall and brick market hall opposite and cradled her arms around herself, thinking of the riches she would enjoy one day. Walking over to the single gas bracket to lower the meagre flame, she glanced at the corner cupboard and saw her life mapped out just as she planned. Tomorrow she would start implementing her plans to secure her position. Now that silly fool Nellie had angered Joseph in public, Vanna could get closer to the gullible girl by telling Joseph she thought that his wife could use more female company.

It was almost too easy! But Vanna soon discovered Violet wasn't easy – or gullible.

Violet watched Vanna as she gradually wormed her way into their lives over the next few weeks. There could be no doubt the woman was almost as bright as Joseph when it came to business matters, but why she would go out of her way to engage Nellie in friendship had to be questioned. Her son's harebrained wife had no gumption and chattered for hours at a time without saying anything worth listening to. The two women seemed poles apart, and sometimes Violet caught Vanna off guard as they sat together in the drawing room, Nellie fussing and fretting about rags for Gabrielle's ringlets, or indulging in some silly gossip she'd read in her periodicals. Violet noticed the bored look on Vanna's face. Then she'd pull herself together, realising Violet was watching her closely. 'Oh, Nellie, dearest – that is quite the thing. You really must send away for the lace edged one and not the silk,' she'd say, as they perused fashion magazines together.

Joseph respected Vanna and was glad he had her to attend to the theatre. He was still distracted by the lack of correspondence from Lillie; his mental health was beginning to suffer again as dreams of her distorted into nightmares. Why didn't she write? Perhaps his letters had not arrived and she thought he had snubbed her? Every evening, he sat in his study, scribbling letter after letter to Lillie until his hand hurt too much to carry on writing. Sometimes he replicated the same letter ten times hoping that at least one copy would find her.

Joseph had banned the rest of his family and the servants from entering his study, saying he did not want his things disturbing; he trusted no-one.

There had been a terrible altercation recently. Shortly before opening night, the parlour maid Poppy had told the housekeeper about an unopened letter that had gone missing from the silver tray in the hallway before the master had chance to read it. The housekeeper informed her mistress and the mistress told the master. The servant was adamant she'd left it out for him. Joseph's outburst shocked her. 'You

silly, useless girl! Why in the devil's name didn't you bring it to me when it first arrived, Poppy?'

Nellie tried to calm her raging husband who looked as though he would attack the trembling servant. She restrained his arm. 'Please dear, it's not the maid's fault!'

Violet looked on shrewdly and wondered what all this meant.

'I'm s-sorry, sir. You were out at the theatre. I left it in the hallway on the table by the d-door,' stuttered the tearful maid.

'What was it like? Did it bear a British stamp?' Joseph challenged.

The maid noticed white spittle at the corners of his twisted mouth. 'I-I didn't notice. I'm sorry sir, it was just a letter I put out on the tray as usual, sir,' she cried.

Joseph was frantic and had the house searched high and low. He interrogated each member of the family and the staff in turn. Nellie assumed it was an important business letter but Violet knew exactly what was going through her son's mind.

After Nellie had gone to bed, Violet knocked gently on Joseph's study door. He answered it and stepped into the corridor, pulling the door closed behind him. In his stained smoking jacket, he looked dishevelled and pale. 'Could we go into the parlour for a moment or two, if you don't mind, son?' Violet asked. Joseph followed her and Violet told him to shut the door.

'You have to give this up, lad,' she instructed. 'I know how you are hurting, but look at you. Lillie Langtry is not worthy of this pain. She's gone—'

'She has *not* gone!' he shouted.

'Joseph, you have to look to the future. You have a business to run.'

'You took the letter! Is that it?' he demanded. 'You know how much she means to me – but all you care about is yourself and living here!'

'For pete's sakes lad, keep yer voice down, yer'll

wake everybody up with yer racket!' Violet was upset at his belligerence; he'd never attacked her verbally like this before. Her careful speaking voice dropped back into its native Lancashire dialect. 'Tha's got believe me, lad, I 'aven't 'ad yer letter,' she cried.

'Who else could it be? You knew all about Lillie – and if Nellie or the children had taken it, why, we'd know for sure!'

'I swear it ain't me, son, I swear it!' Violet was now in floods of tears.

Joseph gazed at her for a second of two, his face set into a grim mask. 'You know what, Mother, when Lillie returns and we marry, we shall need to find suitable accommodation for you. I was hoping you might remain here but I cannot tolerate you interfering in my private affairs. I am not having it. I have a good mind to report the matter to the police.'

Violet said nothing and waited to see what would come next.

'Well, what have you to say for yourself, Mother?' demanded Joseph.

When no response came, he marched to the door and left her standing alone in tears. She sank down on the sofa. Whoever took the missing letter must have their own reasons for doing so; Violet intended to find out what they were and exactly what the letter contained. She rooted through her mind to identify the people who had called at the house that particular day.

And, from that night on, she kept a much closer watch on Vanna Boston.

# ACT 24

Joseph was an entirely different man these days. Nellie had secretly read a copy of Robert Louis Stevenson's *Doctor Jekyll and Mr Hyde* and she fretted in case her husband had somehow been possessed by an evil character. She had nightmares about the tale and burned the book one evening.

Gone was Joseph's amiable and flamboyant style which had once set tongues wagging as he strutted the streets of Oldham. He'd also lost that invincible air he'd had when he climbed into the sky as a steeplejack. Gone was the handsome, rough-diamond of a gentleman with vivid dancing eyes that twinkled like mischievous stars, seeking to hold one enthralled.

Instead, he was a broken man weighed down by problems and tortured thoughts; a haunted being who shuffled through the house late at night and slept through the day in his study. His demons would not allow him to rest alongside his wife at night. No-one could pinpoint what was wrong; it was as if a curse had been placed upon his soul.

The Wragg household was never calm, for nothing would quell the two bickering women in his life. Joseph barely spoke to his mother and avoided her whenever he could. Nellie still loved him dearly and during his particularly bad periods she waited patiently in the parlour for him to spend some time with her. He would sit without speaking, staring at the wall or mumbling some gibberish she could not

understand. Other times he would cling to her, whimpering like a frightened child and demanding that she never leave him. The complexity of his strange behaviour was beyond understanding so Nellie took it as a sign of his devotion to her and his fear that his new business venture would fail.

His children could see that their father was ill. His sunken eyes and sallow complexion under the mop of long, greying hair which straggled beneath his top hat whenever he dressed for the theatre upset them. Mostly, he sat alone in his study writing…writing…writing…

The doctor examined him when Violet finally sent for him. She was concerned at his behaviour; he refused to eat, accusing her of poisoning his mind, then his food. He screamed at her for hours and insisted she wanted him dead. His mood swings were frightening, and he complained frequently of headaches.

Dr Edmund Farrow MD shook his head and put away his stethoscope. 'I can find no physical problem. Except for a raised heartbeat and slight malnutrition, he is in reasonably good order for someone who has neglected himself. But it's the same as last time, I'm afraid,' he said. 'Shattered nerves and fatigue. He needs complete rest.'

Joseph lay wide-eyed and staring, perspiring and writhing on the bed, struggling for breath. He looked right through the doctor as if he weren't there. Then he doubled up as painful cramps overtook his body, his arms thrashing about as if warding off demons. Nellie soothed his forehead with a wet flannel, and gently tucked his lank hair behind his ears. As before, she would be a dutiful wife and nurse him back to heath.

Violet's face was ashen. Only she knew how poorly her son really was, but she didn't say anything to the doctor or the rest of family. Recently, when Joseph was on an errand to meet the buyers of his Pullman coach which he was selling to settle household debts, she'd crept silently into his study, curious to see what he did all the time he was in there. She was horrified at what she found.

The thick, sour odour of unwashed linen and un-emptied chamber pots was choking; Violet looked away in disgust, noticing the organic contents of one under a chair. The heavy velvet drapes were closed, keeping the rankness of the room trapped within its gloomy shadows. The floor was strewn with soiled blankets. Dozens of empty laudanum bottles littered the hearth rug, and some had dribbled their thick contents onto the polished parquetry floor, leaving dark stains on the wood.

A mountain of unread correspondence spilled over the top of the desk and hundreds of sheets of crumpled writing paper littered the floor in a pile almost a foot deep. She picked up a sheet, unfolded it and read Joseph's almost undecipherable scrawl: *'Lillie, My own, my darling own Lillie, my Lillie of lilies, my sweetheart…'*

Violet threw the letter down as if it had stung her. She glanced up; every inch of space on the wall opposite was covered in pictures, yellowing cuttings and poster bills of Lillie Langtry. Violet sucked in her breath deeply and put a trembling hand up to her mouth. 'Oh Joseph, my poor, poor boy…' she whispered. 'What has she done to you?'

Now, as she watched kindly Dr Farrow minister to her precious son, she knew Joseph was suffering withdrawal symptoms from the powerful opiate drug he was addicted to. She realised that Joseph was trying to wean himself off it.

As the doctor left by the front door and walked towards his carriage, Violet ran up to him. 'Please, Doctor Farrow may I have a word?'

'Yes, of course Mrs Wragg, how may I help?'

'I am concerned for my son, but didn't want to say anything in front of the rest of family. You see, he's been taking laudanum.'

'Laudanum?' the doctor asked. 'It is a tincture of opium. You mean he's addicted to it? This is a serious matter; can you be absolutely certain?'

'Yes, I can,' Violet insisted, and handed him two brown hexagonal bottles. 'I found these in his study along with

many others.'

The doctor examined them. 'How long has he been suffering symptoms of confusion and irritability?' he asked. 'I think I'd better come back indoors, Mrs Wragg, and you can tell me more about the situation.'

Missing out the part about Lillie Langtry, Violet told the doctor of the immense pressure Joseph had endured because of the theatre's commercial demise. She said she thought that had caused Joseph to take laudanum.

'This puts a different complexion on things, Mrs Wragg. During my examination, I thought it was simply mental exhaustion as before, but with more severe symptoms this time. Now he must be weaned off the opiate,' he said. 'I shall call regularly to asses his progress but you must watch him carefully and report any degeneration of his condition to me. And ensure all laudanum is removed from the house.'

'Do I have to tell his wife, doctor – our Nellie, I mean? Only, she is rather a highly-strung lass, and I wouldn't want to alarm her unduly.'

The doctored sighed. 'As long as he is tended to properly with plenty of fluids and rest, he should be all right. There may be occasions when you need to strap your son to the bed to avoid him hurting himself as the drug works free of his system. But there is no reason to ascribe this behaviour to misuse of opiate tincture, should you wish to save your son embarrassment or your daughter-in-law more distress.'

'Thank you for calling, doctor,' she said.

The doctor doffed his hat, 'Good day Mrs Wragg. And please do not worry; he will make a full recovery now that we are fully aware of the nature of the problem.'

***

Violet reluctantly called Vanna to Chadderton Hall.

The women detested each other but Violet had no choice but to follow Joseph's instructions when he was slightly less

agitated and explained his wishes. The running of the theatre complex would be completely in Vanna's hands now; there was no-one else qualified or experienced enough. There was no denying she was an excellent manageress, so any objection from Violet was immediately scotched by Joseph, who wouldn't hear a word against his general manageress.

After taking orders at his bedside, Vanna hugged Nellie and told her not to worry. Nellie felt reassured and glad to have an ally against her shrewish mother-in-law.

Every day Vanna sat at her impressive desk in the manager's office at the theatre complex. Because of Joseph's illness, she had kept most of the bad news about the profits —or lack of them – to herself. If things did not improve, she would soon need to keep the main auditorium dark and concentrate on the music hall at weekends. Joseph's error of judgment was revealed in a lack of patrons; the townspeople lacked not only time but money to squander on formal entertainments at his glittering palace.

The complex floundered like a beautiful sinking vessel in a cold northern sea. There was trouble with performing artistes and their representatives; the better-known names insisted on their fees in advance, irrespective of whether the production would run the full contract. Suppliers of goods were loath to deliver foodstuffs for the eating salons and refreshment areas unless they saw their payment first, as were the printers of posters, programmes and hand bills. Vanna juggled them all with a mixture of astute business skill and cunning female wiles.

But the situation could not continue and the venture was doomed to fail. As soon as Joseph was well enough, she would have to put her plans into action before she was out of a job and back to square one – and with no acting experience to fall back on.

Before Joseph fell ill, she had broached the subject of performing on stage but her employer dismissed her suggestion as a 'silly folly', and didn't take her seriously.

'Why, Vanna – what a charming idea that would be, but

264

I fear the theatre would be in great peril without your expert guidance in an administrative role!' Joseph had chuckled. And that was the end of the matter.

Joseph didn't realise that the theatre would have closed much earlier but for Vanna. Granted power of attorney by Joseph's solicitor for all matters relating to the entertainment complex, she somehow kept it going during his long illness by urging firms to extend yet more credit and deferring payments to the bank on their substantial outstanding loans.

Nellie relied on her emotionally, too; the two women often took tea at Chadderton Hall. Violet refused to have anything to do with her, except on one occasion when she was leaving the house. Vanna made a point of being over-charming and gracious, to the point of mocking Violet. The older woman responded, 'You can wipe that smirk off your face, lady! I know what you are about and one day I'll prove it, so help me God if I don't.'

Towards the end of the year, Joseph was well enough to attend to some business matters in his study each day. He seemed more alert and in control. Although he'd lost weight and looked thin and pale, his hair was neatly cut at the back and sides again and his dress remained that of a gentleman. But most importantly, he was entirely free of the laudanum.

During his long recovery, he'd had time to think. It was obvious that Lillie would never respond to his letters, even though she must have received the dozens he'd sent each week. He thought about the mystery of the missing letter and whether it could have really been from her. But, surprisingly, such considerations were becoming less important. Instead of trying to contact Lillie, he needed to resolve his immediate problems with the theatre. He returned to a daily routine of visiting the complex each morning after breakfast.

\*\*\*

Vanna leaned into Joseph's personal space as he stood before her looking at the paperwork on the desk. She needed to

make a closer connection with him and her office at the theatre was as good a place as any. Past attempts at luring him to her bed before his illness had not worked: he'd either missed the signals or simply wasn't interested.

Since she'd become a regular visitor at his home, Joseph's guard was down. She hadn't been able to get him to call her 'Vanna', which would be the next step towards intimacy, but she realised he felt easy with her. Now she would gently nudge him into the second phase of her plan.

Joseph came round to her side of the desk and leaned forward again to examine the box office returns. She felt his warm breath on the side of her cheek and smelled his lemony cologne. She let her eyes linger on his clean-shaven profile for a few seconds too long, but he seemed oblivious to her signals.

'So, Miss Boston, are you telling me the main auditorium has been running at only twenty-five percent capacity for our monthly shows? And yet the music hall is almost full each Saturday evening, although empty the rest of the time,' he asked, scanning the figures with a worried frown. 'Are advance bookings any better for the pantomime for the festive season and the musical productions in spring?'

'Melodramas and light comedies do rather well but the classics do not appear to do so, sir. In fact booking for next week's show – a light operetta – are seventy percent less than anticipated. If I may be so bold as to make a suggestion, perhaps you might consider a lesser-known actress for the lead role in place of Bernhardt in the forthcoming production of *For Green and Country*. Miss Bernhardt *is* rather costly.'

'But how could we hope to fill seats if not with a famous performer?'

'We could use unknown performers, sir. Ticket sales may increase if we lower the admission charges and absorb the deficit by slightly inflating the cost of refreshments and food. We may even turn over a larger profit while appearing to make the theatre accessible to all performers and levels of the community. This would be invaluable in ensuring

publicity for future shows.'

Joseph was silent for a moment. 'I shall consider the matter, Miss Boston.'

Vanna decided to be bold. 'Perhaps you'd care to accompany me to luncheon, Mr Wragg. I was due to meet Nellie but I forgot to arrange a time with her and now I have no choice but to dine alone,' she said, looking a little crestfallen. 'And I do not like to dine alone in public, it's so unseemly,' she added.

Joseph hardly ever bothered with luncheon but he decided to accompany Vanna , if only to continue their conversation about future bookings.

As they pored over the menu in the airy eating room that was full of large green palms and soft music from the resident harpist, Vanna spoke nonchalantly. 'I feel confident that everything will be fine once we've been open for a full year and people know about the theatre. Perhaps then we can afford to book top London artistes.' She sipped her water then added as an afterthought, 'I understand that Mr Wilde has recently written another play. Perhaps he and his friend Mrs Langtry could be persuaded to attend our theatre with his production?'

Joseph immediately stopped reading the menu 'Is she back in England?' he demanded rather too quickly, peering closely at Vanna. He struggled to hide his feelings. 'Have you heard something? Is she back from America?'

Vanna was surprised at his unguarded response but decided to be bold. Lowering her tone so it was barely audible above the music, she leaned forward. 'Mr Wragg, do forgive me sir, but I know all about your relationship with Mrs Langtry.'

Her self-assurance made him recoil in shock. He threw down the menu. 'Sorry – what?' he demanded, raising his eyebrows at her audacity. He waited for further explanation but his manageress remained calm and appraised him with a cool stare as the waitress came to take their orders. He waved her away impatiently. 'What is the meaning of this,

Miss Boston?' he said, angrily.

'As part of my research to better my position at the theatre, sir, I regularly take the publication *Vanity Fair.* I saw an old picture of you and Mrs Langtry during one of your trips to London.'

Joseph breathed out a sigh of relief, believing it was only suspicion on her part. 'Why, that means nothing! Many famous personalities have their photographs taken together, especially if you have friends like Oscar Wilde! It means nothing at all,' he replied.

'But you *were* kissing her, sir, and the picture also bore a brief description of your relationship. It suggested you had rented a house for her and her daughter, where you stayed whenever you were in London,' Vanna said, carefully gauging his reaction. From what Nellie had told her she knew about his temper and was wary of it, but he remained calm.

'So why do you bother to broach the matter now, Miss Boston? You are a good friend of my wife – is this not rather unseemly? What is it you want? If it's money you are after then I cannot hide my disappointment, especially since you have a good position here and have been a credit to me during my long illness.'

'Oh, no, nothing like that, sir. I am loyal to you and shall remain so as long as I am in your employment,' she said. 'But I was hoping we may help each other … and it has mostly to do with our earlier conversation.' She gave her most charming smile.

The hidden barb about her remaining silent while in his employment wasn't lost on Joseph. His heart hammered in his chest as he thought of how close Vanna had become to Nellie recently. 'So what exactly is it you require of me, Miss Boston?'

Vanna told him at length about her time in the music halls and how she considered she would make a fine actress one day. 'And to be fair, sir, I would take a slightly reduced fee while I perfected my craft in smaller roles before taking the

lead. And since Mrs Langtry doesn't seem willing to help you at all... Well, perhaps I can step fully into her shoes.'

Joseph considered her for a moment as she let the implication hang in the air, then decided to call her bluff. 'Miss Boston, I'm afraid you have it all wrong about me and Mrs Langtry,' he said. He picked up his menu again, pretending to read it. 'Perhaps we can end this speculative tittle-tattle? Let's order our luncheon and forget this unfortunate episode. I shall say no more about it.'

'*Have* I been silly, sir?' Vanna enquired , still keeping her voice low. 'Have I *really*?' She leaned conspiratorially towards him. 'Then I think it's best that I immediately inform Mrs Wragg of the situation, in case she happens upon the same publication and *also* forms the wrong idea about the nature of your relationship with Mrs Langtry. After all, I wouldn't want my dear friend Nellie to get upset over something silly, would I sir?' Her hard, glittering eyes left Joseph in no doubt about her intention; he'd misjudged her determination to get her own way and it frightened him. He sensed this over-confident manner concealed something more, and he considered for a moment the missing letter that Violet swore she'd never seen. Joseph quickly cast the thought aside; it chilled him to the bone to contemplate Vanna could be so deceitful. No, surely not...?

'Is that all?' he snapped. He felt ensnared and he backtracked a little. 'And if I *were* to agree to your request, who would run the theatre while you pursue this wild dream of becoming a stage actress?'

Vanna smiled, knowing she'd won. 'I have been training an assistant for several months during your absence. He is very good indeed and comes with excellent references after many years working at The Globe Theatre in Stratford-upon-Avon,' she replied. 'He will be an admirable replacement for me in the managerial role.'

'Well, you'd better leave the matter with me for now, Miss Boston,' Joseph said, his appetite now gone. 'I am sure you agree there is much for me to consider. I need to think

about the implications of what you have just told me.'

'Yes, of course sir. And thank you for your kind understanding.'

# ACT 25

*N*ellie clapped her hands and shrieked delightedly, 'Oh Vanna – that's simply *wonderful* news! I am so happy for you, my dearest.'

Vanna sipped tea from her bone china cup, wiped her mouth delicately on a napkin and then grinned. The two women were discussing her recent good fortune in landing the leading role of Laura in *For Green and Country*. Nellie babbled on, 'I had no idea you were a trained actress, Vanna, and assumed the part would go to Winifred Emery. How did this come about? Pray do tell.'

The would-be actress looked coy. 'Your dear husband said I had been most helpful while he was indisposed and insisted he wanted to repay me in some way. When he found out that I could act and hoped one day to perform at the theatre, well...' She let the words tail off.

'Joseph would be thrilled to give you the part, knowing how close we are. Here, do have another biscuit!' gushed Nellie, hardly pausing for breath. 'Oh, it's simply marvellous, isn't it, Vanna?'

'Joseph – I mean *Mr Wragg* – insisted. It was very kind of him.'

Nellie clapped again. 'We must celebrate with an outing to Manchester to buy new outfits for your opening night.'

Vanna had been victorious and Joseph reluctantly gave her the starring role of Laura after their confrontation in the eating rooms. 'What you do with the damned part is between

you and that bloody fool director,' he'd said coldly, realising he'd been outsmarted. It was his intention to get rid of her as soon as possible but first he must ensure her replacement, Ernest Taylor, could run The Red Rose Palace of Varieties. And he didn't know how to get rid of Vanna without causing a scandal.

As he sat in the back stalls, straight-shouldered, nursing his injured pride and watching rehearsals begin, he saw the confident strength of Vanna Boston unfurl onstage as she skilfully worked through several lines. She was reasonably good, if not exactly lead material. Her voice was distinct and clear, yet each syllable assaulted his ears like a sharp knife; he hated what she'd become, what she could do to him and his family.

He was desperate to be free of her threats. He'd even considered closing the complex for a while so she had no option but to leave. But she was shrewd enough to realise that he'd done that simply to get rid of her. And how would he and his family live? He'd already sold off his shares in Stapes Steeplejacks, as well as his treasured Pullman, to pay the household bills during his illness. His operatives had been reluctant to band together and buy him out. Logan and Rudy were beside themselves with sorrow; it was only when the operatives said they could become part of the cooperative when they were old enough that they cheered up. It was their dearest wish to become master steeplejacks. They both showed little interest in the theatre business, which was a relief to Joseph since he now felt sure his venture into the world of entertainment would fail. The question was: what could he do instead? He was far too old to climb chimneys and all his other assets had been sold off.

As he studied Vanna, he found no answers to his problems.

\*\*\*

Violet was incandescent with rage. 'What do you mean *she's* got the role of leading lady at *our* theatre?' she'd fumed at

Nellie, who took spiteful pleasure in sharing her friend's good news.

Joseph hardly spoke to his mother and didn't realise she knew about his problems with laudanum. When he'd recovered enough, he'd secretly cleared his study of all the drug bottles and the fading posters of Lillie and allowed Poppy to clean the room. It had taken weeks to sift through the mountain of unpaid bills and legal correspondence but finally he was able to function again.

Nellie had been jubilant ever since she learned of Vanna's progress. Each day she goaded her mother-in-law; even the servants were beginning to comment on the strained atmosphere at Chadderton Hall as the two women spat fire at each other.

Joseph could hear the frenzied row as he opened the front door and walked into the drawing room. He'd been watching Vanna rehearse again, wondering where it would all end. All he needed after the sort of day he'd endured was these two at loggerheads. '*Silence!*' he shouted over the raised female voices. Both women turned to look at him. He stood in the doorway glaring at each in turn. 'What in God's good name is going on here?' he demanded.

Nellie and Violet both started talking at once. 'Enough!' shouted Joseph, thumping his cane hard on the floor. 'This is the last straw' he said, looking at Violet. 'I have come the conclusion it is high time you moved to your own premises, Mother. Tomorrow I shall begin an immediate search for suitable property.'

Violet was livid and her cheeks burned in humiliation. She'd endured enough selfish behaviour from her son. He blamed her for all the arguments and had even called her a liar over that mysterious stolen letter. She had kept all his dirty secrets and never been thanked for not telling Nellie about Lillie Langtry and his sordid involvement with her.

'Don't bother, son. I have enough savings of my own from the sale of the house near Alexandra Park when your pa died. I am fed up of taking what you see as charity and

putting up with your double life,' she spat. 'I shall remove myself – as you put it – once I have found my *own* suitable premises!'

'What does she mean, Joseph, a double life?' Nellie wailed, as his mother stormed from the room. '

'It is of no concern, Nellie. We can be alone at last.'

'Oh Joseph, I never thought I'd be happy at someone else's sorrow – but I *am*! Thank you, dearest – and thank you for making my friend Vanna happy too!' It was all her dreams come true: she finally had Joseph to herself.

Much of Joseph's former courage had returned now that he was clear of his terrible addictions – Lillie Langtry and the laudanum. Never a man afraid of taking risks, he contemplated the very worst that could happen. He recalled the times he'd taken risks as a young man to fell an unstable chimney. He'd come up with a careful plan and the dangerous stack fell to the ground without harming anyone. There *had* to be a way to fell Vanna Boston and prevent her from injuring his family.

In three weeks' time, the new play would be launched and her starring role would give her the necessary experience to go on to other touring theatre productions. That was all he could hope for, that she would leave under her own steam...

Until the night he made up with his mother and they hatched a plot.

***

Vanna was in her dressing room with the wardrobe mistress who was tacking up the hem of her blue velvet skirt. 'Come!' she shouted as a knock sounded at the door.

Joseph entered. 'Leave us, for a moment, Ethel, if you will,' Vanna instructed her kneeling assistant. Dressed like a country lady but without a straw bonnet, she turned to face her employer with a beaming grin.

'Joseph, what a pleasant surprise. I have been looking forward to showing off the costumes. So what do you

think?' she said, swirling a full circle in front of him. 'Quite fetching, yes?'

Joseph intended to call her bluff. He would ask her to leave and if she refused, then he would show his hand. It might not be necessary to reveal his duplicitous actions if he was polite but firm and she responded with dignity; that would save them both humiliation and embarrassment.

'Miss Boston, I've been meaning to talk to you,' he said evenly, taking a seat. His tone was grave but gentle as he appraised her. 'I think you realise we have both gained certain favours that perhaps we were never entitled to in the first place.'

'Favour; is *that* what it was, then?' she said, feigning amusement.

'This dangerous game has gone on long enough, Miss Boston. We both know the risks involved in taking something that does not belong to one. I think you know what I'm talking about. I have been good to you, given you a chance—'

'*Jo-seph*' she interrupted, using his first name and dragging out the first syllable insolently. 'May I remind you of your promises to me ... and your wedding vows when you promised to remain faithful?'

Joseph made a gesture of annoyance and furrowed his brow. 'Threats are so ugly and not worthy of a leading actress such as yourself, Vanna,' he said.

'I would not tease if I were you, sir. My role as an actress is merely a stage performance. The role of a loving husband towards a loving wife is one of some significance – especially if the wife of someone else is involved, too!'

He could see that subterfuge would not work and came straight to the point. 'I have decided not to allow you to play the part of Laura. In fact, Miss Boston, I have decided not to allow you to play *any* part, either on stage or front of house in this theatre from now on. I give you one half hour exactly to pack your things and remove yourself from my premises before I call the police and have you arrested for blackmail!'

275

Vanna let out a loud gasp of disbelief. 'So, ever the brave gentleman steeplejack Wragg, eh?' she chided. 'I have a damning letter in my possession which your wife may like to see – from Lillie Langtry herself! Quite the little lover aren't you, sir?'

Joseph looked pained. 'I know, Vanna. I know all about it. And as I say, the police will be here shortly if you do not remove yourself at once from the theatre.'

Vanna stood her ground, puzzled. 'In that case you will be sorry. Nellie will believe me once I show her the copy of *Vanity Fair* and the letter from Mrs Langtry. Do you think I bluff? So now, if you'll excuse me, Mr Wragg – Joseph – I have a dress fitting and rehearsal to attend. Perhaps you can close the door on your way out, and order me some light refreshments.'

Joseph smiled, stood and reached into his pocket. 'Do you mean this?' he asked, holding up the blue envelope with its American stamp. 'Oh, and I'm afraid the copy of *Vanity Fair* is nothing more than ash in the fire-grate of my study by now. But, this letter – it is evidence on both counts of theft and blackmail, is it not?

Vanna glared wide-eyed at the letter in his hand. 'How the devil—'

Joseph relished explaining exactly how he came by it.

\*\*\*

Since the night after the terrible argument about the missing letter, son and mother had grown further apart. Later, as he faced his scheming manageress in the eating rooms and was blackmailed into giving her the leading role of Laura, he knew his mother had been right all along. He realised just how foolish he'd been and saw Violet was right about Vanna and her scheming ways. Later, back home at Chadderton Hall, he'd approached his mother's room to discuss it.

She was sobbing on the edge of her bed, looking at a likeness of him and Nellie. 'I never meant any harm son,

really I didn't,' she wailed. 'I've been so wretched that we've fallen out. Please trust me – that Boston woman is pure evil, not me.'

He put his arm around her and she fell against him.

'I have something to tell you, Mother, but first I must apologise for acting so brutally,' he said. 'What I am about to tell you must never go any further – and I shall need all your help, if you are willing to assist me, that is?'

Violet wiped away her tears and hugged him. Joseph explained about Vanna Boston and the terrible hold she had over him; his hunch about where the letter was. And then they made their plan...

Joseph started to watch the rehearsals, timing Vanna's role to the minute with his gold pocket watch so he knew when she would be on and off stage in acts one and two. Satisfied that he'd learned her routine, he took action when he saw his chance. During her first scene in act one, he ran down the corridor to her dressing room. Seeing Vanna's carpet bag, he searched it and extracted the key to her lodgings. He tucked it into his pocket and dashed back along the corridor to the offices, speaking briefly to Ernest Taylor before leaving again through the opposite door.

Once back in the foyer, he went through the front doors and down the steps to their horse-drawn carriage where Violet sat waiting. 'You have to be back here in less than half hour,' he said, handing her the key. 'You have the address. I shall wait for you in the eating salon upstairs. *Please*, mother, no longer than a half hour.'

Violet left in a clatter of hooves and iron-clad wheels, heading towards Lever Road. She instructed the coachman to remain with the carriage out of sight around the corner by the market hall. She wore the shawl and clogs of a mill-worker. She wished it was foggy as usual, but unusually the day was bright and crisp. Nobody took any notice of her, however, as she walked down Lever Road.

She recognised the single ladies' lodging rooms by the splendid gas lamp directly outside, bearing the number '25'

in gilt numerals. It was lit the last time she'd seen it as they dropped Vanna off on their way home from the theatre on opening night.

Two grubby children were playing on the steps. They nodded in acknowledgement as she held onto the iron handrail and walked up slowly, then she stopped for a moment outside the door, praying it wasn't locked. One boy glanced up, thinking she'd come to see the owner about a room and said, 'She's in, missus, if yer want 'er,' before resuming his game of marbles. He reminded her of Joseph at that age.

Opening the squeaky door with its dull brass knocker in the shape of a laurel wreath, she saw a long, dark hallway. It smelt a little musty and damp, and Violet could hear other occupants – possibly the landlords – coughing and muttering, going about their business. She hoped the boy wouldn't dash indoors and alert anyone to her presence.

She clutched the large iron key and made sure no doors were opening or anyone coming downstairs. Vanna's room was on the first floor opposite the newly-installed Thomas Crapper water closet as Joseph had indicated. The lock turned without difficulty and she entered quickly.

The room was neat and smelt of lavender water. Bright light filtered through the tiny single-sash window, reflecting off the dark polished floorboards and highlighting a pegged rug in a rainbow of muted colours. A ramshackle iron bedstead stood in the corner with a pink chamber-pot underneath. To its side by the wall, under a bare gas bracket, was a balloon-back chair. At the side of the fire-grate stood a wooden coal box, fire-irons and a leather storage case. The mahogany wardrobe at the foot of the neatly-made bed attracted Violet's attention. She opened it but there was nothing inside except three dresses, a winter coat and a hand-me-down fur wrap. The boxes on top held nothing but bedding and a few more items of clothing.

Violet glanced around, wondering where to look next. A mixture of thrill and apprehension coursed through her as

she fanned both her hands and placed them either side of her face. Yes, where to start?

She spotted another shabby leather case pushed under the far side of the bed and drew it gently forward, swiftly opening its unlocked brass catch. It contained old handbills and several curious newspaper cuttings about a chemical works industrialist and his family at a society wedding. But there was no mention of Joseph or Lillie Langtry. She studied some hand-scribbled notes which looked like maps of London and a few personal letters tied with bows, which she discarded after reading the unfamiliar signature.

She heard steps on the landing and thought her heart would burst as they seemed to stop directly outside. Then she heard the door opposite open and close and realised it was someone using the water closet. She continued sifting through the papers and cuttings and was about to abandon her fruitless search when she spotted three copies of *Vanity Fair*. Violet quickly scanned each page and in the last edition she saw pictures of Joseph and Lillie Langtry, with the heading: *'Where are they now?'*

Violet put everything carefully back into the case but placed the periodical in her bag. She looked up and saw the mahogany corner cupboard. Making certain the bed was neat and tidy again, she crossed the room and opened it. A clutter of medicine and calamine lotion bottles, Cephus tonic powders and toilet water, hairbrushes and powder puffs almost spilled out on the floor; she caught a medicine bottle just in time and jammed it firmly back inside. The cupboard was separated by a single middle shelf and Violet stood on tiptoe to peer towards the back of the top section. And there she discovered it, behind three bars of wrapped Sunlight soap and an old tin of shoe polish.

The long blue envelope with an American stamp, bearing a bold, elegant, feminine script, was addressed to: *'Mr Joseph Wragg, Chadderton Hall, Oldham. England.*

Her hunch was right; Vanna *had* stashed the letter in her room! Stuffing it deep inside her carpet bag, Violet felt like

ripping the contents from the cupboard and destroying the room in retaliation for the trouble Vanna had caused. But Joseph insisted that he wanted to try and resolve matters amicably once he had the damning evidence, so she concentrated on restoring the cupboard back to its previous order.

Violet padded silently across the room then placed her ear to the panelled door. She heard no sound on the other side so opened it and stealthily stepped onto the landing. After relocking the door, she scurried down the stairs and out again into the sunny street. The boys looked up from their game of marbles as she started to run along the street.

The coachman was waiting patiently as she approached. 'Back to the theatre as quickly as you can please, Harvey,' she instructed, wheezing. She could hardly stop herself chuckling out loud as they pulled away. Ten minutes later, as they turned into Union Street and approached the theatre, Violet felt jubilant.

Joseph's heart leapt when he saw that his mother was beaming from ear to ear. She handed over the key, the magazine and the missing letter. 'What you do with this is now up to you, son,' Violet advised. 'But I would wait until we've dealt with Miss Boston before reading it, if I were you.'

Joseph hugged her briefly and, as she turned to go down the staircase, she looked back at him and smiled. 'You know, us Wraggs will always stick together and win!' she said and raised her thumb in a gesture of good faith.

Joseph was shocked as he examined the familiar handwriting. For a few moments he was rooted to the spot but he knew he must hurry, so snapped out of his reverie. Needing to return the key to Vanna's bag before she came off stage, he opened the main auditorium door and watched her. She would be on stage for another few minutes yet. Quickly, he returned to the dressing room and replaced the key in Vanna's carpet bag. He could hear her strident voice coming through the speaker system on the wall as he placed the bag

back on top of her woollen cape; her final scene was coming to an end: '...so, one's follies, Gilbert, are of no consequence in these verdant, green pastures of England...'

With little time to think about what he'd done, he headed back up the corridor and entered the manager's office, just as Vanna smiled at a stage-hand and swept off towards her dressing room.

\*\*\*

Now he stood before her, victoriously holding the letter out of reach, taunting her with it. 'So, you see, Miss Boston, I have outwitted you!' he said, relishing her anger.

'I shall report this matter to the police myself!' she shouted.

'Oh? What, exactly?' he smiled back, sure of his position. As he faced his tormentor, he held the letter above her head. 'You have no real proof, only hearsay, and I shall publicly condemn you as a scheming liar if you cause further trouble for me or my family. And who do you think they will believe? An embittered, manipulative woman who frequently tried making passes at me, her married employer?'

Vanna was astonished as he continued with his diatribe. 'And do not think others are unaware of your unseemly behaviour, Miss Boston. Everyone will believe me, a pillar of the community, hounded by a thwarted and scheming charlatan, a common *thief*!'

She lunged for the envelope and he stepped back. 'You bloody arrogant *bastard*!' she shouted. 'This will not be the end of it.'

'Oh, I rather think it will, Miss Boston. You have exactly half an hour to gather your possessions and leave.'

Vanna tore off part of her costume and threw it at him. 'You will live to regret this, I promise,' she spat. 'I shall make you regret ever meeting me.'

'That is perhaps the truest thing you have ever said,

Miss Boston!' Joseph closed the door gently behind him as she screeched obscenities usually heard in the netherworld slums of London's East End.

# ACT 26

*T*he world was at an end for Nellie as they gathered in the parlour. 'And so you see, my dearest, we had no alternative but to let Vanna go…'

Joseph explained as gently as he could and comforted his shocked wife as she cried over the loss of her good friend. His mother stood with an arm around Nellie's shoulder. He glanced at them both and dropped his gaze; the pain of Nellie's emotion was etched on her face. He felt helpless but relieved the situation was over. 'There was nothing I could do, no alternative...'

'We must all remain calm, and look after each other now,' announced Violet.

'She stole from me. It was proven beyond all reasonable doubt, Nellie, and while I cannot go into details, she was untrustworthy and highly unscrupulous,' added Joseph. 'I know you are upset, my darling wife, but you have to believe me: she was bad to the bone and meant to harm us all.'

Violet nodded in agreement and pulled Nellie closer. 'Be brave, our lass.'

'Did you call the p-police?' stuttered Nellie, wiping her eyes.

'No, I decided not to,' said Joseph. 'In many ways she was an excellent member of staff, so I gave her opportunity to leave town without further fuss.'

Nellie blew her nose hard. She couldn't believe her friend Vanna was a common thief. 'But what did she steal, Joseph?

Was it money?' she asked.

Her husband stood sullen and unspeaking.

'Oh, please, why won't you tell me?' Nellie demanded as he remained silent.

Violet shook her head and spoke up instead. 'Here, child, we have never been close friends you and me, but I hope from this day forward we can change all that.' Nellie blew her nose again and Violet continued. 'Idle gossip is irrelevant now. This family is all that matters. She stole something of great importance belonging to your husband, so she can no longer be trusted or welcomed again in this house.'

'Oh, it's not *fair!*' Nellie cried and struggled away from Violet's embrace.

Joseph beckoned his mother into his study as Nellie dashed upstairs, demanding to be left alone. Violet wanted to set off after her but Joseph pulled her back. She reluctantly followed him.

The retired steeplejack avoided his mother's eyes; the humiliation his adulterous actions had caused was close to his thoughts. 'I cannot be anything but extremely grateful that a very highly embarrassing state of affairs has been avoided,' he said, shaking his head at his own stupidity. He explained what had happened after he'd faced Vanna earlier that afternoon.

Violet listened patiently and then nodded her head at Vanna's wicked spitefulness, restraining herself from saying, 'I told you she was evil, son.'

Joseph extracted the slim blue envelope from his pocket and examined it. He turned it around several times, wondering at its contents. Violet didn't speak, just watched as he slowly opened a drawer in his desk. He extracted a bundle of similar envelopes tied with a ribbon. Violet thought for a moment he would add the one in his hand to the pile but he didn't. He closed his eyes for a brief moment or two then inhaled, as though they contained a rare scent, and flung them all into the fire. The flames licked around the single envelope first, consuming it before attacking the heavy bundle. The

red ribbon burned, curling brown at the edges as the flames destroyed the words it contained forever. The only noise was the ticking of the clock and Joseph's deep breathing.

Bits of silver residue floated up the chimney as all was turned to ash. 'It's over, Mam, it's done with. That part of my life is finished forever,' Joseph said, as he watched the fire destroy his dreams of Lillie.

The colour fled from his mother's face. 'I cannot abide seeing the pain you feel, son,' she said, watching him lean against the desk as all strength left his body. He was once able to do the work of ten men but the driving force of his spirit had been weakened by an unattainable love. Love for someone he could never have. Violet decided to be honest with him; it was her only chance to make him see he'd made the right decision. 'I knew of the laudanum problem you had. I saw the bottles and pictures of Lillie Langtry, and decided to tell the doctor.'

He didn't flinch, just continued staring at the fire as he spoke. 'Addiction is a dreadful thing, Mother. But I am finally cured. Life is acquiring new meaning and for it to continue thus, I must turn my back on certain aspects of my past.' He turned from the fire. 'And I'm afraid I've been rather a bad husband to Nellie, yet she's given so much of herself, the poor lass.'

'She loves you so much, son. We can never hurt her with the knowledge of this – any of it. You do understand that, don't you?'

'Yes, I do, Mam. In a way I love her deeply too. I think I always have but I never realised because of my obsessions. There have always been so many … *distractions,*' he added.

Violet knew what he meant. Joseph was ambitious and clever but scarred by rejection and by falling in love with the wrong women.

'I have discovered something I want more than anything,' he said to his mother, 'and perhaps it has always been here within my heart. That is Nellie.'

Violet patted his arm, pleased. 'You've always been a great,

daft lummox,' she jested and he hugged her close. Outside in the hallway, they heard the excited voices of Rudy and Logan, returning back from their day of steeplejacking. At their request, they'd been taken on by Stapes as apprentices. They clamoured to tell him about the state of St Kentergan's Steeple in Preston.

Nellie's voice wafted in after them, composed now and full of affection. 'And, please boys, do *not* walk on the carpet with all that mud and oil on your feet!' She sounded happy to be in charge of her little family.

'Be gentle with her, son,' urged Violet.

'I shall, mother. After all, she is my wife…'

They left the study arm in arm, then Gabrielle came up demanding that Joseph place her on his shoulders, like a queen on a splendid white horse. And like that, the family all went into supper.

Nellie snuggled into Joseph's arms as they sat in the parlour afterwards. Although her eyes were still slightly red from weeping, she was happy. 'I love you, my dearest husband, and shall always respect your wishes,' she whispered. He hugged her close and Violet smiled at them both from her seat opposite. Knowing how Nellie had nursed him and never asked questions nor doubted he would survive, she knew this was spoken from the heart. Such was Nellie's love for Joseph she had tended him constantly, afraid that without her life force he would slip away. She was his candle in the dark.

Violet knew that she'd been far too harsh with the girl and had a lot of making up to do. It would take time, but they'd get through this—

'Who the devil is that at this time, it's almost ten?' Joseph said, alarmed by the loud banging at the front door and hoping it wasn't Vanna here to cause trouble.

Poppy, the parlour-maid, opened the front door and was pushed aside by three men as they dashed inside the house, wild and full or fear, bellowing for Joseph. One spoke up as he came into view. 'You'd better come quickly, lad –there's

a fire at the theatre and it's burning like a ruddy tinder-box!'

For a moment, Joseph didn't register what they were saying or move from the spot. Everything seemed to slow down. The words played in front of him like a zoetrope of moving images.

Violet nudged him into action, 'Look sharp, Joseph – *quick!*'

\*\*\*

The fire took hold much quicker than she'd thought and she was terrified.

Vanna Boston struggled to pull open the small door leading out to the street but it seemed it wouldn't budge. She didn't know that dressing room number one was specially equipped with a door that could only be pushed open from outside once it was unlocked. It was incorporated into the building at Joseph's request, so he could slip in unobtrusively to visit Lillie without having to go through the front foyer. But he stipulated it must only be one way, for he didn't want staff using it as a convenient entrance to and from the theatre.

Vanna had noticed the tiny padded door concealed behind a screen and left it unlocked that day. How could she know about the clever mechanism, designed by Joseph, which prevented it from being pulled inwards? She had thought it would give her easy access for her purpose before she disappeared from Oldham for good.

She'd had no trouble re-entering the theatre after dark with a container of paraffin, some matches and her small suitcase of belongings. Wragg would lose everything dear to him tonight! She'd relished the thought earlier on the omnibus as she returned to the ladies' boarding house. Earlier that evening, she'd gone around each main exit of the theatre securing the doors with stout chains and padlocks so firemen could not gain entry to extinguish the flames that would rob that arrogant bastard of his dreams – as he did

hers. As the newly-appointed general manger locked the staff entrance behind them both, and bade her good evening, she was thrilled.

*Stuff 'em all!* she thought as she slopped paraffin over the plush, red seats of the elegant auditorium where she should have been making her debut in less than a week's time.

There was no way out, as the seats blistered and caught fire.

Now she pushed hard at the quilted door that would not move. There was no alternative but to go back through the manager's office to the foyer. But the corridor was blocked with thick smoke. She turned and ran back into the stage area, entering the wings at the left side, but she could already feel the sweltering heat. The stage was covered with great leaping flames and the swagged front tabs were alive with yellow and red fire.

Vanna panicked.

A small door to her right led into the main auditorium but already most of the seats blazed within, giving off a thick, choking smoke that left her breathless as she ran up the centre aisle towards the back. Overhead, flames consumed the dress and upper circles; the heat was tremendous. She could hardly see for the rolling, sulphurous smoke and felt her skin shrinking as it seared with the intense heat. Coughing and spluttering, almost unable to see, she entered the main foyer and ran towards the outer street doors. She stood for a moment or two, spread-eagled, pushing against them, before realising they were locked and she had no key.

She dashed through a door to the left, entering the smaller music hall foyer, but a roar from the music hall meant it too was being rapidly consumed by fire.

Vanna hurried back through the main foyer and stood panicking, wondering what to do next. Her best plan would be to go upstairs and break the glass frontage of the eating room and climb through onto the signage directly below the widow. That way, she could at least escape from the fire. She ran, taking two steps at a time, the thick carpet deadening her

steps as she screamed in terror. Upstairs was free of the fire so far, but it was impossible to break the widows; Joseph had encapsulated them in three sheets of plate glass to preserve the delicate roundels from Oldham's smoggy atmosphere. She screamed again; the flames were licking at the left leg of the staircase and rising smoke was making it difficult to breathe. Dashing off to the right, she almost fell over an upturned chair but pulled herself up, continued towards the flame-free leg of the right staircase and descended back into the fires of hell.

She shrieked and buried her head in the crook of her right elbow. *'Please! Help me!'* Flames blistered the mahogany frontage of the manager's office and festooned the main front doorway leading to the street. The panels either side lit up like some bizarre fireworks display; the light was so bright that she shielded her eyes against its intensity. The heat made her whimper and scramble back towards the main auditorium where the door opened onto a roaring furnace. She quickly closed it and looked upwards.

The fire was ripping across the fine oil paintings of lilies on the ceiling, giving the delicate blooms an incandescence before they disintegrated into grey flakes of ash and fluttered down like confetti. Two of the huge crystal chandlers suddenly crashed down and smashed into a grand piano near the staircase. Vanna turned to see the left staircase was a waterfall of dripping fire. Her eyes watering, she glanced upwards again as another chandelier crashed down, narrowly missing her.

She screamed again and ran towards the manager's office, pushing through the ring of fire on the varnish of the blazing architrave. It was slightly cooler inside the room, even though it quickly filled with acrid smoke. It wouldn't be long until the flames took hold of the mahogany door, so she pushed through into the corridor beyond that led back down to the dressing rooms. She couldn't breathe properly; her chest felt tight with the effects of the smoke. The way back was now blocked with fire.

The roar from the auditorium was deafening. She could feel the heat penetrating the brick walls as it burst into the passageway connecting the row of dressing rooms. Flames were licking at the door leading to the prompt corner of the stage, and she could see the draught drawing them under the doorway like long, reptilian tongues. She went back into dressing room one and pounded at the padded door again, her fists blooded and raw as she scratched and clawed at the red leather padding. She gagged as more thick smoke poured under the door and flames consumed the corridor outside. There was no-where left to run; she was trapped.

*'Help! Help! I'm dying – please, someone help me!'* she screamed, but no one heard her.

The last thing she saw as her hair crisped and her clothes caught fire was the image of her smouldering suitcase containing all her worldly goods on the blazing golden throne where Joseph had sat earlier that day. As her skin began to blacken, she screamed at the top of her voice, 'DAMN YOU, LILLIE LANGTRY!'

***

Joseph was standing by the side of the Town Hall near the groups of people who had gathered to watch as firemen and their helpers tried to get near the burning building.

When the eating salon window burst outwards, it covered the wet pavement with millions of shards of broken, hand-painted glass, some deep red that looked like blood droplets. The fresh air sucked inwards and oxygen ignited the internal roof structure. Joseph watched helplessly as thousands of tons of lead-work melted and streamed down the side of the building, pooling like mercury and travelling in languid rivulets down drainpipes and stone columns. They reminded him of falling tears.

It was almost too much for him to bear and he tried to push a man out of the way in a desperate bid to move forward

towards the seat of destruction.

'There's nothing you can do, Wragg! Quickly – someone hold him!'

Joseph struggled further, almost knocking over another man.

'Easy, lad, you'll 'ave somebody's eye out if you don't stop wralling about like this!,' shouted a tall man, the red and orange flames reflecting on his face.

As the roof ignited and fell inwards, the huge front signage crashed down. Firemen scurrying down the side of the building tried gaining entry to the side doors, but they were stuck fast. '*Get back!*' they instructed several do-gooders who had formed a human chain passing buckets of water to put out flames. 'The structure could collapse at any time – *get back*.'

The mahogany and glass front doors burst open with the force of the fire. It looked to Joseph like a great, gaping mouth consuming orange sustenance. He distinguished the iron frame of the grand piano, standing like a blazing skeleton amidst marble columns that looked like huge teeth. Sparks floated up into the night sky before dropping as thick, grey ash on several rows of closely-packed terraced houses beneath. Five street lamps directly outside the building exploded in rapid succession and gave off terrible jets of fierce blue and yellow flame as the gas burned off.

A further section of the roof caved in; the noise of the falling structure and the burning smell were similar to those of a chimney-felling operation. Parts of destroyed front elevation toppled outwards revealing the main foyer and some of the music hall. Flames ran along the fallen roof timbers, turning them into nothing but hot, glowing embers. The sides of the building followed; soon the theatre looked like a burning Roman ruin. The only things left standing were great slabs of Portland stone, the marble columns and uneven brickwork.

It took five hours for the complex to burn to the ground.

In bed that night, with the reek of smoke still clinging to

his hair and skin, Joseph thought of the terrible price he'd paid for his stupidity and selfishness. He considered Lillie for a moment and saw clearly that she could never have been his. Had he really loved her? No, it wasn't love for Lillie; it was because she reminded him so much of Tabitha Stark. His determination not to lose a second time had developed into obsession.

He felt guilty about the things he'd done in the past. There was the terrible boiler explosion that occurred because he didn't go in person and inform the board of directors at Stark & Elm Spinning Mill about the serious problems with boiler Number Five. But would that bloody fool Stark have listened? Could the lives of the Stape brothers and many innocent mill operatives have been saved? Would it have made a jot of difference if he had died instead of Les and Ron? He could not prevent fate nor change history but he still felt guilty about the sad turn of events.

The loss of his beautiful black lion Chang and the menagerie – he hadn't intended that to happen either. Hadn't he tried to give the animals the finest care possible? But again, these events were accidental or the result of human misjudgements. He could not take them to heart and let them ruin his life.

His beautiful Red Rose Palace of Varieties could no more thrive in an industrialised northern mill town than his doomed menagerie could survive at Chadderton Hall, no matter how much love poured from him. And now everything was razed to the ground and gone. Perhaps that *was* something to feel guilty about, because the reason he'd built the theatre could have destroyed those closest to him. In some ways, he felt glad it was ruined, a thing of the past.

Nellie moved towards her husband in the dark. He was happy she was there and pulled her close. The ridiculous act of sleeping in separate rooms as refined couples were expected to do made him consider how silly the English class-system was. Joseph was what he was: a simple working man, a steeplejack.

'Joseph, are you all right?' Nellie asked, pushing herself up and leaning against the carved headboard. 'I waited for you, but you were gone so long.'

'There is nothing left, Nellie, my love. Nothing!' he wailed, and then broke down in her arms. He sobbed without embarrassment, for himself, for Nellie and for all the time he'd lost spent trying to be something he could never be.

Nellie kissed him gently and held him. 'Tomorrow we start again, my love,' she said. 'It doesn't matter because we'll always have each other.'

He returned her tenderness with genuine love and affection. That was all that mattered, her simple love and devotion. As she kissed away his tears, it was the sweetest moment of both their lives.

# $\mathcal{ACT}$ 27

$\mathcal{M}$r Gregory Rutledge adjusted his horn-rimmed eyepiece and struggled to find the right words. His client, Mr Wragg, sat in front of him; the news today would undoubtedly destroy him.

The whole thing had been a catastrophe. There would be recriminations and accusations once people knew that the fire had been started deliberately. The solicitor fidgeted with a pen before looking up. 'Mr Wragg, I am not sure how to tell you this but we have received correspondence from the insurance company about the fire at your theatre complex. That is why I have called this meeting today.'

Joseph pursed his lips and waited to see what the man would say. Mr Rutledge continued: 'It seems that letters were sent out to Miss Boston in her capacity as general manageress… Let me see … ah yes, here it is.' He picked up copies of invoices from the insurance company. 'On the 12$^{th}$ and 28$^{th}$ of March this year.'

Joseph remained silent, wondering what was coming next.

'Unfortunately it seems that Miss Boston did *not* renew the insurance premium by the due date. I'm afraid your theatre complex was not covered by any form of insurance the night it caught fire. The policy was null and void.'

Joseph took at sharp intake of breath; the news was harder to accept than he'd expected even though he'd anticipated bad news. He swallowed hard. 'Have you been able to locate

her?' he asked the solicitor. 'Miss Boston, that is?'

'Well, that's just it, Mr Wragg,' replied Mr Rutledge, pursing his lips. 'It seems the fire brigade have discovered human remains in the debris. The police believe it is Miss Boston ... and also that she set the fire deliberately. Several people saw her entering the theatre through a small side door, carrying a can and a suitcase.'

Joseph shook his head in dismay. 'She went through the one-way door leading to dressing room,' he sighed. 'I designed it myself.'

This time he felt no guilt about anything.

Mr Rutledge handed Joseph a document about a Manchester theatre that had been completely destroyed by fire. There was also a newspaper cutting. Joseph saw the similarities and the mention of her name as a possible suspect. 'Good grief! She's done this before then, I take it?'

The solicitor nodded. 'They suspect she perpetrated the crime, yes. Miss Boston worked at that theatre for a while; she left after a ... falling out with the owner. The theatre burned down that very same night and she hasn't been seen since.'

'And then she turned up in Oldham and took the manager's job at the Lyceum.' Joseph sighed. It was terrible to think of her setting fire to his theatre and losing her life in the process. Even she didn't deserve that. 'What happens now?' he asked. 'With what's left of my theatre, I mean?'

'Of course you still own the land, which is a valuable asset. It should be quite attractive to a new buyer, given its town centre location. But the bad news is that you face huge bills to clear the site. Then there is the question of those properties close to the theatre that were damaged by the fire. You will have to dispose of further assets to meet your outstanding loans and ongoing liabilities.' The solicitor let the news sink in as Joseph pulled his mouth into a fine line.

He continued gently after a moment or two. 'It seems that insurance wasn't the only thing Miss Boston neglected. It would appear she hid away a considerable sum of money for

her own use and the police have been unable to determine the whereabouts of the funds she stole from you.' He handed over a pile of paperwork; Joseph recognised accounts not only from the theatre, but unpaid household bills. They were papers that had gathered on his desk at Chadderton Hall when he was in the throes of his laudanum addiction; Violet had become distracted as she cared for her son and neglected the accounts.

'You realise what this means?' the solicitor asked.

Joseph nodded. 'Yes indeed. I must go and break the news to my family at once. We can no longer remain at Chadderton Hall.'

Mr Rutledge agreed. 'I am afraid the extensive borrowing of funds against it to build the theatre complex means that the house and grounds will be repossessed by the bank. There is no other way to meet your legal obligations...'

'I could end up in the debtors' prison in Strangeways? Is that what you are saying, sir?' Joseph asked, suddenly alarmed.

'We should be able to avoid a custodial sentence. However, there *is* the question of bailiffs...'

Joseph realised he was now almost bankrupt. The cost of the theatre complex was staggering in itself, but he hadn't calculated enough to cover the opulent furnishings and decor once work began. He had raised as much capital as he could against Chadderton Hall, until the bank would lend no more.

He left the solicitor's offices with mixed feelings. The thought of having nowhere suitable to live and starting again in middle age terrified him. He was angry at himself for trusting Vanna Boston – but he considered himself lucky that he might avoid a prison term. He walked along the main road in Oldham towards the town centre, wondering where life would take him now.

It was almost dinner time and the streets were busy. Housewives pushed past him carrying baskets full of groceries, 'Yer'll getta clout round't ear'ole if yer don't shurrup!' one woman shouted, as she dragged a screaming

toddler dressed in a coat three sizes too big. Bicycles rang their bells as he tried to cross the cobbled road and he stepped aside to let them pass. Then the omnibus stopped and a crowd of people jumped off at the end of Union Street, not far from the shell of his burned-out theatre. Older men stood talking in groups and smoking on street corners, gathered underneath the gas lamps or outside public houses; the factories belched out smoke and kept the younger men locked to their machines. The thrum of industry was loud, even this close to Oldham town centre.

Joseph stopped outside a greengrocer's and butcher's and gazed across the road to the family baker's where Violet used to take him as a small boy; the one with the metal sign still above the door advertising *TUROG* bread. The rabbits hung up outside the butcher's used to frighten him and now made him think of his menagerie and all the dead animals. People bustled by and a little boy accidentally ran into him, then saw the cut of his fine clothes and said, 'Sorry, your Lordship, sir!'

He spotted an old man he recognised shambling towards him, dressed in scruffy clothes. It was Bert Brandwood, once a cloth finisher at Sturges Bleach Works and a good friend of Aspen's until his father had started hanging around with a wilder crowd. The two men used to have a smoke down by the canal during the blighted days of the cotton famine. Bert shuffled up to the retired steeplejack, limping and broken after a life time of hard work in factories; his face reminded Joseph of the fallen tree opposite where his parents once lived by the park, wrinkled, brown and gnarled.

Bert had fed his family on a few pennies a week during those hard days, and lost four children to starvation. He hadn't a tooth left in his head, but he smiled in recognition. His voice sounded dry and raspy. 'Hey up, if it isn't young Joe! Eeee, ah'm reet sorry ter 'ear about yon fire at yer music hall, tha family must be beggared wi' it all,' he said, genuinely concerned. He looked at Joseph through rheumy eyes that failed to register his smart clothes. He saw only

297

Joseph, the son of Aspen, his dear old mate. 'Tell yer what mi' lad, come on, back to ours an' Ah'll - treat yer ter some fish an' chips. An' if yer still clemmed after that, our Gracie's always got some semolina pud' on the go!'

Joseph could have wept at the kind gesture. Here was a man who had never known anything but hardship and he was willing to spend some of his meagre pittance feeding him. Even though Joseph was dressed in gloves and top hat, the old man saw him as an equal. He pulled Bert towards him and gently patted his hunched back.

Bert pushed him away and said, 'Eee Joe lad, yer fatha always used to say yer were a big soft lummox! Nah then, wipe yer bloody eyes and stop all yer skirkin', and let's get ter that chippy before it shuts!'

Afterwards Joseph caught the omnibus back to Chadderton Hall, having spent the afternoon at Bert's house smoking and playing a couple of games of cards. Some people had doffed their caps as he walked down Bengerman Street where Bert and Gracie lived and a few offered their condolences and enquired about Nellie and his family. He'd stopped off at the newsagents on the corner and bought the *The Oldham Observer*. As the omnibus travelled along the main road towards Chadderton, he listened to the thick Lancashire dialect and studied the paper which carried the front-page story about the fire.

These were real people, he thought. Joseph compared them with the sometimes cruel individuals he'd met in London, who seemed to thrive on the false masks they wore. He smiled to himself and looked out the window, thinking about the duplicitous Septimus Stark who had been publicly shamed after his death when Loma's family had sold the story about his illegitimate child to the Sunday periodicals. Other young mill workers came forward and told anyone who would listen about their abuse at the hands of the shamed industrialist. He imagined Tabitha's shock and the possible effects on her marriage to Captain James.

Watching the scenery go by for a moment or two, he

smiled before glancing at the front story again and the picture of the ruined theatre complex.

***

Nellie came dashing into the hallway. 'Oh, Joseph! Are you all right, my darling? We've been so worried about you!' she said, kissing him and then pulling back. 'Why, you smell of vinegar and chips!'

He returned the hug with genuine affection, laughed then breathed the sweet perfume of her hair and kissed her again. Violet opened the parlour door and came out, followed by Gabrielle who hugged him too. Joseph enquired about Logan and Rudy; they were out still working with the steeplejacks but would be home soon. 'Perhaps some warming tea while we wait for the boys?' he said. 'We all need to talk.'

Each family member took the news far better than Joseph expected. As they sat in the elegant drawing room and heard about the enforced sale of Chadderton Hall, the only person who showed any sign of distress was Gabrielle. She piped up, 'Oh, Papa – I really don't mind moving back to Oldham, but shall we have to change the way we speak?'

Everyone laughed and Violet replied kindly, 'No, my dear. We've done that once already and it won't be happing again, that's for sure!'

'Perhaps you'll excuse me. I need to rest a while, it's been a long day,' said Joseph. He wearily climbed the stairs and changed out of his smart clothes for the last time.

***

Logan and Rudy stood in the hallway after the family meeting. Logan leaned against the polished mahogany banister that Joseph had seen the first time he wandered up the driveway to Chadderton Hall. Rudy listened to his brother as he spoke about their grandmother's outlandish idea.

299

Their father had been mortified at first but Violet persisted, urged on by them all, especially their mother.

Logan said, 'So what do you think? Reckon he can make it?'

'Might be a bit out of practice, but we can give him a whirl,' replied Rudy.

The two brothers laughed and slapped their palms together.

\*\*\*

The family's horse-drawn carriage stopped first at the site of the theatre. Nellie said that unless Joseph linked the past with the future, they would always remain separate in his mind. Joseph protested that he didn't want to see it but Violet supported his wife, as did the boys. Gabrielle was tearful, but she said she would try to be brave to help Papa.

Joseph had spoken privately to Nellie about Vanna's death in the fire; when they broke the news to Gabrielle she was distraught. Gabrielle had liked Vanna and had spent many happy hours with her whenever she visited Nellie at Chadderton Hall. Joseph told her Vanna's death was a tragic accident.

He jumped down from the carriage and left the rest of the family behind for a moment or two. He strolled towards the complex and stopped where the granite steps led up to a fence that blocked access to the destruction where the large foyer once stood. A sign on a fence said 'Danger Keep Out'. He squeezed through a small gap in the stout wooden palings, almost overcome by dread. But he needed to see.

On the other side of the fence, he caught his breath. The white marble columns remained upright, rising like the bleached bones of a stranded giant's ribcage, still supporting some of the steelwork above that hadn't twisted and fallen. An acrid stench of charred timber mingled with other odours which made his nose twitch. Glass crunched underfoot as he

stepped over sooty, fallen masonry and burnt wood. Tangles of cables connecting parts of the complex lighting system lay twisted on the ground, some in thick, melted knots looking like severed arteries of the other-worldly beings he'd often read about in H.G Wells' novels.

Pigeons fluttered off into the gunmetal grey sky as he walked further; they'd been roosting on the iron remnants of the balustrades leading to the eating salon and music rooms. He kicked one of the iron clamps with his work boot. It resembled parts of the machinery from the old factories where he'd once demolished the chimneys. He stepped over part of the piano frame that had fused with the staircase and ventured to where the main auditorium once stood.

It was here that the folly of his dream hit him. Exposed before him were hundreds and hundreds of iron seat frames. The proscenium arch was dislodged and yet still retained its curved shape, held in place with girders of bent steel that had buckled with the intense heat. The destruction made him ponder again his gross stupidity. He looked up at part of the left wall adjacent to the music hall that hadn't fallen and saw that the public boxes and part of the dress circle remained in place. The ornate white plasterwork of lilies and the red rose of Lancashire were destroyed. Water dripped from somewhere in a hypnotic rhythm onto a smashed crystal chandelier below.

Joseph didn't walk any further, but listened. He suddenly thought he could hear the very soul of the theatre mocking him, ridiculing his pretentiousness and stupidity at building such a folly. Then he realised it was voices of small children playing somewhere in the distance; children happy and content with their humble lot in life, like he'd once been.

On the way back to his family, he cut through the rubble where the manager's office was. The bronze statues either side of the doorway now lay damaged, like oversized bodies without arms or faces. He looked around, remembering where he once sat at his huge desk, where Vanna had plotted his demise and made her wicked plans. Something caught

his eye, partly buried under the rubble several feet away. It was the silver trowel given to him by Oscar Wilde. Its ivory handle had almost burned away, appearing dark as old bone, splintered and ruined. Joseph examined it closely and could just read the inscription on the triangle of pitted silver: *To Joseph, for each artist is a creator of beautiful things. With fondness, Oscar Wilde*

'Did I make something beautiful, I wonder?' he said aloud, still examining the trowel, and thinking about his friend who had been arrested on his return to London after the opening night of The Red Rose Palace of Varieties. Oscar had been at the height of his brilliant career when he'd been convicted of gross indecency and sent to prison. Joseph thought about all the times Oscar had supported and listened to him through the long, secret telephone calls about Lillie. Oscar had never once mentioned his own *'love that dare not speak its name'* for Lord Alfred Douglas. Joseph slipped the trowel in his pocket and walked back towards the fence.

No one said anything as they pulled away and Joseph didn't look back.

Continuing towards their old neighbourhood, they turned into a side street and the coachman, Harvey, pulled up the reins. He was starting his new position the following week with the owner of a soda-water works and this was his last outing with the Wraggs. He felt sorry for his employer and his family and wished he could stay with them. But Mr Wragg had said he could no longer afford Harvey's wages and a buyer was coming for the carriage tomorrow.

They slowed down as they came to a junction near the train station. 'Stop the carriage, Harvey!' shouted Violet,

'There it is, Pa!' exclaimed Logan, proudly.

And then Joseph saw it, too.

Outside the King's Head public house was a red placard that announced *Vacant Possession*. The family jumped down from the carriage. Nellie took Joseph's arm as they approached the gothic building. 'Are you *sure* you all want this?' he asked.

A man in a brown bowler hat greeted them at the door. They huddled together on the large granite step of the public house, sheltering from the cool wind. 'Mr Wragg and family. I take it, sir?' the man enquired with a smile. 'Please allow me to introduce myself. Lance Palmer from Nelson's Brewery.' He shook Joseph's hand firmly then extracted a large bunch of keys from his battered briefcase. 'The old tenants got a little long in the tooth,' he remarked, inserting the key into the ornate brass lock-plate. 'It's too busy here for 'em near the central station, you see.'

They stepped inside the red, double doors. It was darker than Joseph expected and the air was rank with stale tobacco and beer. He recalled the many times he'd sat in his Pullman as the train pulled out of the train station and seen the large bay window of the public house with its etched designs in the glass and the word 'saloon' in the middle. Aspen, as a young chimney-sweep, used to drink here with his friends long before the cotton famine.

In the main area the polished parquet floor was haphazardly littered with cast-iron Britannia tables and upturned stools. A doorway led to the snug and opened into a cosy, more private area. The walls were covered in beautiful emerald and gold Minton tiles. The bar itself was made of deep, richly-polished mahogany incorporating embellished ironwork and rich carvings, and a huge acid etched-glass mirror ran along the back wall. Even though the public house was dark and devoid of people, it felt somehow welcoming. Nellie smiled and nodded at Violet.

'Shall we go through to the accommodation upstairs, then?' Mr Palmer asked. The family went up a plain staircase at the back of the main saloon area. The rooms above were connected by a warren of narrow corridors. The public house had been used a lodging-house because of its close proximity to the station.

'As you can see, these rooms need refurbishing if your family were to take the lease,' said Mr Palmer.

The parlour had a small fireplace and Violet went over to

examine it. 'Have to get used to making my own fire again!' she joked.

Joseph smiled tenderly at his mother. Several days ago, the night he'd returned from the solicitors and broken the sad news about them having to give up Chadderton Hall, he'd let the tears fall. 'I really don't know what will become of us now,' he wept. 'I'm so sorry; I seem to have failed you all.'

'Nay lad, God made us Wraggs into fighters,' replied Violet, shaking her head. 'You once told me to remember where we came from, do you remember?'

Joseph dried his eyes, grateful for his mother's steely backbone and abiding love.

Nellie spoke, secretly pleased she could live a normal life at last. 'Yes, and as long as we are all together, why, we can take on the very world itself!'

'What about you two?' Joseph asked his sons.

'Well Pa, you know we never wanted to be gentlemen,' Logan said. 'Our game is steeplejacking through and through.' Rudy nodded in agreement. Gabrielle was the only one who didn't fully understand what was happening; she was too young. She'd never known any other life other than one of luxury since the day she was born. But she smiled as young girls aged twelve often do, happy to be a part of an adventure.

***

When Joseph had returned that evening smelling of fish and chips, he told his family of his afternoon with Bert Branwood and how he missed being a part of the local community. He said he wanted to return to his roots.

Violet listened carefully and the idea came to her in a flash. 'Landlord of a public house would suit you down to the ground, son,' she said. 'You can run your own business, you could be part of the community and it would give us somewhere to live as well. We could help you run the place,

too.'

At first Joseph dismissed the idea as preposterous. 'But why is it preposterous?' asked Nellie, sharp for once. 'We need a new home and have no money to our name. This way we can all make a new start.'

Only Gabrielle looked less than thrilled at the mention of having no money but she didn't say anything, since no-one else seemed to mind. Rudy and Logan thought it was an excellent idea. 'Crikey, our own boozer to enjoy a pint or two after a day's hard graft up top of a chimney!' Logan said, making the best of it.

'Hang on, you two, yer not quite old enough for that just yet,' said Violet, chuckling. The boys grinned back.

Joseph still wasn't sure. Violet spoke again. 'Is it the set-up costs with the brewery and furnishing the place that's worrying you, son?'

'We're not exactly rolling in it now, Mother, are we?' he replied.

'Remember the argument after all the trouble with the missing letter?' she said. 'Don't you recall me saying I still had money from the sale of the Alexandra Park house when your Pa died?'

Joseph cottoned on quickly. 'Oh? I can't ask that of you—'

'I'm telling, son – yer not asking! This is family money and this is a family matter. There is enough to take the lease and make a place of our own without any worry.'

'Ma's right,' urged Nellie. 'We must all remain together and this way we can do so. Please Joseph, I beg you.'

'And where would this daft enterprise be located?' Joseph asked.

'That big public house at the side of the station, the King's Arms,' replied Violet. 'The one with the big sign you can see from platform one as the train pulls out.' Joseph knew immediately where it was.

Rudy spoke up. 'I have an idea how we could open a pub in a blaze of publicity, to drum up interest and make it the

305

most popular in Oldham!'

'I think we've had enough of the biggest and the best for now,' said Violet.

Rudy protested, 'No! You're wrong, Grandma. If we did well, we could eventually think about acquiring the hotel next door. At the side of the station like that, we could make a killing – why, especially with our name!'

Joseph smiled wryly; his sons were following in his footsteps, wanting to be the best at everything. 'Let's just take everything a step at a time for now, eh?' he replied gently.

After the family meeting, Joseph had agreed to view the public house. Now he was there he couldn't hide his fear about the unknown, but he liked the idea. He could see himself propping up the bar, talking to the regulars and enjoying himself.

Mr Palmer waited for Joseph to speak, then became impatient. 'I do have several other people interested, sir.'

The family watched Joseph, waiting for a response. Logan was just about to say something, when his father suddenly put up his hand to stop him. 'No, it's settled – I have made my decision. Yes ... we will take it, Mr. Palmer.'

\*\*\*

Two weeks later, Joseph wandered the rooms at Chadderton Hall. They were devoid of furniture; most of the grander pieces had been sold off to meet crippling debts. All that remained were the few modest items they would take with them to their humble dwelling above the King's Head. The ghosts of their past life could remain here in these large, empty rooms that were never meant for them. The bank was preparing to foreclose on the property and land, and Joseph would hand the keys over to his solicitor later this afternoon. It was time to say goodbye.

The rooms above the public house were soon transformed and a water closet and bathroom installed in place of one

of the smaller bedrooms. Violet had used up all her savings to develop the living quarters into a cosy space; she'd also prevented Joseph being made bankrupt while a buyer was found for his land on Union Street. Most of the money had gone to creditors and he'd narrowly escaped debtors' prison.

Joseph opened the grand front door of Chadderton Hall and strolled down the gravelled driveway towards the back of the house near the stables for one last time. He stopped at the side of the huge black granite obelisk with the name 'CHANG' inscribed on the front in gold leaf.

'Goodbye forever, my brave king. Godspeed in the kingdom of heaven, my beautiful creature,' he said. Then he turned to admire the view over Oldham. The thick smog hid most of the distinguishing landmarks of the town but he could just make out Blinkhorn's chimney, the tallest in the area, belching out thick smoke as always, spiralling upwards and obliterating the blue sky. He thought of his two sons learning their steeplejacking trade – one he'd once loved – and recalled when he'd first proudly designed that same splendid hexagonal chimney and later put the firework staging up to celebrate the Queen's Diamond Jubilee.

HRH Prince Edward Albert, Lillie's former lover, would one day be king of England. Joseph thought it was ironic that his new home was a pub called The King's Head after all that had happened; he hoped it wasn't a bad omen, but quickly dismissed the idea. He strolled a little further as he waited for the removal men to arrive, down to where the boating lake had once been. It was filled in after the menagerie failed. Violet and Nellie had worried he would wander off into the lake when he suffered his nervous breakdown.

He sniffed the spring air, which would be thick and sooty as usual where they were going to live in central Oldham. But he didn't care; he could never take for granted the pleasures of a wealthy industrialist on the outskirts of town. That was for the likes of the disgraced Septimus Stark; the pure air didn't make them untainted as men, did it? He wondered what the new owners of Chadderton Hall would be like

– another Septimus Stark, perhaps. What would they do with all this land? Nothing had thrived here and the human blood of industry owned by men like Stark would taint the soil forever. The wealth it represented was no more a part of Joseph than the gentleman's clothing he'd once worn. He was happy now with his simple flat cap and heavy boots; he looked like someone who'd worked hard all his life, even if his hands were still soft and his nails white and unblemished.

# ACT 28

*J*oseph breathed heavily, exhausted by his exertions, then continued his steady descent down the bright red wooden ladders. The muscles in his arms twitched painfully with cramp-like spasms and his legs and feet were growing numb. At one point more than halfway down the huge chimney, he thought he would lose his grip but he kept on smiling as he moved steadily towards the ground and his keen supporters.

Nellie and Violet had almost missed the occasion because they'd been so busy preparing food for the local community. They ran up just in time to watch Joseph getting off the ladders at the bottom of the smoke stack. The two women waved but remained at the back of the crowd. *So many people present, what a turn out*! thought Violet.

Surrounded by reporters, Logan and Rudy pushed through the crowd to the side of their exhausted father. Joseph lifted his dripping cap and swept away the moisture on his forehead, bending over slightly to get his breath back before standing upright and smiling.

He fiddled with the silver celebratory trowel and held it up for all to see in secret honour of his shamed friend. Logan took hold of the trowel, brandishing it like a talisman. Joseph threw an arm around each boy's shoulder and pulled them close, which brought another huge cheer from the crowd. 'Mr Wragg, this way please—' someone shouted.

The man with the camera stuck his head under a black

cloth and held out his arm. A lightning flash went off as he captured both Wragg boys smiling at the side of their middle-aged father. Another person shoved a pencil in Joseph's hand and asked him to sign a printed likeness, bought from a souvenir stand. People patted him on the back and complimented his brave climb.

The journalists waited patiently until the crowd stopped cheering and then approached Joseph. 'How does it feel to climb your first chimney in years, Mr Wragg?' one asked, genuinely curious.

Joseph assumed an exaggerated grin and replied, 'It feels very wet! Will this rain ever stop, I wonder?' Several people laughed at his good humour after such a terrifying ordeal. He was back on form and entertaining as always. He looked across to Nellie, catching her eye; she nodded her head as if to say, 'I knew you could do it, Joseph.' He winked back at her.

'Tell me, Mr Wragg, do you think you'll ever do it again?' another reporter asked.

'Not if I can help it, lad, I think I'm too old for this lark now. I'll leave it to these two from now one,' he said, hugging his sons again. The boys smiled.

'So how does it feel to become landlord of The King's Head, Mr Wragg?' a journalist from *The Oldham Observer* asked.

'I'd rather pull pints than climb big stacks these days!' said Joseph.

He entertained the crowd for several more minutes and posed for more photographs. He'd eventually agreed to his sons' suggestion that he should climb up the Messrs Longhorn & Co Spinning Mill Chimney as a publicity stunt to celebrate the opening of their new venture. The plan had been the talk of Oldham and beyond.

Tabitha read about it. She smiled as she remembered how determined Joseph was to succeed at everything he did. Her husband, Captain James, sniggered and remarked on how far the mighty had fallen. She gently reminded them of

their own social position now that his family had disowned him and he'd lost his military career as well as most of her inheritance. After the death and public shaming of her father Septimus Stark, her portion of his wealth had been lost in increasingly bad investments by her clueless husband. She sat alone in the parlour of their modest house in the suburbs of Oldham and contemplated what she'd missed out on, which meant more than all the money in the world.

Joseph had left his mark on top of Longhorn's chimney, remembering Les's words when he was a small boy during his first climb up the Cromer weaving shed stack. He'd taken his celebratory trowel that now boasted a new wooden handle and a bucket of his special red mastic, which his operatives at Stapes Steeplejacks always used, and pointed several cracks after carving his initials into the large coping stones of the decorative corbelled top. It was the last chimney he would climb. The long, hard ascent had winded him but it was worthwhile. His life would begin again today and he would celebrate with the locals tonight at the opening of the public house. He didn't mind if he ended up drunk for once because that was part of everyday life in Oldham!

When the reporters and photographers were done with him, it was time for the next bit of the proceedings.

'Did you like that, darling?' asked Nellie, seeing how happy her husband was after his ordeal.

'Aye, I did that, lass.' He laughed and kissed her fondly, not revealing how the effort had almost killed him. Then he turned as the gathering cheered. Stepping into the milling mass of bodies, he threw his hands up into the air to silence the din for a moment or two before bellowing at the top of his voice, 'Right, we're off to the pub!'

The crowd roared and followed Joseph and his family through the streets, cheering, clapping, waving flags, full of admiration at his bravery not only in climbing the chimney but also in bouncing back after being left almost penniless.

A brass band was playing 'Land of Hope and Glory' outside the public house. The street was festooned with

bunting and the pavement quickly filled with people eager to get a closer look at the much-loved gentleman steeplejack. For a second or two, Joseph heard the noise of a thundering locomotive engine pulling away in the distance from Oldham Central Station and thought of his beautiful Pullman coach. Some of the thick smoke drifted towards the grey slate roof of The King's Head then wafted away with his thoughts.

A familiar face appeared; the man handed him a dark, frothy pint of finest Oldham ale. 'First one's on me, stranger,' announced William Croston. Joseph took a deep intake of breath at the sight of his old school friend and ex-business partner. William hugged Joseph hard and slapped his back before letting him go and pointing upwards. The two men hadn't spoken in years and Joseph was overwhelmed at seeing William. At first he didn't register what was happening, then he followed his friend's pointing finger.

'Look at that, mate!' laughed William. 'See it?'

The old metal sign bearing the name The King's Head had been removed. Its shiny new replacement announced: *THE STEEPLEJACK ARMS* in bold copperplate lettering; underneath there was a drawing depicting Joseph as a young man demolishing a chimney. Joseph gasped with surprise, shaking his head delightedly. Overcome with emotion, he wiped his eyes with the back of his trembling hand.

Logan and Ruddy rushed forward and proudly lifted their father high upon their shoulders under the swinging sign as the crowd cheered again. The people began to clap and chant, 'We love Joe! We love Joe! We love Joe!' Nellie and Violet hugged each other and allowed themselves to be swept backwards into the folds of the happy, boisterous crowd.

'Welcome home Joseph,' Will Croston cheered, tears in his eyes by now. 'Welcome back to Oldham, my dear friend.'

# ABOUT THE AUTHOR

Sheila Dibnah was born in Bolton in the north-west of England. As a child – and much to her mother's despair – she was more interested in toy cars, spanners and dirty grid-lids than the more traditional girl's pursuits.

After a successful stage career that took her all over the world, she met Fred Dibnah in 1996 and married him two years later. For the next eight years, Sheila worked with Fred as his business and publicity manager and accompanied him across the country on his public appearances. Following his diagnosis with cancer, she nursed him almost to the time of his death in 2004.

Sheila is now an award-winning public speaker based on the Fylde Coast, North West of England.

Her debut book - A Cast Iron Will (ISBN 978-1-908098-82-5 ) she writes about her life with Fred - the man behind the public image. It follows their first meeting through to the final, troubled days of her husband's life and portrays a moving, funny and sensitive tribute to this great man

Lightning Source UK Ltd.
Milton Keynes UK
UKOW04f1938111214

243024UK00001B/6/P